NORTHERN FRIGHTS

An Anthology from the Horror Writers of Maine

Horror Writers
of Maine

NORTHERN FRIGHTS

An Anthology from the Horror Writers of Maine

Horror Writers
of Maine

**Edited by
David Price**

**Introduction by
Holly Newstein**

A
Grinning Skull Press
Publication

Northern Frights
Compilation Copyright © 2017 Grinning Skull Press

"The Old Guide's Tale" copyright ©2017 Peter N. Dudar
"Giant Wompstah" copyright ©2017 April Hawks
"Purgatory Junction" copyright ©2017 Jeremy Flagg
"Catharine Hill" copyright ©2017 Leslie J Linder
"The Bad Trip" copyright ©2017 Thomas Washburn Jr.
"Teacher's Pet" copyright ©2017 John McIlveen
"Screaming Through Sea Glass" copyright ©2017 Juss Stinson
"Mira's Shop of Peculiarities" copyright ©2017 Harold Hull
"Seeing is Believing" copyright ©2017 Wicker Stone
"The Wait" copyright ©2017 Holly Newstein
"The Janitors Come Out at Night" copyright ©2017 Martin Campbell
"Agony Chamber" copyright ©2017 Morgan Sylvia
"Window of Darkness" copyright ©2017 Duane E. Coffill
"Death Lights (A Lee Buhl Story)" copyright ©2017 Glenn Rolfe
"Rare Birds" copyright ©2017 Katherine Silva
"In the Woods" copyright ©2017 Dale T. Phillips
"Sleep Tight" copyright ©2017 E.J. Fechenda
"The Black Beast of Andover" copyright ©2017 Joshua Goudreau
"A Lovely Little Nash" copyright ©2017 Leon Roy
"Liars and Lies" copyright ©2017 Angi Shearstone
"Confession" copyright ©2017 James Graham
"The Phippsburg Screecher" copyright ©2017 Lynda Styles
"In the Root Cellar" copyright ©2017 GD Dearborn

The Skull logo with stylized lettering was created for Grinning Skull Press by Dan Moran, http://dan-moran-art.com/.
Interior graphic created for Grinning Skull Press by Dan Moran.
Cover designed by Christian Bentulan, http://www.coversbychristian.com.
ISBN: 0-9986912-2-4 (paperback)
ISBN-13: 978-0-9986912-2-0 (paperback)
ISBN: 978-0-9986912-3-7 (e-book)

DEDICATED TO
DEVON AND KAYLEIGH

.

TABLE OF CONTENTS

ACKNOWLEDGMENTS

I would like to acknowledge Scott G. and Karen D.
Scott, you showed me I could do this. Karen, you believed it.

INTRODUCTION

In the nineteen-eighties, two writers put Maine on the map for spine-chilling, insomnia-inducing storytelling. When Stephen King and Rick Hautala wrote about places like Castle Rock and Hilton, and the macabre things that happened there, it ignited a genre and a nation of readers. In the last thirty years, Maine has not lost its cachet as the creepiest state in the nation. And for good reason.

New England in general has a reputation for storytelling. Maybe it's the long winters, spinning tales in front of a flickering fire to pass the time. Maybe it's the deep shadows in the tall pine forests. Maybe it's that Nature itself is so unforgiving up here in the north. Maybe it's cabin fever. But Maine is a place unto itself.

When I first arrived here fifteen years ago, I heard stories about the miserable winters, usually culminating in a spectacular axe murder in late February by someone driven mad by being shut up for months with their family. There is truth to that, I discovered. I also discovered that Maine is home to many gifted writers, who channel their angst in more chillingly constructive ways. Rick Hautala used to say that if he couldn't write, he'd be up on a bell tower with a rifle. Writing scary tales is a much more socially acceptable and occasionally lucrative way to deal with the demons and the shadows that seem to love Maine more than the tourists from away.

This anthology contains some of the best stories from a new generation of Maine and Maine-inspired writers. Peter N. Dudar's *The Old Guide's Tale*, April Hawks' *Giant Wompstah*, and Katherine Silva's *Rare*

Birds are what I call "only in Maine" stories — they could not happen anywhere else but here. There are tales that evoke the haunting, haunted mysteries of our lovely state, like Morgan Sylvia's *Agony Chamber,* Glen Rolfe's *Death Lights,* and Joshua Goudreau's *The Black Beast of Andover.* The peculiarities of some of Maine's residents are illustrated in Dale T. Phillips' *In the Woods* and *Confession* by James Graham. And there are stories that could only come from Maine-bred writers, like Thomas Washburn, Jr.'s *The Bad Trip,* Wicker Stone's *Seeing Is Believing,* and Leslie Linder's *Catharine Hill.*

Mainers have a saying — "You can't get there from here." If it's subzero bone-chills and long winter nightmares you want, you most certainly can get there from here. Enjoy this latest collection of new voices, carrying on with the traditions inspired by our great and most eerie state.

Holly Newstein

THE OLD GUIDE'S TALE

Peter N. Dudar

"We ain't gonna catch nothing today." The Old Guide set his fishing rod between his legs, pulled out a book of matches from his coat pocket, and relit his pipe. A wisp of smoke poured out his nostrils, making him look like an ancient dragon in some storybook illustration. His eyes never left the water as he did this.

"… The water ain't right, that is. And when the lake is in cycle, the fish won't bite."

Skinny Pete threw a glance at him before responding.

"And we *ain't* gonna catch nothing as long as you're running that mouth of yours. You're scaring the fish, dammit!"

I couldn't help but laugh. John (the 'Old Guide' as we preferred to call him, on account of his lifetime of hunting and fishing in Maine) was notorious for running his mouth off. He was the one who could never keep his comments, advice, or stories to himself. And Skinny Pete, who had grown quite restless after an hour without a single bite, was looking for a better reason as to why the fish weren't tugging on his line.

The three of us worked together on the loading platform at the Postal Service. Skinny Pete and I had been planning this trip since fishing season opened. Sebago Lake had just turned over (the dermis of ice that coated the surface for the winter finally fractured and disappeared; gone like another lonesome ghost of winter) and we were hoping to catch at least a few salmon, if only to get some practice in for later on in the summer. And sitting in the cold morning air on the dock of the Portland Water District station can get quite frustrating when there's no action going on.

John is old enough to be either of our dads (myself at forty-four, Skinny Pete at five years less than me) and when Skinny Pete and I went out in public with him, we'd call him 'Dad' just to bust his balls. He served in Vietnam for three tours of duty and had the bullet holes scattered across his abdomen to prove it. Both of us spent countless hours listening to his war stories at work. For John, the bigger his audience, the bigger the stories would get. I suppose with age comes the license to embellish. After all, when you're old enough to start forgetting things that happened in your life, you may as well make the stuff you do remember as unforgettable as possible. So, when he was sure he had you hooked, John's smile would grow even bigger than his story and he'd reel you right in with it, the way he would a fish if one had decided to bite.

When we first started at the post office, the Old Guide had us convinced that the first part of a deer you'd eat once you shot it was its asshole. "You stuff that sombitch with potatoes and carrots, and just roast it right on the fire," he said, his grin practically stretching from ear to ear. John has the smile of an old-timer; the teeth a bit crooked and stained yellow with coffee and tobacco. But it's an honest smile, a smile of general amusement, not fixed and forced like some smiles you get nowadays.

Except this morning, John wasn't smiling. In fact, he treated this fishing trip with apprehension from the moment Skinny Pete and I started planning it. He tried to talk us out of it at first, saying it was still too cold out or that every angler in Southern Maine would be out fishing and it wouldn't be any fun. In the end, he insisted on coming with us. He never showed an ounce of enthusiasm or excitement; totally uncharacteristic of the Old Guide.

"I'm serious," John shot back at Skinny Pete. "I grew up on this lake. I know every inch of it. The water is bad ... It goes in cycles.

Let me ask you something. Other than us, do you see anyone fishing this lake today?"

"That don't mean shit," Skinny Pete set his own rod down long enough to light himself a cigarette. "It's still early. I bet this lake will be jumping by afternoon."

"The fuck it will," the Old Guide snapped. There ain't nobody around but us. There ain't even a game warden around. We are all alone, my friend. Don't you think there's a reason for that?"

"Maybe there's a tournament going on today somewhere else," I offered.

The Old Guide picked up his plastic coffee cup (filled with beer, not coffee) and took a gulp. He set the cup back down, dragged the sleeve of his green L.L. Bean coat against his thick, white beard to wipe it dry, and began reeling in his slack line. His gaze at the water never broke during this transaction. It was as if he was hypnotized.

"If there was a tournament this weekend, I'd be fishing it instead of sitting out here with you two. But there ain't no tournaments going on this early in the season. I didn't want you two to be out on this lake alone. I know that this lake is in cycle." The Old Guide held his pipe to his lips and took another long drag off it. "You two don't realize it, but we're in a lot of danger out here. Skinny Pete didn't grow up on this lake like I did. And Linus ... Well, you're an out-of-stater ..."

I was always thankful that the Old Guide referred to me as Linus; my pledge name from college. Since Skinny Pete and I share the same name, the rest of the crew at the post office call us Pete and Repeat, a moniker I loathe to this day. There are some that refer to us as Pete and Skinny Pete, but I'm told that when I'm not around, I'm always Fat Pete or Big Pete. The truth is I prefer that over Pete and Repeat. If it really bothered me, I'd just go on a diet.

The "out-of-stater" part is true. My being born in New York has been an excuse for the Old Guide to pick on me. If I ever make a mistake, it's because I'm from out-of-state and don't know any better. I've come to learn that the residents of Maine not involved with commercial or tourist trades hate us out-of-staters with a passion. They would prefer we kept our money and our business as far from Maine as possible, which seems counter-intuitive for the state known as Vacationland. I can still recall a time when I first came to Maine and the Old Guide treated me mercilessly, just to try and get me to go back home to New York. It took him at least a year to give up trying, and another year to quit referring to me as an out-of-stater, and start referring to me as being "from away." Somewhere in those two years we became good friends.

The wind picked up and the three of us shivered in unison. Without warning, a strong gust caught Skinny Pete's baseball cap and tossed it into the water just past the dock. Skinny Pete bent down on his knees and reached down to pick it up when the Old Guide's arm shot out like a bullet and caught the back of his neck. With a tremendous yank, the Old Guide sent Skinny Pete tumbling backwards onto the dock.

For the first time since I've known him, I saw a terrified look on the Old Guide's face.

"Goddammit, Pete … Don't touch the fucking water!" John was yelling, and for a moment, I was actually too stunned and too afraid to say anything. When I could speak, I was barely above a whisper.

"Calm down, John … He's just trying to pick his hat up."

"I'll buy him a new one. I don't want either of you to go near the water." The Old Guide sat back down in his folding chair. Skinny Pete stood up and brushed his ass off, sending a cloud of dust adrift in the cold breeze. He shot an angry glance at the Old Guide and muttered something under his breath as he sat back down in his own chair. A few minutes passed by before the Old Guide decided to tell us the story, or rather, the legend of Sebago Lake.

❋ ❋ ❋

"I know you two ain't gonna believe a word I say about this. You both know that I can tell a tall-tale when I'm up to it. Well, I'm telling you the truth right now, so I want you both to pay attention. This lake is in cycle right now … The water is bad."

I glanced over at Skinny Pete, who was now wide-eyed with fascination. He no longer looked upset about being dropped on his ass a few minutes ago, but rather like he knew there was a good explanation coming regardless if an apology was involved or not. I turned back to face the Old Guide again. He had just finished the last of the beer in his coffee cup. He opened up his grotesquely oversized tackle box and removed a fresh can of beer, which he opened and poured into his coffee cup. He placed the empty can back in his tackle box and closed it. When he finished this ritual, he put the lid back on the coffee cup and continued.

"Every five years, this lake takes somebody's life. It's in cycle right now, as it's now been five years since the last accident. All the locals know it, including myself. That's why I didn't want you two to go fishing this morning. The lake is waiting right now. That's why you can't touch the water."

Skinny Pete laughed, breaking the heavy silence around us.

"What are you saying, Old Guide? That the lake is hungry?"

The way these words fell out of Skinny Pete's mouth made me laugh as well. I tried to choke it back, as I could tell from the seriousness on the Old Guide's face that he wasn't amused. But the more I thought about it, the sillier it sounded and the sillier it made me feel for falling for another of John's stories. The last thing I wanted was to be convinced that I should eat a deer's asshole for dinner.

"Well then, fuck you both ... I'm going home." The Old Guide began reeling in the rest of his line.

"No, no ... We're sorry. Please continue," I pleaded between chuckles.

He reeled his bait in, inspected it, and frowned when he saw there wasn't even a nibble on it. He cast it back out into the dark, choppy water and set his rod down.

"A couple hundred years ago, this lake belonged to the Indians. They lived here all year round. Christ, there was enough wildlife to hunt and fish that they could have lived here forever. Everything they could ever need this lake provided for them. This was their paradise.

"Well, the chief of these Indians was named Red Bear. Supposedly, as a boy, this guy was out hunting along Sebago, gathering for his tribe, and he spotted this giant, red bear out along the tree line. The bear spoke to him, and told him that the spirits favored him. The bear told him that if the boy let it free, if he didn't kill it, the spirits would grant him one wish on his deathbed. The boy understood that this was some kind of magic, turned his back on the bear, and it disappeared back into the woods where it came from.

"The boy went back to the camp and told the council of elders about what had happened to him. As a result, he was given the name Red Bear, and was regarded as a holy man among the tribe. Later on, when the chief of the tribe died, Red Bear took his place."

The Old Guide took his eyes off the water and glanced at us to see if we were paying attention. When he saw that we were, he took another drink from his coffee cup and continued.

"Red Bear became a great leader. He was revered by the whole tribe as a wise and honest man. He was courageous in battle; a cunning warrior against the other Maine tribes when they fought for territory and resources. But above all, Red Bear was humble to the spirits. He was what you'd call a righteous person.

"When the French decided to come down from Canada and explore this new land for settlement, they stopped at Sebago. Fucking out-of-staters! They always fuck up everything." John stopped and threw me a glance. "Red Bear offered the French soldiers food and hospitality. Although there was a language barrier between them, the commander of the soldiers accepted the food Red Bear offered under the pretense of friendship. The French dined with the Indians at a great celebration. And when everyone went to sleep, the French commander woke his soldiers and they began slaughtering the sleeping Indians. A few women and children escaped into the woods, but most of the Indian warriors were murdered in cold blood, right over on the beach, over by where we parked the truck."

The Old Guide pointed to the patch of sand just to the right of the dock where we were fishing.

"Their blood ran right into the water of this lake. And Red Bear, after being slain by the French commander's saber, had a vision of the red bear that he'd seen as a boy. The bear spoke to him. 'Greetings, favored one. I have returned to grant your wish. What is it that you desire?' Red Bear responded. 'My people are murdered by my enemy, and I am to blame. I was deceived, and my tribe has all but died because of it. I pray my people shall flourish again someday, but that is not my wish. I wish that for every drop of my people's blood spilled by this lake, a life of my enemies shall be taken in return.' 'So shall it be,' the bear responded. 'For every drop of blood spilled, a life shall be taken. However, as in nature, all things occur in cycles … The sun, the moon, the seasons. As spirit of this lake, I shall only take one life every five years. Thus, nature shall keep its balance.' With that, the bear disappeared and Red Bear died."

The Old Guide inhaled deeply from his pipe, allowed the smoke to escape through his lips, and breathed it back in through his nostrils; a trick that although pretty gross was still neat to watch. As he did this, a noise broke through the silence. A truck with a boat in tow had entered the parking lot. Upon inspection, the Old Guide nodded.

"They're from New Hampshire. Fucking out-of-staters." John

glanced at me. "No offense, Linus."

I shrugged in response, watching as the man in the passenger side of the truck jumped out and hand signaled the driver to back up toward the boat launch. When the stern of the boat was in the water, the passenger unhitched the boat and slid it off the trailer and tied it to the launching dock's post. The driver pulled the truck back into the parking lot, where he parked next to John's GMC and unloaded their fishing gear from the truck's bed. The passenger joined him, and together they loaded and launched the boat. As the wind pushed them by us, the passenger tipped his hat to us and called out, "Any luck this morning?"

The Old Guide answered, "Nah, we ain't caught nothing yet."

The passenger turned his back to us to get situated in the boat. The driver was tugging at the start cord on the Mercury motor. It choked out a few coughs of smoke before begrudgingly turning over. When it roared to life, the two forgot all about us as they sped off to the center of the lake. The Old Guide jumped to his feet, pulling us both off our own chairs with his giant hands. Standing up straight, John was at least 6'4". The guy towered over us, making us two grown men look like children.

"Come on," he bellowed. "Get in my truck."

"What about our fishing gear?" Skinny Pete protested.

"Fuck the gear," the Old guide responded. "We'll get it when it's over!"

"When what's over?" I asked.

"You'll see. I told you, the lake is in cycle. These fucking out-of-staters are about to die."

There was no hint of a smile on John's face to tell us he had us hooked on his story. Instead, he had a look of fear and conviction, and I couldn't help but wonder if this was the look he had when he was fighting against the enemy in Vietnam. Within a few short seconds, he had us piled into the cab of his GMC Sierra.

The Old Guide's truck was a shrine to the Maine outdoorsman. It was decorated with magnets portraying every species of bass, trout and landlocked salmon found in Maine. Hanging off the rearview mirror, a pine tree air freshener, a tiny wicker basket with several variations of trout flies hooked into it, and a few duck feathers fastened together with fishing line. On the back window hung the obligatory gun rack (no rifles, though, as hunting season was far later in the year) which now held a rather large wooden club that one might use if fishing for bluefish or anything with teeth that might take a finger off if one wasn't careful. On the faded upholstery of the seats, several maps, hunting and fishing rule books, and several scattered audio cassettes featuring George Thorogood and Jimi Hendrix. These last few items got shuffled about as we situated ourselves inside the cab.

"It ain't an accident that I survived three tours of duty in 'Nam." The Old Guide had just opened a fresh can of beer (his coffee cup left behind with our abandoned gear). "Hell, I caught a few bullets here and there, but in the end I killed more of them fucks than my whole platoon combined. It was the best hunting I ever did. When I was a kid, I used to go deer hunting all the time, and for the most part, I never even saw a deer until my father taught me how to hunt."

He set the can down on the dashboard and picked up his pipe. He opened the door of the truck just wide enough to knock the dead ashes out of the bowl and examine the inside of the pipe when it was empty. He closed the door, pulled out his tobacco pouch and filled the pipe again.

"Ya see … the deer knows you're out there. He's going by his senses. He can either see you, hear you, or he can smell you. And if he can do any two of those three things, well, you ain't never going to see him. But if you're up in a tree stand, wearing animal urine to throw your scent off, and if you're sitting still and quiet like a mouse, that deer will walk right beneath you. All you have to do is pull the trigger."

The Old Guide swept a match against the strike bar of the matchbook and lit up his pipe.

"The enemy is the same way. Now, I've seen soldiers tearing through the jungle, whooping and hollering like assholes because they think they're scaring the enemy (or at least confusing him into thinking there's a hell of a lot more of us than there really was). Then there were soldiers who wore enough bug juice to wake the dead. You could smell these idiots a mile away. Didn't bother the mosquitoes, though. They kept biting no matter what we smelled like. There were even some who would stop and take a shit in the middle of an open field. These were the assholes that we'd ship home in body bags. Ya see … the enemy knew we were there *all along*. Charlie would be hiding under a bush, counting each pair of legs to march right past him."

John stopped for a moment as he opened his glove compartment and pulled out a pair of binoculars. He handed them to Skinny Pete.

"Now don't take your eyes off the two guys in the boat. You're gonna see the lake eat them alive." Then he glanced at me. "You, too, Linus. Keep your eyes on the boat." He picked his beer up, took a long guzzle, and continued.

"So, when I went into the jungle, I made myself invisible. Charlie was so busy watching the soldiers who were listening to the radio or putting on bug juice or taking a shit, that all I had to do was shoot him first. The enemy was just as foolish and predictable as we were. But ..."

Skinny Pete and I turned in unison, both of us hanging onto every word. A frown spread across his face.

"Don't look at me ... watch the boat!" Our faces snapped back toward the water in unison.

"But, the enemy had a reason to try and kill us. We were invading his home and trying to kill him first. Now, Mother Nature. She has no reason for killing people. She doesn't need one. Like when the tornado drops on someone's trailer house, or when the avalanche buries a family out skiing for the day. She doesn't care. She's a cold, calculating bitch that strikes without reason."

The two men in the boat had just dropped anchor out toward the center of the lake. They were too far away for us to see their faces, but we could see their doomed silhouettes as they baited their hooks and threw their lines in.

"I was a kid when I saw a man die for the first time, right here where we're sitting now. My father took my brother and I out to this very spot to show us what you're about to see. I was only six at the time, but I remember every exact detail. I'll never forget it as long as I live. It was February, and the lake had frozen to at least a foot and a half thick. There was this old guy by the name of Hunnicut that was staying at a camp right down the road from us. He'd come up from New Jersey to do some ice-fishing. He didn't know anything about the lake's history, and he had no idea that the water was in cycle, just like it is now. Why would he? Fucking out-of-stater.

"Well, my dad took me and my brother snowshoeing for the day. Hunnicut told my dad that he was going fishing, even invited him to come along. But my dad knew about the water. He could have told Hunnicut about the water, could have saved the guy's life. Instead, he let the guy go fishing. I doubt Hunnicut would have believed him anyway.

"So, my dad walks us along the bank, trudging through snow that was waist-deep for us, to this spot. And we watched it happen."

I turned to look at the Old Guide again, but he motioned with his hand to look back out at the water. The men in the boat appeared to be having a grand old time. I noticed that the water was no longer choppy with spring whitecaps. It had glazed over smooth, and not so much as a ripple echoed off the boat as the two men moved around. The Old Guide glanced over at me.

"You see it too, don'tcha Linus?" He inhaled on his pipe. "The water is getting ready." He exhaled, and the cab filled with a cloud of smoke. For the first time in my life, I felt truly terrified. My heart was pounding in my chest, and I could feel my skin crackle with goose bumps. It felt like time had stopped moving forward, and that my every breath took deliberated thought just to fill my lungs and exhale.

"Hunnicut was sitting on a folding chair out on the ice. He had five traps set around him, and a sixth hole in the ice that he was jigging a line out of. He had built a fire on the ice with some dead brush he pulled off that small island just starboard of the boat you two are looking at. Hunnicut saw us and stood up. He had the jigging rod in his left hand and a thermos of coffee in his right. He set the coffee down and began waving at us when all at once, the ice beneath him opened."

My eyes left the water again, and I watched the expression on the Old Guide's face turn blank, as if he were staring at a ghost out in the middle of the lake. For a brief instant, he looked as if he were not just telling a story, but as if he was reliving it, and for that moment I was filled with dread. I almost hoped he was pulling our legs with one of his tall-tales. His tired, gray eyes bulged out and he continued talking, but I wasn't quite sure if he was still talking to us or himself.

"The ice didn't just open. Not a break-through like you see on the news, where some idiot snowmobiler thought the ice was thick enough when it wasn't. No, the ice came alive like a giant mouth with huge icicle teeth. Old man Hunnicut never saw it coming. It just happened. He was standing there with that goddamn jigging rod in his hand, waving like an old lady who sees you coming down the street. And the next minute, his body was half-submerged into the ice, and the fucking ice was chewing on him, eating his torso. These huge fangs of ice were ripping him apart, spilling his stomach and intestines all over the pure white surface of the lake.

"And that motherfucker screamed. Not like the soldiers in Vietnam when they got shot. Hell, I never screamed like that when I caught a bullet. Hunnicut's voice shrieked and bellowed across the lake and far into the woods. Christ, I bet they heard it way the hell out in Portland. Every time that frozen mouth opened and closed on him, he'd gasp in just enough air to throw out another scream. He did that all the way until the fangs got a hold of his diaphragm and lungs. After that, either he went into shock or he died outright. But once he stopped breathing, the ice sucked the rest of him down below surface and the lake froze right back over again. The only thing left of Hunnicut was a few patches of red ice and the traps he'd set around him.

"My father made my brother and I watch the whole thing. When it was over, I was paralyzed with fear. I stood there looking at this patch of ice stained red with blood where old man Hunnicut was waving to us moments before. I might have gone into shock myself. My dad carried me home, and when we were inside by the fireplace, he told my mother that he was going back out to bring in Hunnicut's traps. I freaked out. I never felt more afraid in my life than when he walked out the door. Not even in Vietnam. I cried like a baby, begging him not to go back out on the ice, but he swore up and down that the ice was safe again. And when he did come back with the traps, he told me and my brother the lake's history, just like I told you."

The Old Guide turned and looked at us again, and the color was returning to his face. He inhaled on his pipe, and rubbed the whiskers in his thick, white beard as he exhaled.

"I've seen a lot of people die in Vietnam. Mostly kids the same age as you two when you started working at the post office. Hell, I've killed a lot kids. Even babies. I was so good at it that when the war ended I was admitted into Special Forces and was shipped into some other third-world country so I could keep going. I didn't have to come home to a nation that would condemn me and spit on me, and call me a baby killer like they did to the other soldiers. Can you imagine that? Fighting a war for your country and have your country hate you for it? Most Americans think that war is soldiers fighting soldiers, and leave the women and kids alone. In Vietnam, the women and children would try to kill you just as fast as the men would. Let me tell you something … Little enemies become big enemies. In combat, you never take chances. Protest, my ass. If you held a gun in the face of the average American, they'd cry like pussies. They have no concept of what war is. But of all the deaths I've seen while I was in the service, nothing scared me to the point of terror like watching old man Hunnicut die." The Old Guide turned and looked at us.

"Hey, Skinny Pete, how are our friends in the boat doing?"

"They ain't catching anything, that's for sure."

The two men in the boat had been sitting there for almost fifteen minutes, constantly retrieving their lines and casting out again. The water had not made a ripple all the while they were out there.

And then it happened.

One of the men had been drinking coffee, and when he finished, he leaned over the side of the boat to dip his cup into the water and wash it out. The exact moment his hand made contact with the water, the lake exploded into action, in a manner I could never have dreamed possible, except in a nightmare.

The water took the shape of a giant, transparent hand. It pushed the small boat into the air in one huge wave, sending the two men and the boat at least twenty feet into the air, where it held still just long enough for us to watch them squirm in raw fear and disbelief. We could hear them screaming to us for help, although the three of us in the truck knew damn well there was nothing to do except watch helplessly. Their motions inside the boat were pathetic; the two men pitching back and forth, trying to find some form of balance as this aquatic hand held their lives in a chilling grip.

I snatched the binoculars from Skinny Pete, who let them fall out of his grip without a hint of argument. I held them to my own eyes and could see two weeping, trembling faces, their chins quivering and pleading desperately for help that wasn't coming. I had the impression of watching trapped animals, the fight beaten out of them until there is nothing left but a terrible sadness and desperation. I felt helpless, to the point of almost being insignificant, and the fear and sadness began to consume me as well. I was not looking at the Old Guide or Skinny Pete, but I could tell from their breathing that they felt the same as I did. If I could have spoken, I would have asked God to make this vision before us stop, but my throat had knotted and I could barely choke out my own breath.

And then the water moved again; this time parting like the sea before Moses and his people, exposing the jagged rocks at the bottom of the lakebed, dead and solid and black as night, except for a few patches of green growth that made up the vegetation at the bottom of Sebago Lake. For a split second, I could hear the Old Guide's voice in my head telling us that the lake was hungry. Now here it was before us, the water opened like a giant mouth, and a watery hand holding the men in the boat, ready to satisfy its appetite.

The two men in the boat were now in hysterics, and I felt myself wondering what the view they were seeing must have been like. I pushed these thoughts from my mind, waiting to see what I already knew was going to happen.

With the brute strength of nature unleashed, the watery hand rolled the boat so that the two men were turned upside down, and before they could fall out, the watery hand smashed the boat against the rocks below like a human hand would squish a mosquito. From the confines of the truck, we could hear the terrible crunch of the wooden vessel crashing and splintering into the jagged, black rocks in the depths of Sebago Lake. A moment later, the water rushed over the shattered vessel and settled back into the quiet, choppy lake top we'd been fishing out of all morning. The waves had returned and, hesitantly, the broken pieces of the boat's wooden frame floated to the surface and bobbed silently up and down among the whitecaps.

"What the fuck just happened?" Skinny Pete's face had turned a pale shade of blue, and I had to wonder if he had stopped breathing altogether during the horrible spectacle we had just witnessed.

Two small orange shapes bobbed to the surface, and for a sick moment, I thought they were the lifeless bodies of the two men from the boat. I peered through the binoculars again, only to see that they were empty life vests.

"What happened to the bodies?" I turned toward the Old Guide, secretly wishing I hadn't asked.

"We won't see them again. Nobody will," he answered. Despair crept down his spine, and he shivered silently behind the wheel of the truck. John could have prevented all of this from happening, but instead chose to educate us through the obscenity of proof. "Their bodies will never be found. The lake ate them."

Skinny Pete buried his face in his hands and started crying. I reached out to put my hand on his shoulder, but my eyes caught the Old Guide's, and I withdrew.

"What do we do now?" I asked, dreading the response.

"We get our shit and get out of here," he answered. I'll call the Game Warden's office when we get back to Portland ... let them know about the out-of-staters. They'll already know, anyway. None of this is new to them. The state will come down and collect their stuff. They probably won't even bother skimming the lake or nothing. They know about the lake. I bet the incident won't even be in the newspaper. C'mon, let's get our own gear."

The three of us collected our fishing gear as quickly and quietly as possible. There was nothing more to say about the subject, and if there was, well, we just ignored it. And as the old GMC Sierra exited the parking lot, I turned back to face the lake one last time. My eyes scanned across the cold, choppy water and back into the woods along the tree line. For the tiniest second, I thought my eyes were playing tricks on me. I could have sworn I saw a big red bear streak into the woods.

GIANT WOMPSTAH

April Hawks

Prologue

Larry the Lobster (unaware he had been named something as un-imaginative as Larry the Lobster) scuttled around on the silt, looking for tasty bits of things to eat. After searching for a long while, Larry happened upon a cave, unlike any that he had encountered before. There was a flash of an appetizing morsel through the mouth of the cave, and Larry could also see flashes of his fellow lobsters moving around. It looked promising. Once Larry got inside, however, he found he couldn't get himself back out.

* * *

Silas Dirk looked down at the bright red shell on his plate. One of the perks that he appreciated about settling into a small town in Maine

17

was the ease with which he could eat a lobster dinner at prices he had never imagined. Twenty or more dollars a pound for lobster *tail* in the Midwest and on the West Coast. Here, in this little seafood restaurant on a random, rocky beach, he paid twenty dollars *total* for the whole dinner. It was insane. He needed, the first few times he ordered the dish, to look at the placemats for the instructions on opening the whole lobster to get at the meat, but now he was proficient. It was disgusting, but he had learned.

He gave advice to those gathered around the table on how to eat their own lobsters, deciding that he sounded *almost* like a local but better, of course. That was a given. It was also part of why he had picked this particular state for this particular operation.

After only meatless shelled carcasses remained on the plates, all traces of the lobster massacre were swept away by the wait staff, and dessert and coffee were ordered.

"We're close to having the mechanics worked out for the procedure we are all looking to implement." Dirk had no need to expand beyond the vague statement, as everyone in attendance knew the project that was being discussed. It was better that any potential eavesdroppers remained clueless.

Those around the table nodded in satisfaction, except for one disgruntled expression. Dirk focused his attention on this man. He had been the most oppositional through the planning stages but Dirk couldn't just exclude him, as he held sixty percent of the financing. Dirk didn't have time to find a replacement investor so he coddled this one every step of the way.

"What's your hesitation at this point, Jeffries?" Dirk gave him a smile, practiced to perfection in front of the mirror.

All heads turned and focused on Jeffries, who sat thinking about his response.

William Jeffries had made his money the old-fashioned way: hard work ethic, long hours, sweat, and smart investing. He had built his company from the ground up, having bought the perfect piece of land for his first location and working on it in his "spare time" away from his full-time job on a construction crew over the course of four years. In the last thirty years, he had developed it into a multi-million-dollar company. Just two years ago, he sold Lock, Stock and Barrel for a cool billion and retired. Then Dirk approached him with a proposal that his philanthropic side couldn't turn away from. Now he owned sixty percent of Dirk's enterprise.

Jeffries was convinced, based solely on the quirk of Dirk's mouth and the gleam in his eye that there was something — probably something crucial — that the man was withholding. Jeffries knew how to take measure of people. Recently, his gut was screaming at him to pack up and get the hell out. But the magnitude of the impact this project could have and the amount of funds already invested stayed his hand. It was a lot to lose without solid facts.

The board members were all staring at him, so he voiced his concern. "Are we certain that we want to move to the next phase? It seems like a bit of a rush to me."

"I understand your hesitation, Bill. But the research has been solid and this is the next logical step. Jeannie, would you please show the board the report from Monday?"

The woman nodded and passed a copy of the document to each person at the table. She then resumed her seat next to Dirk and consulted the documents in her hand.

"As you can see, on page three, the projected results are ..." She spoke calmly and sent reassuring smiles, as practiced as Dirk's, to Jeffries during her hour-long presentation.

❊ ❊ ❊

Joel Carter liked video games in all the different formats available: Role Playing Games, First Person Shooters, Sandbox, anything. It didn't matter what console it was for. He read all the gamer magazines too. In this, he was like any other thirteen-year-old. He differed in that he was just as comfortable outdoors and spent most of his time out of the house. His mother always encouraged him to take his five-year-old brother along with him as he tromped through the woods. Joel was happy to.

Some of his friends complained about doing anything with their younger siblings. Joel felt bad about that. He and Logan had a great time playing together in the woods behind the house.

They were far enough out in the sticks that their property had plenty of room to explore, and over the years Joel had explored all the corners of their land several times over.

In the beginning, he had gone out with his dad, starting at about Logan's age. As their dad got too sick to leave the house, Joel would

go out on his own partly to stay out of his mother's way and partly because it was hard to see his dad getting thinner and weaker. His mother
didn't stop him, and he appreciated it.

When their dad passed away, Logan was three. Joel decided then
that his brother wouldn't miss out on the experience just because their
dad couldn't take them. When Logan turned five they started their adventures together. Joel felt that their dad was there with them when
they were in the woods. Though Logan could barely remember their
dad, Joel used that time to tell stories about him and to share with
Logan his belief that their dad always watched over them.

* * *

The boys' mother brought them to the beaches on the weekends
when the weather allowed. They took turns picking a beach before loading up the car and heading out. On the way home, they would stop and
see one of their mother's friends — Byron had been friends with both
the boys' mother and father — and he would show the boys his latest
batch of catch. Logan and Joel would peer into the glass tank and each
would pick out one of the lobsters for the next day's meal.

"Wompstah." Logan jammed his finger at the tank, leaving a
smudge of whatever coated the hands of little boys. Joel smiled and
didn't correct him. When Mom was done talking to Byron, they headed
home sea-salted, sun-kissed, wind-whipped, and happy. Logan carried
his wompstah in the same shoe box every week. And he always picked a
name for his short-term companion. This week, he named it Treebump.
Last week's had been Cornnut Peanut. Joel and his mom bit their lips
against the laughter that threatened. They didn't want to hurt Logan's
feelings, but that boy had some craziness come out of his mouth.

Back at home, Joel put his and his mother's lobsters in the refrigerator while Logan put his on the counter. As his mom was making home-
made macaroni and cheese, she could over hear Logan talking away to
Treebump as though he was getting an actual response. She smiled.

Joel went to his room and put his headphones in. He sat at his
computer and entered the server he had created on Minecraft and got
to work adding more buildings to the city he'd been working on, quickly
losing track of time.

* * *

Larry was still unnamed, but he clambered around amongst other lobsters in a strange, smooth cave. The world beyond the walls was blurry, but occasionally, one of his fellows would float away, carried off by some fleshy thing that would reach down and drag it away. Once, Larry had lost three brethren and a patch appeared on the wall, making it even blurrier than it had been already.

For some reason, Larry couldn't open his claws and there wasn't much to do, so sometimes Larry tucked himself into a corner, while others crawled all over him. At other times, he was the crawler.

* * *

Joel's light flickered on and off. He turned to the door of his bedroom and saw Logan flicking the switch with a wide smile. Joel removed his earbuds.

"Hey what's up? Hey, I'm paying attention. Stop flicking the switch. You're gonna break it."

With an impish grin, Logan flipped the light switch down one more time and then up.

"Dinner time." Logan said.

"Okay. I'll be there after I save and exit." Joel turned back to the computer. The light flicked off again, then back on and Joel could hear Logan's laughter fading with the slaps of his feet on the hallway floor. Joel chuckled and clicked on his mouse.

* * *

"Okay, Logan. I need you to please put Treewater in the fridge, now, and go wash your hands.

"Moooommmm. His name's Tree*bump* not Treewater."

"Okay honey, I'm sorry. Now put him away. Scoot."

Logan put the lobster in the box and then into the refrigerator. "Goodnight. Sleep tight. Don't let the bed bugs bite. Sweet dreams and have a good night and I love you." Logan closed the refrigerator door and raced to the bathroom. When he returned, the Carters sat down to eat their food.

* * *

Larry and some of the other lobsters had been moved to several different caves. They were separated and named. Larry paid no attention to the large beings that observed him as he settled into his new home.

* * *

"We've taken your advice and agree that this specimen would be a perfect fit for the program. We'll start first thing in the morning, sir," the deep voice on the other end of the phone line said.

"How long before we see results?"

"Days. Two — three tops."

"Keep me informed." Silas Dirk smiled, an uncharacteristic real expression, as he ended the phone call.

* * *

Larry got more food than he had ever found before. Every once in a while, a shiny thing would poke him near his tail, but overall, life was good. Lobsters have no concept of time, but eventually Larry found him-self back in the silt, in the familiar open spaces he had grown up in.

* * *

The following Sunday it was Logan's turn to pick the location of the family beach trip. As he always did, he thought long and hard about where he wanted to go. As he always did, he chose the beach near Fort Popham. Visiting the fort was one of the few memories Logan had with their father.

The boys played in the water while their mother watched with one eye and read with the other. When Logan's lips were finally bluish, they got out, dried off, and walked the edge of the water — all three of them together — looking for shells, rocks, and sea glass.

As they did at every beach, they all built a large sandcastle and named it Castle Carter. Mom snapped a picture of it on her phone and they left Castle Carter to be devoured by the waves.

The hottest part of the afternoon was spent climbing around the old stone fort. Fort Popham had a series of plaques that told of its history and each visit Logan insisted his mother read the plaques to him. This time as she read, Logan wandered over to Joel and tugged on his shirt to get his attention. Soon he was on his big brother's back and able to see through the giant square holes in the wall, out toward the ocean. He squealed with delight to see the waves on the water and the birds in the air.

When Joel turned his head to have a conversation with his mother, Logan began to bounce up and down on his back in excitement, patting Joel's shoulder with his hand. "Wompstah! Mom! Wompstah! Joel! Wompstah!"

Joel paused his conversation with his mother to readjust Logan's position on his back. "Yeah bud. That's right! That's where Byron gets the lobsters from. The ocean! That's right!" Joel turned his attention back to his mother as Logan poked Joel's shoulder. "Let me down!"

Joel obliged him. Neither Joel nor his mother noticed that Logan was pouting and muttering to himself. "Wompstah gone." After a couple minutes, Logan found a rock with mica in it that was shiny enough to distract him.

* * *

Larry found it harder to move around. He could no longer fit in the cracks and crevices he had once explored. Nor was he content with small bits and pieces, he needed much more to sustain himself. Luckily, his claws were working again, no longer useless. There would have been no way to survive without them.

* * *

"Whatever you did that screwed this up, figure it out and *fix it*." Silas Dirk kept his voice even and low. He never raised it. However, when he was upset his voice frosted over. The man from the lab that was on the phone with Dirk now had no doubt that he was in trouble. He was also under no pretense that if the problem wasn't fixed soon, he would be in *big* trouble. Dirk heard the man on the other end of the line gulp and he smiled. He knew the man understood the consequences. "You'd better figure it out, Tate, before I meet with the board on Wednesday."

"Yes, sir. I'll get right on that, sir ..." He paused.

"What is it, Tate?"

"I'll get started right away, sir ... Now if I may."

Dirk smiled as Tate's voice cracked like he was going through puberty again. Some situations required more finesse. Fear meant results, in this case. He loved that Tate was so eager to get off the phone. He also enjoyed dragging the phone call out for that very reason. He remained silent for a full minute before Tate's voice cracked over the phone again.

"Sir, are you still there?"

"Yes, Tate. Go ahead. Call Jeannie with any results or explanations, as soon as you get them. Understand?"

Dirk ended the call without closing it out. He leaned back in his seat, putting his feet up on the desk, and dialed.

"Jeannie ... we have a problem."

＊ ＊ ＊

Logan was at the coffee table coloring while Joel read a book. Their mom walked in to let them know that their lobsters — Logan had named his Treewater this week — were almost cooked. She wandered over to Logan's picture and rustled his hair. "Is that a picture of Tree Water?" she asked.

Logan looked up at her with his large blue eyes. He shook his head and pointed down at his drawing. "Giant Wompstah" the boy insisted, and when she looked again she could see it. A giant lobster with an island in the background, and a little stick figure in front. If she could trust perspective in the picture (and she knew she couldn't really, because Logan's mind hadn't yet learned to think in proportions) the lobster looked to be the size of a whale. She smiled and leaned down to kiss his forehead. As she walked back to the kitchen, she thought to herself that she was lucky to have boys with such active imaginations.

Joel walked over to the coffee table, intrigued by Logan's description of the picture. "Tell me more about the Giant lobster." He sat next to his little brother at the coffee table and looked at the picture.

"I sawed the giant wompstah at the fort, yesterday, Joel, in the water. I was looking out the window and it poked its head out and then went under the water again." He made a splashing sound to accentuate his story.

Never one to discourage Logan's imaginative stories, all Joel said in response was "Huh". He looked at the picture one more time before their mom announced that dinner was ready. Both boys jumped to their

feet and ran to the table, giant lobster fading from their minds in anticipation of the smallish lobsters they were about to eat.

*   *   *

The little thing in Larry's claw was making more noises, rhythmic
noises, as Larry crushed it. He brought part to his mouth, and the other
part fell away, no longer screaming and begging for help. It was too late,
anyway.

*   *   *

A woman of approximately thirty walked into the office, a smile on
her face and a sparkle in her blue eyes. She reached into the pocket of
her tailored pant suit and pulled out a badge, flashing it in front of the
trooper. He accepted it for study. When he was satisfied that it was legit-
imate, he looked up again at the woman's face, handing her badge back
to her. "How can I help you Miss Devereaux?"
"Can we speak in your office?"
The state trooper nodded and led the way.

*   *   *

"… and in other news, The CDC and Maine's State Troopers have
reportedly closed access to Fort Popham and Popham Beach State Park
in Phippsburg, until further notice. They cite reports of a hallucinogen that has contaminated the water and affected a handful of beach-
goers recently. Fred Jorgensen is live, outside the roadblock. Fred?"
"Thanks, Brenda. As you can see behind me, the road to Fort Popham and to Popham Beach State Park here in Phippsburg, is blocked
from travel. When asked about the restriction on the road, one officer
told me that there has been a hallucinogen introduced into the water.
Fortunately, the currents around the beach front area is keeping the ele-
ment from spreading to other parts of the state. I was able to speak to
Samantha Devereaux, an official from the CDC, earlier. She declined
to be interviewed on camera, but she did say that they are working to
keep the hallucinogen contained. I've gotten no word, yet, whether the
effects were caused intentionally or accidentally or whether they were
from chemical or bacterial side effects.

The hallucinogen even appears to have impacted wildlife. According to an initial exam of the body of Marcus Tate, it seems a shark attacked him in only two feet of water. No one saw the incident, but based on the state of the body, that is the most reasonable explanation. Also of note, is the lack of ducks and sea lions that are typically found frolicking near the beach.

Ms. Devereaux was hopeful that they would have an answer within the next forty-eight hours. If you visited Fort Popham or Popham Beach State Park between last Thursday and today, you are being asked to call the number that has been set up and is being shown at the bottom of the screen. Again, if you or someone you know is experiencing any of the symptoms on the screen right now, please call the number immediately. The symptoms include nausea, visual hallucinations, auditory hallucinations, fever, fatigue, and blistering of the skin. Please call the number at the bottom of your screen. Back to you, Brenda!"

"Thanks Fred! In sports today, the Red Sox played ..."

Dirk shut the television off. He picked up his phone.

"Get Marx on the line ... *now!*"

*   *   *

Mrs. Carter watched the news and began to panic. Ever since their trip to Popham on Saturday, Logan had been insistent that he had seen a giant lobster. The boys had played in the water for a large portion of the day. Was he hallucinating? She spent the next twenty-four hours watching both the boys closely, kissing their foreheads at random intervals to check their temperatures. Neither of them showed any indications of illness, much to her relief. She knew both boys were creative and inventive and the story Logan was telling wasn't unusual from the mouth of the boy. She decided against calling the hotline.

*   *   *

"Bill! Come on in! Have a seat!" Dirk gestured to a chair in front of his desk. "Can I have Jeannie get you anything? Coffee? Tea?"

Jeffries asked for coffee and Dirk echoed the request. They waited until Jeannie had brought their steaming cups before speaking again. Dirk started.

"So, Bill? What brings you here?"

"I just read in the paper that Tate was called in to help out on that beach enzyme thing and that the contaminant in the water killed him. What the hell was the lead scientist from *our project* doing mixed up in that mess?"

"Consulting for the CDC. They asked if we could spare him for a few days to try to isolate the compound in the water. Unfortunately, it has been found to be a bacterium, not a chemical, and it overrode his system. A shame, too. He was a good man."

Jeffries eyed the man and wondered how sincere Dirk's sorrow was. He doubted it ran deeper than his expression. Jeffries shifted in his chair. He glanced over at Jeannie, whose blue eyes were on the notebook and pen in her hand.

"You'll be glad to know, Bill, that our growth formula is working beyond our expectations. Think of the hunger we'll be able to quench with it! We'll be able to make more food with a few drops of the stuff on one plant than a dozen of the normal ones could produce. This phase of the project is going *swimmingly*."

Bill asked questions about percentages and volume before he got up to leave. He still had the feeling that Dirk was keeping something big from him, but he couldn't figure out what so he left it alone until he had proof — or an idea.

As Jeffries walked to the door, Dirk placed his hand on the older man's back. "I just want to thank you again for providing most the funding. We couldn't have done this without you." They said their goodbyes and Jeffries left.

Dirk closed the door. Jeannie spoke, now that they were alone. "What now?"

"We proceed as planned. Marx is looking at Tate's research. He'd been getting sloppy. Looks like he and one of the lab techs let the juiced lobster, the one they named Larry, go in the wild and held on to one that hadn't been introduced to the formula. Without the cessation formula, that fifty-foot lobster's been mucking around, although it does look like the damn thing has finally stopped growing on its own. Marx is working on a way to reverse the growth so we can catch it and move on with the trials. But we're back on track, despite that idiocy. As long as we can neutralize the giant lobster and get rid of the evidence, we're set. It we can't, we bolt. Jeffries can hold the bag for that."

Jeannie smiled and nodded. "And the cessation formula?"

"Worked perfectly. Marx has a thirty-pound lobster in the holding tank, right now. We can reproduce this effect and make lobster — and anything else we want — cheaper than ever before, worldwide. Martin's Market Foods will lead the way in humanitarian efforts to feed the poor and hungry and by undercutting all our competitors, we'll still be pulling in money hand over fist."

Dirk and Jeannie smiled at one another.

*   *   *

One week later

Logan looked up from his picture of a giant lobster to stare at the television screen.

"Mom! Mumma! Joel! Look! Wompstah!"

They walked into the living room, expecting to see Logan holding up one of his pictures. What they saw instead made them freeze.

On the television screen was a lobster the size of a whale. It was washed up on the shore and reporter Fred Jorganson was talking. Joel turned the volume up.

"… washed up this morning on the beach at Fort Popham. State Troopers went to the beach front because the person they had been in contact with from the CDC had not shown up in two days. Stapled to the back of this beast was a paper with the name William Jeffries on it."

"The troopers located the man and brought him to the scene where he was heard mumbling. 'It was only supposed to be plants' over and over.

"When shown a sketch of the CDC liaison Samantha Devereaux, Jeffries identified her as Jeannie Mattheson, assistant to Silas Dirk from Martin's Market Foods. When police checked into the disappearance of Ms. Devereaux, a spokesperson from Atlanta told them there was no employee by that name and that they weren't investigating anything at Popham.

"Ms. Matheson is still at large and the police are looking for any possible leads. If you see this woman …" Joel turned the volume off and looked at Logan, speechless. Their mother did, too. Logan looked at them and held up the picture he'd been coloring.

"Giant Wompstah!" He smiled.

PURGATORY JUNCTION

Jeremy Flagg

Brownville Junction died. No cars passed underneath as she walked along its black steel train trestle. No children played in the overgrown grass near boarded up houses. Shoes stirred the gravel between wooden ties running perpendicular to a pair of metal rails leading to the train station.

The setting sun swallowed the station in the distance, leaving a silhouette where the building belonged. Lily looked over her shoulder, surprised she crossed the lengthy bridge without peering over the side to the rushing water a hundred feet below. Clutching the straps of her backpack, she switched from stepping on gravel to balancing herself on the rail.

With the sun descending into the horizon, lines of heat radiated off the tracks, like tiny specters running along the ground. The familiar red sign for a nearby real estate agent hung outside almost every home. Starved mosquitos attempting to feed spoke to a lack of townspeople.

Being the only person in a six-mile radius left her feeling unsettled.

Lily swatted at the mosquitoes collecting around her face, determined to persevere against the tiny flying vampires. The tween's backpack contained food, water, and a flashlight. Bug spray had slipped her mind. Picking up the pace, she hoped the train station would be insect free.

The water tasted of metal as she chugged from the bottle. Sweat streamed down her forehead as she wiped it away. The day wasn't particularly hot, but she had been walking for almost two miles. The bottle of water dropped as she yelped from the vibrations in her pocket. A text from Caitlyn.

"Survive overnight. We'll know if you didn't. CU2Morrow. <3 :)"

Lily typed at lightning speed. "See you guys tomorrow." The bar at the top of her screen struggled to send the text. After a moment, the one bar faded and a message popped up on the screen. "Could not send. Retry?" She huffed at her phone, holding it up to reclaim her single bar of reception. Finally, she gave up, snatching up the half-emptied water bottle and continued speed walking to her destination.

"Caitlyn." She spoke the girl's name as if she swore. "I hate you so much." She did hate her. A lot. But she wanted to be invited to parties and be able to sit with them at lunch. New town. New School. No friends. Two months in and she still ate her bagged lunch with a teacher. Sixth grade, the biggest catastrophe of her life.

They moved when her dad's company put him in charge of disassembling giant machines in the paper mill. Everybody hated them from the beginning. Her father, proof the mill would never open again. Lily's mother pleaded with her to try harder. Her mom didn't understand the difficulties of sixth grade. Lily had been elated when Caitlyn, Maryanne and Becca offered her a place at their table.

A week later, at a slumber party, she discovered the invitation held ulterior motives. The popular girls offered her the ability to be initiated into what Caitlyn called, 'the inner circle.' The sound of her mother's voice chiding Lily for being solitary echoed in her ear as she approached the massive brick building.

Empty train cars used for hauling lumber littered an empty field next to the station. Dozens of railroad tracks interwove themselves, some leading to another set of tracks and others vanishing into nothingness. Whatever had once moved along the tracks, it seemed all signs pointed to this abandoned train station. Even the town bent around the station, as if the railroad supplied its only reason for existing.

Plywood sealed several of the windows and a small awning covered the main entrance. Grass filled the cracks of the sidewalk and bushes threatened to pierce the orange colored brick. She tried the handle on the door. The cold metal refused to turn, locked from the inside. The second door, smaller, had the wood pulled away in the bottom corner, just as Caitlyn had told her.

"Everybody's done it," she mimicked the girl's whiney voice. Lily pulled at the wood, using the weight of her body to bend it backward. Where the door should have been, it appeared the last occupants, in their haste to vacate the premise, never shut it. With a deep breath, she got down on her hands and knees and squeezed through, making sure not to snag her t-shirt or cut her exposed legs.

Where the outside had been a sea of vibrant oranges and trees filled with green, the interior of the station could only be described as cold. The setting sun fought with the boarded windows, trying to penetrate the dirty glass, casting spots of light in an otherwise dark and dingy station. Dust floated through the air, on the hunt for a clean surface. A sneeze threatened to disturb the silence of the station.

Benches lay scattered about the room. A sliver of light shone on a bench, revealing a thick dust coating. Lily tried to imagine what it would be like, people anxiously waiting for the train to transport them to some far foreign land, away from this small nowhere town. Quietly, she approached the ticket window and found a book filled with dates and times. The pencil had long since faded on the book, but she noted the top read, "Last Passenger to Montreal, 1981." More than twenty years before she existed, the station started to die, and with it, the town.

Caitlyn said the town had been cursed. Rumors said the towns-people vanished. The popular girl made comments about a hooded figure stealing away the residents, each of the people dragged into the train station and never heard of again. The sleepover consisted of the three girls trying to scare Lily before Becca finally said, "I bet she won't go inside." Caitlyn dared Lily to spend the night in the deserted building.

The light inside the station faded. Was being part of the elite worth lying to her parents? Would mom approve of her friend-acquiring methods? The thought of eating lunch in the cafeteria with friends provided motivation. Riding her hand-me-down bike, she left Caitlyn's camp at Ebeemee Lake and headed into the deserted town.

The hair on her arms stood on end. She held her breath, listening.

"Hello?" A squeal escaped her mouth as a pen rolled off the counter, clacking as it hit the ground. Inch by inch she turned, convinced a man might be standing in the doorway. She prayed a cop, or a worse yet, a homeless man who made the station his personal mansion didn't appear.

A quiet nothing.

She walked away from the window, stepping around a group of benches to a wooden door with a textured glass window. Bits of gold flecks clung to the window, perhaps the title of the office, or the name of the person who worked on the other side. She gripped the handle, easing it down. The latch inside the door opened, quiet, but still loud enough to echo in the space. Pulling gently on the door, she coaxed it opened with a creak.

The room, even larger than the last, had tables in the center. Fingers wiped along the edge, a thick dark line carved into the decades of dust. She worked her way around the tables and pulled back the seat in the middle of the giant "U."

The chair groaned as she sat down, dust scattering into the air. Lily squinted to see the fading shaft of light circumventing the plywood nailed against the windows. She didn't have much time before the sun's rays vanished. Thankfully she brought a flashlight in her backpack. With a hearty push of her lungs, a cloud filled the air. The equipment on the table looked like it came from a different era. A microphone with wires leading into a box with switches occupied most of the desk. She touched the microphone, her finger caressing the grooves made into the grip by the operator.

She screamed, retreating from the table. A spider scurried underneath one of the switch boxes. "Spiders? No. Hell no."

A shadow passed by the window outside of the station. Lily got up from the chair and pressed her face against the glass, looking for a break in the wood. Her eyes narrowed as she scanned back and forth, no people moving along the sidewalk next to the station. The last of the light faded. The interior of the station turned from a shadow filled testament to the age of steel to a near pitch black cube sitting next to an abandoned train yard.

Her backpack hit the ground, as she removed her flashlight. With a twist, a column of light cut across the desaturated room. The darkness framed the silence, each making the other even more pronounced. The tween flooded a wall with light, expecting the light to damage the fake wood paneling the building favored. Working her way around the center tables she saw two cages in the corner of the room. Upon closer inspection, she realized they were jail cells like those in a western movie.

"I guess it's like the Wild West."

Lily fished for the phone in her pocket. Inside the open cage, she held the phone through the bars, watching herself on the screen. With a push of the button, the flash lit up the cage, brighter than the flashlight. She squinted to see the screen. A figure, a dark shadow, a person, something, hovering not far behind. Howling, she dropped her phone, scrambling outside of the cage. Defensively, she wielded her flashlight, ready to strike the person inside.

Nothing.

"I hate you Caitlyn. Barely dark and I'm already scaring myself." Through the bars, she grabbed the phone, pulling her arm back quickly in case the shadow reappeared. In her photos, the only scary thing she found was the uncanny red eye caused by the flash. Lily's heart pounded against her ribcage. She wondered if a seat at the lunch table warranted dying from fright.

"Inside," she typed as she hit the send button. The message returned to her, "Could not send. Retry?" Her thumb continued to mash down on the button, holding the phone in the air, trying to get a signal.

"Ugh." With the flashlight in one hand, she walked past the cages to another door. She couldn't imagine there being another room. The door didn't have the glass panel like the others. The flashlight offered little comfort as she gripped it tightly, ready to swing as she pulled at the door. It creaked open and she jumped back, prepared to do her worst. Only a couple of feet beyond the door, a wall greeted her.

Poking her head into the space, a set of stairs on the left led toward a second floor. "Oh, well, that makes sense." From the outside, there had been windows high up, but she didn't think about a second floor. If the downstairs housed the passengers and operators, what might be upstairs?

The narrow stairs groaned with each step. Lily bounced light from her feet to the top of the stairs. The light steadied as she stopped near the top, holding up her phone, attempting to get a signal. Again, the message popped up, refusing to send her photo to Caitlyn. She swore under her breath.

Unlike the downstairs with the large open rooms, the second floor consisted of a long hallway with doors on either side. With her hands stretched out, she could touch the walls. Without the flashlight, the darkness swallowed her. The downstairs should be scarier, with all the old stuff littering the space, but the cramped upstairs gave her goose-bumps.

Downstairs she could run and hide from her imagination. Here, behind every door, she already started to dream up the scary things waiting for her. None of it good.

She rested her fingers on the porcelain doorknob, taking a deep breath as she tightened her grip. With a click of the handle, she thrust the door open. Lily squeaked as something across the room moved. Unable to move, her feet acted as if they were encased in cement. The flashlight slipped from her hand as she made a fist to protect herself. With her eyes clenched shut, she waited for something, anything to approach.

Each second dragged. With eyes like narrow slits, she stole a glance at the room. A bed. A boudoir. A chair. She scooped up the flashlight and penetrated the shadows about the room. White lace curtains framed the windows, nearly identical to the ones her grandmother so proudly displayed in her living room when she was alive. Lily forced her foot to lift, take a step, enter the room. The small room had all the amenities needed for a comfortable visit, but it suffered from the same cramp feeling found in the hallway.

Across the hall, she repeated the maneuver, only flinching a little as her eyes adjusted. The rooms held identical furnishings. Lily froze at the final door. Tap. Tap. Tap. The distant rapping reminded her of rain. She shone her light up and down the hall, paranoid.

With the last door pushed open, she stepped into the room. The sense of déjà vu wormed its way into her mind, same linens, same lace curtains. The last occupant had left the door open to the closet. The light reflected off a full-length mirror attached to the inside on the left door. Confused, she cocked her head to the side realizing she didn't see her reflection. The light shone back at her, but the source of the light seemed to be missing.

She touched the surface of the mirror, squinting in an attempt to catch her own hand in the reflection. Gasping, she realized there was no trick of the light. The mirror was broken, swallowing her image. Again, the hair along the top of her outstretched arm stood on end, as if the static in the room doubled. Where she should have been in the mirror, a black hooded figure emerged from the shadows.

Lily screamed.

Her hand flung backward, attempting to knock away the phantom. Her lungs ran out of air screaming, sucking in another breath. Her chest heaved as she panted from panic. The flashlight waved back and forth, looking for the figure, worried it had scurried underneath the bed. She refused to check. The terrifying figure could be waiting, ready to lunge from under the bed frame. Fear forced her into the hallway, putting her back against the wall, clutching the flashlight so tight her hand shook.

"It's my imagination," she said between breaths.

Lily shut her eyes tight, scared of what she might see. She didn't want to witness dark things. She wanted to be home. Caitlyn's friendship was not worth it. Nothing could make her talk to the girl again. The tapping sound grew louder. Down the hallway, in the darkness, she heard it again. Tap. Tap. Tap.

Tears started as something moved against her hip, her phone. Fumbling in her pocket for the device, her light reflected off something down the hallway. She didn't want to know what blocked her from retreating to the stairs. The phone vibrated again, reminding her she had a text message.

In a moment of bravery she shone the light down the hallway toward the tapping. The shadows at the end of the hall swallowed the light. At the edge of the darkness, two hands extended along the floor, the pointer finger of one hand rapping on the floorboards.

The rhythmic tapping stopped.

Fingernails sank into the wood. Nails cut into the hardwood floors. Something materialized from the darkness. A smokey shadow moved. It was alive. Hands shot forward, pulling it closer.

Her mouth opened to scream, but she couldn't force her vocal chords to function. Dragging itself along the ground, the shadow took on a life of its own. Claw-like hands drove their nails into the walls slithering closer to Lily.

She ran.

Lily stumbled through a doorway giving way to a small kitchen. She didn't have time to stop and look through drawers for a weapon. Running through the tiny space, she hit a door on the far side of the kitchen. The doorknob resisted her frantic twisting while pulling at the stuck door. It wrenched open with a loud groan. Inside, she pulled it shut, wedging it back into place as she frantically searched for any locks.

The phone buzzed again. Caitlyn sent another text. "Hope ur not scared." I fucking hate you. She called 911 and watched the phone attempt to connect. Lily swore quietly at the phone, the word "dialing," never actually dialed.

Her thumbs punched in a message to Caitlyn. "Help. Not alone." The phone rejected the message, refusing to grant her access to the outside world. Despite having a signal, her phone failed her.

Lily listened for the tapping noise. Nothing. She decided not to wait for the thing to pull at the door and find her. She worried she had stepped inside a closet. A quick inspection of the space revealed a stairway. The stairs led down, giving her a chance to reach the first floor and maybe flee the train station.

Descending, the flashlight made it difficult to gauge the distance of each step. She needed to make it into the waiting room, then the boarded door. Freedom. She'd run along the tracks as fast as her feet allowed. If Caitlyn made fun of her or if she was left eating lunch with the teacher for the rest of middle school, she didn't care. Lily would rather be alive.

The final step, steeper than the others, sent her into a downward spin. The flashlight fell to the ground as she reached out for the wall. The tween hissed, a sharp pain shooting through her ankle. Moments passed before she realized the stairwell landing had gone dark. She tried to ignore the pain lowering herself to all fours. Her hand brushed the metal of the handle. Her fingers clutched it as if it were her lifeline. Pressing the power button repeatedly her lifeline refused to shine.

Lily held the flashlight to her chest as she pushed herself into the corner. Tears turned into sniffling, causing her chest to heave. The flashlight slipped from her fingers and clanked against the floor. In the darkness, she couldn't see the thing upstairs come after her. She wondered if that made it less or more scary. The bony fingers would go unseen, touching her leg or brushing against her cheek. Never knowing until it was too late.

Her phone vibrated. The flashing screen blinded her. Waving the phone about, she made sure the thing didn't lurk in the shadows. She hated Caitlyn. She hated her more than she ever hated anything. Not because she made her come to a haunted train station, but because she convinced Lily she wanted to. It had been easier in elementary school, when getting the good swing at recess was the biggest obstacle in life.

Unknown number. Swipe. "I'm coming for you, Lily."

A panicked swipe shut off her screen. The blackness swallowed her. A crash upstairs in the kitchen forced her back on her feet. Pushing buttons on her phone and a couple swipes later, a light came on.

Twelve percent battery life. Enough for her to run out of the building.

Every time she stepped on her right foot, pain radiated throughout her leg. Pain, pain was okay, death scared her more. Up the stairs, the tapping returned. She imagined gnarly nails tapping against the door she had forced shut. Opening the door a crack gave her enough space to glimpse into the room.

Lily shielded herself with the door, fearful the thing might be waiting for her. Every shadow stretched on for eternity, any of them could be the thing. She waved her light about, vanquishing one shadow after another. It took a moment to orient herself in the room realizing she stood inside the ticket booth adjacent to the lobby. The counter held dozens of travel books, tickets, technical stuff, and a clock. No door was visible, allowing her an escape.

"They wouldn't make you go all the way upstairs to get in here." Her fists pounded on the walls closest to the waiting area. Under the counter, she looked for a lever or a doorknob hidden amongst the furniture.

A bang. The door upstairs must have opened, the tapping noise growing louder. She imagined the shadow pulling itself along the walls, seeking her out. With a quick shove, she slammed the downstairs door shut, happy for a hefty lock on the door. With a loud click, the door sat securely in place. Now, back to her prison, she had to find a way to get out.

She pushed a stool out of the way and eyed the opening where the ticket taker exchanged money with the passengers. Lily leaned close enough to compare the width of her shoulders to the opening. Pushing off with her good foot, she tried to balance the phone in one hand while she pulled at the desk with the other. Her shoulders fit through the opening, knocking books to the ground as she wiggled through. Her hips stuck as she dangled helplessly from the window.

The door behind her shook, the hinges struggling to remain attached to the wall. It. What was it? The question quickened her pulse. Whatever it was, it was coming. The thought of those sickly fingers clawing at her legs prompted her to start wiggling. Her legs kicked furiously in the air. Inch by inch she squeezed through the opening.

Smash.

The door strained. She screamed as the door broke open. A final push and she fell to the floor, her feet safely clear of the ticket taker's window. Dragging herself along the ground, she scrambled to put distance between her and the thing. Expecting a dark shadow, arm extended, reaching through the window, she turned over. Lily held up her cell phone like a sword, ready to swing at the beast. Nothing but an open door to the stairs. Waving the light back and forth, she desperately tried to find the thing chasing her.

It took a moment for freedom to sink in. She could run. The door to liberation waited for her less than ten feet away. If her tired arms could drag her through the opening, then she could spend the night walking back to Caitlyn's camp. Anything, anything but here, she thought.

On hands and knees, she crawled along the floor, until one last barrier separated her from the open fields. Her small hands shook the boards covering the exit. The wood held firmly in place. The pain in her ankle throbbed. She hurled her small frame against it, the boards refusing to move. It might be the wrong door, she thought. She tried the next, but wasn't any luckier. Her muscles ached, preventing her from another aggressive assault on the door.

Lily tried to hold back the tears. She wanted friends. But they shouldn't be the death of her. Somewhere in this dark, the shadow monster searched for her. "It's hopeless."

Her phone buzzed. She feared another message. Instead, a warning sign alerted her the battery approached death. Before she turned off the light, it died, leaving her in a dark, unfamiliar room. Minutes passed. The silence surrounding the deserted station seemed even more eerie knowing somewhere in the building, a monster lurked. Her eyes adjusted. She followed the faint lines of light from the window through the upturned dust. It almost felt peaceful.

The light flickered. Her body froze as she waited for the shadows to start moving. It happened again, whatever the cause, it came from outside of the station. She inched closer to the break in the plywood, fearing the shadow thing might be outside, waiting. Nearing the glass, she let out a breath she didn't realize she had been holding.

People. Outside the station, a handful of people moved back and forth. Lily instinctively banged on the window, trying to draw their attention. She didn't dare yell, fearful the shadow might find her before they rescued her from the station. Despite the loud rapping, none of them turned in her direction.

"Nana," she whispered, confused by the presence of the old woman. Her breath coated the window, fogging it over for a moment before it faded. The people outside milled about, looking down the track time after time. Men reached for their pockets, shimmering pocket watches were inspected. Under the dim moonlight the people glowed a faint blue. She stepped back from the glass. Nana died three years ago, complications from diabetes.

In the glass, the reflection of a shadow grew larger. Her body tensed as elongated digits wrapped themselves over her shoulder, the tips digging into her t-shirt. She didn't have the ability to scream, her breath caught in her chest. The hand clenched tighter as she whimpered. She imagined a skull floating in the air, surrounded by a robe, but only a darkness hovered above her. The narrow beams of moonlight vanished as they touched the figure, too scared to violate its space.

Lily let go of the cell phone and raised her hands. The moonlight reflected against her skin as she stared in awe. The tips of her fingers shimmered as if made from glass. With concentration, she could make out the window through her palm. The reality of the situation set in, a calm washing over her. The thumping heart in her chest slowed to a crawl until it thumped one last time. Even if not by train, she readied herself to catch the last passage from the Junction.

Brownville Junction died. No cars passed underneath as she walked along its black steel train trestle. No children played in the overgrown grass near boarded up houses. Shoes stirred the gravel between wooden ties running perpendicular to a pair of metal rails leading to the train station ...

CATHARINE HILL

Leslie J Linder

Down East Maine has many views that are worthy of a Christmas card. Fox Pond, nestled under Catharine Hill, has long been one of them. But in the case of this landscape, the card would be a distinctly gothic one. For how many idyllic settings like this are named after a famous ghost? How many are populated with tales of mysterious deaths and missing corpses?

This scenic wonderland is situated in unorganized territory known as Township Ten, on the border between Hancock and Washington counties, half way up Maine's rocky coast. But this is not the only reason the place is a borderland.

The native tribes always knew it, and told stories to warn travelers away. It is a liminal gateway, populated by spectral beings and unexplained mists. The locals call this stretch of Highway 182 "the Black Woods Road" for a reason. The dangerously labyrinthine path cuts through more than one type of shadow.

On the night this story began, Fox Pond glittered with an icy sheen under a moonless sky. Snowflakes wafted down, as fluffy as feathers. It looked as if a flock of angels was molting. Perhaps this would explain the moody atmosphere. Or perhaps there was more; because another white figure was flitting across the frozen pond. And this one was no angel.

Catharine herself was out on the lake. It happened every December twenty-ninth, like clockwork. She wasn't sure why.

She was also unclear on where she spent the rest of her time. But having been raised a Catholic (dependable if not devout); she supposed one could call it Limbo. She wasn't sure where it was situated in relation to Township Ten, but it felt like it was below. So, when she came back to this old and familiar haunt, she called it "going topside."

She didn't only go topside on the anniversary of her death. She popped in and out when she felt like it. Often, she would thumb a ride from some traveler. She didn't really plan to go anywhere. She just wanted to check out the latest fashions and listen in on modern trends. She always asked them to turn on the radio. But if that failed, people who picked up hitchers were generally prone to nervous chatter.

When she'd had her fill, she simply disappeared from the vehicle. Stories of the woman in white, who demanded rides upon threat of curses, had been passed down for more than a hundred and fifty years. But Catharine wasn't interested in doling out random curses. When she hunted, she did it for a reason.

Tonight, she was hunting. And it was for a reason. Both her personal milestone and the holiday season made her inclined to practice a particular type of charity work. She would walk the Black Woods Road, reading the souls of passing travelers.

For spirits, this is as easy as blinking. All souls share the same source, and can therefore "sync" with one another, like smartphones. And what Catharine was looking for was a bad soul. In the common parlance, she was trolling for assholes.

If she could remove one of those from the earth plane tonight, she figured the benefit was twofold. She would be doing humankind a favor. Additionally, she might put another star in her crown.

Catharine had never tried to "cross over," whatever that really meant. She didn't dare. Not after what she had done. But her Catholic guilt told her there would be an accounting, and she believed in doubling down.

Rather than beg forgiveness for killing her noxious fiancé, for which she was emphatically unapologetic, she figured she would kill more of the same. Doing some good deeds couldn't hurt, either way. Then if she ever decided to present herself at "the Pearly Gates," or whatever was really out there, she'd have something to show for herself.

So now she walked across the silver ice, hunting for the source of her absolution. Her alabaster skin offered a dim substitute for the moon, while her red hair hinted at an apocalyptic comet. And all of her was exposed, because she was bared to the elements. She was a century and a half past being bothered by the cold.

She wasn't naked to shock or scintillate. She wouldn't be seen unless and until she wished to be. She was nude because she came topside as a blank canvas. She read the souls of travelers before she decided whether to approach them, and how to appear.

She walked across Fox Pond for a while. A few cars passed, but no dice. Then she sensed an old, brown Buick turning onto 182 in Harrington. It was headed right for her, and it was putrid with evil. She thought she may just have found her ride.

Catharine stilled her mind and allowed herself to sync with the souls in the car. It took a minute or two for their stories to unfold. And as she let them, a sinister smile blossomed across her pale face.

"*Oh, yeah*," she thought, as her plan took shape. "*This is going to be fun.*"

* * *

Tammy tried to focus on her white knuckles clutching the passenger side door. That way she didn't have to see the danger. She knew what was outside the car windows; death. Because "death" was synonymous with the Black Woods Road during pitch black conditions and subzero temps.

This time of year it got dark by four-thirty, so six PM may as well have been the witching hour. It was as dark in the woods with no moon, as if someone had thrown a black sack over the car. But total blindness might have been a relief for the trembling passenger, for danger was always around her.

The meager light cast by the headlamps was hardly helpful, illuminating only about six feet in front of the car, adding to her terror. And what this revealed were the steep curves and giant boulders of the Black Woods, punctuated by glaring ice and bare trees. A shroud of snow covered it all; a Hellish wilderness of ice, stone, and deciduous bones.

The car took a hairpin curve at about sixty-five miles per hour. Dan always drove this way. He thought he was God's first cousin; impervious to harm. So far no one and nothing had stepped up to disillusion him.

Tammy clenched on the door handle, knowing Dan would be pissed if she leaned into him. If she let gravity take its course in such a careless manner, he called it "being a goddamned drama queen."

She watched the headlights careen past a yellow sign beseeching drivers to go only thirty-five. Boulders as large as trucks sat perched on the mountain above, threatening to crush them like bugs. Tammy recognized this as Catharine Hill.

The next sign that flashed into view read "Township 10SD." The headlights revealed a patch of Tunk Lake glittering under a thick, icy sheen. The terrifying trip was about half over.

Hopefully the silent treatment Dan had been administering would hold out. The last words he had uttered had been delivered on their icy front steps from between clenched teeth, in an unpunctuated stream.

This was Dan's way of telling her that he could only be so patient and long-suffering before she made him totally lose his shit. She never fully absorbed the words. They were like stones, and she was ducking. But they were something to the effect of:

"Goddamn it Tammy you'd better just move your lazy fat ass if you want to go to this goddamned thing 'cause I sure don't wanna spend one hot second with your asshole parents but you'll be the one to call them if you're too fucking lazy to get into the car 'cause they'd never believe me if I said it wasn't my idea."

His breath had spread hot upon her neck, along with the words. She had wondered for a moment if he would push her down the front steps. No; not on a party day. He would know not to leave bruises.

She held her breath as the car lost contact with the road; skimming over about four feet of black ice. The floating sensation ended when the tires made contact with asphalt again, shuddering.

Dan jerked the car back to the right and they avoided destruction. But Tammy could see Tunk Lake gleaming under the precarious embankment that they climbed. When they crested the hillside and started down again, the water would be from Fox Pond. Both looked pretty much the same; like yawning, icy graves.

She could almost desensitize herself to the fear of it; the inevitable cataclysm of a crash. But that was the kind of stinking thinking that got her locked up for postpartum after Aidan was born. She couldn't give in to that shit.

"*You can do this,*" she told herself.

After all, she had survived it six times before. They went to Franklin to do a "second Christmas" with Tammy's family every year.

She only saw them at these Christmas parties, getting even this limited contact because her parents gifted Dan and her with large checks instead of gifts. And they would only pay up if they got to see Tammy in person. So, while Dan was drinking or fishing, they would try to convince Tammy to leave him. But she couldn't, and they just didn't get it.

Tammy's mother had called child welfare on Dan, due to what Tammy revealed during her postpartum hospitalization. Tammy knew she had been stupid to tell her mother the horror stories. It had been the drugs; they made her loose-lipped and sloppy. But now that her family had "tried to ruin his life," Dan's wrath was unrelenting.

She had to stay with him if she was going to raise her son. Tammy knew that if he had smooth-talked his way past the nosy social worker, he could fool anyone. Tammy was the one who looked bad; with her glassy eyes, vague answers, and history of mental illness.

Aidan was with Dan's parents tonight. Dan was making good on his vow to never let Tammy's parents see their grandson again. Aidan was six now. She had twelve years to go. *Twelve years.*

She stared into the bony trees that clawed at the dim glow of their headlights and contemplated her sentence. Six years of Christmas parties behind them. Then another six, and then another. She smiled at the thought of it. *Six, six, six.* That captured it; her own personal Hell.

They rounded another sharp turn and a white object glared in the lights.

"Shit!" Dan yelled, and jerked the car away from the obstruction.

"Is it a deer?" Tammy asked, but she immediately knew that it wasn't.

It was a woman, and she was apparently hitchhiking. She had red hair piled high over her head, and she wore a full length white coat.

This coat was unbuttoned, revealing an outfit that could best be described as "Goth." The girl looked as if she had (barely) survived a head-on collision between Halloween and Christmas.

She looked young; maybe even adolescent. But there was nothing childish in the way she pulled back her coat to reveal her white corset and black-and-white striped mini-skirt. She stuck one leg out in the road. The gesture revealed torn up gray stockings and knee-high boots.

"Goddamn!" Dan exclaimed, stomping on the brakes with both feet.

Tammy bit her lip and stared out her window. The "goddamn" her husband had uttered might as well have been, "Hell, yes!" His tone was dripping with lust.

The hitcher sashayed past the headlights and into the darkness. Then her corseted busts loomed up over the edge of Dan's open window. Tammy assumed there was a face above them somewhere.

"Thanks for stopping, Hun," a woman's voice purred. "How far ya going?"

Dan fumbled with his parking gear as well as his words, suddenly transformed into an awkward teenager.

"Well, we can take you to Franklin, at least," he said.

"It'll do," the girl replied.

After another brief silence, the back door opened. The hellish burlesque act loaded in. Dan stomped on the accelerator the second the door slammed, as if afraid to lose his prize.

"Thanks for stopping," the vixen said. "I don't know what I would've done if you hadn't come along."

"Car trouble?" Dan asked. He smiled lecherously and adjusted the rearview mirror to give him a clear view of cleavage.

The redhead gave a little snort of derision from somewhere behind Tammy, in the darkness.

"Man trouble," she replied. "Same old, same old."

Dan laughed and shot a warning glance at Tammy. He didn't have to worry; she wanted as little to do with the two of them as possible.

"So, what's your name?" he asked the stranger.

"Catharine," she replied, "but my friends call me Kat."

She flipped on the reading light in the backseat and used the rear view to apply some lipstick that was so red, it was almost black. The movement of the tip over her lips made Dan's jaw drop and his hands go slack on the wheel. Tammy would be so pissed if she died this way, after all these years of terrifying car rides. It really was the last straw.

"Well, ah, I'll call you Kat, if you don't mind," Dan replied. "I'm pretty friendly."

Kat laughed. She leaned into the back seat like a porn star; clearly enjoying the fact that the reading light gave her a spotlight in the otherwise dark car.

"You *are* pretty friendly," she replied. "Sure, you can call me Kat. You'd just better hope you never make me use my claws."

She fluttered her fingers in the air to display her ridiculously long nails. They were filed into tips and painted the same reddish black as her lips. Those things were no joke. They sure didn't look like press-ons.

Dan didn't take offense at her teasing little threat. He let out a blast of obsequious laughter and then started sprucing up his comb-over. Tammy thought she might be sick.

"So, you know my name," Kat said. "And you are … ?"

"*Absolutely disgusted*," Tammy thought to herself. But Dan was already giving her their names.

As humiliating as it was to watch him throwing himself at this girl, it was pretty educational. Tammy thought back to how he acted when they first met. He had been charming and kind. Had he been this sleazy? She hoped not.

Either way, it stung to see that he could still be pleasant and charming. He just didn't *want* to any more, when it came to her.

A wild hope occurred to her; that he might leave her for this woman, and let her keep Aidan. But her heart fell as fast as it had risen. His vindictive determination to keep "his son" away from her family made that dream seem impossible. And the thought of Kitty Kat from Route 182 raising her son instead of her made Tammy feel crazy. She had the brief impulse to grab the wheel and send them all over the embankment. Maybe she really *was* losing it.

"Romance is a cut-throat business," Kat said, as if reading her mind. But she had only been telling Dan how she came to be standing on the side of the road.

"I hate car fights," she was saying, "but it happens every year. We head for Somesville to see my parents, and all Hell breaks loose. I don't know what it is about the holiday that makes people want to fight."

"Yeah," Dan replied. "I don't know, either."

He shot Tammy another dirty look through the corner of his eye. It was almost as if he thought she had been telling his new girlfriend stories, behind his back.

"I'm so sorry that happened to you," Tammy said to the woman.

"Yeah," Dan agreed, "he sounds like a dick."

Kat laughed for quite a while. Then she took a long and languid pull off a cigarette that seemed to have appeared out of thin air.

"Something about men and cars," Kat replied. "They always wind up losing their heads. You're right. Maybe it's a dick thing."

Dan didn't laugh or otherwise reply. The veins in his neck were throbbing as he looked at the smoke spiraling toward the front seat.

"*Oh, boy,*" Tammy thought to herself. "*Now you've done it, Kitty Kat.*"

Dan hated cigarettes. He thought he was allergic, though a doctor had never said so. He blamed this on his mother, who chain-smoked all through his childhood. This perceived attack upon him was one of the many things that he seemed to hold against all of womankind.

And where had that cigarette come from? Tammy had been watching the other woman. She hadn't seen her take it out, or light it. But the thick tobacco smoke was very real.

"A smoker, are you?" Dan said.

As hard as he tried, he couldn't put the light-hearted charm back in his voice. Tammy could hear the anger in his taut vocal chords. Anybody could. But Kat didn't look concerned. If anything, she found his change in mood amusing. Dan didn't seem to notice.

"It's a filthy habit," he said. "That shit will kill you, if you do it long enough."

Kat laughed again and took another deep pull from her smoke. Tammy wasn't sure, but it seemed like their passenger deliberately exhaled in Dan's direction.

"What *won't* kill you if you do it long enough?" Kat replied. "*Living* will kill you if you do it long enough. I like my odds, though, Hun. I may just outlast you."

Dan didn't know how to reply to this. Either that or he was fighting with his demons. Because he tried to stay calm, but his lead foot returned.

They had just started descending the Franklin side of Catharine Hill, the Buick pelting downward like a runaway train.

Taking a deep breath, Tammy gripped the door handle tightly. In the glare of the headlights she saw old, rusted guard rails flashing past, looking like a long row of rotten, gnashing teeth. The icy water of Fox Pond glittered below a steep embankment on Dan's side of the road and Tammy didn't know if they were going to get out of this one alive. This was extremely reckless even for Dan.

She glanced in the rear-view mirror, hoping by now Kat would have realized her peril. This didn't seem to be the case. Instead, the red-head took another long drag off her smoldering coffin nail.

"Oh, come on, don't be mad," she said to Dan. "I don't know what it is. I guess I just like to suck on something."

For a split second, shocked bafflement registered on Dan's face, but then in a heartbeat his switch flipped from rage to lust. Relaxing, he roared with crude laughter. But he didn't slow down.

"Oh, man," he said, "You're a pistol!"

Kat smiled and shrugged. She took a placid look out the window, at the blur of guard rails.

"A pistol?" she repeated. "Well, I don't know. Guns just seem too easy."

Dan snorted again. He seemed to think she was joking, but he didn't quite get her meaning. Neither did Tammy, but she did catch the threat.

Kat's eyes met Tammy's through the mirror before the former asked, "You got your seatbelt on, Honey?"

Tammy nodded. The look in Kat's eyes frightened but transfixed her. There was something otherworldly there.

"Good," Kat continued, and smiled at her. "They save lives, I've heard."

"Don't worry about seatbelts," Dan said. "You're in good hands."

He tried to send a seductive glance into the back seat. But his flares of temper had eroded his reserves.

Kat looked back at him with veiled disgust, thinly smiling as she flicked a glowing ash off the tip of her cigarette. It shone red from between her black-tipped nails.

"You've got a real eye for the ladies, don't you, Dan?" she asked.

Dan blinked, clearly unsure whether her question was indicative of a door opening or slamming shut. But he slicked his hair back again, just in case.

"Well, sure," he said. "I suppose. It depends on the lady."

"Well," Kat said, "we'll just have to see about that."

She laughed once more. Then she leaned forward and jammed the red tip of the cigarette squarely into Dan's right eyeball.

The car filled with a hellish cacophony; Dan howling in agony, Kat shrieking in demonic glee. The rest of the noise must have been Tammy, herself, because the car had spun in a circle and broken through the decrepit guard rails easier than a hot knife through butter.

The trip down the embankment was a shock-blunted, terrifying blur. The Buick pelted over and through every obstacle. Boulders ground beneath the undercarriage, spitting out stony teeth. Tree branches and whole saplings snapped in their wake. One huge bough covered with spiking branches smashed the windshield into glittering powder, and then impaled the back seat like a spear.

A hot spray of liquid splattered across Tammy's face, coming from Dan's direction. Had the branch caught him? She glanced over, but there was too much chaos and confusion.

What she could make out was that Dan cupped his eye where the hot cigarette had fused into his flesh, his fingers encircling the protruding filter tip. And Kat was attacking him around his head and neck.

Tammy saw that this attack was the origin of the blood, but she couldn't tell what Kat was doing apart from the fact that it involved her manicured claws, and her teeth.

With one more spectacular smash of shattered boulders, they hit the ice on Fox Pond. The watery depths echoed beneath them; like the growls of an icy monster that threatened to crack its mouth open and swallow the car whole.

For at least a full minute they sped smoothly across the ice. It might have been a relief from the terror of their descent, if not for the groaning ice and Dan's animalistic screams.

But everything else was blasted from Tammy's head when the car hit a large boulder that protruded from the water — the iceberg to their Titanic — flipping the car into the air like a quarter in some late-night drinking game.

The last thing she remembered was her airbag punching the wind out of her lungs and slamming straight into her face. Then there was nothing, for who knew how long.

When Tammy opened her eyes again, she was upside down. She could see through the hole where the windshield should be that a row of emergency vehicles was lined up on the shore, their lights flashing on the snow like Christmas decorations. A snowmobile and rescue sled sped toward her.

It took Tammy a moment to remember the details. But when she did, she gasped for breath, her eyes flying in terror to the back seat.

She scanned the whole car, looking for a monster in the darkness. Nothing. Kat was gone.

Sore and cold, ribs hurting, nose dripping blood, Tammy fumbled with her seatbelt. She was getting the Hell out of that car.

Dan's body sprawled beneath her. He didn't seem to be breathing, but it was too dark to tell. Then the seatbelt gave way and she crashed down onto his stiff, cold form.

He had to be dead. But as soon as she recovered from the fall, she searched for his pulse while the roar of the snowmobile grew closer.

She felt a pool of liquid below them and her heart skipped. Was the ice breaking? No; it was sticky. She raised her hand, squinting into the glimmer of the rescue lights.

Blood. It coated her hand like a glove. It coated *everything.*

"Oh, god," she said, and looked down at Dan.

Her eyes were more accustomed to the darkness, now. She could see his broad shoulders, but nothing above them. His head was gone.

Tammy screamed bloody murder, scrambling through the broken windshield as if she'd been shot from a canon. Her feet spun on the ice, but she was saved from falling when a park ranger who had just disembarked from the snowmobile scooped her up in his arms.

"He's dead!" she screamed. "Oh, my god, there's so much blood!"

"Easy, now," the ranger said. "You're all right. Just breathe. It's gonna be all right."

Tammy clung to him, fighting for breath and fighting the relief that was boiling up inside her heart. It was indecent to feel happy about Dan's horrible death. But she was thinking of her son now, and her family.

"Oh, god," she said, again and again. She didn't know what else to say.

"I know," the ranger said, and patted her back. "These things are terrible. And I don't mean to sound inconsiderate, but you should be happy you're alive. I haven't seen a wreck this bad in ... ever. The way you came down that hill ..."

He trailed off, and Tammy understood his meaning. As she looked over his shoulder, she saw the long scar they had made in the hillside. Then, halfway up Catharine Hill, she thought she caught a hint of whiteness moving through the trees.

"Seatbelts save lives," she said, softly. "At least, that's what I've heard."

*　*　*

The white figure on that mountainside was indeed Catharine, admiring her good work. She squatted in the snow, her bare thighs glittering from the illumination of the recently unclouded moon.

She was glad the mousy little housewife had survived, though she'd have been better off after the crash, either way. Catharine knew from her own hard experience. But the fates were aligned with Tammy. The ice had been unusually thick for this time of year.

Dan's head was perched on the ground, bloodying the snow beneath her. The skin around his neck was shredded like an old lobster net. There he sat; another jewel for her crown.

She had mauled him severely before she conjured up a Civil War era bone saw and finished the job. This was poetic license, of course. She could have summoned any tool that she wished, just like she summoned her clothes. But she figured a guy like Dan deserved a death as old-fashioned as his views on women.

She met his eyes, which gaped open, the pupils rolled upwards. The cigarette poked out of one like a toothpick in a hors d'oeuvre. She raised her eyebrows as if asking him what he thought. But she didn't want or need an answer. She had a good idea how he felt about his evening, and she wasn't a damned bit sorry. He could join her fiancé, and the others.

Henry, her intended, had been a lot like Dan. In their case, the fight had been in a horse-drawn wagon. She had tried to end their engagement, and he in turn had tried to end her. He had stabbed her, and she had known she was dying. But she managed to get the knife away from him and retaliate in kind.

Once he was dead, the rage that had been slow-boiling in her erupted. It had taken her last energy to saw off his head. She would never forget the sight of the blood-soaked snow, or his body sliding into the pond. It had been the last thing her living eyes had seen. Then her mission had begun.

After Henry came that asshole wife-beater from 1922. His Model T was still rotting on the bottom of Tunk Lake, along with his headless corpse. And then there had been the rapist from 1968, and the child molester from '89.

Catharine had hitched a lot of rides in her time, but these three had been the only other terminal cases. Now Dan had joined their illustrious company, having earned the privilege.

There would be more, at least a dozen. Then she would see if she had enough stars in her crown. One could never be too careful; at least not with one's own immortal soul.

Maybe she'd go a dozen more, after that. And after all, what were six more? *Six, six, six.* She had gotten that idea from Tammy's head, and it appealed to her. Some would say her aspirations made her the beast. Some would call her a hero. She'd let God and the Devil sort out the details.

The rescue sled hauled Tammy off the ice, away from her horrible ex. Catharine watched, then dissolved into the ether, along with Dan's baffled-looking head.

The hunt was over, for this year. She was headed back to Limbo. She didn't know where Dan was headed, although she had a very satisfying guess. She hoped he liked it hot.

Catharine still hunts; maybe for eternity. So, if you ever take the Black Woods Road, especially during the holidays, you'd better play nice. If not, you'd better watch your head.

THE BAD TRIP

Thomas Washburn, Jr.

Caleb Rogan was sure Jess had summoned the creature that had attacked them. Not intentionally, but that didn't change the fact she had. It was all just a big joke, at least that's what they thought.

They had come to their favorite camping spot in Greenstone, Maine to eat 'shrooms and talk about religion, the supernatural, monsters and the possibility of an afterlife. Usually the mushrooms enhanced the experience and made for better conversation. Not today though, today it turned into Jess and Savannah getting into an argument about the validity of the spirit world.

Savannah had been pissed when Jess told her there was no such thing. It got to the point they were shouting back and forth like a couple of kids about to fight on the playground.

Jess had hollered out, "Let me prove it. I'll try and summon something right now! If you're so damn sure this stuff is real, it should happen, right?"

Savannah never even got to respond before Jess started babbling random gibberish. That's when things started to get really weird. Jess's normal voice deepened, becoming sullen. It sounded like there was more than speech trying to come out.

Caleb couldn't understand a word of it, it sounded like Latin, but he wasn't sure. At that same moment time slowed like a record player winding down and everything around him paused. Moments later, time wound back up again and something warm was running down Caleb's face. He wiped it away, smearing blood across the back of his hand. A sense of dread filled him, his heart thumping with each panicked breath. What was going on?

Slowly he scanned the campsite. His eyes widened in horror as they locked on the body of Savannah slumped over an old pine log, her Portland Seadogs hat still resting upon her head. She had nearly been torn in half or rather it looked as though something had *bitten* her in half, just above her hips.

Her dead eyes screamed, *"Run!"*

As much as wanted to, he couldn't. Caleb's legs felt as though they were held to the ground by cinder blocks. No matter how hard he tried they wouldn't respond. Off to his left a long drawn out scream tore his attention away from Savannah's dead pleading eyes.

He watched in shock as a large bipedal creature stood over his best friend Peter. It manically slashed at his lifeless body with razor sharp claws.

The creature looked almost human. It stood about five feet tall and was covered in black leathery skin. Its eyes shone a dark crimson hue. A row of small bone like horns lined its head like a thorny crown. A lizard's snout protruded from its face.

A warm wetness ran down Caleb's leg as his bladder emptied.

The creature barked at him in a voice from the depths of hell. "Fools. Now you die."

His fight or flight instinct kicked in as the imminent fear of death made his immobile legs spring to life. The creature lunged toward him, tearing Caleb's shirt as he turned and ran.

"You will pay for your impertinence."

The creature's voice drilled into his head like a choir of angry cicadas.

"You will pay for your impertinence."

Again, the voice called out to him from the distance.

"You can't run from me! Die, die, die!"

He was not even sure if it was the creature who now spoke to him. It had almost sounded like Jess's voice that time. His mind raced, blurry and confused.

Something hard smacked against the side of his head knocking him from his feet. He violently skidded across the ground, rocks, sticks and debris tearing at his flesh.

"You're weak and unworthy."

That had sounded like Jess. Pain shot through his body as he forced himself to one knee and looked in the direction from which it came.

The creature stood only five feet away from him now, holding a severed arm in its clawed hand. It was wearing the clothes and skin of his girlfriend Jess, with only its demon head and black talons revealing its true nature. He knew it was Jess because that was her favorite sweater, the one he'd bought her last Christmas. *Why was she wearing a sweater in July?*

"What did you do to Jess?"

The creature licked at its bloody talon and grabbed at its crotch. "Sliced diced and made me a Jess suit. That's what I did. Fucked her good first though, gave her what you couldn't."

His lips trembled and his body began to shake as his adrenaline surged. "I'll kill you, you slimy demon fuck!"

With beast-like fury Caleb sprung forward, charging the creature. His fist slammed into the bridge of its snout and felt the sickening crack of bone beneath his knuckles. Blood sprayed forth and covered his face as both he and the creature crumpled to the ground.

The weight of his body had the creature pinned. Anger clouded his senses and a vengeful wrath took control. His beloved was dead and this evil hell beast had done it.

"Caleb stop, you're hurting me."

He was confused how did it know his name?

"Don't you love me anymore?"

The monster sounded just like Jess. It was just trying to play tricks with his mind. He wouldn't let it. He wouldn't become another of its victims.

"We didn't do anything to you," he screamed over and over as he locked his hands and swung down like a hammer at the creature's face. With each swing bones broke and skin ripped apart. The creature's face was soon a sickening puddle of indistinguishable gore.

Tears flowed from his eyes as he sobbed harder and harder with each downward thrust of his locked hands. Again, his head filled with that strange chaotic buzz. The world around him went fuzzy, like a television channel full of static as the buzzing increased.

* * *

When the world cleared and came back into focus he was sitting upright against a large pine tree that had fallen over. The creature was nowhere to be seen. Nor was there any sign it had ever been there.

Where did it go? Had it wandered off? Did it just simply disappear back to where it came from? He tried to search his mind, but found no answers, only a whispered echo of the buzzing that had grated at his brain.

He took several deep breaths as he tried to regain his wits and reign in the fear and horror that had overtaken him. How much time had passed he didn't know, but darkness rapidly approached.

His head throbbed and it hurt to think. A panicked voice ran through his head and screamed, *Why the hell did you have to go and do that Jess? Why?*

Faint voices caught his attention and snapped him back to the here and now. The smell of smoke then caught his nostrils. Slowly and cautiously he turned and peered over the log. Through the trees a thick line of white smoke drifted towards him.

"Hello."

There was no response.

"Hello, is anyone there?"

Still there was no response. Was this some sort of trick? Where was the creature? Was it toying with him?

Slowly he began to move in the direction of the smoke. He stayed low to the ground, doing his best to remain quiet. The last thing he wanted to do was alert whomever or whatever might be ahead of him. The voices grew louder and he heard laughter. A small clearing came into view. It looked oddly familiar.

"Caleb, can you pass me a beer?"

That was Peter's voice. He would know that voice anywhere. They had been best friends since the third grade.

"Sure thing man. Jess, Savannah, you guys want one?"

What the hell was going on? That was his voice.

"Yeah sure," Savannah responded.

"I'm going to spark up a J, no thanks."

His heart nearly jumped into his throat. That was Jess, his Jess, she was alive. His legs began to feel weak and unsteady. But the creature had killed her. How was that possible? How was any of this possible?

He stepped into the opening. "Jess."

One step forward was all he managed as his legs gave out and he crumpled to the ground.

Peter's voice called out. "What was that?"

"I dunno," Savannah replied.

"I swear I just heard something in the brush over there. I'm going to check it out."

Jess spoke. "It was nothing. Caleb, will you tell him it's nothing!"

"Dude it's nothing, relax, you're freaking everyone out."

"Sorry bro, must be the 'shrooms we did earlier?"

He was Caleb, why did Jess keep saying his name when he was over here? Who was that over there with them? It took every ounce of his willpower, but he managed to get back on his feet. Like a drunken zombie, he slowly stumbled forward toward his friends.

The painful buzz in his head returned and in a chilling crescendo grew louder with each step.

As he entered the campsite he fell to his knees in shock. Jess, Peter, Savannah and someone that looked exactly like him stared in his direction.

Peter pointed directly at him. "Did you guys see something? I swear to God I just saw something."

The buzz continued to amplify. It now sounded and felt like a swarm of angry bees were attacking the base of his skull.

Confused, everyone looked at Peter and shook their heads no.

"Maybe I'm still tripping balls. I guess that shit's just making me paranoid."

The buzz seemed to speak to him now. *"You will pay for your impertinence."*

Bright spurts of light blinded his mind like the flash from a camera. Paralyzed he could not move. He tried to speak, but his lips seemed to be glued together and he could not separate them.

Caleb watched as the version of him in the camp suddenly picked up a hatchet from the small woodpile beside him. Without warning Caleb ran full speed towards Peter, except Peter wasn't really Peter anymore he had turned into some sort of Gargoyle type creature.

The buzz continued to grow louder.

"You will pay for your impertinence."

He struck Peter in the head with the hatchet and then turned toward Jess who had morphed into the demonic beast he'd fought earlier. He watched as she grabbed Savannah and ripped her apart.

Blood began to run from his nose, the buzz grew even louder.

"Die, die, die you fool!"

What had once been the love of his life turned towards Caleb and began to slowly move forward. He watched as that Caleb looked at the ripped apart Savannah and ran right towards him.

His head felt like it was going to explode as the buzz grew to a deafening roar.

"Fuck her good, that I will, die, die, die, kill, kill, kill!"

He tried to move, but couldn't. Caleb ran right through him. The Demon only a few feet behind as he gasped for breath. All the oxygen felt like it had been sucked out of his body.

His eyes burned. It felt like someone was driving a red-hot poker into them. The smell of charred flesh filled his nostrils. He wanted to scream, wanted this nightmare to end. A violent overload of all his senses tore into his brain. The world faded to nothingness.

*　*　*

In the darkness, Caleb Rogan sat propped against a large fallen pine tree covered in blood and gore. A few feet away four bodies lay piled atop of one another, each one had been mutilated nearly beyond recognition. An empty gas can lay on its side by his feet.

He was soaked in the fluid and so were the bodies. From his pocket, he pulled out a lighter and placed his thumb upon the striker. Slowly and calmly he stood and walked over to the pile of bodies.

How had it all come to this? They had just wanted a break from the rigors of their daily lives at The University of Maine before finals. How had an innocent day of fun turned into the gruesome slaughter before him?

He looked down at the bodies of Peter, Jess, and Savannah. Numb to the world around him.

Peter still clutched a bottle of Impertinence Ale, their favorite drink at Gargoyle Brewery, a small local tap house located just up the road in Orono. There was a picture of a small black leathery demon with a horned crown on its head staring back at him from the bottle. "You're not worthy," it growled at him.

A memory suddenly struck him. He was in the brewery, chatting with his friends distractedly when the clerk at the cash register had asked him, "How will you pay for your Impertinence?"

"Um, what?" he had replied.

"Cash or charge? How do you want to pay for your Impertinence Ale?"

"Oh, uh, cash ..." The memory faded away.

A Ziploc baggie lay open on the ground near the bodies, half-eaten psychedelic mushrooms were scattered about the campsite. What the hell had been wrong with them?

Savannah's eyes still pleaded with him to run. She had always looked out for everyone else and seemed to still be doing so in death. Her Portland Seadogs hat was still on her head. They had bought that when they'd all gone to a game together last year.

Jess, the love of his life, he couldn't even recognize her anymore other than the now blood soaked sweater he had bought her for Christmas. He had planned to ask her to marry him this weekend, the ring still in his pocket.

Caleb's listless eyes stared at the pile, a cartoonish smile slowly spread across his gore spattered face. He turned and held the lighter against his chest and let himself fall backward. As he fell his thumb sparked the lighter sending a giant fireball into the night sky.

A loud buzz filled the darkness of the forest. It grew louder and louder until it seemed to whisper in a devilish voice, "You will pay for your impertinence."

TEACHER'S PET

John McIlveen

In Noel's experience, few things compared with the first day of school, but root canals, third degree burns, and amputation could be on the list. School held nothing redeemable for him; nothing to look forward to, for what was enjoyable about busting your hump to keep your head above water? He managed to maintain passing grades, but the phrase *skin of your teeth* was generous in his case. His parents accused him of being lazy and an underachiever. He figured, what was the sense in trying when his best efforts were met with criticism?

A ninety? Why, heck son, that's still ten away from a hundred! When I was a junior, a ninety would have been unacceptable because I was class president, captain of the debate team, and star quarterback on the football team ...

... and I could juggle six, double bladed chainsaws while running full throttle and carrying three unconscious mountain climbers to safety from the stormy summit of Everest, Noel amended bitterly.

In truth, his parents were average folk who cared for him deeply and wished him to achieve greatness. The fact was ... Noel *was* lazy and an underachiever, but he knew that would all change once he escaped this crappy, mundane town. He thought if the world ended right then, he would have wasted nearly his whole life in school.

Kyle Grainger had the right idea. He had hit the road earlier that summer and never looked back. Noel dreamed about doing the same.

He scanned his mindless classmates from his remote throne at the far back of the classroom. He had nothing in common with them and probably never would. Their juvenile ways irritated him, with their odd lingo and embellished gestures; it was all like some bizarre mating ritual that lowered the IQ. Sure, some of the girls were hot, with their overly made-up faces, artery-choking jeans, and skimpy tops that accentuated and manipulated their assets to the fullest affect ... *making mountains out of molehills*. Besides, it was easier to hate them than to obsess over the reality that such girls wanted nothing to do with him.

At the far wall, Ben Molina jokingly slapped a girl's ass. The girl smiled prettily and fluttered cable thick eyelashes, cranking up her feminine appeal. He could almost hear her pheromones kick into overdrive. If Noel ever tried anything *that* nervy, he'd surely be slapped. Hell, he'd be arrested.

"Morons," Noel mumbled.

"Who?" asked a girl seated beside him.

He recognized her from previous years but didn't know her name. She was on the pretty side of plain, but wore simple clothing and used no makeup. *Trowel on some Mary Kay, squeeze her into skinny-jeans two sizes too small, and she'd go from not so hot to hot-to-trot*, thought Noel.

"Everyone. You're all morons," Noel said with a sneer.

She searched his face for a moment, rose, and moved to another desk.

Good, he thought, tilting back in his seat. He was bored senseless. He wanted to be somewhere exciting, doing exhilarating things. He wanted adventure — anything besides whiling away another year in this abhorrent classroom, humiliated and hated ... hating himself.

And then ... school got interesting.

The classroom went silent as she walked through the doorway — girls and boys alike. Even *Molina the Weena* stopped to watch her glide confidently past the teacher's desk to the chalkboard. With tantalizingly long and delicate fingers, she lifted a piece of chalk from the tray and wrote *Ms. Dewer.*

Oh, the implication of that name will be problematic, Noel thought. Sure enough, a few titters arose from the classroom. He wondered if her first name might be Ivana. Unperturbed, Ms. Dewer faced her new students.

"Good morning, Homeroom 544. You may have noticed the new name on your schedules. I am she, and I might be your History or Social Studies teacher, as well. Before moving here in June, I taught for four years at Gray-New Gloucester High School in Gray, Maine. Gray's sister town, New Gloucester, has only one claim to fame, the Sabbathday Lake Shaker Village, which is the last active Shaker village in the United States. Both Gray and New Gloucester combined have about half the population of Taylor's Falls, New Hampshire."

"Nowhereville," someone opined. Noel agreed.

"Has anybody here been to Fryeburg, Maine?" Ms. Dewer pleasantly asked. When no one replied, she said, "I was born in Fryeburg, where there are more people than teeth. Now *that* is Nowhereville." She smiled, flashing her perfect set of bright whites. Noel couldn't look away.

Her age was difficult to assess. She could be anywhere from twenty-five, to a youthful thirty-five. She had friendly, yet dark, penetrating eyes that demanded his undivided attention ... as did the rest of her. She was an oddity, classy and exotic, unlike any teacher he'd seen outside of the idealistic realm of movies and television, and completely unlike any of those at Nottingham High. Thick black hair tumbled down her back in turbulent waves, contrasting nicely with her navy blue dress, which was tasteful, fashionable, and subtly stimulating. The way the fabric sensually draped the smooth curve of her hips, accentuating her figure, was hypnotic; it beckoned notice but didn't scream for it. She looked Hispanic, but the name *Ms. Dewer* implied she might be unmarried, maybe of Welsh or Scottish descent, both of which tended to be fair skinned, not a shoe-in for Selena Gomez's big sister.

Abrupt laughter caught Noel's attention and he noticed every eye in the classroom was on him. Humiliation warmed his face as he realized Ms. Dewer was talking to him.

"What?" he asked, sounding daft instead of the cool indifference he hoped to display. *More laughter.*

"Welcome back, cosmonaut, I'm sorry to interrupt your reverie, Mister ..." She waited.

"Knob!" someone said.

"Uh, Noel Keating," he said, ignoring the heckler.

"See? That was practically painless," she said. "It seems I'm having a hard time holding your attention."

"Got mine," someone murmured loud enough to be heard.

"Get a napkin!" said another.

Ms. Dewer ignored them, never looking away from Noel. "Move here so you can better hear me, Mr. Keating," she said, pointing to a seat directly in front of her desk.

Noel considered refusing, but being in close proximity to her had a definite appeal. He moved, trying to appear unbothered. He was no stranger to targeting by teachers who considered him a trouble-maker. He didn't think himself one, just a nonconformist, and a non-participant with zero desire to be present.

"Thank you, Mr. Keating," she smiled.

Noel didn't respond, which didn't seem to bother her in the least.

She was even better looking from his new seat and he could smell her perfume, which was captivating to the point of irresistible.

* * *

Noel lay on his bedroom floor, his head resting on a pile of dis-carded clothing and his feet propped on his bed. The thunderous riffs of Mastodon traumatized his eardrums through his headphones, cut-ting off anything outside his personal universe. He tried to disappear within the thrumming bass and machine-gunning drums, but he couldn't drown out his fixation on Ms. Dewer.

He'd had crushes before — realistic ones on girls his age — but this was over the top. Like Van Halen's video "Hot for Teacher," he had an all-consuming mega-crush on Ms. Dewer.

This is insane! I'm hot for my history teacher! It made him laugh, espe-cially when he thought of his prior history teacher, Mrs. Hurley, who resembled the love child of a Shar Pei and a toad, somehow retaining bulgy eyes through her profusion of wrinkles. Mrs. Hurley joked that she was the world's best history teacher, not because of her schooling, but because she had "been there," and by gosh, she looked it.

Noel removed his headphones, closed his eyes, and his thoughts returned to Ms. Dewer. It was understandable. She was amazing, worthy of magazine covers or make-up ads. He fantasized about her clad in a minuscule bikini, lying on a beach beside him and sharing drinks on some tropical paradise.

Noel rolled over, trying to return to reality. He needed a more realistic obsession, one where he had a sliver of a chance.

Maybe if I toned. I could stand to lose a few pounds, but I'm not bad looking, he reasoned. Noel pressed his palms against the floor and pushed. No time like the present.

One … two …

When he reached his fifth pushup, he was nauseous and his arms shook.

Not bad, he thought. *Two better than last time I tried.*

He dropped to the floor and slammed his fist to the carpet. "Come on! Get over it, dude!" he growled. "Get real!"

But Noel didn't "get real." He got far worse as the end week rolled around, but something incredible was happening, something that worsened his obsession; as improbable as it was, it seemed Ms. Dewer was flirting with him. He wasn't sure if his overactive imagination was responding to his libidinous hopes, but her subtle smiles seemed meaningful, and whenever she walked past his desk, she'd pause slightly, letting her delicate scent engulf him before moving on, never faltering in her lessons.

On the third day, Ms. Dewer returned an assignment with "Good Job!" and a winking smiley face on it. It was intriguing and probably meant nothing, but what occurred Friday convinced Noel her flirtations were real.

She had handed out their first test, an involved assessment she called a feeler exam. It didn't count toward their grades, but it gave her a good indication of where her students stood in their knowledge of world history. As the class labored silently, save for a few shuffling feet and a sneeze or a mumble, Noel chanced a look at Ms. Dewer. She sat at her desk holding a few papers, not reading them but staring directly at Noel with that slight, evocative smile. Noel returned her gaze, but her eyes never wavered. Twice more Noel looked at Ms. Dewer whose ebony eyes pinned him to the spot. They made promises and knew his deepest secrets. If someone coughed or lifted their eyes, she would casually avert her own, and then return them to Noel once the interruption was over. It made him nervous, but excited him.

She was out of his league in so many ways; could he really be attractive to her? It seemed so unlikely. If nothing else, it was a brilliant tactic to improve his attendance and grades. He needed to know if Ms. Dewer's flirtations were legit, but to do so, he'd have to get more enterprising.

＊ ＊ ＊

He arrived at school Monday planning to stare brazenly and flirt with Ms. Dewer, just as she had with him.

It didn't work.

When he'd meet her eyes she'd ignore him, dismissively sweeping her gaze over him or looking clear through him, but at other times, he'd catch her staring in that beguiling way. She seemed to be making a game of it.

During Wednesday's history quiz, she ran her hand softly over his back as she walked past his desk. He checked to see if anyone noticed, but all eyes were focused on their desktops. He wondered if she got off on driving schoolboys mad, or maybe she just had some weird kink that made her horny during exams. He'd heard stranger stories, like the woman who cried uncontrollably whenever she touched satin, or the man who became violent when he smelled cinnamon. But this was different … it involved him.

By Thursday, Noel was perplexed and nearly feverish with frustration. During homeroom, Ben the Goon walked into class, looked at him, and shook his head as if Noel were the saddest person he ever met. Noel returned a challenging stare, saying nothing.

"Hey Romeo, do you have any idea how stupid you look drooling all over yourself?" Ben asked. Those in the classroom laughed. "You're pathetic."

"Screw you," Noel said.

"You wish! No wait … I bet you're saving yourself for Ms. Dewer," the Goon went on, provoking another round of laughter.

Noel did nothing. He'd get no backing in an altercation, and "Mr. Popular" needed only to blow his dog whistle to have the football team there within seconds, face-planting Noel to the floor. As Ben walked to his desk, he smacked Noel smartly on the back of the head. Noel sprung to his feet and gave the Goon a double-handed shove to the back, sending him comically sprawling over two desks and onto the floor.

"Stop!" someone demanded from the classroom doorway.

Ben the Goon jumped to his feet, his face contorted with rage, and whipped a textbook at Noel, who deflected it with his left arm.

"I said *stop!*"

They obeyed, but held their positions as Ms. Dewer walked coolly to her desk.

"Your *pet* attacked me from behind," Ben the Goon said.

Ms. Dewer held up her hand, shushing him. "I saw, but I'm sure there's more to it than meets the eye ... or my eye." She looked from Noel to Ben and then back. "I should send you both to the office, but that would waste time and could end up in suspensions, which wouldn't please your little buddies on the football team, would it, Mr. Leeds."

She aimed her well-manicured finger at Noel. "Since I saw you doing the shoving, I expect to see you in detention after school today.

"But ..." Noel started.

Ms. Dewer raised an eyebrow and said, "Do you have a problem with this, Mr. Keating, or would you prefer a visit to the office?"

"No," Noel said with an annoyed breath.

"Bring your bib, douche," Ben the Goon said as he walked to his seat.

"Enough," Ms. Dewer said, but the look in her eyes did the shouting.

Noel stewed in aggravation throughout the day, and his mood had reached rock bottom by the time he arrived at Ms. Dewer's class after school. She stood with her back to him, her body moving rhythmically as she erased the chalkboard. Noel watched, entranced.

"Sit," she directed, showing no indication that she had seen him.

Noel took the seat closest to the door.

"Not there. Your assigned seat, please."

Noel considered walking out, but as provoked as he was, he had finally gathered the gumption to ask her what her game was. He obligingly sat in front of her desk.

Ms. Dewer — always graceful, always smooth, always in command — walked to the door and gently closed it. She glided to her desk and sat — or more aptly — drifted into her chair. Noel's resolve was slipping, but he held on, trying to look defiant and put out. She looked at him and winked.

"Well, Mr. Frumpy Face," she said, her voice silky, her lips playfully pouted. "You know, if anything is to become of us, we need to be careful."

Noel's every thought derailed and tumbled into a tortured smoldering heap. "What are you talking about?" he demanded, utterly confounded.

"Discretion, Noel. Pull out a notepad and look busy," she instructed. Noel did as she asked. "Okay, I like you, and unless I'm blind, you like me, but if you want this *thing* to work, we need to be discrete."

"What thing?"

"Who knows until we try, but we won't get that chance if you make it so obvious." She looked quickly to the door and back to Noel. "I'm a teacher who likes her job and wants to keep it, so if anyone finds out about us, my career is over. If you can keep us absolutely top-secret, this could turn into something fun and adventurous."

Adventurous! The word hooked him. It's what he'd been looking for.

"I ..." he mumbled.

"So, are you *up* for it?" she asked.

The insinuation was blatant enough, but he had a hard time believing it. Could this ... *goddess* really want him? No woman had ever shown interest in him, not for long, at least, and especially not like *that* ... which posed another problem.

"Uh, yeah. Of course I am," he said. "But I've never ..."

"Oh, I'll take care of that," Ms. Dewer reassured him, her promise departing her lips like a kiss.

Noel was thrilled yet clueless on how to proceed. "Okay, where do we go?" he asked.

"The perfect place," his teacher said. "Nowhereville."

It took a moment before it clicked. "You mean where you were born?" he asked. That town in Maine?"

"Yes, Fryeburg. My parents own a house there, but they're in Florida until April," Ms. Dewer explained. "We could spend the day and get to know each other without any interruptions. We'd be out of sight there."

It was mind blowing, this conversation in the classroom that, to anyone who peered in, would be just a teacher and student having a discussion.

"The most important thing is we don't raise suspicions. Keep it quiet and don't act foolish. I'm thinking I'll want this to last a while."

Dozens of questions and concerns came to mind. "How will we get there? When would we leave? When would we get back?"

She smiled and said, "My car, Saturday morning, Saturday night ... late. There's a wonderful deck and it's magical under the stars. Full moon, very romantic. Do you work this Saturday?"

"No," Noel said.

"Perfect! You live on Belknap Road, right?" she asked.

"Yes," Noel said, surprised and flattered she knew his address.

"Good, nine o'clock Saturday morning. Be walking on Ferry Street towards Dairy Queen. I'll drive by. If it's safe, I'll pull over and you get in ... quickly." She looked at the wall clock and again at the door. "If it isn't, I'll loop around until it is, all right?"

Noel nodded.

"Do us a favor. Pack some snacks and drinks, it's a two and a half hour drive," she said.

Noel nodded and she flashed her wonderful smile.

"Good, and remember, discretion is everything. Oh, and a little something to think about until Saturday ... a vocabulary lesson of sorts. The word *pet* is both a noun and a verb." She gave him a teasing wink. "Detention is over."

Numb, Noel stood and left the room without looking back.

* * *

Noel lumbered along Ferry Street, eyes to the ground, trying to look inconspicuous. His backpack rode low, heavy with a variety of snacks. His normal snack preferences leaned toward Doritos, Starburst, and Mountain Dew, but hoping to appear more sophisticated, he brought a block of good cheese, gourmet crackers, apples, Lindt chocolate balls, two bottles of Cocoa Cola, and two bottles of iced tea. He had showered, shaved, and splashed on his father's Drakkar cologne. His hair was still wet and the cool morning breeze made it uncomfortable.

By quarter past nine, he was sure Ms. Dewer was playing him. He imagined her, the Goon, and rows of laughing and jeering faces, mocking the pathetic, love-struck boy. There would be no returning to school, he'd be the laughing stock! His only choice would be taking the Kyle Grainger route and hit the highway in search of greener pastures. Maybe Los Angeles or somewhere warm like Tampa Bay. He'd start at the bottom, flipping burgers or cleaning toilets, since he'd never exceled at anything, or even tried. He'd live on the streets until he settled, but there had to be places he could hole up.

A car approached from behind but he didn't look, fearful it might be the police or some turd-cake intent on harassing him. If so, he wished he had a baseball sized stone in hand so he could sail it through their windshield.

A gray Honda Accord pulled beside him. Ms. Dewer pushed open the passenger side door and said, "Hey, lonesome traveler, going my way?"

Noel tossed the backpack on the back seat and practically fell into the car, his legs weak from nerves and the acknowledgement that it was really happening, Mrs. Dewer actually showed up.

She looked phenomenal in red casual jeans and a low-cut black top that validated the endowed figure Noel had fantasized about. She kissed him quickly on the cheek and accelerated onto Ferry Street. Where her lips brushed him burned with the reality of her touch and he buzzed in anticipation for what the day might bring.

This was too good to be true, he thought, and as they drove toward their promising day, he understood it was also probably too good to last. At some point, Ms. Dewer — or Isobel, as she insisted he call her — would tire of this and be through with him, but he decided he wouldn't let that happen. She had her job and her reputation, both of which he would soon have the power to destroy. This would provide him with enough blackmailing muscle to hold her captive; he could make her his veritable sex slave. If she protested, he would go public and he was okay with that. In most cases of *hot teacher seduces student*, society vilified the teacher and labeled the student a victim, regardless if they were willing participants, or not.

Who wouldn't be willing, with a knockout like Isobel Dewer? Noel wondered. *Who wouldn't billboard that he was with her?* It would be a badge of honor that even Ben "The Goon" Molina couldn't downplay.

✳ ✳ ✳

They drove through Windham NH, taking Route 93 to 495 to 95, which they seemed to stay on forever. About ninety minutes later, Isobel exited the highway and then drove even farther. Each turn led to narrower roads, finally turning onto what, despite being little more than a dirt path, had a street sign. Blue Goose Drive led to a picturesque log home perched upon a knoll that overlooked a pond. It was nicely kept, with freshly painted trim, well-tended flowers, and a large, uncluttered farmer's porch.

They climbed from the car and Isobel looked at Noel over the roof and said, "Hey, boyfriend. Are you ready for an adventure?"

Noel smiled, feeling nervous, yet oddly confident. Isobel tapped a code on a keyless lock and led them into the house, which was *very* country. The house smelled fresh, the kitchen appliances looked new, and counters were empty and spotless. Copper pots and pans and assorted utensils hung from overhead hooks secured into thick beams.

"You come here often?" Noel asked. He wondered if she brought others here, like Ben the Goon ... a disturbing thought.

"Often enough, it's my childhood home. I'm very attached to it."

She took his jacket and hung it with hers on a coat rack mounted to the wall, across from which was an open doorway leading to the basement; it appeared nicely finished.

"Before we get to fun and games, how about if I make my signature turkey and Swiss panini? I'm famished."

"Sure," Noel said, a little disappointed, but considering his inexperience with all things female, he figured he'd best let Isobel lead.

"Do you prefer beer or wine?" she asked, pulling a Panini press from within a cabinet.

Another thing in which Noel was inexperienced; wine was more refined, but beer was what most guys seemed to prefer. He chose beer.

"Great! I'll have one, too." She opened the refrigerator and searched the shelves. "Huh, we're out up here. Be a dear and grab some from the media room refrigerator at the foot of the basement stairs. I'll have Sam Adams and take whatever you like. We have about a dozen choices," she said.

The basement was the ultimate man cave, with a wet bar, couches, a pool table, and a sixty-inch wide screen.

Nice! Noel thought. He opened the fridge door and perused the shelves for his quarry, but it was empty, the shelves were warm, and the interior light hadn't lit. "Is there another fridge?" he called up the stairs, but the slam of the door silenced him and then he was thrust into total darkness.

.

＊　＊　＊

Noel had no sense of time or place. He'd surely been there more than an hour, but he had no idea if it was three, five, or ten hours. When the door slammed and the lights went out, his first thought was that Isobel had an odd sense of humor. He carefully worked his way up the stairs, feeling for a light switch, but found only a blank cover plate. Someone had removed the switch. The door was locked, as he had feared, and unusually solid for a basement door; his fists making little sound as he pummeled it.

He was in utter darkness, which convinced him this predicament was intentional … planned. There should have *some* light, the laser outline of sunlight around a curtain or shade, from the gap beneath the door at the head of the stairs, or from some kind of electronic device. There was nothing. His mind went in numerous directions, but when the true ramifications of the situation hit home, panic sank steely talons into him.

He hollered his way through a series of emotions, from a light-hearted *okay, that was funny, now let me out*, to an angry, *let me out, now*, to terrified pleading, and finally tears. He had settled on the top step, his throat raw and his fists sore and bleeding, before he calmed enough to seek other routes of escape.

He blindly felt his way down the stairway and around the perimeter of the room until he found a doorway near the bar. He turned the knob and was surprised to find it unlocked. The door, like the one at the head of the stairway, was disconcertingly heavy, but it opened easily, allowing him entrance to another space as dark as the first, but dank and much cooler. He shuffled his way around the room, feeling for a light switch, windows, or anything he could use as a weapon, but it was empty, save for a pile of discarded rags against one wall. He found the outline of another door, which was steel and had no knob or handle.

Anxious to leave the cold emptiness of the second room, he returned to the first. A complete search turned up nothing; no bottles or glasses at the bar, no balls or cues at the pool table, and not a single pen to stab with or a damned book to throw.

Distraught, Noel sat atop the pool table, waiting and praying he was the target of some elaborate prank. He would embrace the laughter and mockery if Ben the Goon and the rest of the class appeared.

Nothing occurred for hours, until he heard a loud *clack* and scraping from the other room. Noel tensed, frightened, yet hoping Isobel appeared. He knew he could take her, and he'd revel in the chance to sock her a good one. The door near the bar opened and Noel leapt to his feet, backing away until his back met the wall. Nothing moved within the room, but he heard the sound of something breathing, waiting.

... and then the lights flared on.

Noel raised an arm to block the light, squinting and blinking against the sudden glare, helpless if anything attacked. An outline appeared and resolved into the form of a man — an ordinary man, thirtyish, of average height and build, with commonly handsome features. He was leaning on the bar top. He waved cheerily to Noel.

"What do you want? Who are you?" asked Noel.

"Hi, loverboy. I'd like you to meet my husband, James."

Noel spun towards Isobel, who sat on the stairway, six steps from the basement floor. He hadn't heard her open the door or come down.

"Your husband?" He looked back at the man, who waved again and offered a friendly smile, similar to Isobel's. "I didn't know you ... you didn't ..." Noel sputtered.

"No harm, mate, I'm cool with it," said James Dewer in a British accent as thick as stew. He took a step in Noel's direction, which, despite his amiable demeanor, frightened the heck out of Noel.

"I think I should go," Noel said, edging away from the advancing man.

"Oh, you aren't going anywhere. We have plans for you," said Isobel.

That damned smile.

"Plans?" asked Noel.

"We 'aven't even eaten, yet," said James.

"I'm not really hungry. Just let me go, okay? I won't say a word to anyone."

"I don't think so," Isobel said.

Noel prepared to spring toward Isobel but James Dewer, sensing Noel's intention, had him in an arm lock within seconds. Noel had never seen anyone move so quickly and *damn* he was strong.

"Why are you doing this?" Noel asked, struggling fruitlessly to get free.

"You were easy," said Isobel. "So unbelievably easy."

"People know I'm here. My parents ... my friends. I told them I was going to Fryeburg, Maine."

"No you didn't. Besides, you have no friends, Noel, that's one of the reasons I chose you," said Isobel. "And, well ... I told you a little white lie. We're in Turner, Maine, fifty miles from Fryeburg, which, of course, *you* wouldn't know. All anyone back in Taylor's Falls might know is that you were seen walking along Ferry Street carrying a backpack. Gee, it appears you ran away from home, Noel, unhappy boy like you. It makes sense."

Isobel strode to the outer wall of the room and slid what looked like a letter opener into a small slot. A spring activated and a small seam appeared. She slid back a panel, exposing a window. She repeated the process on another window and pulled a thin remote from her pocket. With a jab of her thumb, the lights in the room went dark, although the room remained lit by silvery spears of moonlight through the windows.

Noel thrashed wildly, but James Dewer's grip tightened and his breathing became guttural, a growl. The man's arms thickened as he squeezed Noel's chest. His ribs compressed and the pain was excruciating. Noel twisted, frantically trying to face his captor to reach for his eyes, but when he saw James Dewer's face all strength left him. The man's mouth, now a gnarled maw, twisted and elongated. Long protuberances sprouted from within, curving into feral, ivory spikes. Hair sprouted from his crevices and pores, turning the ghastly sight beastly.

"Almost dinnertime," said Isobel. "The full moon makes my man hungry. The disadvantage of living in a small town is that everybody knows everybody's business. Too many missing sheep, cattle, or people, becomes painfully obvious. With small town mentality and mass hysteria, hell, one person cries werewolf and next thing you know there's a lynch mob. I've had to find alternate means to feed my man when he gets hungry. Fortunately, full moons only happen about once a month." She smiled her too pretty smile at Noel and winked. "I'll leave you men alone to get acquainted."

Hot breath moistened the back of Noel's neck as the beast lifted him into the air.

"Oh, Honey. Hold it a moment," Isobel said, pausing on the stairway.

The creature halted, long ropes of drool spilling from its maw. It snarled its hunger but held Noel suspended against the ceiling.

"Sorry Noel, but there's only *one* teacher's pet for me." Isobel disappeared up the stairway, her exit finalized by the solid clack of the door closing. The now moonlit room offered Noel a view of the creature, transformation complete. It resembled no creature Noel had ever seen.

It slammed Noel's body to the tiled floor, driving the wind from him and snapping a bone in his forearm. It dragged him into the back room and slammed the door. The pain was brutal and blinding as Noel's fractured arm flopped to and fro. Huge and terrifying, it leapt onto Noel's back and embedded long, brutal tusks into his neck, severing Noel's spinal cord from his brain stem. All feeling fled from his extremities, and as the creature feasted, Noel opened his eyes one final time and saw the pile of clothing he had come across earlier in the darkness. Within the pile lay a maroon and gold jacket, the team colors of Nottingham High School. On the torn and blood-streaked sleeve was the name *Kyle,* embroidered in a fine white turned grey.

Kyle Grainger.

SCREAMING THROUGH SEA GLASS

Juss Stinson

Della

The ride to the beach was pretty and peaceful. I always enjoyed driving with my window down, especially here in Maine. The moving shadows from trees that battled against the sun were relaxing to watch on the secluded back roads. The month of June was proving to be a great time of year. It felt like fall weather and it wasn't too hot or too cold. The radio continued playing some good ol' rock while I hummed and occasionally played air guitar on the steering wheel; only when a solo came on that I clearly needed to participate in of course.

My jam out session was interrupted when ringing came from my bag in the passenger seat. Reaching in with my right hand, I continued to fish for it until the vibrating met my fingertips. Quickly, I answered and put the phone to my ear. "Hello? Griffin?"

"Della, why do you sound surprised that I'm calling you? How much longer are you going to be?" My brother already sounded irritated with me; go figure.

"You sound like a pissed off teenager. I know you are the youngest of the three of us but you do know that you're in your twenties, right? Give me ten more minutes and I'll be there. Did everyone else get there okay?" I was already pretty sure that Mom, Dad, my sister Dina, and her husband Gavin were already in attendance.

"As always you are the only one left to arrive." His tone had stiffness to it.

"Do I detect sarcasm in that tone of yours? Seriously, I am not ALWAYS late." Inside, I was laughing hysterically. I was so lying and we both knew it.

"Just get here already." Griffin hung up before I could get another snappy remark in.

I went back to my jamming out until I pulled into a parking spot. From where I was parked in the lot I could already see everyone on the beach. I adjusted my extremely round sunglasses that were too big for my face and threw my keys into my rugged bag before putting the strap across my shoulder and my chest. I stumbled a bit out of my car and then shut the door before running down to the beach to join everyone.

"Oh Griffin, you were right. Your sister showed up." Mom chuckled and my eyes rolled in reflex.

"Funny. Mom, you really are quite the comedian." I grumbled out as my dad squeezed me up in a bear hug. "I'm going to go and say hello to Dina and Gavin." I made a quick getaway to my sister who was goofing about with her husband by the water.

"DINA!" I threw my arms around her neck, colliding into her. We tipped over, falling to the ground.

"Mom and her vicious dog Griffin already sank their teeth into you, didn't they?" She laughed as we sat up cross-legged in the sand.

"I think I got away quick enough. Can't I just be happy to see you and not be accused of using you as an escape plan?" She knew me better than anyone in our family.

"Della, I see you all the time. Hell, I'm the only one who does. Not to mention we even shared a womb for nine months. It's safe to say that you're faking it. Shouldn't we be happy that even though we're twins we look completely different, we're nothing alike, and our parents treat us like the separate individuals that we are?" She lowered her brow. There she was trying to be the logical one in the family again. Damn, she really was though, so disagreeing with her was always a chore.

"It's only happy for you because you aren't the black sheep in this family." I lowered my brow to the level she was giving me. Game matched.

"To be fair, you're like the three-headed wombat in this herd of sheep. You're lucky I love you, my sweet little screwed up animal." She stood and winked as she grabbed my hand and helped me up.

I do really love Dina and her husband. They really were perfect for each other. So, while I did only let Dina into my life, Gavin was always welcomed too. We goofed off while Mom, Dad, and Griffin ate. We found ourselves jumping around a small formation of rocks on the water, almost like we were six years old again. We kicked off our shoes as we explored, talked, and laughed. As I was sliding down one of the larger rocks trying to touch the water, I cried out with a shriek.

"Ouch! Dammit!" I cursed under my breath. Picking my foot up, I examined the wound. It was pretty deep and I groaned as I gave it a generous yank to free it from my flesh. The piece I removed had a jagged triangular shape to it and was a light green; at least it was before it entered my foot. I dropped it into the back of my shorts and hopped closer to the water. I dipped my foot to clean it off a bit.

"Did you really just pocket that bloody piece of sea glass?" Her worried expression quickly melted into a comical disbelief.

"It's a battle trophy. The sea glass won this round but I'll be on high alert for an attack next time," I said seriously as I continued to rinse my foot.

"You do realize how freaking weird you are right?" she asked, but she already knew my answer without a doubt in either of our minds.

"Unfortunately," I groaned and Gavin helped me off the rocks and into the sand as I slid my flip flops back on. "Gavin, do you still have your paramedic kit in the car? Do you mind just giving this a quick couple of stitches?"

Gavin dashed off to their car and was back in a minute. He prepped the gash as I talked to Dina. Like birds of prey, the rest of the family descended on us.

"Should we be surprised that you were the one who got injured?" A smile was spread across my mother's face.

"Hmm, interesting. I had my suspicions that you were a man-eating shark but now I'm positive. I'm impressed with how quickly you smelled blood in the water." I could hear Dina chuckle after my comment. I continued, "Anyway, thanks for the concern. I think that Gavin took care of it, you never know though. Perhaps now I have a zombie virus. Who knows where that sea glass could have been? Humanity is doomed; we should put them down easy. It's too bad we don't know a vicious shark that can begin thinning the world's population sgarting from the water! Wait, Mom! I have a job for you!"

"I think you're safe, zombie viruses affect the brain, something you lack. Your humor proves it." My mother was a pro at comebacks; there was no doubt about that.

That pretty much summed up the hours ahead. We bickered, joked, talked, and now we were all just walking around by old rock formations once again. As the sun sank below the horizon, something caught my eye and I stopped. I turned around and where I had cut my foot earlier there was someone standing in the same place.

I squinted a bit, it was hard to make out anything at that distance in the fading light. It appeared to be a woman looking down at the rocks and the water below them. Every now and again, she would crouch down and run her hand over the surface by her feet. My Dad finally caught my attention by calling out to me, "Dellabell? You okay?"

I glanced back, but there was no one in the distance now. People constantly take small walks on the beach here in Maine; I have no idea why that woman seemed to interest me. Everyone helped pack up and load it into Mom and Dad's car. Someone spoke my name behind me as I was shoving a bag into the trunk like a lame-ass puzzle piece. I groaned, "Yeah?"

I heard the mumbled reply of, "Meet me back at the rocks?"

"I thought we were all leaving now?" I answered, about to win this terrible game of bag Tetris.

A hissed response made me jump a bit, "Now!"

Startled, I whirled around angrily aborting the mission with the bag and letting it crash to the ground. Having started a minor avalanche, a few more items fell to the ground.

"Della! What the hell is your problem?!" my mother yelled.

"Was Dina just behind me being a bossy jackass?" I got on my knees and picked up my mess, maneuvered everything more success-fully into the trunk, and then shut it tight.

"No, do you ever pay attention? She yelled goodbye to all of us when her and Gavin left. No wonder you got hurt today! You have absolutely no knowledge of your surroundings."

"Sorry." I rubbed my head, feeling fuzzy. I could have sworn that Dina was just talking to me. Maybe I was just tired. To be fair this was more family time than I was used to.

"Contrary to what you believe, I do worry about you." She kissed my forehead, "Go home and get some sleep. It was nice seeing you today. I love you."

I kissed her cheek and said I loved her before doing the same for Dad and Griffin. They drove off and my car was the only one remaining in the parking area. I took another look out on the beach. Nothing.

I got into the car and started it. As I was pulling out, something familiar caught my eye again. In the distance, there was the outline of the woman in the same place as earlier. I blinked and the image faded away. Dammit. I stayed put for a moment but the sight didn't return to me so I started driving.

Driving home proved to be harder than I thought. I think the hallucinations from earlier sparked some type of weird anxiety because I was constantly catching shadows dancing around my car. By the time I was home, thankfully only a twenty-minute drive, I ran into the house and locked the door behind me. I seriously needed to relax before I cracked. I ran some hot water in the tub and looked in the mirror. Shoulder length auburn hair, bluish-gray eyes, thick but healthy body features, but most of all a worried expression looking back at me. I looked pale and shaky.

I stripped off my clothes and focused on my fingertips grazing over my skin as I did so. I was hoping that by focusing on the sense of touch that I wouldn't think of much else, even if it was just for a moment. I slid my jeans down over my hips and took my lacey blue panties with them all the way to the floor. I kicked them aside while peeling off my gray tank top and black bra, also throwing them in my messy clothes pile.

I jumped back as I caught another glance of myself in the mirror. It was my reflection but with completely blackened eyes staring back at me. I quickly leaned into the mirror and the dark vision remained. Gripping the sides of the sink, my hands shook. A hot bath would melt all of this away. I needed to get out of this mental funk. The bath. Do. Not. Think. About. Anything. Else.

I sunk into the hot water and it felt sharp against my goosebumps. Leaning back, the water warmed up my cold and trembling skin. I was getting my grip on reality back and I was thankful for that. When the side of my foot throbbed, I remembered the cut and stitches. I sat up and brought my left foot out of the water to examine it. The wound was black and it looked like black ink had crawled in a vein-like pattern through my foot and up my lower leg. I panicked.

"I promise you that it isn't going to look much worse than that." A soft voice caused my eyes to shoot up.

"The beach. You're her. The rocks," my voice gasped out in broken segments as I bolted up into a standing position. Unseen hands plunged me back into the tub. I choked on a mouthful of water before I found myself pulled into a lounging position with an arm on each side of the tub. No matter how much I thrashed I couldn't move. Even my screams were halted in my throat.

Quietly, a voice said, "I am so sorry; I had to do this. I tried to get you to venture back to the rocks but then you came here and brought me with you. I need you to take us back."

Without being able to speak or move my body, I shifted my eyes to look over in her direction. Her hair was long and dark brown. Her eyes were as black as mine were in the mirror a moment ago. She was as pale as death but her features were all extremely feminine. Her left forearm contained what looked like black inked symbols; tattoos? It was strange though. The more I looked at her, the more I calmed down. My mind was foggy and oddly tranquil, almost like my control was in someone else's hands.

At the moment I felt my mind relax, so did the rest of my body and I felt the pressure on my mouth become loosened enough to speak. "Who are you? Why ..."

I was quickly cut off. "Reeny, my name is Reeny. I'm stuck, and I need your help Della. Please, I had no other choice to get your attention." Her cold hand touched my cheek causing me a jolt. She tucked a piece of hair behind my ear and pulled her hand back.

Mental and physical feeling was returning. This couldn't be real. I shook my head and heard a nervous laugh escape my lips. Standing up, I walked past my "Reeny" hallucination and grabbed a towel off the bathroom shelf. I was drying myself when I glanced again at the mirror in front of me. My eyes were clear but there was a cold black stare behind me. My imaginary, not-so-friendly friend did not find my mental breakdown entertaining.

I spoke up, "So, tell me why the hell I am now stuck with a 'Reeny'? You seem so damn keen on sharing, so why don't you give it a go?

Enlighten me." I could just imagine my mother's face when I told her that I needed to check into a psychiatric ward.

"You think this is a joke? That's cute." Reeny took a step forward causing me to back into the wall behind me. Before I even had a chance to answer, her hand was gripped tightly around my throat. I gasped, so she lightened her hold enough to offer a small oxygen supply.

"You think I chose this for myself? Six years ago, I was at the beach with my fiancé, and it was just another day together. Hell, after a rough patch we really needed one good night. It was dark and quiet as we sat on a pile of rocks by the water. He looked at me and said that I should realize that things weren't going well between us. All I could do was cry as he told me that I wasn't enough for him. Crying led to anger, I shoved him until we were both waist deep in the water. He shoved me back and I lunged forward, knocking him over and pushing him under the water. It was like something had taken over me and I couldn't let my grip lighten up. His hand was frantically feeling over the rocks to find leverage to pull himself up. He found a sharpened piece of sea glass and slashed my throat. I let go of him and gripped my severed neck. All I can remember was the wave of red trailing heavily down over my neck, chest, and hands. It was the last warmth that I ever felt."

I stared blankly, stunned. I was actually feeling sympathetic to the story. There was too much detail to conclude that this was just a hallucination. I cautiously questioned further, "You said that I brought you here?"

Reeny held up a bloodied piece of sea glass, "Earlier, you stepped on this, and then took it with you. I need you to put it back where you found it. I need you to take me back so I can remain where my body found its end. My body is now gone, this is what was left, and it has its place. Moving it unnaturally brings me back to this world to wander. Don't doom me to this zombie-like existence. Put me back. Please." Her hand dropped from my throat.

I pulled away from the wall, scrambling out of the bathroom and into the bedroom without looking up. I didn't need to see the spirit breathing down my neck. I was gripping hard on the sea glass that Reeny had held in front of my face and given back to me. I tossed the towel down and quickly threw on a black sundress. I blushed because a zombie was watching me get dressed, and then ran from the room snatching my bag and the keys from the door-side table on the way out of the house.

In the car, I kept my eyes fixed strictly on the road. With the music off, I could hear shifting in the passenger seat next to me. I was still holding this spirit's vessel. Adrenaline was surging. My hold on the steering wheel and the shard of sea glass was viciously trembling so I tightened my grip. The glass buried into my palm and still I stayed silent. I bit my lip as it cut into my skin, and glanced over at Reeny. Her softened moan made me turn. It looked as if her eyes had sunk inward, creating two pits of darkness. There were small versions of the black veins from my foot around her eye sockets. I snapped my attention back to the road, my lip quivering.

It wasn't until twenty minutes later that I spoke up, "We're here. Time to end this nightmare. I just put this back where I found it and that's it, right?" And then what? Call Dina? Drive myself straight to the hospital? Not until after I saw this delusion through. Maybe it would bring me some kind of closure before the inevitable shock therapy. A broken brain isn't easy to fix.

Reeny sounded flat, "You know where to go."

I didn't reply, I was just keeping my eye on the prize; getting this done. I hurried over to the rock formation from earlier. I was looking over the place I had slipped and zoned out until I heard anxious groaning behind me. I carefully stepped on the rocks until I was where I needed to be. I got down on my knees to find the place where I believed my foot caught onto this damned piece of sea glass.

"Hold on! Don't let it go yet, this has to be exactly right!" Reeny demanded, fear in her voice. I looked up to see the dead girl standing in front of me. She crouched down, took the glass from my hand and sighed.

"Are you ready to be put back?" I was more than ready but I gave her a moment. I reached out for the glass to take it back but she snapped her arm back and an evil smile crept over her face.

"You moronic girl. Yes, I needed you back here to grant me my freedom, but it was certainly not to remain here. This is your tomb, not mine." She held the sea glass between two fingers in front of me. "This was a blood sacrifice. You stepped on this and your blood was a donation to me, a beautiful portal. Thank you, by the way." Her snicker made my heart drop.

"Go back to your ghostly games, I did what was asked and I'm leaving." I was surprised at how strong my words were. I cautiously stood up on the slick rocks. One wrong step and I might fall in, probably smashing my head on the way down. Then my body would be lost at sea too.

"I told you that to get you back here. Don't call me a fucking ghost; I'm not one of those frumpy little nitwits. A demon is what I am. We try to break free from Hell in order to fulfill our purpose. Nightmares are needed in humanity's realm of reality; think of it as a poison that brings you one step closer to the place that we call home. We need a blood sacrifice to summon us. It needs to be where the portal was placed and with the demon who created it. Why do you think you have so many bloody disasters your world? They're usually strategically planned by the most intelligent of my kind, even though most of us settle for the occasional 'accident.' We booby trap the world with trinkets like glass, nails, needles, and anything that can draw even one simple drop of blood. That is all we need. It was all I needed."

"Then you got what you wanted." I tried to keep my tone steady and harsh.

"Not exactly, I got out, but I desire completion. Please be a dear?" Reeny gripped my hair and pulled me into the cold, sharp water. I was plunged under the rolling waves and it disoriented me as I scrambled back up for air. My hair was still wrapped around her clenched fist. She slammed my head against the stone I was previously kneeling on and kept it pressed there.

She tightened her grip as I whimpered. "There we go, so willing to help me. You are just so perfect." She mockingly traced the sea glass from my temple, down my face, all the way to my shoulder. "When it comes to bloodshed, one drop is never enough."

She pulled the glass across my neck and my screams were soon replaced by a grotesque gurgling. My vision was blurring but I could catch glimpses of Reeny licking her fingers in clear satisfaction. I wanted to fade away but the agony held me there. It was hard to determine if the sound of rushing liquids over the rocks was the sea or the blood pouring from my throat. Reeny leaned down and rested her chin on the rock so she was eye level with me. The ink I had spotted on her earlier was shifting, as if the black lines were snakes that slithered through her forearm. I could see that she was watching for the lights go out in my eyes as she reached up with the sea glass again. She stuck it into the gash in my flesh and released it creating a lump in my already brutalized jugular. My shrill squeaks didn't help.

My eyes fluttered and I prayed that this meant I was finally drifting off for good, but prayers were useless here. Hell destroyed hope. Reeny crushed her lips to mine and my eyes flew open. My body got a shot of pure adrenaline and within my throat I felt an unbearable heat building. It was searing through my neck and the ink on her arm danced as if in celebration. I felt like every particle of my body were being ripped apart and consumed. Blaring red flames kissed my skin, taking my sight from me.

I felt numb. I felt alone. Everything fell quiet. A faint green light surrounded me and I stumbled forward until I was against what felt like a wall. My vision was back but I couldn't wrap my head around what I was looking at. Squinting through the transparent-ish barrier that I was leaning against, I could see my own self dancing around the sands of the beach. My left arm had black symbols all over it. My body wasn't mine, it was Reeny's.

I pulled back and noticed I could catch some reflection in the wall. I was looking into a face with two deep, blackened, and evil cavities. I wasn't me any longer. First my mind had left me and now so had my soul. I noticed carvings in a section of this glass prison.

I read aloud, "Tomb sweet tomb."

I wasn't sure if it was the loss of myself or the reality that I had set loose a carrier of chaos into the world, but at that moment I was sure this very well may be the last burst of raw humanity that I could muster. I couldn't stop banging my reddened fists against the translucent green wall again and again. Over and over, I pounded and yelled for help, not even sure if help was possible. My lungs burned and my ears rang from my continuous screeching, but my mind knew the truth. It really didn't matter anymore. All I was doing was screaming through sea glass.

* * *

Dina

Mom walked into the waiting room, her eyes bloodshot. It was clear we wouldn't be going anywhere for a while until we had more answers. We sent the rest of the family home and Mom and I were planning on staying in hopes of progress.

Mom sat down and opened up before I had a chance to ask. "Dina, they said there are no signs of consciousness. They said it's all just a waiting game right now. You can go in and see her if you want, I'm going to call your father and let him know that nothing has changed."

I didn't know what to expect when she fell at the beach. I knew that she hit her head hard enough on the rocks to knock her out but I didn't know it would put her in a coma. Without a word, I found my way into Della's room. I sat beside her on the left side so that I could still see the door. I think that deep down I was just hoping that a doctor would rush in and fix this, even though I knew that it was just wishful thinking. Prayers were useless here. Hell destroyed hope.

I caught a glimpse of movement on Della's left side, almost as if something was slithering through her forearm. I wrote it off as an exhausted delusion. Reaching out, I took her hand. I quickly pulled it away when I grasped something that she was clenching in her palm. I examined it until I heard what I swore was a faraway scream. I slipped it into my back pocket to bring it home with me. Maybe it would help me feel closer to my sister when I couldn't be here with her. I looked at her lying on that hospital bed, feeling helpless that my sister was trapped in her own mental tomb. Maybe she was still at the beach in there and hadn't left that moment? I tried to clear my head, not to get depressed. I reached into my pocket and pulled out the item I had put there a minute ago. I heard distant screams as I held the sea glass.

MIRA'S SHOP OF PECULIARITIES

Harold Hull

It must be a trick, James Pictou thought.

He stood in the store's entryway and watched the eyes — blue and unattached — peer around the room. Collecting strange items happened to be his hobby, and he'd traveled all over the world in search of oddities, but he'd never come across a display like this one. This was unique and hilarious in a grotesque way.

The pair of eyeballs floated in the center of a square glass case. They turned with the movement of the customers, following them as they wandered down the rows.

James took a step forward and the eyes locked onto him. Grinning, he walked over to the front counter, where a tall, middle-aged woman with dark hair stood. "How do you do it?" asked James. "Animatronics?"

She said nothing, but allowed her mouth to curl back into a smile.

There was a thin metal plate on the glass case and inscribed on it were the words: *My ex-boyfriend's eyeballs.* James pointed at the plate and chuckled. "That's funny. Quite the novelty."

The woman watched him amusedly.

He took a couple of steps to the right to see if the eyes would follow him. They did. James moved back against the counter and the eyes shifted to him yet again. *Must be battery operated or something.* He looked around the case and noticed there was no price tag. "How much do you want for the eyes?"

"They're not for sale," the woman said. "Display only."

"Really?" James said. He didn't like the answer. He'd flown from California to Maine looking for something interesting to add to his collection, and while this wasn't the sort of thing he usually bought — he typically went after things that were real — the eyeballs would make for an interesting conversation starter at his dinner parties. "You're the owner, right? Mira? I can offer you a lot of money, Mira. I owned a tech company in my younger days, and now I travel around finding the weirdest shit I can —" He paused to let out an obnoxious chuckle. "— and this is just too hilarious not to bring home. How much would I have to spend to persuade you to sell it to me?"

"Again, I must insist it's not for sale. How could I part with something so personal?"

"How is —?" He let himself trail off, his eyes focusing back on the metal plate and its words. *My ex-boyfriend's eyes.* "You mean?"

"I could never get rid of my beloved's eyes. It would be a betrayal, don't you think?"

She's fucking crazy, James thought, backing away from the counter. "All right," he said. "I'll just take a look at what else you're selling then."

He walked down an aisle, inspecting the items with genuine interest. The back wall had built-in shelving, while three tall, wooden shelves occupied the middle space of the shop. Glass cabinets were placed as endcaps to each row. James moved alongside the mahogany shelves, smiling every time he stumbled upon something eerie or gross, and rolling his eyes every time he came across the same old things he always came across in these kinds of shops. There was the usual stuff: calcite and vanadinite and an array of other rocks and minerals. A buffalo skull glared down at him, and beside it was the skin of a cobra, extending all along the back wall. There were fossils of fish and crinoids. And there were also more common items like handmade bowls, jewelry, beard oil, and key chains.

Someone is fond of taxidermy, he thought, as he passed a series of bats hanging upside down in Plexiglas casings. There were jars of green and red and orange powder, each with a description and various uses. One description read: *Sparrow Bone. A multi-spell powder made from the crushed bone of a sparrow, mixed with scorpion venom and a touch of virgin blood. Most potent purpose: immobilization.* The price tag: $59.99 a gram.

"Christ," James whispered. It was some expensive bullshit Mira was selling. Some might find the 'magic dust' amusing, but it was still nonsense.

He looked back at the front counter. Mira stood expressionless and watching. It unsettled James the way she stared at him, as if he were one of her specimen trapped inside a glass encasement.

And then there were the eyeballs. They'd shifted slightly in their glass case and now rested diagonally so they could keep watch of James's movement.

In a corner toward the back of the shop was a section that was blocked off with a chain. A sign read: *Warning! Grotesqueries Ahead. Restricted.* And as James crossed over the chain — he just couldn't help himself — he soon realized the warning was not without merit. Vials of blood lined the wall with various tags indicating the origins of that blood: lizard, rat, leper, fetus. There were more glass cases filled with eyeballs, all of them moving in jarring synchronicity. Situated on top of a glass display was a severed head covered in tumors and boils. The head looked mutated, like the ugliest circus freak James had ever seen. He reached out with his right hand, nearly touching the head. It appeared so lifelike, but he knew it couldn't be. Retracting his hand, he moved on to a stand labeled: Voodoo. Three dolls sat on top, pins puncturing their cloth skin. Beside them were three shrunken heads, none of which looked like wax. The skin had color to it and a certain amount of elasticity that made it appear strikingly like human flesh. Again, James could not help himself from touching and moved his hand closer to the shrunken heads.

Slowly, an eye opened on one of the tiny heads. A quiet, scratchy voice uttered, "Help me." Then the eyes of the head beside it opened and the same words came out. The third shrunken head soon joined in and now there was a harmony of desperate voices begging James for help.

A part of him wanted to run, but another part wouldn't allow it, a perverse fascination having settled into him. He needed to know how it all worked, how everything seemed so real. If necessary, he would beg Mira for a glimpse behind the curtain, offer her more money than she'd make all year. He would do whatever it took to add these peculiarities to his collection.

He left the restricted area and headed to the counter, where Mira awaited him with a cold, unwelcoming stare. "Did you find what you were looking for?" she asked.

"This place is incredible. It's like a freak show back there. Stuff looks so real."

"That's because it is," she deadpanned.

"Yeah, sure. Don't want to share your secrets. I get it. You don't want to sell me these eyeballs, but what about one of those teensy heads? Name a price and I'll pay it."

"The restricted area is — like the eyes — a mood setter, if you will. The items for sale are clearly marked and set on the shelves before you."

"You're a difficult woman to persuade, you know that? What's it going to take for me to get something exotic for my collection? There must be something that will change your mind."

"The price is too steep, even for you I'm afraid."

James nodded, then backed away from the counter. "All right," he said. "Can't change your mind. That's fine. Unfortunate, but hey, what are you going to do, right? Guess I'll be on my way then."

She gave a curt nod.

Leaving the shop, James stepped onto Wharf Street and pushed through a flock of hipsters until he'd made it to the other side, then turned back so he could take a good look at the place. The whole street was just one shop after another, a restaurant or bar peppered in after every couple of stores. And everywhere he turned he saw brick: brick buildings, brick streets. A wooden sign attached to a pole that connected onto the side of one of those brick buildings read: Mira's Shop of Peculiarities.

Indeed, James thought. That was exactly what it was, and he wanted one of those peculiarities in the worst way. For a moment, back when he stood in the restricted area, he contemplated taking something and stuffing it inside his coat. But it would be too easy for Mira to track him down or identify him to the police. He wouldn't risk it, but there were other ways of getting what he wanted.

There were men he could hire, professionals who'd done things like this countless times, and he just so happened to know one in the area. A low-level guy named Jay Cole, who did jobs for a city councilor James had gone to school with, was known to be reasonably priced and efficient. He reached into his coat pocket and pulled out his cell phone, then searched through his contact list for Jay Cole's number.

An hour later, James was inside his suite at The Press Hotel meeting with Cole. Short and rib-showing skinny, Cole sat on a cream-colored couch, a leg draped over the side, and took in the room. He had a crop of blonde hair that was a month overdue for a cut, and just enough hair on his chin to say he had a goatee. "I've never stayed here," he said. "Too high rollin' for me, you know?"

"Yeah," James said. "So, are you able to do the job or not?"

Cole shook his head. "I can do it. Bunch of weird shit you've got me looking for though. Don't you want some money like everybody else?"

"I've got money. I don't, however, have these things. Once you've got them in your possession, bring them to the airport. I'm leaving in the morning. I'll give you your money and I'll be on a private jet back to California. Everyone is happy."

Cole smiled and said, "Everyone is happy." He stood up and walked over to the door. "You're into some freaky shit, you know that?"

"Yes," James said. He did, in fact, know that. It was an observation many people felt the need to expound upon repeatedly. "I'll see you in the morning." He shook Cole's hand, then showed him out.

Once he was alone, James sat down in a chair and stared at the elevated fireplace built into the wall opposite him. Doubts were beginning to fill his mind. There were other shops in New England he could visit, and while they might not have the same level of eccentricities, they would undoubtedly have items he did not already have in his collection. He could easily walk away. That would be the smart thing to do, instead of risking a criminal charge.

James had good lawyers, so even if the theft could be traced back to him, it wasn't likely he'd spend time in jail, but the legal process would be bothersome. A nuisance. He posed the question: What were some stupid animatronic eyeballs and shrunken heads worth to him? And for what? To add to his glorified Halloween collection?

He went into the kitchen and got a beer out of the mini-fridge. Downing an entire bottle, he slammed it on the countertop and bent for another. Yes, he decided. He would take the minor risk — the nuisance — in the hope that he might add some truly novel showcases to his dinner parties. Picturing himself back in his San Francisco home, he imagined standing next to a beautiful woman — a model maybe — and chatting her up about his discovery of eyeballs that would follow a person around. She'd marvel at them and ask how they worked, and James, who would now understand Mira's secret, would explain the mechanics of it to the young model.

Beyond wanting to impress people, James craved the chase, the rush of scouring the planet in the hunt for the weird. He fashioned himself a connoisseur, but also a big-game hunter, oddities being his trophies instead of the head of a lion or rhinoceros. Usually the price of obtaining an item would come in the form of a ridiculously high price tag, but in this case, the price would be breaking the law. Which was all the same to James. It came down to cost.

The price is too steep, even for you I'm afraid. He remembered Mira's words and wondered what she'd meant. Hyperbole, he guessed. "One hard bitch," he whispered, then bit his bottom lip. A challenge. Her icy disposition turned him on. If he hadn't wanted to arouse suspicion, he might've returned to the shop in the morning and tried his hand at getting to know her better. He might even ask her out to dinner. His experience taught him that if he tried long enough he could almost always get someone to respond to his advances with a yes.

He finished the second beer and headed into the bedroom. Not about to lose sleep over the situation, he slipped under the covers, read for a few minutes to wind down, then felt himself drifting off.

Awaking to the alarm clock's annoying beeping, James lifted his arm straight up, held it there for a second, and then dropped it onto the top of the clock. The beeping was no more.

4:30 a.m.

By now, if everything had gone well, Cole would be heading to the airport with a suitcase filled with some very bizarre contents. James would meet him in less than an hour.

He opened the curtains. Taxi headlights moved through the blackened city, bringing home the last handful of drunks from the Old Port.

His cell vibrated on the nightstand. He went over, saw the ID come up as JAY COLE, and answered: "Hello?"

Silence.

"Cole?" he said. "Are you there?"

Again nothing, and now it dawned on him what he'd done. Cole had been caught — maybe police, maybe Mira — and they'd called the last number on Cole's cell log. Now they knew the connection.

He felt worried for a moment, then shrugged and started to pack. So, what if the police knew what had transpired? They could provide him with a summons and he'd call his lawyers, make a deal out of court that might result in him paying a settlement, but that was fine. The risk had been worth it.

Poor Cole, though. He might end up spending some time in jail. The thought crossed James's mind that he could pay an attorney to represent Cole. Yes, he decided. He would do that. It was the least he could do, really.

Once packed, he carried his bags down the hallway to the elevator. His cell went off again. Pulling it from his pocket, he checked the ID and saw a number he didn't recognize. "Go to hell," he said, and hit the ignore button. The elevator doors opened and he stepped inside. When they reopened, he moved out into the lobby of The Press and started toward the front desk.

Again, his cell vibrated.

Same number.

He pressed the send key, lifted the cell to his ear, and listened.

Mira spoke to him. "I will sell you one item," she said. "On the condition that you do not pester me anymore. No more questions; no more break-ins. You never step foot in my store again. Do you find that an agreeable condition?"

"Yes," James said.

"Then come to my shop and you may buy one piece from the restricted area."

"How do I know you're not setting me up?" he asked.

"I know who you are, James Pictou. I know the amount of money you have and the lawyers you retain. I will not waste my time pressing charges against you or your thief."

He ended the call and left the hotel.

On the way to Mira's, James ran through different scenarios in his head. He might arrive only to be handcuffed and taken away in a police car. A worse possibility crossed his mind, though. Knowing she had little hope of legal recourse, Mira might shoot him on the spot, or have men waiting to take him out back and beat him half to death. Although that could, of course, happen, James found it unlikely. Mira didn't strike him as a killer. She was crazy in her own way, but murdering people had a way of ruining a person's business and she didn't seem the type to risk her own personal gain in exchange for revenge. More and more, he kept coming back to what he deemed the most likely option: Mira was being honest. One item, and in return, he'd leave her alone. Simple enough.

He parked and made his way onto Wharf Street. It wasn't dark anymore, but the sun had yet to rise, leaving the streets dim, with a faint mist.

The lights were on inside Mira's Shop of Peculiarities. James pulled the door open, a bell signifying his presence with a clang, then he stepped in and glanced around the shop for Mira.

His eyes met the glass case near the front counter. He was being watched intently.

"Hello?" James called out.

"I'm in the restricted area," Mira said. Her voice was even, unthreatening.

As he moved along one of the shelves, he worried once more that he might be walking into a trap. Police officers — or large men with baseball bats — could be waiting. But as he turned the corner, he saw that his fear had been unfounded. It was only Mira standing in the restricted area.

She raised her eyebrows, unfurled her arms, and said, "Come find what you want."

Maybe I've gotten lucky, James thought, as he moved cautiously toward Mira. "I didn't mean to cause you trouble," he said. "I'm just … fascinated with this sort of stuff, you know?"

"I tend to believe it has more to do with your inability to take no for an answer."

Stepping over the chain, James peered around the section, trying to decide what he wanted but also attempting to avoid eye contact with Mira. "Like I told you before, I want those peepers. No need to look around here." He swallowed hard. "The eyeballs are what I want."

"Were you not delighted by the shrunken heads?" she asked.

"I was. They were incredible … truly, but —"

"Let me show you how they're made. A parting gift, if you will. Then, you can bring the eyeballs back to your home, but you'll also know the secret on how to make my shrunken heads."

He took a step back. "That's okay, really."

"I insist," Mira said. "All my best inventory is in the basement anyway."

"I think I'll be satisfied with the eyes, but thank you." James turned and walked back over to the chain that blocked off the restricted area.

"Inquam," Mira said.

His muscles tensed. As soon as he heard the word, his feet stopped moving. Then he spun around and followed Mira to the basement door. "I don't want to go down there." He sounded pathetic, his words coming out in a prolonged whimper.

She touched his face and said, "I don't care what you want." Opening the door, she descended a flight of wooden steps.

James had no choice but to move down into the darkness behind her. He was no longer in control of his body. "Please," he said. "Let me go."

She clapped her hands. "Come now. I have things I want to show you."

By the time he reached the bottom of the stairs, James realized how monumentally he had screwed up, how severe a mistake he'd made, and knew he would pay dearly for his miscalculation. A tear ran down his cheek, curving toward the chin. *Beg,* he thought. *Goddamn it, beg her for mercy.* But he never did. The words failed him, but he also believed they would do him no good. He now saw something in Mira that he hadn't before, a cruelness in her eyes, a loathing she directed toward him. No, begging would be pointless.

The walls were lined with mahogany shelves, just like the ones upstairs, and were crammed with merchandise: colorful powders, vials of blood, fossils, crystals and minerals. There were more shelving units in the center of the basement, and these spaces were occupied with an assortment of animal heads — an abnormally large wolf head stuck out to him — and glass cases similar to the one which held the eyes. But in these cases, there were no eyes. There were severed arms and legs. The largest case held part of a man, everything above the waist. He sat without legs, without arms, just torso and head. Bubbles sputtered out of the man's mouth, and that was enough to make James want to scream. But he couldn't.

He was unable to do anything, except when Mira wanted him to do something.

Another stairway — this time stone instead of wood — lead them further down into another space, nearly as large as the basement. *This is where I'll die,* James thought. There were no peculiarities on this level. The stone chamber consisted of seven separate sections. Cells. The light dimmed; each exhalation of breath sent out a tiny puff of smoke. A long table had been set out in the middle of the chamber, with smaller tables situated around it.

Jay Cole lay on the long table, his arms and legs strapped. His head was held firmly in place by a vice. "Christ, lady, come on," he said. "You don't want to do this. You seem like a nice lady. Just let me go and we'll forget about this whole thing. I swear."

Even in such a terrible predicament, Cole was still trying to negotiate his way out. James wished he could help the man, but he'd been reduced to a slave.

Mira put on a pair of surgical gloves, then began applying a cream-colored lotion to Cole's face and scalp. She locked his head into the vice again. Holding a hand over Cole, she looked up at James and said, "Now I will show you my secret." She uttered a few nonsensical sounding words and then pulled her hand back.

Cole's jaw pushed upward, his teeth coming together like magnets. The top of his skull dropped an inch, freeing him from the vice. His cranium compressed, tears and blood streaming out of his eyes. Several teeth snapped, leaving little white chips across his chin. Cole tried to scream, but couldn't open his jaw to do so. All he could do was make a low groaning noise and hiss the word: "Help." His head was half the size it had been, and still it shrunk, crushed like a soda can. Every centimeter was a rush of agony. Effectively braindead, Cole stared blankly at the ceiling above, no longer moaning in pain, but just waiting for the process to be over. And when it finally ended, his head had fallen to the size of a fist.

Taking a machete off one of the smaller tables, Mira swung and brought the blade down over Cole's throat, detaching what was left of the head from the rest of the body.

Cole's eyes still moved, and his mouth opened slightly to let out a breath, which made no sense seeing as he had no lungs to pump out oxygen. But breathe the shrunken head did, just as all the others had.

"Here is your gift from me," Mira said, tossing the head at James.

Still unable to move, James could not catch Cole's head and was powerless to do anything other than allow it to hit him in the stomach, then fall to the ground.

Mira shoved Cole's body off the table. "Now it is your turn," she said.

"Please," James said. It took effort to speak. "I'm sorry." He had told himself it would be pointless to beg, but now he couldn't help it.

There was nothing else he could do. "I'm sorry," he said again. "I'm so sorry."

"I know you are, but it's too late."

He felt his body move against his will. Tensing, locking up, none of it worked. Falling onto the table, he watched as Mira poured red powder into a glass of water, then brought it to his lips.

"Sparrow Bone," she said. "Now open your mouth and drink."

His jaw was forced open and the water spilled into him. Instinctively, he swallowed, gulping down every last drop.

"I could hold you like this for hours," Mira said, "but this is easier. I'll need to focus while I'm doing the extraction." She looked down at him and smiled.

Extraction. The word stirred him into a panic. *Christ Almighty, Lord Jesus, save me. Dear God, savior, my redeemer, please, I beg you, save me. Don't let me die like this. Please. Please.*

No one answered his thoughts. Not a single entity, human or cosmic, cared about his prayers. He was alone in this place, his fate sealed.

Mira took a scalpel off the small table, holding it in her right hand. With the left, she gently pulled down on the lower lid to James's left eye, then wedged the scalpel between eyeball and lid. "You will not die," she said. "You should know that before we begin. Will that ease your mind? No, you won't die for a very long time, but you will see everything and feel everything. It'll be an out of body experience. You've heard people talk about seeing themselves on the operating table, right? Watching themselves being operated on, halfway between living and death. Then they rush back into their body and tell everybody about their experience, as if this was all the proof we needed that there must truly be an afterlife." She bent down and kissed his forehead. "Well, this will be sort of like that, except you won't ever want to re-enter your body. Not ever. You'll want to die and I won't let you." She pressed the scalpel deeper into the eye socket. "Now, let's begin."

*   *   *

James could see.

Through the blur of liquid and glass, he could see his body lying on the table. Today, she'd flayed part of his hand. Yesterday, it had been a couple of toes. It hurt, but he couldn't cry. Not now. He wanted to scream and curse, but he never spoke again. At first, she simply would not permit it, then on the fifth day, she removed his tongue and placed it in a jar with the words *Liar's Tongue* written on it. She told him it could be used in certain brews. James believed her. He wished he'd believed her words from the beginning. Now he could only watch from a distance as she stood over his body, the scalpel once again in her hand.

He watched and learned her secrets.

SEEING IS BELIEVING

Wicker Stone

I always suspected that somewhere along my father's life his wires got crossed, for as far back as I can remember he used to cut himself ... a lot, and on purpose, believing something or some, *thing*, lived just beneath his skin. Sounds pretty crazy, right? That's okay. Like I said, I also thought the same.

Despite how horrible my father's urges would get he never once did his cutting in front of me, my mother, or younger brother, Jacob. He attended to his addiction in private, choosing either the garage, bedroom, or bathroom. Although his absence did nothing to deaden the screams that periodically echoed throughout our humble abode in Newport, Maine while the razor or knife delivered its part of the bargain. His body became a road map of fresh and old sores and we were all fairly certain plenty more hid underneath his clothing. Whether we were afraid of what he might say or do, none of us mentioned the cuts. We all just pretended they were not even there.

And then came that dreary April morning my father didn't show up for breakfast. We all knew something terrible had happened. I'll never forget my mother's expression, when she excused herself from the table and ventured upstairs to check on him. Whenever his cutting worsened my father always slept in the spare room across from me and my brother's room, which is where he had been that night. From downstairs, we heard her repeatedly call out his name and then the heavy void that followed.

When she finally returned to the kitchen, she had on her ratty green bathrobe and instructed we wait here, while she went out to the garage.

This time it was her screams (not my father's for a change) that startled us and turned our worst fear into reality. She found him in the garage, lying in a pool of his own blood that seeped from two red rivulets carved into the inside of both arms. She arrived too late to save him and while my father's private hell finally came to an end, ours had just begun.

For my mother, his death became her downfall. Whether she couldn't accept the fact he was gone or just couldn't remove the grizzly image of how she found him from her head. Either way, she never recovered and chased anti-depressants with Jack Daniels, until she withered into an empty vessel that hid away up in her bedroom. Years later my brother, Jacob, followed suit. Hooked on medication of his own he quickly became as vacant as she was. By sixteen, he lost his battle and hung himself in the very place dad took his life. I overheard mother had found him also. By then, I had already graduated high school and moved to Portland, nearly one hundred miles away. I haven't been back since, not even for the funeral, having no desire to reopen old wounds or visiting a place I see only in my nightmares.

As for myself, I managed to escape my twisted, corrupt, childhood with only a few minor bumps and bruises and set a course, determined not to let the tragedy ruin me like it did the others. My father, despite holding down a custodian job at the grammar school, was a disturbed individual and suffered greatly from mental illness. It was delusional of him to believe something lived buried beneath his skin, festering and growing inside him like cancer. He believed the creatures inside of him came from all sorts of different places unseen by the naked eye … the wood pile in the basement, the dust bunnies in the corners, the dirt we carried in on our shoes from outside. I remember him pulling me near and saying, "It's the pine trees, Jerry. They turned the soil too acidic, forcing these … these things to rise to the surface. I got them in me now. You and your brother have to move away before it's too late."

Ludicrous, spoken by a madman, I thought, until the day the so-called dreaded family curse befell upon me.

I distinctly remember lying on the couch, watching the greatest rivalry in sports, the Red Sox versus the dreaded New York Yankees, when my fingers discovered a lump on the bottom of my right leg. The spot wasn't large by any means, the size of a dime at best, yet foreign just the same. Without realizing it, I began rubbing the area, probing it with my finger, and found the mass to be spongy, possibly filled with fluid, but something else led me astray.

I tried telling myself it was probably just a bug bite, a lone mosquito that had somehow gotten inside the house, except my mind wouldn't accept that possibility, considering what my father had gone through. I made up the excuse it was late, that I was just over tired, and simply over embellishing things, only it didn't work and I slowly found myself slipping into that off-kilter world my father rightly called home.

By the seventh inning I made a terrible mess of my leg. What little nails I had dug lines into my skin and caused the area to break out in reddish-purple splotches. It appeared like I had a severe case of poison oak. But despite how badly the area looked, I couldn't keep my hands away. My skin felt as though it were on fire, along with the prickling sensation that tiny teeth were gnawing away at me. Plus, the blip on my leg seemed to be getting bigger. I tried convincing myself it was only because I wouldn't leave the area alone, but again, I had a hard time believing that.

So … what are you going to do about it? I heard the voice of my dead father ask me as though he were standing right beside me. *I see you didn't take my advice and move far, far away, since you're here. I got ourselves an idea, how about you go into the kitchen, grab a knife, and let's open this pig-fucker up and see what's really under there. I think you'll be genuinely surprised with what you find.*

The thought of doing so sickened me, although I couldn't say I ruled it out entirely. I teetered between sanity and insanity, recalling my father's screaming when he would do his cutting and how that howling used to riddle me with terror in the dark, wondering if it me if he'd be coming for next. Most kids feared the boogeyman, while I feared my father's frame of mind. Every so often, like now, I can sometimes still hear him as if he were in the other room, picking up where he last left off.

What do you say, son … let's do some cutting, for old time's sake?

I closed the book on my father's proposal. I wouldn't partake in the activity that eventually led to his demise. Not tonight. I needed only sleep and believed by tomorrow things would be better. Yet the air conditioner in my bedroom seemed to be on fire, making me even more miserable. Maine may not be Florida but there were some days you wouldn't know the difference. I tossed and turned unable to get comfortable as the itching sensation on my leg increased. I had no choice except to scratch it, while the realm of sleep eluded me.

However, I must have dozed off, for I woke the next morning to the sound of fists hammering upon my front door. When I finally swung out of bed and strode across my apartment, I was startled to find my ex-wife, Sharon, and our son, Trevor, standing on my doorstep. In the midst of all that transpired I had forgotten what day it was. Sharon kept Trevor five days of the week, while I had him over the weekend, but I could tell, after she took a good look at me, that Sharon wasn't sure if leaving him here was such a good idea.

"What the hell happened to you?" she asked, as Trevor, seemingly unaffected, trudged past me into the living room, peeled off his knapsack, and then plopped himself onto the couch, where he reached for the television remote. "Are you okay?"

"Yes, I'm fine," I answered and explained how I just couldn't get any sleep last night. I blamed it on the air conditioner going to hell, which technically wasn't a lie.

"My God, what on earth happened to your leg?" she asked, pointing. I really didn't have the energy to explain or listen to her lecture me. That's one of the reasons why the divorce happened in the first place.

Curious, I glanced down and stared at the horrific sight that had once been my leg, but now resembled something a Saint Bernard had mistaken for a bone. The bump, which started this whole nightmare, had ballooned to about five times the original size and could feel it throbbing in unison with my heartbeat. I became sickened by what I had done, but underneath my guilt, I still possessed an urge to scratch the itch that ran through me like an electrical charge.

"Just a bug bite," I stated. "Nothing serious."

"Nothing serious, Jerry? Have you looked at it? Jesus, it looks awful."

I saw that flash of worry in her eyes, the kind that showed concern for Trevor's safety and she had every right to be, my frame of mind was anything, but stable. I watched her scan my living quarters, as if stalling, so she could fully gauge the situation.

"I'm fine. Really, I am," I reaffirmed, yet deep down I hoped she wouldn't buy it and would take Trevor away, leaving me to contend with my problem alone.

Strangely, that did not happen. She eventually went into the living room, gave Trevor a kiss, and then left. Before she was even out the door, my hand automatically went to my leg, scratching like a flea-infested dog.

By the time evening rolled around my entire body felt as though someone had poured sulfuric acid all over me. The irritation had spread from my leg to all points of my body. Nothing was spared. My skin became a fireball of pain, while my hands tried desperately to put out the blaze. The harder I dug, the better I felt and there were areas where I had broken through the skin. The blood seeping from my wounds was like poison that needed to be flushed out and I welcomed the release.

I felt my sanity breaking, hearing my dead father's voice begging me to just go get a knife and begin cutting. He assured me the pain would go away once I did and I almost listened. If it wasn't for Trevor sitting in the next room, I honestly believed I would've done anything my father had asked. I needed to find something, before I cracked completely.

I scoured the bathroom searching for the right antidote and then came across a container of peroxide. Uncapping the bottle, I poured a heavy stream onto my leg dangling over the tub and immediately an orchestra of bubbling and popping erupted. A frothy river of cleansing oozed over my foot and around the drain, where even there the medicine continued to fizzle, illustrating just how dire my condition became. My pain slowly subsided, sitting in ecstasy as the liquid worked its magic beneath my skin.

The morning began to feel normal again, that is until I ran out of peroxide. Now the areas where I applied the medicine itched ten times as worse. My fingers immediately went back to work, scratching, digging, reopening sores, and bleeding. I knew I wouldn't last the next hour if I didn't find something else in a hurry and then I remembered purchasing calamine lotion last year when Trevor got poison ivy on the last day at Camp Ketcha. Sure enough, the plastic bottle rested in the back of the cabinet beneath the kitchen sink.

I began applying liberal amounts of the pink lotion all over me, until it felt like I was wearing pancake batter. Although unlike the peroxide, the ointment provided no dramatic fizzling show, the burning desire to scratch had sufficiently lightened and that was the important part.

I left the kitchen believing this probably could work. When Trevor saw me he howled with laughter, chanting how I looked like the Energizer bunny. I knew he meant well, except at the time, I didn't find the humor and told him in a harsh tone, "Just watch your friggin' cartoons, smartass."

I felt horrible afterwards, figuring life must be hard enough on him, shuffling back and forth between parents. My heart went out to him and I allowed Trevor to stay up an extra half hour past his bedtime. It was my way of saying, I'm sorry, and Trevor seemed to accept the apology.

After Trevor went to bed, I took over the TV and quickly turned off the cartoony crap. I needed something to distract me from scratching, now that I was out of Calamine lotion and the irritation had started creeping back. It was too late to run to the store and I swore at myself for not planning ahead. Before the hour was up, I went right back at it, worse than ever. I felt extremely uncomfortable within my own skin and wished somehow I could just remove the hurting layers and my father, who had been listening, couldn't have agreed more.

Just when things couldn't seem to get any worse, a yawning wedge of pain broke out beneath my right cheek, causing me to open my mouth widely to help distribute the throbbing torment swarming down from my temple, but before I could bring my hand up to inspect the area, I had lost the vision in my right eye. Terror besieged me like never before as I blinked repeatedly with still no affect and I don't think I've ever been so frightened in all my life. There was no forewarning, just instant blindness, and my fingers soon confirmed what I had feared all along ... some, *thing*, had crept out from beneath my skin and covered my cornea like a leech.

I ran to the bathroom and stared into the mirror. What I saw was something I would never forget, yet at the same time never want to remember. The *thing* that wrapped over my eye was molten gray in color and glistened with a clear frothy fluid that pooled around the bottom of my eye. Whatever this was, it began squeezing my eye socket like a Boa constrictor, causing an immense deal of pressure. Having a hard time comprehending what my good eye showed me, my father quickly jumped in and told me how I needed to remove this *thing*.

Drawing my face closer to the mirror, I prepared myself for the next step. Positioning my hand inches in front of my eye, my fingers mimicked a pair of needle-nosed pliers, ready to pinch and pull on command. I was sweating and shaking all over. I took a moment to collect myself, and, after several deep breaths, I acted, only to discover the revulsion was more than I imagined. My hand reeled back the moment my fingers touched its slimy hollowed body and my inability to execute had cost me my chance at capture.

You gotta be quicker than that, son. A lot quicker.

The dark mass slipped beneath my eye with the quickness of a water snake, tunneling its way across my forehead, around the back of my skull, where it stopped just beneath the hair line on my neck. I took my hand and lightly touched the bump that had settled there as if to confirm it was there.

You need to get this thing out of you, son. You need to get something to stab it, that's the only way. Stab it and then pull it out, before this thing goes deeper inside you, so deep you may never be able to find it again!

This time, I listened to the only voice that had any experience with this sort of madness. I ran to the kitchen, opened the top drawer beside the stove, and stared at the glimmering collection of possibilities. I grabbed a small pear knife, but my father suggested taking something bigger. Taking them both, I ran back to the bathroom and closed the door shut behind me, not believing what I was about to do. My thoughts were taking me places I didn't think were possible twenty-four hours ago. I turned desperate and believed if this attempt failed, then all would be doomed. There was no time to hesitate.

I dumped the larger knife into the sink, determined the small blade would do the trick. *Remember, son, don't think about it too much. Strike quickly and the pain would be over.* I couldn't agree more. I held the pear knife into position, while my other hand once again combed the back of my skull, fingers moving slowly, yet purposefully, like a cat stalking a bird. When I came to the unnatural growth on my neck, my fingers firmly took hold, squeezing as hard as a teenager would popping a zit, while the foreign mass within my grip tried to slither away, but this time I was quicker.

If I prepared myself for what came next, I suppose, by closing my eyes and biting down. I didn't, however, plunge the knife down as hard as my father instructed. Instead, I kind of dragged the tiny blade across the lump like skinning a potato and that mistake turned out to be costly.

The explosion of burning heat caused my left hand to loosen, just enough for this echinoid-like creature to escape. As I put the pain on hold, I tried to catch this strange parasite, but again it disappeared. I glanced down at my hands, mesmerized at the amount of blood covering them. The mangled piece of flesh I severed was still wedged between the knife and my thumb like some odd prize. I tossed the small blade into the sink in exchange for the bigger one. Apparently, my father had the right idea.

You've got to slam that knife home, son. You just can't dilly dally around. When you get the chance, you need to take it, no second guessing.

The coppery scent of blood filled my nostrils like a drug as I stared at my naked upper half within the mirror, waiting, watching, and hoping for another opportunity at redemption. My deep and steady breathing reverberated loudly within the confines of the bathroom. A line of blood ran down my back, feeling cooler than the heat coming off from me.

At that moment, I saw the creature moving along my neck and this time I acted promptly. My screams filled the bathroom, as I sent the knife not once, but twice, into the meaty side of my neck, the blade releasing streams of blood. The mirror displayed two inches of gore on the blade, yet no creature. Once again, the *thing* had gotten away and was angry at myself for going soft at the last second. That hesitation could've meant the difference.

A sudden rap on the bathroom door startled me and I released an unexpected scream in fear.

"Dad, are you all right?" the nervous voice on the other side of the door asked.

I had forgotten all about my son trying to sleep in the other room and I silently commended him on his courage. I never had the gall to check on my dad when his screams echoed throughout the house. I turned to the door, but didn't open it, and told Trevor, as calmly as I could, that I was fine, just really sick. I suggested he go back to bed and I promised to be quieter. I waited and then silently rejoiced when I heard his footsteps retreating.

Returning to the mirror, I pressed the fact that I needed to be quicker, more patient, and now quieter. Although when I stuck myself again at what turned out to be false movement, I felt I hadn't learned anything. More blood pissed from the area near my collar bone, making it an absolute nightmare to see anything clearly. I ran a face cloth under some cold water and did my best to clean my chest, but it was nearly impossible. The blood was really trickling down at an alarming rate.

Regardless, I was not giving up now and would stay here all night if needed. It turned into a waiting game for I fully believed this *thing* would eventually rise to the surface and show its ugly self. I kept the knife poised and ready, while I continued mopping up fresh blood, hoping for a sign. And then I noticed a small blip near my left nipple and I trembled with excitement. My eyes grew to the size of saucers, watching my skin expand and bulge, but unlike my other failed attempts, this time I showed restraint and didn't strike right away. I waited and my father delivered praise.

That's it, son, let it completely come to the surface, wait for it to stop, and then attack.

I shifted the knife so it was in the best possible position, the tip inches from the rising mass. I became filled with a bloodlust that wouldn't go away. Not until I removed the *thing* inside of me. I watched the orb settle just underneath my left breast and began counting down from ten. I felt like a hunter staring down at a trophy buck through the scope of a rifle, just waiting for the animal to take that extra step so the shot could be perfect.

Four ...

Three ...

Two ...

One!

I zealously plunged the blade into my chest, no doubt deeper than I should have, but was hell bent in putting an end to this creature's existence and lapsed momentarily for my own safety. Inside my head, I swore I heard this entity shrill out in pain, a high-pitched whistling sound that got me even more excited. I jammed the knife further and, for a moment, my eyes flickered like house lights during a massive storm. But a storm was indeed brewing inside of me, dark and angry, while warm blood ran down my leg like an opened faucet. I changed up my technique and began using the tip of the blade to scrape and dig, sensing that I was almost there. I no longer needed the mirror, knowing precisely what needed to be done, and, through the bloody mess, I caught a glimpse of its dark gray body coming through the fresh wound. At that moment, I used the knife more like a spoon and began scooping.

That's it, boy! That's it! Dig ... dig ... dig ... you're almost, there!

I dropped the knife, in exchange for my fingers, and placing them inside the wound, I fished around, until I finally grabbed ahold of it. The *thing* was slippery like holding onto an eel and it wiggled and squirmed, desperately trying to flee, but I wouldn't let go. As I tugged, the thing stretched out like a rubber band, and, as with an elastic, it had its breaking point. I heard something snap. My hand flung back unexpectedly, although within my grip I still held the mysterious creature.

I anxiously opened my hand and curiously stared at the now oily-black blob, smelling of rotten meat, and pulsed as though I was holding a still-beating heart. The *thing* turned out to be a lot bigger than I had imagined, nearly six inches in length and looked more like a squid, with one end thicker and thinning towards the bottom where it branched off into three curly tentacles. Through the slimy mixture, a crown-like mouth opened, displaying several tiny rows of pin-like teeth and laid upon my hand, gasping, as though it couldn't breathe.

Everything inside of me told me to get rid of this damnation as quickly as possible and I did, tossing it into the toilet bowl where it sank like a stone. I hit the flush lever and watched as the rolling water jostled the creature around like fish bait, before being swallowed whole and disappeared. I believed the nightmare to be over.

I took one step towards the sink and then everything spun around on me. I was out cold, before I hit the floor.

* * *

I woke the next morning, groggy and sore, in a hospital room at Maine General, hooked to an IV, hearing a stream of steady beeps. I automatically reached out to touch my chest and found it bandaged. A voice called out to me.

"Leave it be, Jerry," my ex-wife informed.

I glanced to my right and was surprised to find both her and Trevor sitting across the room. They looked happy to see that I was awake, yet frightened at the same time.

"You're lucky to be alive. Luckily for you, Trevor had the smarts to call me. Doctor said you severed a main artery and would have bled out in no time." She paused, folded her hands and then unfolded them. "Jesus, Jerry what on earth were you thinking? Trevor could've ..." She stopped and turned to our son with the making of tears in her eyes. I guess she decided now was not the time to push the issue. She got up, ruffled Trevor's hair, and then stated, "You owe your son a big round of thanks."

My smile lengthened as I held out my good arm and welcomed him over. Trevor did not need any coaxing. He skittered across the room, buried his head into my chest, and began to cry. I tried to hush him by promising everything was going to be fine. I ran my hand over his back and gave him a strong hug. He looked up at me with those doll-like eyes of his, glistening with tears and I felt nothing but eternal love for the boy.

As he pulled away from me, I alarmingly noticed a horrible reddened rash covering Trevor's left hand.

"What's wrong?" Sharon asked, seeing the concern in my eyes.

"What happened to Trevor's hand?"

Almost on cue, Trevor began scratching at it and I felt the boy's pain.

"I don't know really. Poison Ivy? Hives? But seeing what you've just been through I'm going to have a doctor take a look at him since we're already here."

"Sounds like a good idea," I blurted out, as tears of my own welled, knowing the horror that awaited him.

THE WAIT

Holly Newstein

"BOOM! Phssh!" I cried, as the dirt bomb burst into a million pieces, burying the Nazis in a cloud of dust. The Panzer tank overturned too, its plastic wheels spinning helplessly.

"Yeah," I said under my breath. It was summer, my brother was gone to camp, and I was re-enacting the Battle of the Bulge with toy soldiers, dirt bombs, and pebbles in my backyard.

"Hey, Joey! Wanna go into town with me?" My father's voice boomed across the backyard.

"Sure, Dad!" I scrambled to my feet and brushed the dust and dry grass off my shorts. The afternoon sun was hot, and my scalp felt like sparks were arcing from the roots of my hair. A ride in Dad's almost-new Catalina convertible would feel like heaven.

My mother came out through the kitchen door. Her hair was rolled tightly in pink plastic curlers, and her makeup didn't quite cover the purple bruise under her left eye.

"Make sure your Daddy doesn't forget the ice. We need it for to-night," she said. She looked at me again and sighed. "How on earth did you get so filthy?"

"Sorry, Mom," I said. My dad pulled a handkerchief from his pock-et and rubbed it over my sweaty, grime-streaked face.

"Now you're ready. Let's go," he said.

I slid into the passenger seat, wincing as my bare legs made con-tact with the hot vinyl upholstery. Dad started the engine and opened the clips that held the convertible top in place and pushed a button on the dashboard. I watched, fascinated, as it lifted from the windshield up into the air and folded back on itself behind the passenger seat. Dad lit a cigarette and backed the car out of the driveway, half-turned in the seat, the cigarette dangling from his lips.

My dad was a big man, and his muscles stretched against the fabric of his t-shirt. He had a job at the Warren Paper Mill, and his body was accustomed to hard physical work. He was handsome, but he could be ugly. Especially after he'd had a few shots of Seagram's. I had learned early on, through many tense family dinners, to shut my mouth when he began pounding the table. And, after a few too many whippings, that the best place to be in the evenings was at my friends' houses. Or under my bed, reading books with a flashlight.

Since I wasn't big and strong enough to fight him, I settled for be-ing hard to find.

But he was my dad, he hadn't been drinking yet today, and a ride into town was a lot more fun than the Nazis.

Dad fiddled with the radio until he found the ballgame, and the play-by-play crackled from the tinny speakers. We had tuned in just in time to hear the Yankees score another run on the Sox.

"God damn it," my father growled as we turned onto Main Street. The air felt cool as it rushed past my face, and I rolled down my win-dow and breathed deeply of the river smells as we went over the bridge. Since it was a Saturday, the pulper wasn't running, so there were none of the usual rotten-egg smells masking the brown-water smell of the Pre-sumpscot as it flowed toward Portland and the sea.

We pulled into the parking lot of Shaw's Groceries. I tagged after Dad as he marched up and down the aisles, picking up the few items my mother needed for the party that evening. My parents often had cocktail parties in the summer, and I would fall asleep listening to the chatter in the living room, the clink of glasses, and the sound of Mantovani playing on our big console stereo. My mother would fix plates of cheese and crackers, onion dip made with sour cream and Lipton's soup, and bowls of potato chips. Then she would put on a full-skirted summer dress with gold leather sandals, red lipstick and big silver earrings. She looked beautiful to my ten-year-old eyes, and she was.

Dad pulled a bag of ice from the cooler at the front of the store and put it on the cashier's belt along with the other items. I wordlessly put a Hershey bar on the belt too, from the display rack at the end of the checkout counter. I half-expected my dad to say NO, but he let it go, and grabbed it before the bag clerk could pack it in the bag and handed it to me.

"Thanks, Dad," I said. He grinned and roughed up my hair.

"Don't tell your mother," he said.

We got back into the car, the seats even hotter and stickier from being open to the sun. I imagined I could feel the back of my legs bubbling up with blisters from the heat, but as we began to drive and the wind blew in our faces again, everything cooled off.

We stopped at the light on Main Street. A blue Chevy convertible pulled up on the other side of the street. A woman was driving, wearing a chiffon scarf over her blonde hair and big sunglasses. She grinned and tooted her horn. My dad looked up, and she blew him a kiss. The light turned green, and my dad did a U-turn, tires, screeching, and followed the woman up the street, his bumper almost touching hers.

"What's going on, Dad?"

"Be quiet," he said. His face was intent, his eyes narrowed. I wanted to ask why the strange woman would blow a kiss at him, but the expression on my dad's face was a little scary. So, I did what I was told.

The woman pulled into a parking space on the street by the bakery, and my dad pulled in a few spaces down, under a shade tree.

"Wait here," he said. He got out of the car and went over to the woman's car. He opened the door and pulled her out, then lifted her into his arms. They were laughing. My father carried her as easily as he carried me, and she reached up and put her arms around his neck. He carried her into the building, through a door marked APARTMENTS 1-3, and closed the door behind them.

I sat in my seat for a minute or two, but my dad did not come out. I turned the radio on and found a rock n'roll station.

It's my party and I'll cry if I want to.

You would cry too if it happened to you.

I ate my Hershey bar, softened in the summer heat, and licked the melted chocolate from my fingers. I opened the glove compartment and played with the tire gauge. I thumbed through the owner's manual and found nothing interesting. There was a handful of change, and I looked at the dates and mint marks on each coin, and put them back. I ate a stale Certs from the half-gone roll tucked in the back of the glove compartment.

I watched the melting ice leak through the insulated paper bag and stain the red carpet a deeper red. Blood-red. I watched the minute hand on the dashboard clock go around, and around again.

What's taking so long? What was wrong with that woman that my dad had to carry her out of her car? Why were they laughing? What will Mom say if we don't get back before the ice melts?

I thought about getting out of the car and walking home, but my dad had told me to wait. Disobedience would cost me raised red welts on my backside, and sitting down would be painful for days. I thought about going to get my dad, but I didn't know which apartment they'd gone into, and it would be kind of embarrassing to go the wrong one. Plus, I would probably still get whipped. So I waited.

The sun streamed down through the leaves, making dappled shadows on the car and on my legs. I watched a family walking toward me on the sidewalk. A mom, a dad, and two girls dressed in pink sundresses. The girls pointed at the bakery window, and I could hear them pleading for cookies. A blue jay screamed rudely right over my head, and I jumped.

What if someone I know sees me? What if they ask where my dad is? What do I tell them?

In a sudden panic, I scrambled over the front seat and lay down on the back seat so no one could see me. I could smell the slight mildewy smell of the convertible top and the plastic smell of the car seats. I flattened myself into the seat, and watched the leaves and the clouds overhead.

What if he never comes back? What if I die here?

I imagined my mother and brother finding my skeleton in the back seat, like something out of a Vincent Price movie. A big hairy spider would crawl out of my mouth, and snakes would slither around my ribs. I amused myself thinking of their horrified faces.

The deejay's cheerful, antic voice squawked through the speakers.

"Hey, you sun worshippers on Revere Beach! It's time to turn! And here's a brand-new hit from Jan and Dean!"

Two girls for every boy ...

And still no dad for me.

Suddenly the car door opened.

"You taking a nap?" my dad asked.

I tumbled back into the front seat.

"Nope," I said.

My dad pulled his handkerchief from his pocket and wiped his face. I saw traces of pink lipstick smeared on the white fabric. He smelled of sweat and perfume, and a musky smell I couldn't place.

"I got you a chocolate chip cookie from the bakery," he said, and handed me a small white bag.

"The ice is melted," I replied. I pushed the toe of my sneaker into the squishy wet stain on the floor of the car.

"It's a hot one. I need a shower as soon as we get home."

I pulled the cookie out of the bag and took a bite. It was still warm, and the chips were gooey.

"Hey, don't eat that. It'll spoil you for dinner."

A flash of anger surged through me. *You left me. You left me in the car to die.*

I looked straight into my father's face. I no longer cared if he was going to hit me.

"Should I tell Mom about how you helped that lady while I waited in the car and the ice got melted? Or is this another thing I shouldn't tell her?"

My father looked back at me, and his eyes narrowed. I raised my arm to block the smack I was sure I was going to get, but I kept my eyes fixed on his.

He blew out his breath in a whoosh.

"Right, Joey. Don't tell your mother."

He suddenly looked smaller to me.

Someday soon I'll be bigger than you. I'll take you, and you'll never hit me or Mom again.

The thought was both scary and exhilarating. I took another bite from my cookie, and we drove home in silence.

THE JANITORS COME OUT AT NIGHT

Martin Campbell

Okay, so I will admit I have not always been the best student that I could be. Like many before me, I was unable to self-evaluate my career at Sanford High School until it was far too late. I should have taken more pride in being a Spartan, but instead I chose an opposite path.

Often, I did not do homework, teased the underclassman and participated in more than my share of stupidity. There was no doubt in my mind that I spent more time serving detentions than attending classes.

School pranks happened to be my specialty: spreading glue on the teacher's chairs, clogging the teacher's bathroom and occasionally sticking my chewed-up gum on doorknobs. Admittedly I did that last one more than just occasionally.

What I failed to realize was that my behavior did more than just immediately effect those I targeted. After the smoke cleared, the laughs stopped and the detentions were handed out, someone had to do damage control.

Whose job was that? Whose job was I unintentionally making tougher. Not the teachers, that was intentional, not the other students. The Janitors.

They really have a lot of power within the school. But it's not power given to them, it's a power they seized. Think about who cleans the school, the bathrooms and does all the grunt work that makes the school day run so smooth. The Janitors. They know this and silently use it to their advantage. Janitors patrol the school, abiding to no laws but their own.

Another interesting fact about Janitors is that they often mark students. That's something I wish I had known way back when I was planning my first prank. Freshman year I was looking to get immediately noticed by my peers, being something of an attention whore. I wanted first crack at the title of class clown.

So, I snuck into the principal's office, locked myself in and went all Shawshank Redemption. I was in Maine after all. Turning on the PA system, I introduced myself so there was no mistaking who was the mastermind behind this prank.

"Hello students of Sanford High. This is none other than the coolest freshman, possibly ever, Sam Franklin."

I knew I didn't have much time to follow through with what I had planned. The principal was in a meeting at the other end of the building and the office ladies were in a panic trying to find a Janitor to unlock the door.

This was my third day of school and I was already acquainted with everything I needed to be. I had sat through all my class introductions. Met all my teachers. Made good with the lunch ladies and even scouted out the administration. From all those observations, I put together a little rap that I wanted to share with the staff and student body.

"*Let me tell you about my first couple days of school. If it's a reflection of anything, I won't make it out any less of a fool.*

The teachers all smell and my goodness they are as boring as hell.

Mrs. Wellington from English Lit should not be wearing tanks. I think Principal John wants to give her a spank."

That's all I could get out before Principal John finally made his away across the school. He busted the door open with his shoulder since no one could find an available Janitor.

I froze as the door swung open. Principal John was a big guy, he looked more like a Northern Maine woodsman than someone in charge of a school. With his massive chest and Tony Atlas arms, he put every seam on his black and red Sanford Spartan polo at risk.

When his gigantic shoulder busted the door open, a freak accident happened. Well not as much of a freak accident as an unfortunate one which did not bode well for me. The large window glass displaying Principal Johns name across it slipped out of place and crashed to the floor. Pieces of all sizes shot out into the air and scattered around the office.

Pure anger twisted his face as everything unfolded. The vein in the middle of his forehead was starting to pulsate as he held his breath, flexing in frustration. His jaw just trembled mightily. If there wasn't a gathering of employees and students who had stopped to observe the spectacle, then I'm sure he would have attempted ripping my head off.

That hilarious little prank of mine ended up getting me a ten-day suspension, marking me amongst the administrators. It also catapulted my name into the stratosphere amongst the school population. Every student, teacher and school employee had started talking about my insane feat. Want it or not, the spotlight was mine.

One thing I did not account for while reveling in my newfound fame was how it affected the Janitors and all the time and effort they were going to have to put into cleaning up the unnecessary mess that I made. Sweeping, disposing of the large shards properly and combing the floor for as many tiny slivers as they could. It was a tedious job that none of them appreciated having to do.

That was just the first of many pranks and acts of rebellion I displayed throughout my four years. On the grand scale of things picking up glass off the floor was probably a treat compared to what I eventually would put them through.

Looking back, I realize that moment was the most important because it was the day that the Janitors marked me. I didn't know their names or faces, at the time, but like everyone else in the school after my Shawshank moment, they knew mine.

At the time, I didn't realize that the Janitors had marked me as enemy number one. It wasn't till later in my high school career that I realized that I, Sam Franklin, a man who strived to be loved by everyone, was so hated by a group other than administration.

No, I had the pleasure of fully coming to that conclusion one weekend before graduation. Despite my not so stellar performance as a student, only one weekend, two days, stood in between me and getting the hell out of those miserable hallways.

College, surprisingly was also knocking on my door. It didn't matter that I could barely pass a class, write a paper or even read a book because I had one smooth jump shot. The only reason I wasn't expelled from school had to do with the fact I lead the basketball team to two Maine state championships.

The University of Southern Maine was willing to look past my low GPA and offer me an "Academic Scholarship" to play division three basketball. Really there were several schools but USM, although not high on the competitive side boasted one of the best party scenes in the in Maine. And it didn't hurt that the coach was recruiting me like I was the next Larry Bird or something.

So, there I was, fifth period study hall, my last class as a senior. Quietly I was filling out class enrollment paperwork for my first semester when that troublemaking lightbulb started blinking inside my head. I had skated through this school causing mischief and mayhem and now I was set to ride off into the sunset. I wanted to go out the same way I came in, with a bang.

That was an idea I would soon come to regret, it would change the course of my life. 6/7/1981, 1:45 pm. All those numbers have since been carved into my arm as a constant reminder, an attempt at keeping the biggest mistake in my life fresh to memory.

As I stared at the clock and watched the minute hand tick past the eight onto the nine, signaling it was forty-five minutes past one, the seed for the greatest idea ever sprouted roots in my head. That seed started with the age old traditional senior prank. A tradition that brought the whole class together to come up with an innovative prank to pull on the teachers and administration.

Over the year's seniors have put together and pulled off some pretty noteworthy pranks. One year they hid alarm clocks throughout every corner of the school and every two minutes one would go off. Last year the seniors snuck into the school early and set up a noel scene in the front office; equipped with a Christmas tree and a town drunk paid to dress up like Jesus.

My senior class, instead of doing something cool and memorable, opted to put together one of the lamest pranks in school history.

Class president Suzie Ayers, the uninspired, following the rules of kissing ass was the one spearheading the whole thing, unfortunately. This girl was the definition of dull.

She came up with this AMAZING idea or at least that's what she wanted everyone to believe that it was. We all met on the football field one morning instead of reporting to homeroom. Once the bell rang signaling the start of first period, all the seniors ran straight for our classes, making everyone late. It was completely underwhelming and a bit embarrassing to have attached my name to.

I decided that I was going to leave this school on my own terms, leave my own mark just like I did my freshman year. It would be an independent senior prank on such an innovating level that senior's decades after my departure would strive to reach my greatness.

The plan was to break into the school, alone. This was going to be my shining moment and mine alone to bask in. Once I was inside the school I was going to graffiti art as many of the walls as I could with scenes from the greatest movie of that year, The Goonies. Graffiti art was all the craze now and I was going to capitalize on its popularity.

I had had some practice *tagging* (which is slang for graffiti) around town, and was pretty good at it.

"Dude. They will never let you graduate if they catch you. You will end up being a fifth-year senior," my buddy Billy warned when I told him about my plan.

"They won't catch me. Not to mention it's not something they can't fix without a little paint and elbow grease."

"Yeah, well once they fix the mess you are about to make, I am sure the cops will "fix" any chance you have at a collegiate future with a few misdemeanor charges. The Sanford Police department does not mess around."

I looked at Billy and let out a little laugh. "Look, I'll be fine. Ninjas like myself move within the shadows, unseen like ghosts."

"If the idea of getting caught by the cops doesn't scare you, then getting caught by the Janitors should. They'll tie you up and take turns beating you like a piñata."

Looking back, I should have listened to his advice but I was stubborn, my mind was made up and it wasn't going to change. Searching my room, I found and old duffel bag that I used for my basketball gear during freshman year. I filled it up with everything I would need to create my masterpiece; a few cans of spray paint, some still photos of the movie, plastic, painters tape and a couple pop tarts, just in case hunger came knocking at an awkward time. I was more than prepared to execute my plan.

I really didn't have too many concerns about getting caught. This was way before security cameras were being plastered throughout schools across the country. Not to mention it was also Hempfest weekend two towns over in Lebanon. All walks of life from all corners of Maine flocked to enjoy the food, music and other festivities.

This meant Sanford police would be busy patrolling the streets, fields and town watering holes rather than wasting time cruising by the High School.

There was a tool shed on the backside of the school. I could easily access the roof by climbing up it. I had done it periodically throughout my four years when me and my friends wanted to smoke a joint during school hours or break into the gym to shoot hoops.

We would crawl through a small hatch that was easily unlocked by a paperclip. It dropped us into the back hallway which was only a few steps from both the cafeteria and the gym.

I entered through that access for my little prank because no one would see me, it also meant I wouldn't have to break in a door, which could cause suspicion if by chance someone did stop by to check on the building.

Most people were spending time at the lake, hanging with family or enjoying the festivities put on to honor the spirit of Hempfest. My family wasn't the festive type, mom always drank the weekend away in the kitchen and my old man, well he would do the same, just at one of the many local bars.

At least I knew they wouldn't be suspicious that I wasn't home. Honestly if I went missing for real, it wouldn't surprise me if it took a couple days for them to notice.

I wasted no time getting down to business once I got inside, taping a roll of plastic on the floor, pulling out my arsenal of colors and a stick of gum. I always did my best work when I had a piece to chew on. It eased my nerves. The fruity flavors were always my favorite, melon, cherry.

The first spray felt great. My fingertip pressed down on the stem of the can and out came a steady stream of black paint. I could feel my mind instantaneously go to that place that only artists can go. A place where some of the greatest works have been accomplished and brought to the real world for the human race to enjoy. What a rush. What a feeling.

I had decided to make my first mural of Chunk wearing his iconic

Hawaiian t-shirt and biting into a candy bar. Chunk was my favorite character from the movie. He was probably everyone's favorite treasure hunter from the movie.

As the minutes passed, I was moving along at a great pace, impressing myself with my ability to craft such a phenomenal looking piece of art. I was already playing in my head what everyone's reaction was going to be once they saw my finished product. I fantasized that it would be received so well that they would keep the graffiti up to show future freshman the fruits of my labor.

All those feelings of future glory, triumph and praise came to a crashing halt when something happened that I never saw coming.

"Hello Sam" a voice from the end of the hallway yelled. I looked up and dropped my spray can. It was one of the Janitors, his name was Joe. His voice was clearly agitated as he stood in the distance with a roll of trash bags in one hand and a small waste basket in the other.

"What do you think you are doing?" Another voice coming from the other entrance to the hallway. I swung my head to see whose voice it was. It was Etna, the toughest broad to ever mop a floor.

They had me blocked in with one at each end. Etna was holding a broom stick in her hand. The expression on her face as she looked at me and then at the wall I was tagging made me cringe. It resembled the look your mother would give if she caught you stealing a couple bills out of her purse.

Trying to process how I was going to get out of the situation, I said the first string of words that came to mind.

"Look. I know I'm trespassing but this is in the name of a good spirited senior prank. I mean, what's the harm if you let me finish my work and let me go? No harm, no foul." I chucked nervously.

Neither Joe nor Etna seemed moved by my plea. Etna balled her free hand into a fist. Her knuckles turned white as she squeezed them tight. This woman was an intimidating presence when she wasn't angry, so I was petrified.

She was a short woman, standing maybe five feet tall with shoulder length grey hair and extra thick bifocals. Cigarette burns covered her arms, small black burn circles peppered her right forearm and there was the scattering of tattoos on her left arm, all faded and almost unrecognizable from age. They resembled the tattoos my old man got when he was in prison.

"Ok, I can see that you guys are upset. I don't want any trouble."

I continued pleading, trying to get a response from one of them.

I could feel the tension in the air. I thought Etna was going to say something as her lips started to form the shape of a word but instead she gritted her teeth. The intensity on her face would have frozen a charging linebacker in his tracks. She snapped the broomstick over her knee and snarled. Then for real dramatic effect she snapped one of the half pieces in half, really letting out some frustration.

"What the fuck. I can see you guys being a little upset with this but it's just a little spray paint. Nothing that can't be easily fixed."

That was possibly the worst response I could have given. I never really was any good at defusing situations, only making them worse.

"Look here you little teenage prick, for the last four years, ever since you stepped foot in this school, all we've done is clean up after you. Gum on the doorknobs, things you threw on the roof and the glue, the fucking glue! I can't even count how many hours I've had to spend on my hands and knees, arm deep in the teacher's room toilet fishing out whatever random object you decided to flush down it! No more! This mural, this "harmless" senior prank, who the fuck do you think will be stuck cleaning it up? You? The teachers? Administration? NONE of them, it will be us, the Janitors. ENOUGH is enough. It's time to teach you a lesson," Etna spat out in unbridled fury.

I was shitting myself. At each of the exits a janitor blocked my escape routes. I wasn't sure how serious Etna's words were and how far her and her associate would be willing to take this. Judging only by their voices and demeanor, I felt like I was fucked, about to get a serious beat down.

Afraid as I was, the sensible young man in me knew that they couldn't really do anything. I mean, if those two toilet scrubbers did anything crazy such as beat me to a pulp, perhaps shove a piece of the broken broomstick handle where it doesn't belong, they'd be in some serious trouble. Would they be willing to risk legal ramifications just to get revenge on an eighteen-year-old who caused them some headaches over the years?

If they just detained me and called the cops, that would be enough revenge. A run-in with the law for breaking into and vandalizing the school, would surely prevent me from getting my diploma, most likely ruining my full ride to college as well. Surely that would be punishment enough. Right?

"Ok, would it help if I said I was sorry? I never really knew that I was making your jobs that much harder. I really am sorry," I pleaded.

"Apology not accepted," Joe said.

"Ok, I think you either need to call the cops or let me go. This whole intimidation thing is going a little too far."

But Joe wasn't so much intimidating as he was … creepy. In his fifties, he stood well over six feet tall, looked like he may weigh a hundred pounds with grey scraggly hair spilling off his head. Joe liked to stare at the teenage girls in the hallways, making them very uncomfortable. Cindy Fairland, who was one of the more attractive girls in the school, caught him going through her gym bag once. She reported it to administration but nothing ever came of it.

Things got a lot weirder as I was having a Mexican standoff with the Janitors — a lot weirder. Etna and Joe began slowly, methodically, stepping toward me, closing in.

As they advanced toward me, my heart raced. I never expected what would happen next. Their bodies began contorting in unnatural ways. It reminded me of the little girl from The Exorcist when her body was being possessed by that demon. The scene where she crawled down the staircase backwards.

Etnas eyes started glowing red and her mouth drooped open wide, so wide I expected it to start ripping from the sides. Her canine teeth grew longer, deadlier. I closed my eyes, shaking my head to clear the nightmarish vision. What the hell was in those pop tarts?

Glancing at Joe, the same thing was happening to him, except his skin was turning blue, like a cold corpse. They were transforming into inhuman monstrosities.

Then as Etna let out a huge long, high pitched scream, I saw wings shooting straight out of her back; big, black bat wings.

"Are you guys fucking vampires?" I yelled. I had seen enough movies and had a creative enough imagination to categorize what I was seeing. Neither of the Janitors, who moaned hideously as black leathery wings unfurled from their backs dignified my accusation with an answer. I had to escape.

As they moved closer their slow contorted walk snapped into a full athletic sprint. It happened so fast that before I knew it Etna was airborne coming right at me.

In an act of desperation and instinct I grabbed a can of spray paint with each hand. When Etna was close enough, I unloaded both cans into her eyes, halting her attempt at an assault. She fell to the ground, rubbing at her eyes with black talons and howling in agony. More confident now, I spun on Joe and did the same thing, sending him into a frenzy as well. Both of them momentarily incapacitated, I seized my chance and ran for my life.

My heart pounded as I barreled down the hall. I still remember thinking it might jump out of my chest at any moment. Never had I been more terrified in my life. I moved as fast as my legs would allow, slipping and sliding over the recently waxed floor, slamming against and rattling the trophy case that held those Maine state champs awards.

In the near distance, I could see the roof hatch that I used to get inside the school. If I could reach it, then I could run across the street to where my truck was parked. I was hoping to God that they wouldn't follow me outside.

I peeked over my left shoulder to see if I was in the clear. Neither one of them was in sight, a relief. That relief was short lived when I slammed into a brick wall. Well not exactly a wall, it was Joes chest. When my body crashed into his brick wall-like chest, I flew backwards, right into the arms of a waiting Etna.

She pinned me to the ground and all I could do was start balling my eyes out. "Please do not kill me, Please, PLEASE."

But when I looked into her empty soulless eyes, I could see there was no pleading with her. She opened her mouth wide once again revealing the two huge fangs that stuck out of her mouth. She lunged downward, driving both incisors deep into my neck, so deep. I could feel each fang sucking a stream of blood out of my neck, taking and taking until I passed out.

That's how I became a Janitor, a lifer here at good old Sanford High School. What I wouldn't give to go back to my freshman year and change the piss poor attitude I had. I would have never broken into the principal's office and recited that poem, never stuck gum on the doorknobs, clogged the toilet in the teacher's room or any of that other senseless shit I pulled.

You know if I had even just kept my nose clean for twenty-four hours straight and not aspired to pull off one more memorable prank before I graduated, I would've never fallen victim to this horrible fate, this curse of a "life."

It wasn't just Joe and Etna who were vampires at the school. I found out every Janitor at Sanford High was except for Tommy Borgin. He was a stoner who graduated a few years ago. He sported a poorly groomed beard, scraggly blonde hair and one of the thickest Maine accents I had ever been around, which was a little uncommon in Southern Maine, being in close proximity to Boston and all.

Etna hired him on after he graduated. He handled most of the duties that required being outside during the day such as taking out the trash and sweeping the parking lot.

Although I will say vampires are vulnerable to the sun, it is false that they can't step outside during the daytime. Just not for long periods of time. Sunscreen is surprisingly one of a vampire's best friends. Luckily there was a Reny's only a few miles from the school, so Etna set up some deal where they delivered a couple boxes a month, year-round.

And Etna, well there was a good reason to fear her after all. The old bag wasn't just any vampire; she was the mother of vampires as it turns out. She's the queen bee and all the other vampires (who were all halfblooded like me) were her worker bees.

We aren't allowed to wander far from the queen. Etna requires all of us to work at the school as Janitors and has a small list of general rules we must follow. *The code of the vampire* she calls them.

Etna had created a secret underground passage located in the boiler room of the school. It leads far underneath the damp basement to a cave that we call home, where we all live. It's not the most comfortable of accommodations. Instead of a cozy bedroom at my parents' house or a dorm that I could call my own, I have a damp corner and a cot. Instead of hitting jump shots on the court like I was supposed to at Plymouth, I now prepare the high school gym floor before big games.

For some reason, unknown to me or any of the other halfblooded vampires, Etna does not want to leave the school, the cave, or even the grounds except to feed once a month. What a miserable fucking life, or "unlife" I have found myself living.

No one dares ask her about leaving, moving on to something more dignified for a vampire. Maybe someday I will have the nerve to ask her, find out what is keeping her here at this school. The mother of vampires should be bound to no place, but here she is.

I guess I should be thankful in a way, that night when she was draining my blood, she could have killed me. Apparently while tasting my blood, she saw a premonition, something I was destined for in the future. Something that made her think twice about killing me. I was the first to be converted in almost fifty years.

Thinking back now, reflecting on how I got to the position that I am in, sweeping floors and unclogging toilets for the miserable high school I graduated from (yes, I did make graduation that Monday if I forgot to mention).

I wonder if I deserved this fate? Did making the Janitor's job more difficult justify turning me into the walking dead, a soulless, hell-bound creature.

Part of me says I deserved what I got, but another part says that not in any way, shape or form should anyone have to go through life as a blood sucker. Unfortunately, I have an eternity to ponder it.

AGONY CHAMBER

Morgan Sylvia

We never knew what that place was, until it was too late.

The day started out innocently enough. It was a clear autumn morning in Maine, and the five of us were setting out on a hunting trip, one of dozens, perhaps hundreds, of such outings we had made together over the years since high school. It was an annual tradition, one that had lasted through college, various jobs and relationships, marriages, moves, funerals, the births of several children, and more cars than I could even begin to count.

There weren't many things I could rely on in my life: my knee giving out regularly, my wife complaining, my kids giving me grey hairs, my dog doing dumb shit, lobsters at the coast in summer, Thanksgiving turkey with the in-laws, and autumn hunting with the guys. That was about it. I suppose it was enough, because I always looked forward to October.

It was a perfect day. Fall had painted the woods yellow, red, and

126

amber; the leaves were at their peak, and the forest around us bore the colors of fire and blood. It was just chilly enough for jackets, but winter's bite was still a few weeks off.

Jason and Danny were walking slightly ahead of Tim, Toby, and I. We were planning to split up, to reduce the noise and increase our chances of getting deer. Toby had also finally won the lottery for a moose hunting permit, and was scouting possible locations to return to when the season opened. He'd spent the majority of the morning talking about moose burger recipes and hunting tactics, which only served to remind me that I had, as always, lost the lottery.

I remember talking about my tomato crop, and my disappointment in the meager offerings my garden had presented that summer. Years ago, the conversations would have been about girls, cars, and video games. I guess we'd all grown up.

I was watching the ground to avoid tripping over roots or rocks, but I glanced up just in time to see Danny vanish. One minute he was walking along over a rust-colored carpet of leaves, and then there was a sharp *crack!* and he was just ... gone. The earth had swallowed him whole.

There was a black hole in the ground ahead of us.

We all stopped in our tracks. "What the fuck ..." Jason muttered.

Toby breathed a curse. "Holy shit."

We were never a particularly eloquent bunch.

Jason headed toward the spot where Danny had gone into the ground. Tim stopped him by grabbing his backpack. "Hold up! You want the same thing to happen to you?"

A low moan rose from the night-black depths of the hole. The sun was high and golden in a pale blue sky, the woods bright with daylight. But that pit was black as coal. It was as though it caught the sunlight and sucked it into some whirling black abyss.

Jason shouted at the top of his lungs. "Danny!"

We heard a groan.

Toby grabbed a long, sturdy-looking stick. "Stay behind me," he said. He pushed the stick into the ground before him to determine if it was solid before moving forward. He approached the hole in that manner, the rest of us following single-file.

My skin prickled into goosebumps as we approached the breach. Part of my fear was physical. I half expected the ground to open beneath me and swallow me up too. The ground being solid ... well, that was one thing I had never questioned. Suddenly I felt as though the very earth was just a thin blanket over a bottomless, pitch-black abyss. But there was more to it than that — there was a strangeness to that place that set my nerves on edge. A sense that something was wrong.

Toby reached the hole, and tested the area around it. "Solid rock," he said. "Looks like ... I dunno. An old well or something." He knelt at the edge and peered down into the hole. One by one, we joined him, staring down into the blackness.

Danny hadn't fallen far ... I'd guess no more than a single story. He was lying on solid rock, in a perfect circle of golden sunlight that was a stark contrast to the shadows around him. Around him I could see the remains of what had been a wooden cover to the hole. He'd stepped on a rotted board and gone straight through.

"Danny?" Toby yelled down into the shadows. "Danny, you okay?"

Danny moved and groaned again, then let out a string of curses. "I hurt my ankle."

"Anything else hurt?"

"Just my leg, I think."

"How many fingers am I holding up?" Toby called down.

Danny wasn't amused. "Fuck you!"

"He's not hurt bad, other than the ankle," Jason said. "At least, I don't see any blood."

I grew painfully aware of a sense of *wrongness* about the place. The air felt heavy, oppressive, as though it were alive. I looked around, scanning the woods, noting that the trees in the immediate vicinity grew gnarled and twisted, and the vast majority of them were dead. Two of the trees nearby were particularly strange. One had branches growing along the sides of its trunk, evenly spaced, in a manner that made it look like an insect. The other had snapped, but the massive trunk that remained bore a faint resemblance to a stoic face.

My skin prickled into gooseflesh. I shuddered.

Down in the pit, Danny looked around. "Wow, guys. This place is crazy."

"What is it?" I asked.

Danny shook his head. "I don't know. Some kind of chamber."

"Do you see any stairs or exits?" Jason yelled.

"I can't see shit," Danny snapped. "Throw me a flashlight." He hesitated, and started patting his pockets. A moment later, he pulled out his phone. "Wait, never mind. I have a flashlight app."

"Guys." Jason pointed at the curved wall of the shaft. "Look."

Every inch of the curved shaft had carvings on it. To call the marking runes would be an understatement. The text included pictures, shapes, and strange dots. The script lined the shaft in perfect rings. It wasn't in English, or French.

A panicked shout came from below. "This place is wicked fucking creepy. Get me out of here." Danny groaned again. "Get me out now!"

Jason pulled out his phone. "I'm calling rescue." He tried dialing, and then frowned. "No signal. We're in a dead zone."

None of us had any better luck.

"Let's see if we can get him out." Tim stood up. "I've got all my camping gear and snowshoes in the SUV. I think we can rig a gurney-type thing."

After a short debate, Tim and Toby went back to the SUV. This left Jason and I staring down into the hole.

"Get me out of here," Danny called. I could hear the fear in his voice. "I think I heard something."

"Probably just a bear," Jason joked. The tension in his voice made the humor fall flat.

The place had a heavy air to it. The longer we stayed, the more palpable it became. Tension was rising, both above and below the surface. I felt as though I were being watched by a hundred eyes. My hair stood on end, and my skin crawled. Jason was sweating bullets, and I could tell by his face that he felt uneasy too. I was suddenly more than ready to be out of the woods, enjoying a microbrew and lobster roll at some local bar.

Danny was really getting agitated by this point. "Get me the fuck out of here." He tried to move, and jarred his leg. Apparently, that didn't feel too good, because he let out a shriek. "Screw this. I want to get out of here! I want to go home!"

And then he was gone. He didn't walk or crawl away. He just vanished.

Jason and I exchanged looks, and I saw the fear in his eyes. He looked away from me, staring down into the hole. "Danny?"

No answer. There wasn't a sound in the forest. A thick, impenetrable stillness clung to the little glade.

Jason and I screamed down into the hole, calling for Danny. Over and over again, we called his name. Nothing. The earth swallowed our voices. There was only silence below.

The sounds of rustling leaves and branches cracking underfoot announced Tim and Toby's approach as they returned, carrying ropes and snowshoes. Tim reached us first. "What happened?"

"Damned if I know." Jason shook his head. "Danny's gone. He just vanished."

Toby frowned. "What do you mean, 'vanished'?"

Tim leaned over to look back down into the hole. "He's gone. I can see the spot where he hit the ground."

"Yeah, and it's pitch black right next to it," Toby said. "Somebody's got to go down there. Maybe he fell further in and lost consciousness."

They all looked at me. I was the skinniest, and the only one with rock climbing experience. I won't bother with a word-for-word recap of the conversation, save to say that it ended with Tim tying one end of the rope around me and the other around a tree. They all grabbed the rope to support me as I climbed over the edge and descended into the darkness.

The air hung thick with malevolence. I felt a heavy, pressing sense of rage and pain, so palpable that I could almost taste it. When I finally reached the bottom and my feet touched earth, I kept a tight grip on the rope, my only connection to the world above.

As my eyes adjusted to the gloom, I made out pale shapes in the blackness within. At first I thought they were people, and my heart hammered in my chest. Then I realized the figures were statues. Thirteen statues stood along the chamber's curving walls, placed in evenly-spaced intervals. I'm no art expert, but I could tell that they were the work of a master carver ... and a madman. The sight of them made my skin crawl. The beings depicted in stone before me were not human. They had never been human. They owned a terrible beauty that belonged to dream and nightmare, but had no place in the world above.

Tim yelled down at me. "You see Danny?"

My throat was dry. I swallowed. "No." The word came out in a croak, which echoed eerily off the stone walls of the chamber. I shone my flashlight around the chamber. "He's not here."

"What *do* you see?" Toby yelled down to me. "Any tunnels?"

My spine tingled, as though some unearthly being was standing behind me. "No. There's no passageways or anything. Just one round room. Guys, this place is really fucking weird."

At the far side, I saw something that resembled a table. I took a few steps closer and then stopped, unable to process what I was seeing. An altar, intricately carved with strange glyphs that I found at once both attractive and repelling. Dark splotches stained the sides and top of the thing. Piled around and behind it were stacks of what I thought at first were branches. Then I realized they were bones.

The faces of the dead stared out of a pallid tangle of limbs. Thighs and arms and fingers all lay piled atop one another.

I wanted nothing more than to get out of that place, but I was worried about Danny, so I inspected the room, looking for passages or doors that I may have missed. I don't know how long I stayed down there, encased in darkness. It felt like an eternity. On a whim, I pulled out my phone. I had no service, but the camera worked just fine. I took photo after photo. Video too.

The statues watched in silence.

Every moment I spent down there, I grew more uneasy. The air felt thick, livid, almost electric with power. After a few minutes, my phone shorted and died. I couldn't stand it anymore, and called up for my friends to pull me out. It seemed to take forever for them to haul me back up, though it couldn't have been more than a few minutes. I still remember the moment. As I rose out of the pit, I felt as though something demonic was right below me, about to grab my ankles and yank me back down into that foul hole. A feeling of relief washed over me when I stood once more in the autumn light. I tilted my head back, gasping for air, feeling the sun on my face. I hadn't realized it, but I had been holding my breath on the way up.

There was nothing to do but return to the SUV, drive to a spot with signal, and call for help. As we walked away, I turned to look back, and noticed again the two bizarre trees.

The Watcher and the Centipede, something whispered.

I remember only flashes of that ride. My mind was still swarming with the images of what I had seen. We bounced back down the muddy dirt road, all of us checking our phones, waiting for bars.

Toby was the first to get a signal. "Finally," he said, manipulating his home screen.

I'm not sure how I knew, but I had a gut feeling, and spoke up as he was about to call for help. "Try calling Danny before you call rescue."

Toby shot me an odd look, but he obliged, putting the phone on speaker so we could all hear it.

To our surprise, Danny answered.

"Danny?" Toby's face was the definition of shock. "Where are you? What hap —"

He was cut off by a string of expletives as Danny exploded. "What the fuck kind of bullshit was that? What did you guys do, slip me some shit?"

"What are you talking —"

"I fucking hurt my ankle, and I just woke up here. You could have at least brought me to the hospital! Dumping me on the doorstep? Really? After fucking 20 years of friendship?"

"Danny, we didn't do anything to you. Where are you?"

There was a rustle in the background, and then Danny's wife got on the phone. We'd all seen her get belligerent when she hit the coffee brandy too hard, but this time she was really in a rage. She spent the next several minutes cursing us out at the top of her lungs and demanding to know what happened. When all we had in answer to her questions were more questions, she hung up on us.

We sat in stunned silence, looking at each other and breathing expletives.

"How the fuck could he be at his house?" Jason muttered. "How is that even possible?"

None of us had any answers.

By the time we all got back to our respective homes, Danny had blocked us all from his social media sites, and refused to answer our calls.

That night the first god visited me.

That dream was blood and fire and stone. The god was a thing of shadow and light, beautiful and terrible, and he spoke dark truths in a language I had never known, but somehow understood perfectly. He spoke of pain and death, and the gifts of agony. His voice shivered with powers that course through the universe and, perhaps, through our veins. Truth, drenched in blood: burning words of apocalypse, the turning of ages, the death of the mammoth and the return of the dragon. *Wisdom,* he whispered, *dark enlightenment and pale truth. The wheel is turning again. This age is ending. The gate will open soon.*

I wondered what truths the dead in that accursed chamber had found.

* * *

Everyone has a dorky friend or two. You know the type: the book-worm/gamer/nerd who turns out to be the most level-headed person you know, the socially-awkward brainiac who is actually really cool, the quiet savant — the person you go to when you want advice.

Ken was that guy in our crowd. He'd moved to Boston after college to teach history, but we'd all stayed in touch. After spending countless hours staring at the photos I'd taken in the chamber, I decided to call in the brain squad, and rang him up. I didn't tell him about Danny. I just said we'd found a weird chamber at the bottom of a hole, and emailed him the entire gallery of photos.

It took him a few days to get back to me. I was just sitting down to eat lunch — a tomato sandwich, iced tea, and a Whoopie pie — when he called.

"Where is this place?" he asked by way of greeting, when I answered.

"Allagash," I said, deliberately vague. "Did you figure anything out?"

"Yeah. Some of the inscriptions are Celtic. Some are Egyptian. Some are Roman. Some are Viking. Some are Aztec. I don't even know what the others are."

I took a bite of the sandwich, and sighed at the cardboard taste of my latest crop. "That doesn't make any sense." I wasn't a history buff, by any means, but I knew that Egyptian and Aztec artifacts had no business being in the backwoods of Maine.

"None whatsoever," he agreed. "It's highly unlikely that Celts, Vikings, Aztecs, Vikings, and Romans all came to this spot. What makes more sense is that one person — or group of people — made this place in homage to all these things. The names on the bottom of the statues are in old French. So is the inscription on the altar."

I pulled up the photo gallery on my laptop and looked again. Apparently, the camera on my phone had noticed more than I had. The inscription was clear, and I knew enough French to make it out.

La chambre d'agonie.

Agony Chamber.

"The inscriptions on the statue bases are legible," Ken continued. "Some of them, anyway. These are all statues of gods. Kivutar. The Algea. Odyne."

I tried the sandwich again, then tossed it in the trash. "Whose gods were they?"

"The Algea and Odyne were Greek. Kivutar was Finnish. Chantico was Aztec. There's one common thread, though." Ken hesitated. "They're all gods of pain."

I felt the blood drain from my face, and fought to keep my voice calm. "What about the others?"

"I'm still digging. But they don't match anything I've ever seen. My guess is that some rich, eclectic settler brought the statues over from the old world. The chamber itself ... he probably hired laborers for that. Is this thing near a town?"

"Kinda. If you can call it that." The place wasn't too far from one of the hundreds of tiny, unremarkable backwoods towns that peppered Maine. New England was dotted with such places: tiny towns with long histories and lots of old houses. Many of those old towns had been around since before the Civil War.

"Does this have anything to do with Danny?" Ken asked. "He's been ranting on Facebook about alien abductions and conspiracy theories. Says he's having nightmares. Something about a centipede?"

"I gotta go," I said.

*　*　*

The next dream was of a great upheaval. The ground swelled and rose as though moved by a giant wave. The sky bled fire. The centipede was the size of a whale, and it reared into the air, guarding the old king. Shadowy figures stood in a ring around them. Behind them, some vast, prehistoric animal tried to flee, only to be blasted into ash.

The second god turned to me, his burning eyes fixated upon me. *This is the path to obliteration. This is the road of truth. The secrets of the universe are waiting in the cells of human flesh.*

As he spoke, the mountains behind him collapsed, and trees snapped like twigs under a charnel wind. And then everything went up in flames.

The dream melted away, white-hot.

*　*　*

It didn't take long to put the pieces together.

To get curious.

To fall into madness.

They came to me in dream after dream, whispering secrets of the abyss. They whispered dreams of hellwords. I searched the internet, visited the town's nearest library, scoured occult manuals, looking for answers. I only found more questions.

But in time, I answered the call.

I found myself staring at the Watcher and The Centipede again a few weeks later, when I was no longer able to resist the growing urge to return to that blighted wood. The Centipede was a black silhouette against a grey November sky, its branches still looking remarkably insect-like. Behind him, the Watcher stood silent guard, his face a faint but menacing outline in ancient bark.

An inhuman voice whispered through my thoughts. *The Watcher and the Centipede stood through the churning of the earth at the falling of the first age. This is the place where worlds collide. This is the door.*

I gathered some liquid courage — whiskey — and managed to force myself to go back down into that cursed pit. Alone. Afraid of getting trapped, I brought two ladders and three ropes with me.

I started small. Just a test, to see if it worked.

I took the hammer out of the tool belt I was wearing, and gingerly placed my hand upon the altar. I remember drawing a deep breath of musty, damp air, and hesitating. Delaying. Was there a ritual? Some chant I was supposed to utter? I had no idea. Up until that point, I was just a normal guy. I had never delved into the dark arts.

But I did enjoy gambling.

"Gods of the abyss," I muttered, "I give you my pain."

And then I brought the hammer down hard on my thumb.

My scream echoed eerily — perfectly — off the chamber's walls. For the next few moments, the world was obscured by black and red pain spots. I felt something change in the atmosphere. The air began to shiver with whispers. The statues stood unmoving, but I felt a presence there.

I turned and looked behind me. Had one of the statues moved? I couldn't be sure. A livid silence filled the air.

I sensed that it was time for my request.

I asked for something little. My daughter's cat had been missing for a few days. "Bring Fomper home," I said.

I waited a few more minutes. Nothing happened, so I climbed back up. The woods were silent around me. Too silent. I had the feeling that I was being watched, but nothing appeared. At one point there was a sharp *crack* behind me, but when I turned, there was nobody there.

Despite my creeping terror of the place, I hid the rope ladders nearby.

When I got home, I found Fomper's body in the driveway.

I guess the old gods were not generous in their interpretation of human wishes.

* * *

To this day, I cannot explain what the chamber is, or how it works. I was pretty scared after that, and vowed never to return. But day after day, the burning curiosity grew, until, in time, I found I had to go back once more.

The chamber wasn't empty this time.

I smelled the corpse before I got to the bottom. The man, whoever he was, had been killed slowly, horribly. The energy in the chamber had grown stronger, more malevolent.

Which one of my friends had done it? I turned it over and over in my head.

The next few months proved ... interesting.

Two locals went missing in our area. Another four disappeared in Portland. Three in Bangor. When I went back to the agony chamber, there were many more bodies than those poor souls could account for.

I waited to see who won the lotto, got a new job, scored a hot new girlfriend. The results, however, were far less obvious. Tim got a new truck. Jason got a job promotion. And Toby's wife finally got pregnant. No one hit the Megabucks, or inherited a vast fortune.

Pain, the gods said in my dream. *Give us pain.*

I should have gone to the authorities. But we don't always take the high road. That's why murders happen, and rape, and child abuse, and all the other terrible hatreds mankind wreaks upon the world.

I told myself to stay away.

The dreams continued. I found myself plagued by a growing urge to return. Though I fought it off for months, when the snow was gone and the moon was full, I found myself drawn back one more time to that cursed pit. Once I had climbed back down into the shadows, I found myself yet again in the company of the dead.

There were clues, this time. The killer had taken few precautions, and hadn't bothered covering his tracks. I held my nose and pulled a wallet out of a dead man's jeans. The address left little doubt as to who had been there before me. One of the corpses had a Red Sox cap, and another wore a *Cheers* sweatshirt.

"That little bastard," I muttered.

* * *

That night, I drove down to Boston. I rarely use my concealed-carry permit, but I went armed, out of precaution. I wasn't sure what to expect: I'd never confronted a murderer before.

Ken opened the door and stood there in his pajama bottoms and a white tank top, his pale, pudgy face set off by the way the flickering blue light from his television reflected on his glasses. He didn't seem particularly surprised to find me on his doorstep.

He stepped aside and waved me in, then shut the door behind me, silent.

"How did you find the place?" I asked.

Ken apparently saw no point in fudging. He didn't try to deny anything, or evade the question. He'd always been honest, to a fault. "I went to visit Toby, and brought him a bottle of whiskey. He told me everything. Then I brought Danny vodka. He told me everything too."

"What did you ask for?"

The expression on his face didn't change. "Happiness," he said.

I frowned. "I don't get it."

"Come on," he said. "I'll show you."

He had kept trophies, like all good serial killers. Jewelry, in his case. He pointed at the rings and necklaces and watches one by one, ticking them off as though he were reading tarot cards. "The rapist, the hangman, the judge, the brute, the whore, the murderer. And the worst of them all: the aspiring politician."

I remember hearing a ringing in my ears.

Pain.

"They speak to me, you know," he said. "They need one for each full moon. That's when they're strongest, collectively. They told me things … things that would make your blood run cold. Things that would set the world afire."

"But what did you ask for? Danny only asked to go home."

"For myself? Nothing. I've funded three schools in third world countries, helped a blind child see, brought a soldier home safe to his family. It's a great feeling to know you're doing something good in the world."

I blinked. "Is that what you've become? Justice?"

He smiled. "I always wanted to be a superhero."

Memory offered a collection of childhood Halloweens, juxtaposed atop one another. He had always dressed as a comic-book hero. Every year.

The next moment is an out-of-focus snapshot in my memory. He reached for something. I panicked, thinking it was a gun. And so I pulled out my own weapon and shot him.

He slumped against the wall, then slid down it, leaving a smear of blood on the white wall. He looked up at me, wide-eyed, his expression strangely childlike. His hand flopped onto his leg like a fish, and he dropped the object he was holding.

It was a cell phone.

Oops.

I told him I was sorry, that it was an accident, that I would take him to the hospital. I repeated those words over and over again, though I'm not sure if it was him or myself I was trying to reassure.

I helped him into the car, laid him down carefully in the back seat, then ran back inside and grabbed some blankets from his bed to keep him comfortable.

I fully intended to drive to Mass General. But the gods whispered into my soul, and took control. At least, that's what I tell myself. But, to be honest ... I wasn't that nice. I wasn't that good.

And it seemed a shame to waste such agony.

Just across the Maine border, I pulled off the interstate and found a dark parking lot which offered the brief privacy I needed. I tied him up with a bungee cord I kept in the trunk, wrapped him in the bloody blankets, and stuffed him into the trunk. He woke up briefly, but he was too weak to struggle much.

I don't remember much about the drive back to the Allagash. Just the moon, guiding me like a beacon. I vaguely recall pulling Ken out of the trunk, hoisting him over my shoulders, and making the short walk through the night-dark wood.

The Watcher and the Centipede were waiting, cloaked in moon-light.

Rather than try to figure out how to let Ken down gently, I just dropped him into the hole. When he hit bottom, I heard a thud, a harsh cry, and a crack which I am fairly sure was the sound of bone breaking.

A bit more pain couldn't hurt.

Once I climbed down myself, I hesitated. Part of me screamed that this was madness. Ken was my friend, after all. But *They* stood before me, and I knew, when I looked at *Their* terrible beauty, that I had gone too far to turn back.

What to ask for? I turned the options over in my mind. World peace? Money? A classic car? What is worth the loss of a friend? What exactly should one request, in exchange for the blackening of a soul?

Ken's last scream made the gods very happy. That shriek lingers in my thoughts, echoing through every moment of my life. When I am awake, trying to go through the paces of being a decent human being — if there is such a thing — it waits silently in the darkest corner of my mind. In my dreams, it goes on forever.

You're no doubt wondering what I wished for. I wished with all my being that we had never found that place. I wished myself back to that sunny October day, hoping that I could turn back time.

But they could not give me that. Nothing changed. In the end, Ken died in vain.

In the daylight hours, I felt the impact of what I had done. The weight of it, the horror of it, eats at me constantly. I battled with the thought of turning myself in, and decided that it wouldn't bring Ken back. I thought maybe the best thing to do was to continue Ken's work. It isn't hard to find child molesters these days. Or to locate good folk that need a little luck.

The last time I went back, I found three fresh bodies. I'm not sure who is responsible, who figured it out. In a way, it doesn't matter. Maybe we all had the dreams. Maybe we're all killers now, servants to the silent gods that wait in the darkness. Maybe there are agony chambers peppered throughout the world, not just in the dark Maine woods.

Maybe that's where the vanished ones are, in piles of bones far below the reach of the sun.

Danny still rants about alien abductions. I haven't spoken to him since that day, but his rapid descent into madness is a hot topic in a small town like ours.

At first, killing Ken changed both everything and nothing. I still went to work every day, and came home to my wife's nagging and my kids acting out. My dog was — and is — still dumb as a box of rocks. I never thought of myself as innocent. I realize now that I was, but I left that there to rot with the corpses in that cursed chamber.

Perhaps you never know what innocence is until you've lost it.

I miss my friends. I miss the days that I didn't fear to close my eyes, or to turn around in response to a faint noise. I miss our hunting trips. I know I'll never be the same man who set out into the woods that autumn day. Ken died in agony, but my pain is eternal.

Every full moon, I hear them, calling me, whispering. They want more pain. More blood. More death. The Watcher and The Centipede still visit my dreams. With them stands the pale, angry ghost of a dead thing I once called friend.

They feed off me, even now. I can feel them around the edges of my anger, the rage, the pain and self-loathing I try to hide. And every time I wish for something — good tomatoes, bright weather, a little more battery life on my phone — I get it, regardless of what it is. I've hit the lotto twice, and got the promotion I'd been wanting for years. These things mean nothing. They are as shallow and empty as the eyes of the dead that haunt my dreams. Everyone tells me that I have the best tomatoes around, but they taste like ashes and blood to me now.

I know what they're doing. They're toying with me. Tempting me. Teaching me that the pain of the soul is even sweeter to them than physical agony. In my dreams, they tell me to kill, and they promise me that, if I serve them well, one day I, too, can become a god. All I have to do is kill. Not rapists or murderers or child molesters, but innocents.

I don't know how long I can resist. Days, weeks, and months I have lasted, and with each passing moment, my resolve weakens.

The Agony Chamber waits for me in the frozen north, whispering the bloody dreams of forgotten gods.

Someday I will be one of them.

WINDOW OF DARKNESS

Duane E. Coffill

Mark Stevens was working on his third novel when it happened. A thirty-year-old writer, Mark lived with his wife, Marie, a teacher, on the third floor of an apartment complex in South Portland, Maine. On the day it began, he sat at his monitor, pushing his medium length blonde hair out of his face. His word processing program reflected in his wire-framed glasses.

Marie sat on the couch, reading a magazine article about the rise of women's eye replacements. "Honey, do you like my eyes? Are they beautiful?"

Mark stopped typing. *If I answer this question wrong, I'll be sleeping on the couch tonight!* He turned slowly towards her, and found her smirking at him. "Babe, your eyes are the windows to your beauty and intelligence."

He turned back to the monitor, anticipating her response.

She approached from behind, embracing him. "Nice answer. That was so sweet of you." She kissed the back of his head. "I'm going to bed.

Have a good night, honey."

Marie was beautiful with her light blonde hair and ocean-blue eyes. She made him feel special, and he was lucky to have her. "Good night, beautiful."

As he resumed writing, she walked towards the bedroom.

Hours later, having fallen asleep on the keyboard, Mark woke up, and found that he had created twenty pages worth of letters and numbers. He chuckled a little and started deleting them.

As he was doing this, a flash of silver light caught his eyes. He turned and looked out the window. Peering down onto the street, he noticed some people and an odd silver light moving around. *Someone must have one of those fancy, silver beam flashlights, I guess.*

Suddenly, the silver light shined up, blinding him. "SHIT! DAMN PEOPLE!" he shouted.

The silver light vanished completely.

Reaching underneath his glasses, Mark wiped his eyes. He looked out the window again — no silver light. Sitting back down, he checked the time on his computer: 2 AM.

The next day Mark woke up at noon, already missing a half of day of writing. The success of his two books brought in some money to the household, but he still worked part-time in the Gray/New Gloucester Schools district. Someday he hoped to write full time, but he couldn't quit his day job yet. He needed coffee desperately, so he made an extra-large cup, and went into the living room to start writing.

It was the last normal day of his life.

By 7 PM Friday night, Marie had fallen asleep on the couch while watching TV, her glass of wine only half-finished. She looked forward to weekends. As a teacher, fall was the hardest, because both students and teachers were still adjusting to their schedules.

She woke to the sounds of screaming.

Still shaking off sleep, Marie peeked out the window and saw a man and a woman shouting at each other while walking down the street. As she looked down at them, the screaming abruptly stopped. The couple turned towards her, their eyes ablaze with a red glow. Marie hid behind the curtain, but she knew she had been seen.

Heart pounding, she scooted over to the couch and guzzled what was left of her wine. Still shaking, she filled another glass. *What the hell was that? Oh, my God! When does Mark get home?*

She sat on the couch nervously. A few minutes later, she checked the window again. The couple was gone, so she sat down and had another glass of wine.

Two hours later Mark walked in. Marie ran up to him, throwing her arms around him. "What's the matter, honey?" he asked, frowning.

When Marie told him what had happened, Mark had trouble believing what she claimed to have seen. "I didn't see anyone down there while I drove into the garage." He dropped his work stuff onto the floor and noticed her shaking, the smell of wine strong on her breath. He sank into the couch, and Marie cuddled up next to him with a severe case of the shivers. "It's okay, honey. I'm home. You sure it wasn't the wine?"

"NO! Their eyes were glowing red! And they looked right at me!"

He chuckled, and Marie rolled her eyes, not the least bit surprised that her husband didn't believe her. They snuggled on the couch watching one of her favorite shows, Empire. She eventually calmed down, so Mark made them a couple microwave dinners. They fell asleep on the couch.

In the middle of the night, Marie got up to use the bathroom. She glanced out the window, and spotted five people on the street. She froze, trying to see what they were doing.

Mark rolled over and saw Marie staring out the window. He yawned, wiped his eyes and stretched. "Hey, what are you doing?"

"Remember what I told you?" she whispered.

"Yeah."

"It seems they brought friends."

He walked over to her, looking down onto the street through sleepy eyes. All five people turned and looked up at them, red eyes blazing.

Marie's hand flew to her mouth as she gasped.

"HOLY SHIT!" Mark yelled. "WHAT THE HELL?"

All Marie could see were their flaming red eyes and their ghastly teeth, which seemed to glow a sickly yellow in the dark.

Mark glanced out the window again, but they were gone. Marie sat down on the couch, shaking, terrified.

"Okay, let's calm down." Mark paced back and forth. "Should we call the police?"

"They won't believe us. You didn't see those creeps when you drove into the garage?"

"No. There was no one," he said, rubbing his hair. "We have to think. Are we the only ones who have seen these people? And WHAT THE HELL ARE THEY?"

Mark sat down next to his shaking wife, putting his arm around her while trying to calm himself down "Should we ask our nearest neighbors if they've noticed those weirdos?"

"How are we going to ask them that and not look like idiots?" Marie said. "Oh, excuse me, Mrs. Baker, have you seen those people on the street with glowing red eyes? Right!"

"Maybe it's a prank?" Mark said.

"That's not a *prank*, Mark!"

They sat on the couch drinking wine and passed out form alcohol induced exhaustion within an hour.

Marie woke up to the sound of rain. 10 AM, they had slept in. It was the weekend, and neither of them had to go to work, so she went into the kitchen to make coffee, contemplating the events of the past night. With Mark still asleep on the couch, she sat down at the computer with her cup of coffee, and Googled "People with glowing red eyes."

Mark slowly stirred and woke up. Seeing Marie on the computer, he asked, "Hey, what are you looking up?"

She slowly turned in his chair and said, "I'm trying to see if any of those things have been sighted anywhere else. So far, nothing."

Mark walked around the room, his thoughts a tornado of confusion. *Maybe we were just hallucinating*, he thought. *Because if not, this shit was fuckin' insane!*

"Let's ask Marge and Hunter if they saw anything strange," Marie said. She got up off the chair and headed to the door.

"Wait. You mean right now?" Mark asked nervously. "I thought you said we'd look like idiots?"

"I changed my mind. Are you coming with me?"

Mark looked at her and hesitated, but followed her out into the teal-colored hallway.

Marge answered the door, her dirty blonde hair covered with small red clips. "Hi."

"Sorry to bother you," Marie said to Marge. "We've been seeing strange things outside our window and were wondering if you'd seen anything."

Marge looked at Hunter, who was shuffling to the door in his Captain America slippers, his hair an uncombed rat's nest. "Honey, have you noticed anything unusual?"

"Nope," he said, and shuffled back to the living room.

"What did you see?" Marge asked.

Marie opened her mouth, but couldn't quite bring herself to say what she had seen. "Oh, it's probably nothing," she said quickly. "Never mind. Sorry to bother you."

Marie and Mark started to walk away. As Marge closed her apartment door, they heard noises from down the hall. Someone was running up the stairwell.

"Do you hear that?" Mark said.

Marie nodded. "Shhh," she whispered.

The footsteps grew closer, and they heard the stairwell door's rusty hinges creak in protest as it flew open suddenly.

On edge from the night before, Marie and Mark rushed to their apartment, ripping open the door and diving in quickly as the phantom running footfalls of multiple people approached their apartment, stopping just outside their door.

Mark snapped the deadbolt in place. "There's more than one," Mark whispered.

Marie rolled her eyes, as if to say, "Obviously."

They stood still by the door and waited for someone to knock, but then heard the footsteps moving away. The couple let out a big sigh of relief, embracing each other, still unsure of what had just happened.

The rest of the day was uneventful, and they went to bed wondering if the strangeness had passed.

At 3 AM, the TV was still on, playing infomercials. Except for the light near Mark's desk and the kitchen night light, the apartment was dark as they slept. The window in the bedroom was open slightly, a cool breeze gently blowing the curtains, a window that Marie had closed and locked before going to bed.

On the side of the building, a thumping sound was getting closer to Mark and Marie's room.

A silhouette moved across the window, temporarily blocking out the moonlight and casting a dark shadow into the room. Suddenly the bedroom window rattled, and something peeked into the window with one red eye, pulling back its lips and revealing fangs. The creature reached down and tried to pry open the window wider, but a security lock prevented the window from opening more than six inches.

It looked into the room and glared at Marie and Mark, snarling as it crawled back down the side of building.

Sunday morning, Mark woke first. He yawned, stretched, and headed for the bathroom. The sound of the sink running woke Marie, so she rose from bed and opened the window to let in some fresh autumn air. Mark made coffee, then sat down at his computer to do some research.

He started to look for "red-eyed street creatures." To his surprise, he got a couple of hits. He started reading one article, and quickly got excited.

"Marie! There's an article here by someone named Wally Aarons. He talks about creatures with red eyes and fangs that drip poisonous green saliva. No one knows what they are. Wally claims to have killed one of them with bright light. He says that's why they only come out at night. Some sort of weakness to light." He looked at Marie. "It says that once you see them, they come for you."

Mark quickly tapped out an email to Wally, detailing his and Marie's experience, and hoping for a prompt response.

Later that day, they went to the Army/Navy store and bought several flashlights, two baseball bats and other assorted weapons.

"I think we have enough," she said, smiling, as they unloaded everything.

Mark was focused on securing the apartment. "We have to try to remain calm," he said, double checking the door latch. "Why hasn't this been on the news?"

She looked at him and gently touched his face. She could feel him shaking, and knew that he was just as scared as she was.

Mark grabbed a bottle of wine from the cupboard, corkscrewed it open, and drank it straight from the bottle before offering his wife some. At first she hesitated, but then she drank as well.

By 11 PM, it was raining heavily. Mark paced back and forth, revving up like a car, repeatedly checking to make sure their baseball bats were close at hand.

Marie pulled her chair near the window and sat down, watching outside. "Honey, you need to relax."

Her voice was soft. She was calm. He wasn't.

Mark checked his computer and noticed an email from Wally Aarons. As he clicked on it, something caught his attention out of the corner of his eye. One of the creatures was just outside the window, glaring at him.

"Oh, shit! There's one right there!"

Marie screamed.

The creature's face was revolting. Slimy green mucus dripped from its ghastly jaw as it gazed at Mark and Marie with mesmerizing red eyes.

Marie broke eye contact with the thing, only to see that Mark was in some sort of a trance. "MARK!? MARK!?" She shook him, then slapped him.

His eyes gradually focused on Marie. "What happened?"

"I don't know. You were in a trance or something."

She glanced back at the window, but the creature was gone.

She looked at Mark's computer and read the email, her jaw dropping.

"Well, what does it say?" Mark asked.

"The creatures are vulnerable to light, like vampires. Wally says light will keep them away, but we should run." Her voice was low and empty. "Keep all the lights on."

"This doesn't make any sense. Vampires aren't real!"

"There's one more thing," Marie said. "They can enter without permission. We have to leave the lights on and stay armed."

"He didn't specify what can kill these fuckers? Or why they might have targeted us?"

Marie shook her head. Mark went to the pantry and emerged a few minutes later, holding a crucifix.

"Where did you get that?" Marie asked.

"It was my grandmother's. I got it when she died, but I never hung it up."

"What if that's just superstition? Don't you think we need something else?"

He put the cross down onto the armrest of the couch and went over to their wooden bench. Flipping it upside down, Mark started breaking the legs off. He spent the next hour whittling the legs down to a point with a sharp kitchen knife. Marie sat on the couch with the crucifix in her lap, watching the window while Mark worked. When he finished, the carpet was covered with wood scraps and shavings, and he had four wooden stakes.

Sweating a little, Mark handed his wife two stakes, keeping the other two for himself.

"I hope you're right about this, Mark."

"Don't worry. We have some protection now." He kept looking towards the door, wanting to go hunting in the hallway.

The lights went out and Marie screamed. They froze, listening for something, anything. "Honey," Marie said. "Why is your hand so cold?"

There was silence.

"I'm not touching you," Mark whispered.

She gasped. Mark shouted, trying to push at whatever was near her, but there was nothing. "Honey? Honey?"

"It's gone," Marie said.

"What the fuck was touching you!?"

"I don't know," Marie cried. "What was it? Where did it go?"

"Calm down," he said, guiding her into the kitchen. "I'm getting a flashlight."

Holding the wooden stakes under his arm, he grabbed the flashlight and pointed it towards her. Something was right behind her.

"Marie, look out!" Mark yelled. "It's right behind you!"

She ducked. Mark lunged at the creature, pushing Marie aside. The creature growled, then there was silence.

"Mark? Mark?"

No answer.

The flashlight rolled across the floor, the beam casting strobe light shadows on the wall. Marie grabbed it, shivering with fear. She cried out for Mark, but he didn't answer. She pointed the flashlight towards the floor and searched the room carefully.

Marie tripped over something and her knee banged hard off the coffee table. She would have landed on her face if she had not raised her hands at the last second.

Marie pointed the flashlight at what she had tripped over, and then stifled a scream.

The creature was serpent-like, with a cobra's face and red eyes. Its skin was gray, like a rhino's, but covered in scales ... and blood. Marie slowly stood up, grimacing through the extreme pain in her left knee. As the beam of light moved, she realized the awful truth of what had happened.

The creature was impaled, a wooden stake buried deep in its chest. Mark lay beside it, his throat ripped open. His blood covered both bodies.

Tears streamed down Marie's face. She wanted to touch Mark, but didn't dare to. She reached down and picked up the crucifix, and then limped to the window.

Many red eyes stared at her from the dark, lonely night.

"Come on, you bastards!" she yelled. "Let's do this!"

The next moments were a chaotic blur. The window glass erupted inward as the snake creatures lunged into her apartment. For just a moment they stopped, noticing that the struggle had taken the life of one of their own. Then the growling started as the scaly demons lifted their blazing red eyes toward Marie.

Suddenly, the front door burst open, gunshots blazed and rang out in the apartment.

The creatures scattered, fleeing back out the shattered window.

"That's right, run, you fuckers!" It was Hunter and Marge, both wielding shotguns. Buckshot and shotgun shells littered the floor.

Marge saw Mark's body and gasped. "What the hell happened?"

Marie glanced at her dead husband, and choked, "He saved me."

"These bastards are everywhere," Hunter said. "Are you ok?"

Marie nodded.

"I am so sorry, Marie," Marge said.

"Did you know about them?" Marie asked, nodding at their shotguns.

Marge and Hunter exchanged uneasy eye contact.

"The landlord had imprisoned at least one in this apartment building," Hunter said. "It was locked in a secret chamber behind the closet. That creature," he pointed at the thing's corpse "killed our son. We thought it was already dead."

Turning the lights on, they escorted Marie to the bedroom. The closet was open. Looking inside, Marie saw a compartment inside it. There were scratches on the inside of the door. "Is that why the creatures were drawn to the building?" she asked, still crying.

"Maybe it was dormant," Marge said. "We thought it was gone. But when those things started appearing out on the street every night, we knew it must still be here."

"What do you mean?"

"The creature was alive, but asleep. Our research has found that these things hibernate sometimes. The other ones must have picked up its scent and awakened it. That's why they were concentrating on this building."

"The landlord had one imprisoned?" Marie asked.

Marge nodded. "We've dug up all we can on him. Dr. Rudolph

Schlanger used to work for a genetics lab, before being fired for multiple ethics violations over the years. He was brilliant and way ahead of his time, but I guess Genoscope finally had enough of his erratic behavior and canned him. He has doctorates in both genetics and herpetology."

Marie shook her head and raised her hands questioningly.

"That's the study of reptiles and amphibians," Marge explained, and then continued. "He went off the grid for a couple years after that, and we think that's when the government, maybe even the CIA, recruited him for some black projects. After he resurfaced, he bought this building. Some of the locals say strange construction crews worked odd hours here for months. They also say that a lot of bizarre looking lab equipment was delivered to this building, usually in the middle of the night." Marge looked at her husband.

"I think there's an illegal genetics lab hidden deep in the bowels of this building somewhere, probably even a set of secret passages throughout the complex," Hunter said. "And those things that have been terrorizing you and killed Mark and ... and our son, we think Dr. Schlanger created them, somehow."

"But he must have needed some funding for his experiments, because he started renting out the apartments after all of his mysterious 'renovations' were completed," Marge said.

"No one has seen Dr. Schlanger for a few months now," Hunter said. "And it looks like some of his experiments may have escaped."

Marie sat on the bed crying, looking at a picture of her and Mark on the Merry-Go-Round at Old Orchard Beach. Her voice hitched, "If you two knew about, or at least suspected all this, then why the hell would you stay here, especially after your son was killed?!"

"Are you kidding?" Hunter said, shaking his head. "You can't find rent this affordable anywhere else in South Portland."

DEATH LIGHTS

(A Lee Buhl Story)

Glenn Rolfe

The bright sun sinking from the sky was a lie. There was no warmth here. Only the light of the dead. Lee Buhl lit a cigarette and waited for the owner of the home to arrive. Bob Dylan's voice creaked through the Rambler's stereo promising a hard rain. Something was gonna fall all right, a storm was coming. Gazing up at the attic window, Lee swallowed a mouth full of smoke and waited for the blue shadow behind the glass to fade.

Maine. He hadn't been back to the state since his time at the Bruton Inn. He'd vowed never to return. There was nothing up here. Not for him anyway. Rhiannon was his only connection and she high-tailed it out and moved to New York shortly after surviving the fight of their lives. They'd remained friends, though he hadn't spoken to her in almost a year.

Carl Owens's blue Focus pulled in behind him.

Lee tossed his cigarette out the window, killed the engine, and stepped out.

"Mr. Buhl?" Owens said. He reached out his hand. "Carl Owens, Hidden Realty."

Lee had only spoken to him over the phone. Carl Owens was in his thirties, short, his black hair receding from a set of thick eyebrows over brown eyes. Round in the middle, dressed in black slacks, a white shirt and black tie, Owens looked just as likely to try and sell you on God's good grace as he was the haunted house on the hill.

"Mr. Owens," Lee said, lighting another cigarette, leaving the man's hand searching for a partner. The black and white clad realtor pulled his hand back and reached inside his pants pockets. Lee noticed that Owens refused to look at the home. He also failed to stifle the tremor in the hand as he held out the keys to the property.

"It's all yours for as long as it takes."

Lee let the keys tremble and craned his head back to the attic window. "You've seen it."

"I ... I just want it gone. Whatever it takes. I need to move this house, this land. Please ..."

Lee turned to see Owens's eyes begging him to take the keys. More than that, he saw the dread eating at the man. Bad spirits stain a person, left a mark.

Lee took the proffered keys. Owens spun on his heels and reached through the driver's side window of his Ford. He hauled out a white envelope.

"Don't bother with the money," Lee said.

"I ... I got the first half here. You get the —"

"That won't do me any good if I don't make it out."

Owens held the envelope, lost in the statement.

Lee nodded. "You're fine to leave, Mr. Owens. I'll come collect, one way or another, when I'm finished."

Owens nodded, got in his car, and pulled out of the driveway without so much as a second glance.

Lee stamped out his cigarette and faced the farmhouse.

"I'm a fucking idiot."

Pocketing the house keys in exchange for the Rambler's, he went behind the car, opened the trunk, and plucked a flashlight from the milk crate on the right. His gaze lingering on the gold picture frame poking up from behind his other supplies. He traced the edge of the frame with his fingertips.

Emma would be his reward, someday.

In his mind, he saw her brown eyes, her long dark hair, and her smile. The memory shattered by his mistake, leaving her alone with that goddam devil in the mirror. Her screams echoed like a ghost in a hallway. He took a deep breath, clenched his fist, and let her go for the hundredth time.

He considered the wicker basket. His tools of the trade so to speak. The sage, salts, smudge sticks, candles, and chalk. He decided to scope the place out first, size up his opponent.

Slamming the trunk shut, he headed for the house.

Cobwebs and cracks filled the clouded windows. The porch stood wrapped in greyed roots and pale vines holding the boards in a final embrace. Lee took the three moaning stairs, stopping at the big red door.

A late afternoon breeze clattered the dangling skeletal fingers of a nearby tree, wind chimes of the damned. Darkness rose from the depths. The earth stopped cold as he slid the key into place. The door creaked inward before his hand could make the turn. A frozen breath brushed the fine hairs on his fingers.

Pale blue haze illuminated the foyer, communing with each hair across the back of his neck and prickling to life every goose bump in his possession. The light inside, shifting and fluttering like the flame of a candle catching the cold, receded deeper into the home.

Lee turned on the flashlight, sweeping the bright, dust particle-filled beam across the room as he crossed the threshold. The blue light disappeared up the stairwell across the room. The entryway was cluttered with the shambles of someone else's life — furniture lined both walls beneath canvas coverings, like bodies on slabs in a morgue, he expected them each to rise, one after another. Turning, reaching for the keys still hanging in the door, he jerked his hand back. They were iced over. Extending his hand, the visible part of the key broke away and shattered upon impact with the wood floor.

The door slammed shut causing the hair on his neck to rise. His stomach tensed.

Before he could make a move, his flashlight flew from his hand and smashed against the wall.

"No warm up, I guess."

Cracking his knuckles, Lee gritted his teeth and tasted the charge in the room. There was a bite to it, like the flavor in the air before a mid-summer thunderstorm. For the hell of it, he tried the door. The knob, still cold, refused to budge. A strong wind shook the house, rattling loose shutters, sending a vibration through the soles of his boots. He moved to the window left of the door and gazed out at the decrepit trees being thrashed around. Fat rain drops slapped against the clouded glass. In seconds, the downpour blurred the outside world.

He needed his supplies, but it looked like he may have to get acquainted with the spirit of the house first. That could go one of two ways, either they made their introductions, maybe poked at one another a few times until he could get back outside, or … well, he was trapped here for the night without access to his weapons. Death, or something worse, could come before the dawn.

Lee lit another cigarette. The black clouds coming on outside made it nearly pitch dark in the already gloomy house. Passing the staircase, he could make out enough shapes, the ghostly furniture ended just beyond the bannister. He pulled his zippo, sparked it to life, and followed the light to the next doorway.

A living room, piled with more canvas covered creatures, shelves of books and knickknacks, and a mantle over a long-closed up hearth. Two partially burned white candles set atop the mantle on either side of a portrait. He found a skinny box of fresh ones behind the one on the left. White candles held many great strengths. He lit the two on the mantle flicked his zippo closed, and picked up the picture frame, and turned allowing the candlelight to shine on the woman in the photo.

His jaw dropped, his cigarette dangling from his bottom lip. The woman in the portrait was identical to the one in the picture in his trunk.

Emma?

Smoke drifted into his eye. He shut them tight and remembered her …

Back when he'd been using his abilities to make money, back when the money is all that mattered, he'd met plenty of girls, plenty of women eager to share his bed. Then, he'd met Jeff and Rhiannon. And the Bruton Inn. Everything changed. He changed. He learned the true ways and power of shamanism, and how he could make a difference in people's lives.

He sought out those in need of his services, those in actual danger. He wound up saving a woman from a haunted mirror and the demons sheltered within it. That woman, Emma Pierce, introduced him to another side of life, a wonderful and fragile thing some sick bastard called love. The beautiful woman in the portrait in his hands had her brown eyes, long dark hair, and matched her freckle for freckle.

Soft laughter echoed somewhere deep in the house.

Lee returned the portrait to the mantle and backed away peering into the darkness outside of the room. The ceiling fan above his head rocked back and forth and dropped. He brought his arm up just in time to deflect the damn thing off his elbow. The jolt sent a stream of numbness from his elbow to his fingertips. The laughter came again.

"Well, hello to you, too," he said, shaking out his arm. There was a droplet of blood that looked like a black teardrop in the dim candle-light as it slid down his arm. He grabbed one of the candles from the mantle when he noticed the portrait again. The woman looked nothing like Emma. She had black hair that hung just above her bare shoulders, a dark complexion, maybe Native, maybe something else, but her strik-ing blue eyes cut through like sunshine through the rain. He stamped the remains of his cigarette in a bronze plate to the right of the candles.

Whatever was here could see inside of him. It was fucking with him. And it knew his Achilles.

After he failed to keep Emma safe, his promise broken, his shield tarnished, he let the doubt roll in with the guilt. And for the second time in as many years, he changed. It took months to answer another call for help.

And here he was. *Ease your way back in*, he told himself. A haunted farmhouse in Bumfuck, Maine. Of course, whatever rotten spirit was here could see into him. Test him. See how much give the shaman had in him, how much grit. Lee cracked his knuckles. He hadn't jumped back in the saddle to fall off and snap his neck.

The shadows cast from his candle leaned back as he made his way to another room off the foyer. This one appeared to be a study. More shelves, more books, a trunk set next to another covered corpse, most likely a chair. A lamp, some ugly, tall ashtray, and a roll-top desk placed squarely before a boarded-up window.

Lee walked over and raised the hood of the desk. A book, the cover all black, devoid of any title or author, sat beneath a layer of dust. He tilted the book so he could see the binding. No title or author there, either. He opened the cover and sucked in a breath.

He'd only read of this book's existence.

Nex Susurrus

Death Whisper

The legend revolved around the book's main purpose — to summon the Death Lights. Evil spirits that promised to take the living in exchange for bringing back the dead. They were tricksters, but far from your average poltergeist. They were not to be fucked with. Fools thought they could control the conjured spirits, thought they could wield the power. It never worked that way.

The cover of the book snapped shut. The roll top, rattled and slammed down. Lee tried to lift the lid, but it refused to budge. A loud scraping sound, like furniture moving across the floor, came from the room above. Whatever was here had his full-attention.

Lee left the room to find a way out. Hurrying down the shadow-filled hall, he tried the door again. It didn't budge. He moved back to the living room, set the candle back on the mantle, and tried each window. They were all sealed shut. He tugged the canvas covering off a heavy looking end table and discarded it to the floor. The piece was made of two thick pieces of oak and had a set of green metal legs, similar to the desk he'd had in grade school. Bending down to heft the piece, he heard *her* voice.

"Lee."

Emma

Raising the end table over his head, he smashed it through the living room window. The storm outside rushed in, a force against his intentions. He found the canvas cover he'd thrown from the end table and used it to clear the remaining shards from the sill. Throwing one leg over the ledge, he was ready to escape when an icy hand grabbed hold of his neck. The broken window fell away as he found himself hurled backwards. He landed flat on his back, the wind knocked from his lungs as an immense chill spread from his neck, through his shoulders and arms, and down his spine. The strange blue fog engulfed the room around him.

The Death Lights.

Lee tried to pull himself up from the floor, but his entire body felt like it was made of concrete. He focused on catching his breath and calming his nerves. The blue fog began to swirl, a tornado of death's glow. He knew what was coming next. The funnel began to take form. When it was finished, Emma, or some demonic version of the woman he loved, stood cold, smiling like a shark, deep in the ocean blue.

"Hello, Lee," it said with her voice.

"You shall not —" His voice suddenly cut out. His ability to speak frozen in the thing's presence.

"Ah, ah, ah … None of that, magic man."

Fuck.

"Oh, while that sounds like fun, I'm afraid we have a few things to get to first."

Let me go and maybe I won't destroy you.

The spirit cackled, holding Emma's delicate hand to its filthy mouth.

"Let's be honest, magic man, you're in no position to make threats." The thing rose inches from the floor. "I can see inside you. I feel your fear, your cowardice, your *doubt.*"

I fear no evil, especially a second-rate apparition with no imagination.

The spirit flew face-to-face with him, floating prone above his body, cold lips centimeters from his own. Emma's brow furrowed, darkness flooded her eyes before its shark-toothed grin reappeared. Lee could smell a familiar odor resonating off the thing …

"I'm going to have fun snuffing the fight from your flesh and bones from the inside out, magic man."

Lee sensed its motives too late. He sucked in the coldest breath. The world fell into a midnight blue before fading to black as the Death Lights entered his body.

✽ ✽ ✽

He was somewhere he recognized … The hulking figure of the Bruton Inn stood before him. It was blackened, signs of the fire Rhiannon had set, yet still there. There were no lights, no voices, no signs of life. The building abandoned, left to rot alone. He'd not returned since leaving it to burn. He'd been too afraid. The demon that called itself Sarah had nearly killed him … Jeff hadn't been as lucky. He'd only known Jeff a few hours that day, fate bringing them together, death separating them eternally, but it was long enough. He'd seen Jeff in his visions from time to time in the years since and Lee was grateful. Though Jeff had pardoned Lee for any miscalculation made that horrible night, Lee held the bitter pill deep within.

A light flipped on in the window in front of him illuminating the pool room. Icy claws scraped his spine. A figure appeared in a housecoat. Lee watched the silk robe slip from her bare shoulders. Emma pulled her dark locks back into a ponytail and began a stretching routine Lee had witnessed many times. The clear pool bubbled. Steam rising to the ceiling and beginning to fog the windows.

"No ..."

Lee reached forward and wiped at the cloud. His arm went through the vision, his balance lost as he tumbled forward and into the pool room. He raised his chin in time to see Emma dive. The clear water was gone, replaced by a pond of crimson thickness.

"Emma!"

She disappeared into the pool of blood with a sickening *slurp*.

He pulled his knees beneath him and climbed to the pool's edge. It hit him. This wasn't happening, yet the demon had him. Fooled and terrified.

Lee stood.

The pool began to drain. The blood swirled until there was nothing left.

A wave of lightheadedness washed over him. Stumbling forward, Lee's right foot found the edge. He fell, raising his hands and shutting his eyelids in preparation of the impact.

There was nothing.

*　*　*

He opened his eyes to candlelight. He was back at Emma's. The mirror across from him burned the blood in his veins.

"No, no, no," he cried.

He gritted his teeth and clenched his fists.

Emma sat on her feet, head bowed, naked and so alive, before the black reflection. He hadn't been there. He'd been on his way back from another case. She'd promised him she would get out of the house if she felt its presence. She'd swore that she could handle things. That he should go help someone that couldn't. She would see him when he returned.

The strategic vision and its deceit were lost in his flood of heartache and regret.

Dropping to his knees, tears filled his eyes. Emma's voice grew from a whisper to a scream. Her refusal morphing into agony. Lee tried to go to her as the black reflection reached out and clutched her by the head. He couldn't move a muscle. He couldn't save her. All of his knowledge, his heritage, his gifts ... Useless.

Emma was pulled into the mirror as the front door opened. Lee heard himself yell her name charging into the room as the glass shattered and exploded everywhere.

Lee's sight blurred behind the tears that refused to fall. He tried again to move. The other him across the room turned.

"You let this happen."

Despite the blue hue shining in the whites of his eyes, the words were what stuck him like a dagger over and over again.

Lee's doppelganger raged toward him, screaming the devil's cry until his ears felt like they would bleed. He saw the blue flame within its mouth burst outward like dragon's breath.

The cold, blue light — the dead light — engulfed him.

❋ ❋ ❋

When Lee opened his eyes, he found himself back in the living room of the Maine farmhouse. The storm continued to swirl outside, rain and wind blowing in from the broken window.

He could move. He rolled onto his side. His head filled with a buzzing, his bones with an ache, and his insides with spoiled milk. On shaky arms, he pushed himself to a sitting position.

The demons could take his body, his voice, but they couldn't conquer his soul unless he let them.

He hurried to the mantle. He re-lit the candle, the source of power.

"Spirits, I ask for your protection and guidance."

The cold laughter echoed through the dark house.

"You have never let me down. I give myself to your strength for my strength. I give myself to your power for my power. I call on your light to chase the dark."

The flame in his hand grew brighter and taller.

Turning to the broken window, he found nothing but a concrete wall.

Trapped.

Lee would have to use whatever he could find in the house to fight the demons, and whatever he could muster from within.

He snatched up two more white candles from the open box and grabbed the bronze plate he'd put his cigarette out upon. Swiping the butt and the ashes clear, he set the plate on the floor and began lighting one candle at a time. He dripped three globs of wax onto the plate to hold each lit candle in place.

"Here is my light. Here is my power. Fear not the darkness. Spirits, light my way."

He stood with the plate and paused. A series of wet *splootch* sounds hit the floor behind him. Lee glanced over his shoulder and saw the ceiling darkening. Black teardrops began to leak from above. Blood ran down the concrete wall as the droplets from the ceiling began coming down like the pouring rain outside. Lee put his arm up, hunching over the plate of candles and hurried from the room.

Blue lights raged above illuminating the top of the staircase. He ignored the lightshow and returned to the study. He needed the book or he stood no chance of defeating the Death Lights.

An old lady's voice, a screechy rasp, filled the room.

"You'll not find what you're looking for, magic man."

Lee ignored its lies and searched the room for something he could use to help him open the roll top desk.

Some old books upon built-in wooden shelving, an ugly ashtray featuring a carved horse's head for a body, the short glass lamp upon a skinny wooden stand, another canvas-covered chair, and beside it, the black trunk. Lee pulled the furniture cover, revealing indeed a brown, suede upholstered chair. He set the plate of candles down on the chair, and reached for the handle on the side of the trunk. It was heavy, but nothing he couldn't lift.

He dragged it to the desk.

"Lee," the creaky old voice became Emma's.

He hesitated for a split second, then with a grunt, hefted the trunk upon his shoulder. Pain shot through his back, his bicep burned, he'd deal with his body later, if he made it out.

"Lee, please don't do this. Be with me."

Twisting his hips, his back muscles screaming in sharp protest, he brought the trunk down with every bit of force he could muster.

The hood of the roll top shattered beneath the trunk's impact.

"Noooooo!" multiple voices screamed at once.

Lee dropped the trunk and reached for the book.

He caught something flying toward him in his peripherals, but didn't have time block the object. The black, horse-faced ashtray slammed into his cheek, temple, and jaw. Staggered, Lee gripped the edge of the desk. The glass lamp fired at him next, shattering as it hit his raised elbow and delivering more pain in its wake. He could feel blood trickling down the side of his face and neck from the ashtray, his elbow would be black and blue, but not broken. The books began hurtling off the shelves in rapid succession. He did his best to protect his head as he turned his back to the flying hard covers and picked the *Nex Susurrus* up from the desk. Cradling the book in his arms and keeping his chin tucked to his chest, he backed across the room toward the plate of candles. He clutched the *Next Susurrus* to his chest with one hand, and reached back for the plate.

The corner of a book caught him in the eye.

"Fuck," he gasped.

His hand found the plate. Picking it up, he hurried toward the door. The chair slammed into his back just before he crossed the threshold, sending him flailing forward into the hallway. Lee hit the floor. The air escaped his lungs as the book drove into him. He managed to keep the plate upright, but two of the candles broke free, rolled to the wall, going out along the way.

The front door opened.

Rain whipped inside from the thrashing storm beyond.

"Leave the book and we'll spare your life."

Able to breathe again, Lee gathered himself. Still protecting the *Nex Susurrus*, he reached for the candles that had broken free. The bronze plate flew down the hall and out into the wild night.

"Last chance, magic man."

Emma walked from the living room.

"Go, Lee. Just go. Leave this place," she said.

Every ache pulsed in his injured body, his heart most of all. He could listen. He could walk away. He didn't owe anybody anything.

"That's right, Lee. Look what it did to me, to us," Emma said.

The house held its breath, silent and poised. Lee dragged his knees up beneath him, his back screaming out for surrender. Hanging his head, Lee closed his eyes.

"Lee ..." Emma cried. *"no, no, no ... Lee, why?"*

Eyes still closed, he sat up with the *Nex Susurrus* in his hands.

He allowed his mind to reach out toward the place he called *home*. The spirit world. His grandmother's voice met him with a single whispered word: *"Rise."*

Emma's voice croaked out, *"Lee, look what you've done."*

He reached across the floor and grabbed one of the candles that had broken off. He used his zippo to relight it. Flame in hand, wielding the one true power he knew, Lee stood and gazed upon the false apparition. The whites of her eyes went black. Arms at her side, he watched in horror as a slit drew across the milky flesh of her throat and seeped the life that had dried up many moons ago. His heartbeat skipped. Taking a deep breath, he moved forward. The apparition reached out for him. Ignoring it, he started up the stairs.

The thing pretending to be Emma howled in agony behind him. The front door slammed shut, opened, then slammed shut again and again. He held the candle out as he reached the second floor, and the Death Lights.

Three balls of light circled before him. The blue luminance grew brighter. Lee stepped to the side, being sure to place a wall at his back rather than the stairs. Kneeling down, holding the candle out ward off the demons, he lay the book on the floor and opened the cover.

"Many have tried, all have failed. As will you," the voices screeched.

"I have faced many evils. I have conquered them all."

"Not all ..."

Lee saw Emma being pulled inside the mirror.

"All that I have faced have succumbed to the light," he said.

"You're a failure, a quitter, a fraud."

Lee ignored the taunts, held the candle above the open pages of the *Nex Susurrus* and called upon those he trusted most. "Find the spark, the flickering light. Show me the path to shut out the night."

The pages began to turn.

"You will never see her again!"

The house shuddered.

The pages stopped. Lee read the words as best he could.

"Libero haec malum. Acccipere eius potestatem."

The spirit lights twirled and shivered in a frenzied whirlwind, flickering like a strobe light all around him. The pages of the book fluttered, threatening to turn or tear, but did neither. The flame from the white candle in his hand grew in intensity.

Lee continued: "Exilium haec daemon."

Hundreds of screams tore through the air around him at once. The blue light engulfed him. His body filled with a numbing coldness. Lee gasped, unable to breath. The warm flame in his hand dimmed.

Tears wept from his closed eyes. Lee tried to grip the candle tighter, but couldn't feel anything. He couldn't tell if his hand was working or not.

Please ... guide me ...

Finding his voice, he repeated the chant ...

"Libero haec malum. Acccipere eius potestatem. Exilium haec daemon."

The demons hissed one last time. *"You have damned her, magi —"*

The screaming blue lights exploded. The force lifted him from his spot on the floor and sent him flying into the wall at his back. The candle spun from his hand and over the railing down to the floor below. As he dropped back to the ground, a swelling *whoosh* sounded from below.

He tried to move, but couldn't feel a thing.

Thoughts of paralysis floated among the jumbled debris swimming in his dizzy mind. Is this where it ended? Was it over?

He could hear the crackling fire below. The canvas coverings, the furniture ... it was all ablaze.

Lee closed his eyes, ready to join his family.

"Rise."

"Grandmother?" he said.

"Rise."

A warmth flooded his body. His fingers twitched, his legs followed.

On his feet, he looked for the *Nex Susurrus*. It was gone. He stumbled to the stairs, bracing himself as he made his way down. The heat from the fire scorched the walls around him. The billowing smoke made it impossible to see and nearly as hard to breath. He held the railing until his foot missed a step and sent him tumbling down the remaining stairs. He heard the deep, thick crack, and felt heat light up his collar bone as he came to stop at the bottom. Each cough made the ache from his broken clavicle worse. Getting to his feet, hunched over, and disoriented, Lee did his best to shut out the pain. The runner leading to the front door, like the wall to its right, was engulfed in flames.

He felt his way to the living room. The bloody concrete wall had vanished with the Death Lights. The broken window his beacon in night. He stumbled to its promised freedom.

✳ ✳ ✳

Lee landed in the wet grass and crumbled to his knees holding his hand over his collarbone. He could feel the bone jutting up just beneath the tented shirt. His stomach roiled. After all he'd just been through he didn't think anything could trigger his body into shock. The rain soaked him to the bone as he made his way to his car and climbed in. Exhausted, beaten down but not out, he reached for the fresh pack of cigarettes in the center console, gingerly opened the pack and drew out a cigarette with his teeth.

As he lit up and watched the farmhouse burning from the inside out, he was swallowed by an overwhelming sense of déjà vu. He should have known better than to come back to Maine. There was nothing out here but rednecks, shitty weather, and fucking demons. He sent a prayer that the conflagration took the Death Lights and the *Nex Susurrus* with it.

He thought of Emma. He had failed her, but that would neither define nor ruin him. He *needed* this. Needed to snuff out any dark spirits he could. His body would heal. Then, he would engage any malevolent force he could find. *For her.*

His heritage told him one thing: though there will always be light … evil never dies.

*　*　*

Miles away, in the Augusta office of Hidden Realty, Carl Owens obeyed the black reflection in the bathroom mirror. His chin quivered, tears rolled down his chubby red cheeks, his hand trembled as it guided the cold, hard steel of the handgun to his temple, and pulled the trigger.

RARE BIRDS

Katherine Silva

They're supposed to be quite beautiful, you know. Plumage as colorful as a September sky, red throats, and black breasts shimmering like oil. You can only ever see them this far north, and only this early in the season, when the winter is crisp, bitter, and ready to bite down. You can look for them, and look for them, but they will always find you.

I tipped my thermos back and swallowed the luke-warm remnants of my coffee. Grounds get stuck in my teeth. I crunched on them and I stared at the thicket ahead. Bare maple trees scar the white landscape, creaking and groaning in the wind.

This is the place, the only location in the whole US where one can catch a glimpse of the Red Wailer, in the northern-most woods of Maine, far from any tourist-visited campgrounds, where the names of the towns all have a flavor of Québécois, and the residents are usually spread far and wide across the dark, snow-laden forests.

It's an ornithologist's dream to glimpse a Red Wailer, that one bird too elusive to be caught on film. It's so rare, there isn't even an estimation on its population numbers. My mind spins with glee at the thought of finally seeing one for myself. I've followed the chatter online, investigating various bird-watching forums for some inkling that this marvelous creature is still alive. Many people think the Red Wailer was endangered when it was first acknowledged in the 20's by Maine naturalist Frank Thibodeau. Now, being thirty years from its last sighting, many fear it's gone completely extinct.

It was last glimpsed in the 80's by two men on a weekend hunting trip, Dallas Marquand and Phil Seaver. The Red Wailer is purportedly nocturnal and because both Marquand and Seaver were too drunk to confirm exactly what the specimen looked like, there's still no clear picture of what type of bird the Red Wailer is. Is it a passerine as small as a nuthatch or as big as a blue jay? A galliforme like a turkey? Or perhaps it's more like an owl? Is it capable of flight or does it hop, walk, or flutter at ground level? Is its beak for probing, tearing at flesh, or for coniferous seed-eating?

Despite the hunters not being the least bit interested in birds, even they were impacted by the sighting; stunned by its splendor, no doubt, that they felt compelled to rave about it to anyone who would hear them. Seaver became alienated from most of his family just because he wouldn't stop talking about it, and Marquand? Last I heard, he was running some kind of bird-watchers anonymous club with two other guys. A hobby turned into the most diabolical of addictions. Did they have meetings and sponsors? Exactly how did one become five years sober from "bird-watching?"

Most professional ornithologists disregarded the hunters' claims anyhow, because among other things that same night, Marquand and Seaver also thought they'd had a conversation with Abraham Lincoln and Bono about the complexities of fruitcake.

Teeth chattering, I cupped my hands together in front of my mouth and blew hot air into them. Finding this bird was worth the numbness, the sore feet, and my aching shoulders from hefting my twenty-pound pack for hours on end. I swung it off for a moment, flexed my arms wide, and gazed miserably at the thin grungy canvas that held it all together. I shouldn't have brought it. One day, the straps would cut right down to my bones, unless the whole thing burst open like a rotten tomato first. But, if I returned home with a photo of a Red Wailer, I wouldn't have to worry about money for a while. Nat Geo would probably drop a hefty sum for that photo, at least a few thousand. Hell, maybe they would ask for more bird profiles. I had dozens. I could give them almost anything they wanted as long as it was from Maine.

Renewed by this thought, I swung the pack back on and tightened the hip belt, hoping to take some of the pressure from the straps off my shoulders. Checking to ensure that my camera's batteries hadn't died, I stepped into the grass, down the embankment and toward the tree line of the forest.

The camera was my father's, a Pentax Spotmatic 35 mm. He had an eye for a perfectly framed shot. His photos hang around my apartment, matted, framed, signed. Each one is crisp, bright and pulls you in. I knew my shots were nothing special, certainly nothing like his. I hoped whatever magic he'd worked to take those photos had rubbed off and would give me a chance to take the one shot I needed of the Wailer.

Where the woods behind my office felt welcoming and familiar, these trees inspired a different kind of response, an impression I sometimes caught a hint of when gazing at Dad's old photographs: reverence. They exuded an inkling of power that had permanence and was perhaps wisely left alone. The grey sky dimmed as I ventured further inside where the pines grew taller, and more claustrophobic.

I spent the afternoon following my ancient map of the area, one that hadn't been updated in the last decade. Nothing had changed despite that. The trees were older, their branches more gnarled and blackened. The river that ran from the northwest was still there, though it was shallow. It had been a dry summer. I was surprised the entire thing hadn't frozen over yet. Wherever there wasn't snow, a thick bed of dried leaves coated the earth.

After the river, the greenery ceased. Bare pine trees stretched up from the earth, like spines silhouetted against the silver sky. I couldn't figure out why this sudden and inexplicable change had occurred. There were no signs of a fire, or any other kind of environmental trauma. I continued forward into the seemingly black and white portion, my eyes and ears open. Soon, I ventured across a glade, a small clearing in the midst of the desolate pines. A deer recoiled across the clearing from me and dashed into the thicket, crunching snow and breaking twigs in its escape.

The unusual empty space was where those two hunters had camped nearly thirty years ago, and it was where they had witnessed the Red

Wailer. If I was ever going to come across this bird, this was the place.

Over the next few hours, I walked the perimeter of five miles-square around the glade, my camera out and eyes searching. I caught a cardinal about ten paces away, perched on the spindly branch of a barberry bush, pecking at the crimson berries there. Squirrels chattered in the canopy up above. As I made my way around, I marked each tree with a stick of chalk, lines for the border trees, x's for the corners. It was a trick my father had used, in the off chance that he found himself away from camp without his map.

Darkness fell and I returned to the glade. The clearing was in a section between two hills which made it naturally protected from harsh gusts and a good place to set up my camp for the evening. The ultralight polyester of the tent canopy flapped as I finished securing the stakes into the snow. I'd torn a section of it on my last trip to Moosehead Lake when a branch came down. Thankfully, I was out shooting when it happened, but a jagged L-shaped hole had to be Frankenstein-stitched back together with fishing line and then sealed with duct tape. The only man in town who repaired tents wouldn't do it because he hated lawyers. I told him I wasn't one. It hadn't mattered.

By the time the sky burned down to a smoldering orange, I was boiling water in my camp stove. Dehydrated beef stroganoff: nothing but chewy noodles and watery sauce but still infinitely better than the "Alaskan Salmon" I'd eaten the night before. My stomach revolved on cue with the thought and I almost thought I tasted it.

Crows cawed in the distance. I sighed. There was probably a roost nearby, which meant I might not see the Red Wailer that night. Despite not knowing much about the bird, I had it in my mind that it was a dainty little thing, pretty and perfect, about the size of a chickadee. The kind of bird that if you blinked, you would miss altogether. It had to be for no one to have seen it in almost thirty years. Either that or it was dead. If I didn't come across it that night, I'd know for sure.

The conditions were similar to the ones the hunters had encountered. It was late December. I was in the same location as they'd been and the temperatures were dipping into the single digits. Most birds would seek shelter in those conditions, even the crows. But not the Red Wailer.

So, I settled down for the evening in my tent, with a battery-powered space heater and a whole mug of freshly made coffee to keep me awake through the long night. I pushed far into the downy sleeping bag, zipped it up around me, dimmed the light on my Coleman lantern and waited, waited so patiently that I thought the sound of my breathing was the loudest thing out there in those woods. I waited until the sky was dowsed in a blackness so pure that not even the stars could cut through it. I waited for the Wailer.

*　*　*

I didn't do this for a living. God, how I wished I did. Being bound to an office chair, eyes glued to a computer screen was about as deadening to the mind as reruns of the Brady Bunch Hour. (I was subjected to them in my youth by Great Aunt Mallory. She had an affinity for Florence Henderson, sequins, and horrible one-liners). My menial tasks at Whitiker, Diamond, and Associates included fielding phone calls, retrieving coffee for the higher ups, and making hundreds of copies that were destined for the paper shredder in a week's time.

The printers stood in the north-east corner of the second story and faced a large expanse of trees on the edge of our township. One could get an almost perfect panoramic view from there. I say "almost" because a small patch of the wall separates the corner windows. I'd seen hawks and falcons sweeping through the autumn sky after swallows, buzzards circling over the small graveyard next to Alan's General Store, and crows flying in like ominous harbingers from the sunset.

I used to take my lunch break out in the field that separated the building from those trees. Someone had cleared a trail there years ago, and despite it being a little overgrown and sometimes blocked by downed limbs, it was a welcome escape from my lackluster occupation. A fallen, moss-covered oak tree became my coveted seat amongst nature. I've observed the birds from there each and every day for three years. I'd spend whole days there on my weekends, ogling through my binoculars, writing down each different species I saw and snapping the best shots I could manage. It was my heaven inside of the doldrums of my existence.

Until someone noticed, that is. Why couldn't they just let it be? It's not like I lean over their shoulders reading their text messages or push through their mail to see what they've been sent. Why did it matter what I do on my lunch break? But Betty Elraine, nosiest conniving demon that she was, got it into her head that I must be doing something sinister out in those woods. She followed me, kept her distance of course, because if I'd seen her … But I didn't see her. It was all over the office the next day. Betty had yapped to everyone that I wanted to be Richard Attenborough. I told her she meant David, but that only seemed to confirm my stardom as a "bird-gawping pansy." I'd tried to defend myself. "Ornithology is a highly intelligent hobby and profession," I'd declared. It was even a competitive event on certain days of the year. Jimmy Carter, Paul McCartney, and Mick Jagger were all bird-watchers. Once a rousing rendition of "Happiness is a Warm Gull" set in, I knew it was pointless to continue. Over the week, I was subjected to various birdified versions of Beatles classics including "All You Need is Dove" and "Yellow Submar-eagle" (that one was a stretch, even for Betty).

I didn't enjoy going out anymore, not when I knew I was in for 60's subjection the moment I returned. My escape was ruined. It would never be the same unless I got out of there. But the only way I knew how to evolve from a grossly-misunderstood copy/print man was if I went in the direction of my only other skill; photography. And birds were my passion.

Though the birds intrigued me, to the average layman, a blackbird was a black bird. A crow was also a black bird. They were basically the same thing to people like Betty. Unless I got a shot of a bald eagle conveniently perched in front of a billowing American flag, or I went vacationing in some tropical paradise to capture parakeets, bee-eaters, and macaws, I wasn't going to make much money from these shots. I couldn't afford to jet off to the Amazon any time soon, nor could I afford to get a better camera. Short of hitchhiking my way out of town in the mail truck, I was stuck in a cold and obscure township with no name, just a number. Even my car was out of commission and the repair shop was so backed up with work that I probably wouldn't see it working for close to a year. I had to find something within my grasp. I had to make the shot come to me.

That was where my search began. It was where I discovered the whisperings of the Red Wailer, the perfect and convenient ghost in the birding world. I was going to be the one that found it. I was finally going to get the hell out of that place.

＊　＊　＊

One A.M. I tipped the thermos to pour myself another cup of coffee. No sign of anything yet. The fire had burned down about an hour ago, but the stench of smoke was still strong. It was stupid to have lit it in the first place. My cold aching limbs had won out over my rationality though. My fingers and toes felt raw and even my own body heat in the sleeping bag wasn't enough to stifle my shivering; if that was what I was shivering about. As much as I feared losing my fingers due to frostbite, blowing the whole trip due to some stupid oversight was my biggest concern. I was ready to face physical pain if it meant finally getting somewhere away from Whitiker, Diamond and Associates. After all, frostbite could add to the adventure, tell a more exciting story. I was the Shackleton of birders as far as I was concerned.

But had I already screwed everything up? If I was upwind of this bird, which I hoped to God I was, it meant that the fire might not have perturbed it; it might still not know that I'm here. If *it's* here, that is.

There.

I heard something just now. It sounded like a crunch of snow. Not a prolonged sound, very short, almost too short. Maybe some snow had just fallen from the canopy.

No. It was there again. Slower, the crunching almost squealed as it passed slowly through the snow. I tried to keep as still as possible. Too much rustling around might scare whatever it was off. There was every likelihood this was that same deer from earlier. I flashed a glance toward the far end of the tent, searching for a silhouette. Not yet. Still too far away.

Tunneling my hand up from the abyss of my sleeping bag, I blindly reached into my pack until my fingers touched one of the smooth lenses on my binoculars. I brought them up to my eyes and swept them slowly along the snowy glade, searching for some origin to the sound.

And again. It was on my far right. I settled the binoculars on a particularly wiry tree with few limbs and waited. Was that a hazy shape in the darkness there? Was it just a strange shadow being cast from … well … no. It couldn't be that. There was no moon in the sky. It had to be a shape.

Crunch.

But if that was a shape, it was bigger than a petite chickadee-sized bird.

Crunch.

The weight in the step was heavier, too. Was it a bear? My entire body tensed and I almost lost my grip on the binoculars. I had been so feverishly convinced that I would see the bird and only the bird that I hadn't stopped to think about the possibility that I'd encounter something else out here.

Crunch.

The misty shape seemed to gather together as if it were formed by particles right then and there. As it did, I became aware of not just the crunch in footsteps but also a very tell-tale shuffle, as though someone was dragging a rug behind them through the snow.

Crunch.

Shhhhh.

It had a shape now, this mystery beast that had ruined my chance at ever catching the Red Wailer on film. It was big. The thing stood about where I'd stand if I had the cojones to be intimidating with anyone. I didn't though and shortly after making that observation, I took it back. This thing was much, much bigger than me. But it didn't move like a bear. Bears had a tell-tale shuffle, a lumber where they swung from side to side, unavoidable when you are a two-hundred and forty-pound fuzz-ball that roars and can't properly spin around with all that junk in its trunk (a phrase I feel perturbed about ever using again in the foreseeable future, as it immediately reminds me of Betty).

Crunch.

Shah.

Beads of sweat simultaneously formed and froze on my forehead. I tried turning the gears in my head, trying to come up with an escape to the ridiculous situation. This could still be an adventure piece, if I changed the aim of the story. Instead of finding the elusive Red Wailer, I could be attacked by a bear, gravely wounded, all for the sake of biological study. It might not get me a Nat Geo story but it would give me a place to start. The media liked all stories that reeked of animals attacking humans. I wouldn't just be a photographer; I'd be a photographer *and* a victim all in one.

Crunch.

Screeeeeeeeee—

God, what is that? What in the holy ...

But I know what it is. The knowledge of it permeates me, fills me full of red absolute terror. My mind denies it. There isn't a chance.

It.

Can't.

Be.

By now, every fiber of me was trembling. I didn't feel the cold anymore, I couldn't focus on it. The thing standing at the edge of the clearing had stopped moving for now, and my binoculars could take in its entirety.

Hulking was a strange descriptor, but the only one I could think of at the moment to describe its frame. A wreath of quills encircled its craned neck, fluffed for warmth and bursting with a hint of red. They merged into darker plumes along its hind quarters and down the large dreary wings that dragged at its sides. Nipping at the first branch on the tree beside it told me its height; at least eight feet. I couldn't reach that branch even if I jumped.

The beak curved around like a smooth dull meat hook and the eyes, though rather birdlike in their empty blackness, had the profound effect of making it difficult for me to swallow. They were deep gorges; there was no beauty in them at all. At the very ends of its three-toed feet, sickle sharp talons scratched at the snow.

I reverted to a child then. In my head, I was a boy who could crawl under the covers and pretend it was all a bad dream. The monsters were not real. When I woke up, it would be morning. Light would pierce the memory of this nightmare. All would be well.

Except it wouldn't be, because I couldn't make myself move. Instead I remained frozen, the binoculars glued to my face, forcing myself to swallow back any gasps of fright. I watched the featherless head turn, and the eyes rotate in their sockets until they fixed on mine.

The beak opened, it tilted its head back, and —

Screeeeee!

All my natural instincts buckled. I practically threw the binoculars from my hands. I tried to wriggle out of the sleeping bag but I'd entrenched myself inside it too far — a worm dangling like bait. I did the only thing I could. I reached up, pulled the zipper for the tent all the way down, the sound ear-piercingly loud in the night.

The screeching stopped.

I swallowed and felt around in my bag as quietly as I could. I had a hatchet. I'd gathered kindling for the fire with it though it was as dull as Betty's skull. It was all I had.

Crunch.

Shhhhh.

Crunch.

It was coming toward me.

A stench assaulted me. I envisioned viscous crimson rolling down its beak, the stripped rotten flesh of previous kills caught in its jaws, feathers bathed in gore. My beef stroganoff was jumping hurdles in my stomach.

Despite there being no light, I thought I could see the creature's outline through the thin material, accentuated by the taped stitches of my tent flap. I closed my eyes and tightened my fists and prayed to and swore at whatever God might be listing.

A flare of light exploded inside the tent.

The snow outside seemed to burst up all around me. That abominable scream tore across the sky and I squeezed my camera more. More flashes of light popped through my closed lids. The logs in the fireplace scattered and hit the outside of the tent in the commotion. Before I knew what I was doing, I was pressing the button over and over, the light like a never-ending god-sent strobe.

In a flurry of feather and squawking and screeching, the footfalls dissipated in the snow. The pungent aroma had soon vanished.

I didn't stop. I couldn't stop. My finger was like a broken trigger, firing the flash until the muscle was so sore I couldn't imagine ever using it again. I lay cowered in a ball in my tent until daybreak and only then was my decision to leave as swift as it had been for me to come.

I left the tent. I left my ratty old pack. I left my sleeping bag and the strewn remnants of the campfire, blackened sticks tossed about the pink-stained snow.

I took the camera and the axe.

＊　＊　＊

Naturalist Frank Thibodeau was a hermit, who worked and lived out of a shack outside of a camp in the northern woods of Maine. He drank, he gambled away whatever fortune he had … he isolated himself. He spent long hours out here reconnecting with who he'd once been but also identifying with everything that he encountered. From the moose, to the bears, coyotes, and badgers, the journal he kept had been filled with comparisons. But Thibodeau's notes on the Red Wailer were by far the most cryptic.

No, besides color, the only thing Thibodeau had remarked upon was its call. It didn't sing like a songbird nor did it mimic the sounds of other birds to communicate. It wailed, hence the name, an eerie wild cry that Thibodeau thought at first to be an animal in distress, some poor creature caught in a trap or about to be eaten.

As though this was merely a detriment to its overall splendor, Thibodeau had included the following passage: "Their plumage is as colorful as a September sky. Their throats are red, and their black breasts shimmer like oil." Poetry. He makes it seem like its living poetry.

That fucking liar.

IN THE WOODS

Dale T. Phillips

In the tiny convenience store, Carson scanned the off-kilter shelves, but the stocked items seemed to have no particular arrangement. Cans of stew were stacked next to batteries, and potato chips sat by the cleaning products.

"He'p ya find somethin'?" The storekeeper's voice came from the front.

Carson stood up. "Do you have any sriracha?"

The man frowned. "Ah, nope, nothin' like that."

"Oh." These little country places had their charm, but only carried the basics. There was a lot more that Carson wanted, but this would have to do. He went to the counter.

The storekeeper adjusted his glasses. "Big supermarket down in Bangor prolly have some."

"Yeah, thank you." *Damn.* That would take several hours, round trip. Well, he should go anyway, as the only thing they had in the pro-

176

duce section here was tiny cans of fruit cocktail.

"Anythin' else I can he'p ya with?"

"No thanks."

The storekeeper punched in numbers on the register. "Call me Bert. You took that Lapointe place up on Noseeum Road, didn't ya?"

"Yes, I did. By the way, I was curious. What's that road name mean? Some Native American name? I heard you've got some of those folks around still."

The storekeeper chuckled. "The name's from some damn little bugs we get up this way. We call 'em *no-see-ums* because they'll bite ya, and you won't even see that they're there."

"Ah. That explains it. Well, I got bit plenty yesterday when I was moving in."

"That was the skeeters. You'll want some Woodsman fly dope." The storekeeper held up a small, flat plastic bottle.

"Bug repellant?"

The storekeeper smiled. "Best kind. Smells like shit, but works great."

Carson unscrewed the cap and took a whiff. "Holy cow, you're right."

"Ayuh. Needs to be strong. They can bite mighty fierce this time 'a year."

Carson laughed. "Well, nobody's going to smell me anyway. Sure, I'll take some. Oh, and now that you mention it, do you have any duct tape? I can tape over the holes in the screens until I get them fixed. That should keep some out."

"That row behind you, bottom shelf."

Carson turned and saw the roll of tape and reached down to take one. When he straightened up, a man was standing by the door a few feet away, scowling at him. He wore a dirty flannel shirt that was unbuttoned, showing an even dirtier T-shirt. The blue jeans and work boots were worn, and the bill cap had a John Deere logo. His unshaven face was complete with a drooping mustache, and shark-like black eyes glared at Carson.

"Doobie," said the storekeeper. "How ya doin'? This here fella took the Lapointe cabin, up near you."

"I know that," the man said. Carson noticed the man had a missing canine tooth.

"So, you're neighbors. Doobie Harlow, say hello to … what's your name, young fella?"

"Carson Schmidt," Carson said, extending his hand.

Harlow ignored the hand. "Schmidt? That's a kraut name."

Carson's eyes narrowed. "German origin, yes, but we've been here for generations. Is that a problem?"

"My granddaddy fought the krauts. Weren't never right in the head when he got back."

Probably wasn't to begin with, judging by you, thought Carson. "My grandfather fought, too, in Patton's Third. He got a Bronze Star." *Suck on that, you redneck asshole.*

"That make you somethin' special?"

Carson sighed. "Nope." He turned back to the register.

"Don't you turn your back on me." The violence in the smaller man's voice took Carson by surprise. "I ain't scared of you."

"No one said you were supposed to be." His voice came out steady, but Carson was afraid. This man seemed genuinely psychotic.

"You just keep the fuck out of my way," the man snarled and stalked off, slamming the front door of the market behind him.

Carson shook his head. "Jesus, is he the town nutter, or what?"

"Ah, Doobie's just a little high strung."

"That what they're calling it these days?"

"You don't want to get on his bad side."

"He's got another side?"

Bert finished his tally. "That'll be eighteen-fifty."

Carson handed him a twenty and took the change. "That diner I saw on the way in any good?"

"Not too shabby. Stay away from the meatloaf, though. You never know what they ran over recently."

Carson looked at him to see if he was joking, but couldn't tell, as Bert kept a straight face. He decided the storekeeper was having some fun with him.

Bert placed the items in a paper sack. "So, what brings you up this way?"

"I wanted a place to write."

"Write?"

"Yes. I'm working on a novel." Carson couldn't help but feel self-conscious saying it.

"Is that so?" Bert's lower lip pushed out a little, with the corners down, as if he was impressed. "What's it about?"

The dreaded question. "About a man trying to find his place in the world."

"And you came all the way up here to do that."

"Well, no distractions," said Carson smiling. *No Internet access, hell, not even a cellphone signal up where I am.*

"Ayuh, gets pretty quiet, you're right about that. Say, you know how to run that gennie?"

"The what?"

"Gennie. The generator. They got one out in the garage. Power goes out a lot, so ya gotta know how to start 'er up."

"No, I have no idea."

"Okay, I'll send Ronnie out this afternoon. He'll show you how."

"That would be great, thank you."

"Been a real pleasure making your acquaintance, Mr. Schmidt."

"Likewise, Bert." Carson put out his hand. This time, the gesture was accepted. "But call me Carson."

"Like Kit Carson."

"Just like that," Carson said. He picked up his bag and left. *Well, so far, the townsfolk are only fifty percent assholes. Way better than New York.* He smiled.

✻ ✻ ✻

The diner looked like some throwback joint from a retro movie. Sitting in a booth, Carson gazed around in wonder. It was like a place stuck in amber, fifty years in the past, even to the Moxie ad. They had the requisite old-time chrome jukebox selector on the wall, five plays for a dollar. Carson found some quarters in his pocket and slid them in, and started selecting songs he hadn't heard in years. The voice of Bobby Darin came through the speakers, singing of Mack the Knife. Carson smiled and scanned the plastic menu.

A middle-aged woman appeared next to the booth, and set down a glass of water. "Hey there," she said. "What can I get you, hon?"

Carson looked up. Swear to God, she had a bit of a beehive hair-do going, and her name tag said *Mabel*. Perfect. She wasn't wearing a starched polyester uniform, at least, but a pair of jeans and an untucked shirt.

"What's good?"

"Well, the meatloaf's fresh."

Carson pursed his lips, thinking of Bert's admonition. "Think I'll try the chicken salad sandwich. On whole wheat. And an iced tea."

"Comin' right up."

The last notes of Johnny Cash had just ended when she brought the sandwich and ice tea over. "Here ya go."

"Thank you."

"Say, you the fella took the old Lapointe place?"

"News travels fast here."

"Well, ain't like there's much else to do, ya know? I'll let you eat your sandwich now."

The sandwich might have been from fifty years in the past as well, Carson thought. Even the chips were stale. *Ah well, didn't move up here for the cuisine.*

A big-bellied man was now standing next to the booth. Carson looked up. "Hello?"

"Hey there. I'm Marty, but everybody calls me Chief. I'm what passes for law in these parts. Just wanted to say welcome to town."

He stuck out a hand, and Carson shook it. "Carson Schmidt."

The man's eyebrows knitted together. "You a German fella?"

"As American as apple pie," said Carson. He doubted this guy would know that apple pie was actually a Bavarian dish, but it sounded good.

"Well, that's all right then. You're in the old Lapointe place, right?"

"As everyone seems to know."

"Quiet up there."

"That's what I was hoping."

The man nodded. There was a bit of uncomfortable silence. "Well, my office is right across the street. You need anything, just drop in."

"I will, thanks," said Carson. "Nice to meet you."

* * *

Inside the cabin, Carson stared at his laptop, reading over the paragraph he'd just typed when the sound of a truck in the driveway distracted him.

He stepped outside to see a tall, cadaverous man with a bad comb-over alight from a pickup.

"I'm Ronnie," the man said. "Bert said you needed a lesson."

"I appreciate your coming out. I've never run a generator before."

They found the generator in the back of the garage. The tall man squatted to look the machine over, put his hands on it in various places, and nodded. "They left her in pretty good shape. It's all hooked up. When you need it, just start her up, and she'll run."

"Okay. How do I do that?"

"Give a pull on that handle of the starter cord there. Just like on a skidoo."

"A what?"

The man looked at him. "Ain't you ever rode a snowmobile?"

"Can't say that I have."

"Hmph. Okay, just like a lawnmower, then." Seeing Carson's look, he rolled his eyes. "Don't tell me you never started a lawnmower? Jesus, where you from anyway?"

"New York City. We don't have lawns."

"You ain't telling me you're a Yankees fan, are ya?"

"No, I don't follow baseball."

The man rolled his eyes again. "Well, better that than loving the Yankees. Then we'd have to shoot ya for sure."

Carson hoped the man was joking, but like Bert, his face was so deadpan Carson wasn't really sure.

"How do I shut it off?"

"That button there. And you'll need gas to run it." The man opened a lid and pointed. "Goes in there. Looks like you need some. Got any around?"

"Uh, I don't know." Carson saw a red can with a yellow spout and brought it over. "This is gas, right?"

The man gave him a look, but unscrewed the top and sniffed. "Yup." He filled it and replaced the cap. "It'll run the lights and fridge."

Carson stepped back and bumped into a chain hanging from the rafter. "What's this?"

Ronnie laughed. "For your deer."

"What?"

"When you shoot your deer in the Fall. You dress it out, get it back here, and hang it before you carve it up."

"They hang dead animals in the garage?" Carson was repulsed.

The tall man shrugged. "That's how people eat through the winter here."

Carson shivered. He had never known a world like this.

❋ ❋ ❋

Carson tried to get back to the writing after the tall man had gone, but it was no use. This world was too new, too strange, and it distracted him. A mosquito whined in his ear, and he swatted at the intruder. He took out the duct tape and patched the holes in the screens. Supper was from a can of stew that he poured into a pot and heated on the stove. Without a television or radio playing, the place was deathly quiet, and if he wasn't writing, there was nothing to do. Maybe coming here had been a mistake, but he'd have to give it time. The utter boredom would force him to write eventually, he told himself. With nothing else to do, he went to bed a little after eight o'clock.

* * *

Carson awoke before dawn. He decided to make the drive down to Bangor and get some supplies, maybe find an Internet café and check his email. He could be down there, have some breakfast, be back before lunch, and still get a full day of writing in.

With headlights on, Carson threaded his way down to the blacktop. A blur of motion from the side of the road startled him, and his stomach lurched at the thump of something smacking into the side of the vehicle. He put the car in park, and got out to see what he had hit.

A doe was lying on its side, panting. Carson knelt to inspect the injured creature, and it thrashed, gashing Carson's arm with a sharp hoof, tearing the shirt and the skin beneath. "Easy now, easy," he said, ignoring the pain to himself. He felt terrible, responsible for hurting this beautiful animal. The creature looked wild but fragile, the eyes showing panic. Carson was behind it now, away from the slash of a hoof, and he stroked the deer's side and murmured soft words.

He thought of the chain in the garage, and shuddered. A plan flashed in his mind, and he scooped up the doe in his arms and carried it to the car. It now lay docile, possibly in shock. Carson opened the back of the vehicle and with some difficulty, got the animal inside.

Carson drove to town and parked. The diner was lit, as was the Chief's office. Carson knocked and walked in. The Chief looked up from his paper, a cup of coffee and a doughnut before him. "Well now, you're an early bird. What brings you out?"

"I hit a deer with my car. Is there a vet in town?"

"A vet? For a *deer*? Sounds like you need someone to put it down and dress it out."

Carson pursed his lips. "No, I want a vet. It's just hurt a little."

The Chief just shook his head. "No one around here is gonna patch up a deer." He laughed, and a piece of doughnut sprayed out.

Carson glared at him for a moment and turned to go.

Closer to Bangor, he finally got a cell tower signal, and searched the Internet for an area veterinarian. Then he brought up a map application, and followed the directions. The office was locked, so he waited, checking on the now unconscious doe.

Sometime later, a woman showed up and unlocked the front door. Carson got out of the car and scurried over before she could go inside.

"Excuse me, are you the vet?"

She looked around warily. "Yes."

"I hit a deer with my car. Can you take a look at her, please?"

A few minutes later, Carson had been assured that the doe had not suffered any permanent damage, and should be returned near where Carson had found it. He also got his own wound bandaged, and the vet said he had been lucky, as he could have been seriously injured. Relieved, he drove back north with the sedated doe. He pulled off the blacktop and gently picked up the sleeping deer and placed it in a small clearing. It stirred and lifted its head to look at him before he backed away.

Later that day, while trying to write, the roaring noise of a chainsaw started up, and was a constant irritation. Try as he might, Carson couldn't concentrate. He took out the binoculars he had brought and walked through the woods toward the sound. At a break in the trees, he used the binoculars to scan the terrain, and saw the cabin on a ridge not far away. There was the little shit he had encountered in the store, sawing away on a pile of wood. What was his name? Doobie. *Who in hell names their kid Doobie?* The man had his shirt off, his skinny frame covered in sweat, John Deere cap on backwards. Carson decided it would be a terrible and likely dangerous idea to go over and ask him to stop. Carson would just have to find something else to do.

But the noise continued until about four o'clock that afternoon, and at that point, Carson gave up and decided he couldn't get any work done today. He mixed himself a gin-and-tonic and took it out on the back deck to look at the scenery. He brooded on the memory of the deer, and how the constant noise later kept him from writing. He'd thought to have peace and quiet. The forest was impenetrable, a dark mystery filled with impossible things. He sipped his drink, almost in a trance.

When the long shadows were giving way to dusk, he was on his third drink, still staring out at the trees. A flash of movement caught his eye, and he saw the deer. *Was it the same one?*

Carson got his binoculars and focused in. It certainly looked like the one he had hit and helped. Yes, there was a mark he had seen. The deer was looking at him. Not knowing what else to do, Carson waved. The deer seemed to nod at him, or maybe it was just his imagination. As the last of the sun left the sky, the deer moved off.

*　*　*

Next morning, Carson arose early once more and got in his car to head back down to Bangor. This time there was no incident, and he arrived in the city, found a supermarket, and stocked up on a variety of supplies. He located a coffee shop with a Wi-Fi signal, and checked his email on his laptop. It made him feel connected with the world again.

But the world fell away once more as he drove back up north, like going back in time, the houses and cars becoming sparser and older. Maybe he should be writing with a quill pen and ink. At the cabin, he unloaded his groceries, listening for the sound of the chainsaw, but all he could hear was the singing of the birds.

With the groceries put away, Carson sat and opened his laptop, but the white screen remained empty and mocked him. He typed a sentence, then deleted it. That was the thing about writing on a computer, you could wipe out everything and feel you had done nothing. It wasn't the same as having a pile of crumpled-up sheets of paper to mark the effort.

After a few more minutes, Carson decided to make lunch. Then he'd get back to work, he assured himself. He ate, washing it down with a beer, and felt drowsy afterward. His sleep patterns were all messed up, with the early to bed and rise routine, for in the city he'd been a night owl. So, he stretched out on the bed, just to close his eyes for a minute, he said to himself.

Carson awoke to a fading light and the groggy aftermath of a long nap. He shook his head, unable to believe he'd slept away the entire afternoon. The lunch dishes were still unwashed, and he set to cleaning them while he came back to his senses.

He went to his computer, but saw that he'd left it on without the recharger plugged in, and the battery had drained. Cursing, he connected it to the recharger and realized he'd have to wait for it to regain enough power.

Carson made a drink and took it out to the back deck and sat. He was disappointed to not have got any work done yet, but there was still plenty of time, he told himself. With nothing else to do up here, he'd just have to write to stay sane.

As the sun set, he saw the doe again, edging tentatively from the woods at the back of the property. He raised his drink in a salute. The doe dipped her head and disappeared.

Later, he heard someone on his porch. He opened the door and saw a young Native American woman, dressed in jeans and a flannel shirt. She was barefoot.

"Can I help you?"

She looked past him. "I saw your light."

He was wondering what that meant, when she stepped inside with a quick, fluid motion. Bemused, he closed the door behind her. "Come on in, then."

She looked around as if checking for predators, and he thought he saw her ears twitch. She studied him. He was reminded of the way the deer had looked at him from the edge of the forest.

Her voice was soft. "What are you doing here?"

He laughed. "I see you don't beat around the bush. I'm a writer. I came up here to write."

"Will you be here long?"

He shrugged. "As long as it takes."

She looked around again. "Do you have salt?"

He blinked at the odd request. "Uh, sure." He found the salt shaker and handed it to her. She unscrewed the top, poured some into her hand, and licked it until it was gone. She smiled, and Carson was bewildered. "Say, what's your name?"

She spoke, and he tried to repeat what she had said. "Waweshka?"

She shook her head and tried again, but that was as close as he could get. "I'm Carson."

She looked at the bandage on his arm. "You're hurt."

"Oh, it's not bad. I hit a deer with my car, and it cut me when I tried to help it. It turned out it wasn't badly injured, and I released it."

She came closer and touched the bandage. "You are different. You are a good man."

She put her arms around his neck and kissed him. From outside came a crack of thunder, and suddenly she was gone. Carson shook his head, wondering if he had dreamed her.

Rain pounded the roof of the little cabin, and Carson was concerned for the barefoot woman out in the storm, as he had seen no car, and wondered where she had come from. He went to bed, but his sleep was troubled by visions of a dark-eyed maid of the forest.

Carson was ripped from his dreams by booming thunder. He stumbled in the complete absence of light, realizing the power had gone out. He found the flashlight by the bed, dressed, and went to the garage, as flashes of lightning split the night sky. He put the flashlight on a shelf and filled the generator with gas, and then tried yanking the cord to start it. It barely moved. He braced a foot and used both hands, giving a hard pull. It sputtered, an encouraging sound. He pulled harder, and it coughed louder. Several more tries, and the little engine finally putted to life. Carson smiled with a sense of accomplishment, picked up the flashlight, and went back to the cabin. Now he was wide awake as the thunder crashed outside, and he lay on the bunk, thinking about the woman for a long time before sleep returned.

The next morning, the storm had cleared and the power was back on. Carson finished his breakfast and sat down to the laptop, ready to work. He had typed just one paragraph when the sound of the roaring chainsaw flooded into his senses. Damn the man. Carson couldn't work with that racket. He took a sweater and went for a walk, noting the damage from the storm of the night before.

Carson walked for a long time before he realized he was lost. He'd followed a path which had simply ended, and when he turned back, the path split into two. He took the right-hand fork, but wasn't sure if this was the way back. Bred in the city, he could not distinguish the trees and undergrowth.

An hour later, a sweating and desperate Carson gave up and sat with his back to a tree. He was utterly lost, and couldn't even hear the sound of the chainsaw. He didn't know how far he was from the cabin, or the road. He felt like a fool for getting turned around so easily. He didn't want to spend the night in the woods, so he stood and began to shout for help, his voice quickly being absorbed by the surrounding trees, which seemed to close in around him. After a time, he stopped.

Carson saw a movement on the far side of a clearing. It was the doe. It turned around and slowly moved back along a trail, looking over its shoulder as if to see if Carson would follow. He laughed at the thought that the deer might actually be helping him, but followed anyway. The doe kept ahead of him by a good distance, but never too far as to lose him. After a time, Carson recognized part of the path that led from his cabin, and gave a cheer. The startled doe ran off, as Carson yelled a "Thank you!" feeling more foolish than he ever had.

Carson showered and ate and made himself a drink to calm down, before stretching out on the bed again. Exhausted from his running around, he drifted off, once more dreaming of a brown-skinned woman and her kiss.

He awoke as the last of the afternoon light was fading. After his woodland encounter, Carson had a need to see people, hear voices.

He drove into town, to the one bar. Carson sipped his beer, looking at the various items on the walls: old farm equipment, part of a barrel, some things he couldn't identify, and of course, the ubiquitous deer heads. Three of them, with the glassy stare of the dead, as revived by the taxidermist. Carson shook his head, wondering about the fetish for trophies.

"Hey you. Kraut." The voice of Harlow came sharply, cutting through the bar smoke like a blade.

Carson said nothing.

"I'm talkin' to you, ya lousy rich bastard." The words were slurred.

Carson had to turn to face Harlow. "What is it now?"

"Think you're so damned special, huh? Come up here and buy up our homes." The man's breath stank of stale beer and tobacco. Carson felt ill.

"I'm renting it."

"Yeah, so you can write some stupid book. About life, right? What the hell do you know about life?"

I know you're a piece of shit, Carson thought to himself. He put several dollars on the bar and got off the stool.

"Where do you think you're going?"

"Away from you."

"Think you're better than me?"

"I think just about anybody is."

Carson never even saw the punch coming, just felt a blinding pain, and then nothing. The next thing he knew, he was in a car with an ice-pack against his throbbing head.

Bert was driving, and looked over when Carson moaned. "How're you doing?"

"My head's about to come off."

"Well, I told ya to keep out of his way. Keep that ice on it, take a coupla aspirin, that'll help. We'll bring your car around in the morning."

"Did they at least take the little bastard to jail?"

Bert took his eyes off the road long enough to glance over. "That's not how we do things up here."

In the morning, Carson awoke with a pounding headache. He looked in the mirror and saw a huge bruise around his eye, angry purples and reds. He swallowed more aspirin and drank his coffee, and managed to get down a piece of toast. He showered and felt a little better. His car was back in his driveway, so someone had been good enough to drop it off. He went out and saw the keys in it. He drove to town.

The Chief was behind his desk, reading the paper. He looked up at Carson. "Well, that's some shiner you got there."

"I'd like you to arrest Doobie Harlow for assault and battery."

The Chief put down the paper. "Now hold on there."

"He confronted me, and sucker-punched me without provocation. He should be in jail."

"Well, first off, we don't have a jail. Second, I heard you boys exchanged some words before the fight started."

"Did you also hear that I was minding my own business when that little shit jumped me?"

"I wasn't there. The boys said that you two were arguin', and next thing you was on the floor."

"When he hit me."

"That sometimes happens when two fellas are arguin' in a bar."

"I wasn't arguing. He came up to me and started mouthing off, and I tried to leave."

"But you said somethin' to him, didn't ya? Somethin' to rile him up, maybe?"

Carson took a breath. "What are you getting at? That this is somehow my fault that I was assaulted?"

"I'm just sayin' when two guys are yellin' at each other, tempers can get pretty hot. And then things happen. Now I don't know who started what, but it's over, and best forgotten."

Carson stared at him. "You're not going to do anything?"

"This happens from time to time up here, and it's nothing serious.

All I got is your word that you didn't do anything. Anyone says different, I might have to consider charges on both sides, and I don't want to do that. Things could get ugly."

"Things are already ugly," Carson said, slamming the door behind him.

All that day Carson lay in his bed at the cabin. For a time, he held a raw steak to his injured face, since he'd heard that was good for a black eye. He brooded on possible courses of action, but realized that out here, he would get no justice. He was the outsider, and the locals would support their own. Damn them all.

In the afternoon, he started drinking. His headache had mostly gone away, and he was feeling sorry for himself. Another day shot to hell because of that psychobilly hick.

He cooked up the steak for his dinner. No use letting it go to waste. He looked at the laptop after supper, but instead poured himself another drink.

A noise on his porch after dark startled Carson. He peered out the window to see the woman standing on the porch. She wore the same clothes as before. He opened the door. "You again."

She stepped in with that otherworldly air about her. She put her fingers up to his face, examining his injured eye.

"Ow," he said, pulling back. "That hurts, you know."

"You fought with Harlow."

He gave a grim smile. "It wasn't so much a fight as him hitting me and me hitting the floor."

"He is evil."

"You can say that again. But since the Chief doesn't feel like prosecuting, the little shit won't even have to pay for it."

"They are kin to one another. Nothing would ever be done."

"Well how do you like that?" Carson nodded. "Figures they'd be all inbred. Still, I hoped for something like law, even up here."

"There is no law. Harlow killed my brother, and nothing was done."

"What?" Carson looked at her. "Punching me is one thing, but you're saying they didn't prosecute a murder?"

"Up here is different."

"That's for sure. I need to sit down. Would you like a drink?"

She shook her head. "But you are nothing like them. Where are your people?"

"I have no people," he said. "And I live in the city. How about you? Where do you live?"

"The forest is my home. It has always been."

There was a silence, and Carson felt uncomfortable. "Before, when you kissed me. What was that for?"

"For being a good man."

"I don't know as I'm all that good."

She went to him, and kissed him. Though he still couldn't believe it, she led him over to the bed.

* * *

Carson awoke to daylight, but she was gone. He almost felt like it was another dream, except he could still smell her in the sheets, a clean forest scent. He was drained of all energy and dizzy from the memory of her body, entwining in his, by turns savage and caressing, insistent, intoxicating. He had never known such a wild lover. He craved her yet, and searched for a note, but saw none. Would she return? He didn't know. He couldn't even pronounce her name properly.

Carson showered and ate breakfast, and sat down to his laptop. But he just stared at the screen, unable to create any meaningful sentences. His thoughts froze with the banality of his prose. All this effort to come here and write, and now he had nothing of value to say. He looked with longing at the bottle of whiskey, but morning was too early to start drinking, even for him. He hadn't sunk that low yet.

It was a long day of frustration. He was a failure, a charlatan. He had nothing to say, no story to tell. Finally, a day without the whine of a chainsaw, everything ready and waiting, and no words would come. Carson was disgusted with himself, ready to pack up and leave. If it hadn't been for the woman, he would have. But he had to see her again.

Somehow, he got through the day. He drank that afternoon, pining like a schoolboy, waiting for the dark, hoping she would come.

But the dark brought another visitor. Harlow stood outside, yelling in an angry voice.

"I'm coming for you, kraut! Call the cops on me, willya? Last time was just a taste. "

Harlow kicked open the front door and stormed in, seizing Carson by the shirt. Harlow punched him in the stomach, and again in the back of the head when Carson bent double. Carson fell to the floor as Harlow rained kicks on him. Carson looked up just before losing consciousness, and saw the woman grab Harlow by the throat. Then he blacked out.

* * *

Carson came to in his bed, weak and dizzy. The woman sat in a chair by his side.

"What happened? Where's Harlow?"

"He will not bother you again."

"My head."

"Rest now."

The next time Carson came to, he could sit up with only a bit of dizziness. She showed him a bowl and told him he should eat. She carefully spooned each bit to him, and the soup was warm and nourishing. He felt better by the time he had finished, but he still didn't feel like getting up.

Carson awoke, wondering how much time had passed. It was almost night, and he was alone. He called for her, but no one answered. He staggered up and reached for his laptop, but the battery was drained again. He set it down and sank back onto the bed.

She came in at dark and turned on the lights. "You're feeling better."

"Yes," he said.

"Are you hungry?"

Carson thought about it and found that he was. "Yes."

"I made some stew."

She busied herself at the stove, and a few minutes later brought Carson a steaming bowl and a large spoon. He took it from her gratefully, and ate his first bite. The meat was strong, chewy, but there were potatoes and vegetables. When he had finished, he handed her the bowl. "Thank you. For everything."

"Now you will grow stronger. His strength is now yours."

Her words seemed to have importance. "What do you mean?"

"The one they call Doo-bee. You have his power, but not his evil. That is gone."

He could not make out her meaning. "Where is he?"

She looked out the window. Carson staggered to his feet. He lurched to the door and went out into the night, out to the garage. He found the light switch, and then saw what was hanging from the deer

191

chain, but it took him a moment to recognize it. Hanging there was a blood-smeared, upside-down body, naked, gutted, and skinned, showing that strips had been cut from the flesh.

"What did you do?" He turned to see her face, as she looked matter-of-factly at the swinging corpse. There was no pity or horror in her eyes, and it terrified him.

"He killed and ate my brother. Now it is his turn."

The realization of what she meant hit Carson like a tree falling on him, and he collapsed, mercifully blacking out.

*   *   *

When he awoke, it had all seemed a fever dream. The chain hanging from the rafter was bare, and he made his way back to the cabin in the daylight, with no sign of the woman, or of Harlow's body. Carson slumped into a chair, knowing she would never be back. He touched the wound on his arm, all that he had left from her.

He could go tell the Chief, but they would think him insane or arrest him for murder. Now he had the greatest story ever, but one he could never tell.

SLEEP TIGHT

E.J. Fechenda

"Mommy, I can't sleep."

Colleen opened her eyes and blinked, willing the dark bedroom to come into focus. Enough light emitted from her alarm clock display, which read 3:11 a.m., to see the outline of her son, Ethan.

"Again, honey?" she asked. This had become a nightly occurrence ever since they had moved into their new house less than three weeks earlier. They knew it was an adjustment moving from New Jersey to Maine, but Ethan seemed to be having a particularly hard time.

Her six year old slowly nodded.

"The man keeps waking me up. He won't let me sleep."

"What?" Alarmed, Colleen sat straight up and shook her husband, who was blissfully sleeping through yet another interruption. Burglary was common where they used to live and they had chosen Maine because of the lower crime rate. She expected an occasional mouse in the house as an intruder, but not this.

"Hummm?" Trent mumbled while rolling over to face her.

"Ethan just said a man in his room woke him up," Colleen said in a harsh whisper, loud enough to emphasize the urgency, but not loud enough to scare off whomever was in her son's bedroom.

In less than a second, Trent was up and running down the hall to investigate. Colleen pulled Ethan into bed.

"Stay here. Mommy's going to go check on Daddy."

Picking up a heavy candle holder from the top of her dresser, Colleen crept down the hallway, pausing outside Ethan's door to take a deep breath. She collided with Trent in the doorway.

"Holy shit!" she squealed, dropping the candleholder on top of her bare foot. "Ow!" she cried out as her makeshift weapon rolled into a pile of toy cars.

"Are you my armed back up?" Trent teased and Colleen let out a nervous laugh. "It was nothing. There's no one here and the windows are still locked."

"We should check the rest of the house anyway — just to be safe."

"I got this. You go back to bed. One of us needs a full night's sleep."

Colleen watched her husband descend the stairs to the first floor before heading back to their bedroom. Ethan was sitting up, wide-eyed, in bed.

"Did you tell the man to leave me alone?"

"Honey, your daddy didn't see anyone. He's checking the rest of the house, but nobody was in your room."

"Oh." Ethan's face scrunched up in confusion.

"It was probably a dream. You can sleep in here with me and daddy, okay?" Colleen said, sliding beneath the covers. She tucked Ethan up close to her and kissed his forehead. Ethan fell asleep almost immediately, while Colleen listened for Trent. She heard him moving around downstairs, opening and shutting doors. Finally he returned and crawled into bed.

"Anything?" Colleen whispered.

"No," Trent said and yawned. "Either he had a dream or he's still having a hard time adjusting to the new house."

Colleen gently kissed Ethan one more time on his cheek before falling asleep.

Every night that week, Ethan appeared at Colleen's bedside claiming "the man" kept him awake. He even had dark circles under his eyes to prove it.

Over breakfast Saturday morning, Colleen was determined to find a solution.

"Ethan, can you tell mommy what this man looks like?"

Ethan nodded; his eyes wide. "He's old like Pop Pop."

"So he has gray hair?"

"Uh huh."

"What else?"

"He wears jeans and a sweatshirt."

Okay, so an older man in regular clothing. It doesn't make any sense, Colleen thought to herself, glancing over at Trent. He too seemed puzzled, his brow furrowed as he listened to his son ramble on about how the man sometimes smoked a cigar and it was the smoke that woke Ethan up most nights. Ethan had a vivid imagination, but this disruptive pattern needed to come to an end.

"I've smelled smoke in Ethan's room, but it was so faint, I didn't think anything of it."

"What?" Colleen slammed down her mug, sending a wave of coffee splashing over the lip, onto the table. "Why didn't you say anything before?"

"Like I said before, I didn't think anything of it. I still don't know what to think."

"A ghost?" Colleen posed the question, silencing the room.

Ethan looked up at her with his big brown eyes. "Like in Scooby Doo?"

"Yes, but I don't think he's going to hurt you." Colleen stood up and ruffled Ethan's hair trying to exude an air of calm. *Dealing with an actual person is easier, but how do you keep a ghost away?* She asked herself.

That night they tucked Ethan into bed and told him to ignore the man, that he wasn't real and couldn't hurt him. Before they went to sleep, Trent and Colleen checked on their son. He was hugging his plushy lion, a gift from Trent's parents.

"I hope we solved the problem," Colleen whispered.

"Me too," Trent brushed his lips across Colleen's and he clasped her hand. They walked down the hall toward their bedroom, hand-in-hand, united against whatever forces were affecting their child.

An ear-piercing shriek echoed through the house, causing both Colleen and Trent to sit straight up in bed. The shriek tapered off into hiccupping sobs. Shaking off a deep sleep, Colleen realized the cries were coming from Ethan's room. They both ran down the dark hallway, seconds stretching out like minutes.

Trent flipped on Ethan's light and Colleen immediately noticed how much colder it was, her breath visible as she exhaled. She also detected a hint of the heavy and sweet odor of cigar smoke. Ethan was shivering, curled up in a ball underneath his blankets. His cheeks were damp from tears and the sound of his chattering teeth filled the room. Colleen sat next to him and pulled her trembling son into her arms, keeping him swaddled in his blankets while Trent checked the windows and closet. Satisfied there wasn't anyone else in the room with them, Trent sat down next to Colleen and pulled his family to his side. Ethan's sobs had slowed and his breathing was slowly returning to normal. The room was warming up and soon Ethan stopped shivering.

"Baby boy, what happened?" Colleen cooed.

Sniffling and whimpering, he said, "The man was here and I told him to go away, that he wasn't real and ..." Ethan shivered again so Colleen hugged him even closer.

"What did he do?" Trent asked, his voice tight with emotion; a rare combination of anger and fear.

"He yelled at me and shook me! He ..." Ethan started sobbing again, hiccups wracking his body. The ghost had touched their son. This was no longer a harmless entity. She frantically looked him over and when she removed his pajama top handprints were visible on his upper arms. They faded right before her eyes; the color seeping into pale skin. Colleen leaned into Trent, hoping to draw strength from him. "He said this was his house and he still lived here. He told me we needed to leave. Then he gave me this." Ethan opened up his hand that had been curled into a fist.

Colleen blinked twice unsure of what she was seeing. Trent drew in a deep breath. Lying in the palm of their son's hand was a bone; covered in grime with dirt encrusted joints. It looked like a human finger.

"Oh my God!" She swatted the bone out of her son's hand and it clattered across the hardwood floor.

"That's it, I'm calling the police," Trent announced, jumping up. He left the room and returned moments later with the phone in his hand. He called the non-emergency line and was told an officer would be over later in the morning to take a report. He was asked to not touch the bone further.

He hung up the phone and hoisted Ethan into his arms. "Come

on, we're all sleeping in the big bed again." Ethan smiled up at him and rested his head against Trent's shoulder. The boy fell asleep out of sheer exhaustion, but Trent and Colleen could not. Colleen wanted to talk about what happened, but she didn't want to disturb their son and there was no way in hell she was going to leave him unprotected. Instead, she and Trent stared at each other over Ethan's head, listening to the deep sounds of his breathing. Trent's hand played with her hair and she closed her eyes, drifting off soon after.

The next day a police officer showed up and took a report. They sat around the dining room table, Ethan on Colleen's lap as Trent recounted the week's events leading up to the incident with the bone.

"No offense Mrs. Ricci, but are you sure your kid's not making this up, you know, for attention?" Officer Dan Jenkins asked when he finished writing everything down. His lips twisted up in a smirk. Clearly he doubted their experiences.

"Yes, I'm sure," Colleen snapped at the cop who looked young enough to still be in high school.

"You just moved here, maybe the little guy is having a hard time adjusting?"

"Explain the bone then?" Trent said, pointing at the evidence bag on the table.

"Has he been digging in the yard?"

"No."

"Did he bring it home from school?"

"No, the man gave it me," Ethan spoke up, defending himself. Colleen couldn't help but smirk back at the police officer who clearly was judging them as crazy people from "away."

"All right." Jenkins slapped his notebook shut and slid the chair back. Standing up he extended his hand to Trent, who briefly shook it. "I'll have this bone run through forensics, but it will take a while since they're backed up. It's probably from some animal anyway."

"We understand, thank you," Trent said and walked Officer Jenkins to the door.

"He was helpful," Colleen said when her husband returned to the dining room. Sunlight streamed in through the windows, highlighting the bags under Trent's eyes. He sunk into the chair, wrapping his hands around a mug whose contents had long grown cold.

"Can't say I'm surprised, we sound like lunatics."

"But this is really happening, Trent."

"Don't you think I know that?" he yelled and Colleen flinched. Trent launched out of his chair and left the room. Colleen was glad she had sent Ethan to the den to play with his toys. He didn't need to see his father so angry.

A few minutes later, Colleen found Trent on the treadmill in the basement, running so fast he might have been being chased by a monster.

"I'm sorry," he said, panting. "I'm just so frustrated. How can I protect Ethan against something we can't see?" He hit pause on the treadmill and rode it out until the belt stopped. Stepping off, he walked over to a stack of towels that were on the folding table. He leaned against the washing machine, wiping sweat from his face with a hand towel.

"What if we move?" Colleen suggested.

"With all of the renovations we did to make this house livable, we're upside down and can't afford to move."

Colleen sighed and hopped up on the dryer. Strangely, this is where they did their best talking. Colleen disliked the basement and laundry was her least favorite chore, but for whatever reason whenever they had an argument or something to sort out, they always wound up by the washer and dryer, away from Ethan's ears and away from any distractions like cell phones or the television.

"Ethan sleeps with us until we hear back from Officer Jenkins. We'll look into a paranormal investigator too. Somebody has to know how to deal with this shit," Trent said, placing a hand on Colleen's knee and giving it a light squeeze. "We can't let it get between us, okay?"

She nodded and set her hand on top of his and lacing their fingers together. An image of the dirty finger bone flashed in her mind and she shuddered.

That night they all piled into bed early, Ethan slipping into sleep almost immediately. Sheer exhaustion pulled Colleen under only to be awakened hours later. Smoke filled her nostrils and she woke up coughing. Panic set in briefly that the house was on fire, until she realized that the smoke detectors were silent. Ethan was gone.

"Trent!" she screamed and shook her husband awake. He jumped and sat straight up.

"Ethan's not in bed and do you smell that?"

He turned on the bedside lamp and hopped out of bed. His boxer shorts hung off one hip as he bent over to look underneath the bed.

He ran down the hall, turning lights on as he went and Colleen followed, the cigar smell growing stronger. She used that as her guide and went down the stairs as Trent searched Ethan's room. She flipped on the light in the living room and did a quick glance, but the smoke was leading her away from that side of the house. On the way to the kitchen, Colleen paused. The basement door stood wide open.

"Ethan!" Colleen cried out and darted down the basement stairs.

Trent heard his wife yell and he cursed, running down to the first floor. He saw Colleen just as she started to go down to the basement.

✱ ✱ ✱

Four days later Officer Jenkins was surprised to see an envelope from the forensics department sitting on his desk. He opened it up to discover the DNA results had come back on the bone turned in by the Ricci family. He sprayed coffee all over his desk, narrowly missing the clean white documents in his hand. "Jesus Christ!" Jenkins didn't think much of the "case" he had been assigned since he was a rookie and had accepted the fact that he would be given the weird calls to follow up on as part of his initiation to the force. He also didn't connect it at the time that the Ricci's house was "that" house.

Mainers liked to associate places with those of the past. For example, when giving directions it was common to say make a left where the old Levinsky's used to be. In this particular case, the Ricci's had purchased the old Mason place. The Mason place had a dark history, which Jenkins thought had been exaggerated over the years to grow into urban legend. Considering the evidence sitting on his desk, he decided to do some research to separate fact from fiction.

It didn't take him long to find the cold case file in the archives where they sat waiting to be uploaded into the county's database. Reaching into a banker's box, he pulled out the first related file. The manila folder had yellowed with age and the edges curled from the damp basement. Officer Jenkins set it on the table, under a bright overhead fluorescent light and opened to find notes in faded but familiar slanted handwriting. The first entry date was July 23, 1985 by Officer Mike Rollins. "No shit," Officer Jenkins muttered to himself. "This was one of Chief's first cases." Jenkins read on, impressed with the detail. At the time Chief Mike Rollins had been just Officer Rollins, but even then his investigative skills and attention to historical documentation were strong. Jenkins settled in to read.

Bill Harris, resident of 27 Cumberland Lane called the police to report a foul odor coming from the Mason residence. I was on duty when the call came into dispatch and I was the first to arrive on the scene. Recognizing the smell of decomposition coming from the open windows of the house and after knocking, but not receiving any response, I looked in the front window into the living room and saw a body on the floor. It was covered in flies — so many that I heard the buzzing from twenty feet away. I kicked in the door and rushed over to the body. Kneeling down next to it, I almost gagged from the smell and from the sight before me. The body was so swollen and bloated that the skin stretched out across a man's face, making it unrecognizable (see attached photographs). The deceased was clothed in jeans and a gray sweatshirt. I placed a call to the county Medical Examiner's office before checking the rest of the house.

After a walk through I didn't find anyone else home. There were two bedrooms upstairs, one was the master bedroom and the other was a girl's room based on the pink gingham bedspread and a collection of dolls on the bed. I went back downstairs and the M.E. arrived, the black station wagon stirred up a cloud of dust from the dirt driveway. I made sure to shut the front door behind me to prevent any contamination. While there wasn't any exterior sign of trauma to indicate an unnatural death, I still made sure to follow protocol just in case.

Jenkins smirked when he read that because Chief was still a stickler for proper procedure. Taking a sip from his bottle of water, he continued reading.

The autopsy revealed Gerald Mason had died of a massive heart attack (see enclosed autopsy report). Since it appeared he lived alone, a search for next of kin began. According to neighbors, back in 1953 Cumberland Lane was a dirt road and only had three farms built acres apart. Gerald Mason, his wife and their daughter occupied one. They were of a homesteader mentality and lived off of their land; their daughter, Millie, was homeschooled and the Masons generally kept to themselves. Gerald was known for his monthly trips to town for supplies. His wife and daughter rarely made an appearance.

Over the years the town grew and more homes sprung up on Cumberland Lane. Gerald Mason's cantankerous reputation and bitter disputes with neighbors about trespassing on his land also grew and they learned to give him wide berth. No one really thought much of his wife and daughter and in fact several of the neighbors who moved into the neighborhood later didn't even know Gerald had a family. The only information I could find was a census conducted in 1967 by the U.S. Census Bureau. Millie Mason would have been twenty-one years old according the records and 25 Cumberland Lane was her last recorded address. Same with Ber-

nice Mason, she would have been forty-two. At the time of this census, it was noted that both Bernice and Millie no longer lived there. That was all that was recorded.

Additional paperwork in the file revealed that no one claimed Gerald Mason's body and he had been given a simple burial in the town's cemetery. A clipping of the brief obituary told the story of an aloof man who led a simple life. His wife and daughter were mentioned as survivors, whereabouts unknown. A black and white photograph of Gerald accompanied the obituary and showed a man with sharp features, narrow eyes and thinning hair. There didn't seem to be anything remarkable about the man. A follow up note was added to the file that after sitting in probate for two years, the Mason property was finally sold at auction by the bank.

Officer Jenkins closed the file and set it aside before grabbing a slightly newer manila folder from the banker's box. Once again he recognized the handwriting only this time the ink wasn't that old and Rollins had been promoted to Detective. Jenkins took a few minutes to get up and use the bathroom before reading about the next owners of 25 Cumberland Lane: Bob and Diane Peterson.

A call came into dispatch at 2:03 pm on Sunday, May 20, 1988 from Bob Peterson. He had been doing some home improvement and was in the process of fixing a sunken area of the basement floor that had appeared after a big rainstorm. Suspecting there was a sinkhole forming underneath the concrete; he rented a concrete saw and cut away an opening. Once Bob Peterson had cleared enough of the area to get a glimpse at what he was going to have to deal with, he discovered what appeared to be human remains.

It took months for the state's forensic lab to process everything and when the results came back, I was stunned. The remains were those of two females, one approximately aged eighteen to twenty-five and the other was presumed to be between forty and forty-five. Based on the estimation for how long the remains had been in the ground and the fact that the DNA revealed they were mother and daughter (see enclosed forensic report for details), I was 99.9% sure that Bernice and Millie Mason had never moved out.

Jenkins sifted through the pages and found the forensic reports. The findings made the coffee and bagel he had earlier turn in his stomach. What had been unearthed had basically been skeletal remains since they'd been interred for over twenty years, but the skeletons weren't intact. Evidence indicated the bodies had been dismembered prior to being buried. Rough gouges along the bones were made by an axe or similar tool. Each skull had a web of cracks and fractures with a giant crater at the center, caused by a heavy blunt object. Jenkins picked up one of the pictures for closer examination; eye sockets now dark, empty hollows stared back at him. Their killer was dead and the only justice the department had been able to serve was to have a proper burial. In a small town where usually everyone knows your business, the Masons had succeeded in being invisible. Whatever secret motive or psychosis haunted Gerald Mason and drove him to kill, dismember and hide his family's bodies would never be known.

That was only part of the mystery surrounding this particular address. Jenkins had heard bits and pieces of the story. That Chief Rollins, then still a detective, had been dispatched back out to the house after Bob Peterson had called the police station again. He hadn't discovered more remains, but he called to report his wife missing. Diane Peterson had literally vanished without a trace. Jenkins read through the detailed notes, revealing that Detective Rollins didn't leave any stone unturned. According to Bob Peterson, Diane had gone down to the basement to do laundry and she never came back up. The bulkhead doors were welded shut and dust on the narrow basement window sills remained undisturbed. The area where Bob had cut out the basement floor had already been repaired. Her car was still in the driveway and her purse was on the kitchen counter. There wasn't a history of domestic disturbances or any financial issues. The young couple wanted to start a family and buying a house had been their first step towards this future.

Bob Peterson had been the main suspect, but even after he was thoroughly investigated and cleared, as long as his wife's whereabouts remained unknown, suspicion by neighbors and residents followed his every move. Eighteen months after Diane disappeared, Bob moved away. The case remained open as a cold case. So was the next disappearance associated with the house on Cumberland Lane.

The LePlante family purchased the home from Bob Peterson. Stephen and Celine, along with their thirteen year old daughter, Rihanna, moved in. Stephen was the new high school principal and Celine worked at the town library part time. It was a half-day, not even six-months after they moved in, when Celine went missing. Both Stephen and Celine had been at work when their daughter got home. Her backpack was hanging up on the peg above the shoe rack and the sneakers she wore that day were in their usual slot. Nothing was missing from her room and there weren't any signs of forced entry or a burglary. The only evidence that something was amiss was a drop of fresh blood on the basement floor that forensics matched to Celine. It was only a drop though and without the usual indicators of someone trying to clean up the scene of a crime, like the smell of bleach, extra clean floors or recently replaced items, there hadn't been anything to go on. Celine's diary revealed entry after entry about the spirit of an old man who visited her at night, but her parent's said she never mentioned anything to them about a ghost.

Missing posters were circulated, local and national media surrounded the LePlante's, but public interest died down as time went on. Shortly after the one year anniversary of her disappearance, the LePlantes moved. Celine became one of the many missing and forgotten. She was never seen or heard from again.

Officer Jenkins scratched his head and leaned back in his chair with a yawn. His stomach rumbled and when he looked at the clock, was surprised to see it was after 7:00 pm. While tempted to stop for the day, he had finally reached the folder for the case connected with his: The Smith's. He texted his wife to let her know he wouldn't be home for dinner before opening the file for the last family to live at 25 Cumberland Lane prior to the current residents. Robert and Beverly Smith had two children: Brandon and Emily. The twins attended Grafton Academy, a local private school and both were honor students. Robert and Beverly were attorneys who quickly became fixtures in the community. The Winter Ball, an annual fundraiser to benefit the area animal shelter, had been their idea. They'd been gone ten years, but the ball was still going strong and he remembered reading an announcement in the paper that a date had been set for the next event.

Thinking about the ball jogged something loose in his memory and he flipped back through the file. There it was; the call for a welfare check on the Smiths had been recorded on October 25, 2006. *Exactly ten years ago today,* Jenkins muttered to himself. According to the report, when the responding officer had arrived on the scene he discovered an unlocked front door, not uncommon in the small town, so he entered. Jenkins looked at the pictures from the crime scene. The home was lavishly decorated; the living room and dining room looked untouched as if nobody had ever set foot on the high gloss dark walnut floors. The updated kitchen had top of the line appliances and bright white cabinets. It wasn't sterile like the other rooms though and appeared to be the heart of the home. The table was set for breakfast, indicating the Smiths took their family meals together. The images showed matching bowls filled partially with cereal that had sat too long in milk, becoming a light brown sludge. Mugs of coffee, glasses full of orange juice and a large serving bowl containing a dried out fruit salad completed the scene. According to the notes, a search of the house and property then phone and bank records were inconclusive. The kids' backpacks, Robert's briefcase and Beverly's purse were found by the door, indicating they were planning on going about their day as usual, but they never showed up. The Smiths had seemingly disappeared in the middle of eating breakfast.

After that, none of the real estate agents wanted to deal with the cursed house so it sat empty for almost a decade. There were notes added to the file throughout the years whenever a call came in regarding the residence. Most of the reports were from neighbors complaining about lights being on in the house even though power had been disconnected. By the time an officer was dispatched, the property was dark. Other calls came into the station from neighbors who heard faint screams and a child crying. These were never confirmed and added to the mystery surrounding the house. When an offer came in from out of state to purchase the dilapidated property, the bank fast tracked the sale.

As far as Jenkins knew, the Ricci's didn't know about their new home's history. People only talked about Gerald Mason killing his family and the other disappearances in hushed conversations, concerned about somehow becoming cursed themselves. The Ricci's didn't have any prior connection to the Smiths — not until the bone of one of Beverly's fingers showed up in Ethan's fist.

* * *

The next morning, with a search warrant in hand and with half of the police force parked in the street along with two forensic investigators, Officer Jenkins knocked on the Ricci's door. He waited a few seconds and rang the doorbell, hearing the faint echo of chimes. There was no answer and he didn't have any luck when he tried their cell phones. He dialed the land line and could hear the phone ringing on the other side of the door.

The Ricci's two cars were parked in the driveway and several issues of the Portland Press Herald were piled up on the front step.

"They're not home." Officer Jenkins turned to see an older man standing on the uneven brick walkway by the driveway.

"Do you know where they went?"

The old man shrugged and took a long puff on his cigar. "I just want to be left alone," he growled before continuing on his way with a slow, uneven gait. There was something familiar about the man, but Jenkins couldn't place where he's seen him before.

Jenkins shook his head. He didn't have to time to think about it. They had to get inside the house. The DNA results provided the hottest lead that could potentially solve the Smith case. They broke the door down and officers filed through with their weapons at the ready as a precaution. It was daylight so Officer Jenkins didn't realize right away that all of the lights on the first floor were on. He did notice the basement door was open, emitting freezing cold air into an otherwise cozy environment.

The rest of the house turned up empty and one of the officers reported that it didn't look like anyone had packed for a trip. A signed permission slip for a field trip with Mainely Kids Daycare was on the counter as well as a cell phone being charged. Wherever the Ricci's went, it was sudden and unplanned. "Just like before," he muttered to himself and the fine hairs on the back of his neck prickled.

They only had the basement left to search and Jenkins led a team down the stairs; slowly, cautiously. They all held their breath, anticipating a horrific crime scene.

The basement was normal and tidier than most, except for something that caught Officer Jenkins' attention. He walked over the washer and dryer for a closer look. Lying on top of the washing machine was a bone. This one was cleaner than the other one, almost the same white as the appliances, causing it to blend in.

They searched the home again, took pictures, made the proper documentation and left the premises. As Jenkins was getting into his patrol car, he glanced up to see the old man from earlier. He was standing at the end of the driveway. They made eye contact and the old man grinned widely around the cigar clamped between his teeth. He winked once before vanishing.

THE BLACK BEAST OF ANDOVER

Joshua Goudreau

"Oxford County is creepy," Sarah said.

Darius glanced at her. She sat in the middle of the pickup truck, one hand in his as he drove, the other holding open a paperback novel. He was pretty sure she hadn't lifted her nose from it since they'd left Auburn, so there was no way for her to know if the place was creepy or not. He kept the comment to himself. With the wedding coming up, October 16th 1993 to be exact, he didn't want to argue.

"It's beautiful out here," he said.

She shrugged. "I suppose if you like the color green ..."

He took his eyes from the road only a moment and saw a mischievous smirk play across her lips. Her pale face brightened, and she removed her hand from his to push an errant strand of chocolate hair from her face. Darius smiled. He didn't care what his mother said. Why couldn't he find a nice Greek girl to settle down with? How about Erica from church? She's so sweet and did you know her father runs that deli on Lisbon Street?

"It's not creepy. It's just remote."

"Remote? I don't think there are actually any people out here."

"What about those kids we passed? With the fishing poles? They waved."

"That was like fifteen minutes ago."

He smiled and nudged her with his elbow. "It's going to be fun, I promise. Spending time among the mountains is good for the soul."

She raised an eyebrow at him. "Really? *Among the mountains?* That's the line you're going with to convince me to do this? Did you know the Appalachian Trail through Maine is the most dangerous section of the trail? The library has a whole bunch of books about it."

Darius fought rolling his eyes. She was technically correct. More people disappeared on the AT in Maine than anywhere else on the trail. Most vanished without a trace but some were found days or weeks later, dead or raving about the things they had seen. It was clear to Darius that these cases were wildly exaggerated and due almost entirely to negligence or simple unpreparedness. This trip was a small one, they were prepared, and they would be fine.

Sarah was a self-proclaimed librarian by preference and profession. He needed a bit more action in life and career than surrounding himself with books and reference materials or whatever it was her job entailed. She enjoyed it though, and that was the part that mattered. Adventure was not in her blood. He chuckled to himself, how did a cop and a librarian end up together?

"The mountains can be dangerous if you're not prepared. There's not many people so sometimes you're miles from a telephone and then help is still hours away. Don't look at me like that. You've got me, so we'll be fine."

She turned her face back to her book and turned the page. Her hand found its way back to his. The summer air through the open windows was crisp with a freshness unknown in other parts of the world. They were amid two thousand square miles of rugged mountains, glacial valleys, and fewer people than their hometown. Lewiston/Auburn, the twin cities of the Androscoggin, was a long way away out here.

"Did you know that my Uncle Malik was from Byron?"

Sarah lifted her face from her book again. "Is that a place?"

He laughed. "He was the weirdest. I used to sit behind him at family reunions and watch the way he moved. He had these wicked scars all up his back, all crisscrossing. He said it was from when he was younger but never told me the rest of the story. He was full of other stories though, swore they were all true. He had wacky names for them too; The Witch Curse of Snow Falls, The Shag Pond Monster, that sort of thing."

She narrowed her eyes at him. "I'm pretty sure you don't have an Uncle Malik."

He smiled. "Scout's honor. He used to say that these mountains held more secrets than anyone could really understand. Every mountain, every lake, every town has some ghost story attached to it. He swore it was all true."

"You're not helping."

Darius laughed. "My crazy uncle just liked to scare the kids. It's not like any of his stories were real. Forget I said anything."

She curled up on the seat and focused on her book again. He cursed himself for a moment. He just wanted to have a good time, away from the hectic life behind them. It was only going to get more hectic in the following months as the wedding grew closer. October 16th wasn't so far away. In addition, Darius would finally be able to show the city girl he knew his stuff in the woods.

This weekend away would be good for them.

The road twisted from a narrow whaleback to the floor of a wide, flat valley and Darius knew they were close. Bare, granite cliff faces dominated the view to either side. Daring evergreens clung to crevices and rock tops, creating a carpet of green in every space not occupied by bare rock.

Before long, Andover sprung into view at the far end of the valley. It was as Darius remembered it: tiny, dusty, and quiet. At the cross-roads, across from the wide gravel lot of the volunteer fire department, beside a weed-choked baseball diamond stood the only store in town. It didn't even bear a sign giving it a name. The two gas pumps in front of the store were ancient and streaked with rust. Darius contemplated the risk of a fiery death and chose to go for it anyway.

Sarah looked around. "Are you sure this is a real town?"

He kissed her. "Cute."

He slid from the truck while Sarah pushed herself to the passenger door.

Darius removed the nozzle from the pump, flipped a lever, and began to fuel the truck. The town possessed an eerie silence. Even the gas pump was silent. He released and pressed the handle a few times and flipped the lever but got no response.

He rounded the truck to where Sarah had emerged, stretching the stiffness from her body. In her hand, she clutched the book.

"I'm already tired, D," she said.

"It's gonna be fun, I promise."

"Forgive me as I roll my eyes in disbelief."

"Brat."

She stuck her tongue out at him.

"Anyway, the gas pump's not on. I guess the guy inside is asleep or something."

Sarah looked at the book in her hand, then to the store. She shrugged and followed him.

The glass door of the store opened to a cavern of darkness until Darius removed his sunglasses and let his eyes adjust. Looking about, he saw no one.

Virtually every country store in every small town was home to a stand of coffee canisters and a small table or two that was home to a collection of old men in dusty jeans and flannel shirts, trucker hats tipped back on their heads, conversing about one thing or another. This store however, was home only to dim shadows and an oppressive quiet.

Absent was the hum of lights and coolers. No lights at all, now that he really looked around. Darius could not put his finger on exactly what was out of place but something told him it was more than just a power outage. He moved to the table, beyond the register and snack foods, next to the wall of rental VHS tapes. The coffee dispenser pump handles were up, indicating they were full, but the canisters themselves were cold. He pressed the handle of one and it dripped coffee. What the hell was going on? The only sign of disturbance was a single, toppled chair.

He listened hard.

The dim sounds of leaf bugs and grasshoppers outside, the normal background hum of summer in Maine. Nothing more, however. No vehicles, no electricity. No people.

He didn't need a cop's instinct to tell him something was very, very wrong.

Sarah moved slowly, eyes darting about. "It's like nine AM on a Friday, folks are probably just busy or something."

"Power's out too."

She shrugged. "There might be a line down somewhere."

She was clearly grasping for reason.

"Maybe," he said. "I'm going to look around. Stay here."

Outside the stillness was more eerie now that he was aware of it. The background hum of insects and the faint drone of the wind down from the mountains were the only sounds.

Across the road crouched a row of half a dozen buildings, one of which advertised itself as Little Joan's Diner, though aside from the plate glass window and wide front porch, it looked much the same as the surrounding houses. The road between the rows of buildings was little more than a faded strip of asphalt, crumbling on either side, merging seamlessly with gravel and dirt up to the fronts of the buildings. Without the faint, yellow line down the center, the road would have been nearly impossible to see.

The oppressive lack of the sounds of civilization weighed heavy on him. Such stillness should not exist here, reserved only for the mountains and the deep glens they concealed.

The door to the diner creaked and opened to a cramped dining room, packed tight with tables. Atop each table, the chairs rested up-ended to make the surface of the floor clear. Despite an unlocked front door, it was clear the place had not opened for the day. Perhaps it never would again.

Back outside, the sun warmed the humid air. Darius closed his eyes and tried to figure out exactly what was going on. A town didn't simply empty itself without notice or report. Not even a small remote place like Andover.

Nearby, a creak sounded, as if from an old floorboard. Darius listened. Another. It was coming from the house to his left. Cautiously, he crossed the grass and ascended two steps to the front door. Everything was silent again inside.

He wondered if he should knock or try the doorknob. He chose the latter and reached for it.

The door exploded from its frame, sending a shower of splinters in all directions. It struck him hard, throwing him from the steps and slamming him to the ground. Some great, thrashing weight pressed down on the door, crushing him into the grass. He planted his hands on the door, his muscles throbbing in pain and stress, trying to stop the thing pushing the air from his lungs. Whatever held him down was massive. With all his might, he shoved then rolled aside, freeing himself from the door.

Only a few feet away loomed a great mass of shadow and fur. All description and dimension became lost to a void of lightlessness. Save for the gnashing teeth. The thing lunged.

He rolled aside as the beast's paws hit the ground where he had been only a moment before, tearing vicious furrows in the lawn. It spun and snapped at him without a sound. Darius leapt for a splintered board nearby and rolled onto his feet. He swung as hard as he could at what he guessed was the thing's head. The board connected with a loud snap, shattering and sending shudders up Darius' arms. The thing staggered. Without waiting to see what happened next, Darius spun and ran as fast as his legs would carry him.

Sarah stood in the sun near the entrance to the store, her mouth agape. Terror was barreling down upon her.

Darius shouted as he covered the hundred yards between them. "Get inside!"

She turned and ran for safety.

The beast was fast approaching. He would not make it to the door in time. He veered aside and let the heavy, rushing weight of the beast carry it past him. It spun, strangely not disturbing the gravel beneath it, and raced toward him again, which is exactly what Darius wanted. It hurled itself forward, vile teeth bared and claws out. At the last possible moment, Darius ducked aside and let the thing crash into the steel pylon aside the gas pumps. A resounding clang tore through the silence. Darius was relieved to hear the thing make at least some kind of noise.

Without waiting, he was on his feet and inside the store. Only then did he dare a peek outside. The beast staggered and shook itself. It looked around, lifted its snout and sniffed the air. When it lowered its head, the shape was lost again to shadow, as if the beast were made only of darkness, defying the light of day. Details were difficult to discern, but it was clear the thing was nearly the size of a horse. As it moved, shapes and definition would emerge, momentarily giving it the recognizable appearance of an animal before melding back into the mass. It seemed to ambulate on stout legs though it was impossible to tell if there were four or six. It had a snouted head that extended occasionally to take in its surroundings. The strange teeth seemed to have vanished.

Slowly it made its way back to the shattered front door of the house across the road and disappeared inside. Darius sunk to the floor, his strength drained.

"Darius, move!"

He scrambled to his feet and helped Sarah, who had emptied a nearby display shelf and was pushing it toward the door. In only a few minutes, they had the door and window behind the register blocked with displaced shelves and displays. The makeshift barricades blocked most of the view, hopefully preventing the thing from seeing them moving but still give them small glimpses out.

Once they had a moment of safety, Sarah glanced at him. "You think that will keep it out?"

"I hope so."

"What the hell is that thing?"

Darius shook his head. "I have no idea. I've never seen anything like it."

He looked around and tried to plan their next move. The store had everything from candy to automotive supplies, so assuming the barricades were solid, they should be able to hold out until help came.

Sarah's head snapped up. "Shit, the back door!"

Darius broke into a run, cursing himself for not thinking of the back. Across the length of the store, he moved through an open door next to the coolers. To one side was a small room that seemed to serve double duty as a stock room and office. In front of him was a cramped bathroom. To his left, a door to the outside, propped open with a broken cinderblock. He pulled it closed and slid an ancient metal desk from the office and upturned it to block the door. To cover the sole window in the office they stacked nearby cases of beer until it was completely blocked.

"Good with the quick thinking," he said.

Sarah shrugged. Her arms crossed tightly, she paced about. He approached and put his arms around her.

"We're going to be okay," he said.

Silently, she nodded and leaned into him.

Over the next hour, they scoured the contents of the shelves. A back corner, beside the dark coolers, contained a surprisingly robust collection of camping and hiking supplies. Several the shelves in the middle of the store held dust covered canned goods, so if all else failed, at least they'd have food.

Sarah emerged from the back with a shotgun held before her as if it were some kind of vile creature. "The phone is dead. I found this in the back room."

Darius took it from her and checked to see the weapon was not loaded. He gathered up some shotgun shells found on one of the shelves and loaded the weapon. There was no way to know when help would come.

"I guess I can defend us if that thing comes back."

"Do you think it will come to that?"

"I hope not."

She shifted her feet and looked around, biting her lip.

"We'll be out of here by nightfall," he said. "A whole town doesn't vanish without people noticing. The state police or game wardens or someone will be here soon."

"State police like you?"

"Exactly. See? We'll be fine."

She seemed to relax and moved away to pull water from one of the coolers. Darius wasn't as certain as he let on, and he knew Sarah shared his apprehension, despite his words of encouragement.

"Too bad there's no power," he said. "We could bust out a VCR and watch a movie."

She walked over to him at the rental shelf. "There is nothing here that's even a little recent."

He scoffed. "Look, Terminator 2, Batman Returns. The Bodyguard, you wanted to see that."

"They have Nintendo games too," she said. "Look, Kid Icarus. I played the hell out of this in college. And there is the Darius Rias blank stare again. You play this guy who has wings like Icarus."

He shrugged.

"Really? You're Greek and don't know who Icarus is?"

He thought for a moment. "Was he one of the titans?"

She put the game back on the shelf. "No culture. Your mother would be rolling over in her grave if she happened to be dead."

Darius watched her walk away. His levity dropped out from beneath him. He may never see his mother again. Or anyone.

For now, they were on their own.

The day waned and night came in slowly and deliberately. Sarah collected some of the camping supplies and made a comfortable nest for them. They made a meal of some canned pasta and settled in next to a low burning lantern.

"Do you think the light will draw that thing?" Sarah said.

"Not if we keep it low and on the floor like this."

They ate in silence for a time.

"What if help never comes?" Sarah said.

"It will."

"What makes you so sure?"

"Faith I guess."

"I'm serious."

"Me too. Ghost towns don't just appear overnight without attracting attention. Someone will come looking."

"What about that thing out there?"

Darius shook his head and sighed. "I don't know."

❉ ❉ ❉

"Darius!"

He started awake and it took a moment to piece together where he was. Sleeping bags on the hard floor, the pillow made of clothes wrapped in a t-shirt asking 'Where in the Hell is Andover, Maine?' Shelves surrounding him. Sarah shaking him.

"What is it?"

"It's back."

He stood, the shotgun in his hands, retrieved from its resting place beside him. The store was dark. Moonlight streamed in through the barricades, leaving long trails where dust motes danced about.

Through the window behind the register, he watched the great, black shadow moving near the gas pumps. The light of the moon cast a silver halo around the shaggy blackness. It circled the pumps and sniffed at Darius' truck. When the thing stopped moving, it vanished into the darkness between moonbeams. If he hadn't known it was there, he would never have seen it.

Only a moment later, the shadow moved in a blur, nearly impossible to follow in the dimness of night. The glass of the front door shattered and the shelf blocking it jumped back half a foot, tossing aside the chairs bracing it. Darius ran around the register and brought the shotgun to his shoulder. The boom of the gun reverberated through the quiet of night and put a large hole through the wooden shelf, into the shadow beast on the other side. The shadows shifted, but the thing made no noise.

Without hesitation, Darius jacked the slide and put another slug through the shelf. The thing crashed forward again, toppling the shelf.

The darkness roiled just outside the door. Darius put another slug into it.

The darkness shifted and vanished, leaving only the silver of night behind. Darius pumped the shotgun and moved to the door. Across the gravel lot, the thing passed the pumps and crossed the road, returning to its lair. It left a trail of tar-like blackness in its wake. Each resting like a spot of shadow. More of the viscous blood had splattered on the wall beside the door and across the shards of broken glass.

He placed the shotgun on the counter beside him and, with Sarah's help, replaced the shelf barricade. Sarah then turned the lamp back on, and they used hammer and nails found among the store goods and further barricaded the door.

Once satisfied the door was secure, Darius turned to Sarah. "Are you okay?"

"What do you think?"

"Look, I'm more than a little shaken too."

She was shivering. "Sorry. I'm okay."

He wrapped his arms around her until she breathed a little easier. Once she calmed, he climbed onto the counter next to the register and placed the shotgun across his lap. From his vantage point, he could see through the slits between boards over the window, into the front lot. The door was not far away. That thing would not catch him unaware again. He remained on vigil, his back sore from the seat and his muscles stiff and tired from exhaustion and adrenaline, until the sky turned gold and the sun returned.

When the sunlight touched the ground and warmed the air, the pools of black blood turned an ashy gray and blew away like soot on the breeze. Too exhausted to continue, Darius took Sarah's urging to lie down and rest.

* * *

Darius was not sure how much time had passed when he finally woke. Beside him, the makeshift bed was empty. A surge of panic rose within him and he stood, grabbing the shotgun. Sarah was gone. He looked around, frantic. The barricades were still in place.

Then, from the back, he heard the toilet flush. A moment later, Sarah emerged and smiled at him. She looked harried and tired, her hair pulled back in a sloppy ponytail and her eyes puffy and red. He thought she was beautiful. He swore to himself that he would see her out of this alive.

He stretched. His whole body was sore. His shoulder popped, and an ache coursed through it. Likely from a combination of the shotgun and his fall when the beast first emerged. He looked out the window and saw the sun was high in the sky. The beast was nowhere to be seen.

"How long was I asleep?"

Sarah looked at her watch. "About five hours."

He sighed. "It looks like that thing is gone. We should get out of here."

"It hasn't been back."

Together they dragged the shelf aside and used the hammers to pull the boards from the door. The day was still and that fresh, mountain air drifted lazily inside. Cautiously, they emerged into the sunlight. They were only a few steps into the gravel lot when the beast leapt from its hiding place around the side of the store. It lashed out with its claws, sending Darius and Sarah skidding in opposite directions.

Sarah darted back into the store. Darius turned and fired the shotgun, his blast spraying wildly into the air, completely missing the beast. His balance knocked off from turning and shooting, he staggered and fell hard on his back.

A sharp pain coursed through his arm and shoulder. He fired again from his supine position, unsure if he hit the beast, and scurried back inside. Sarah pushed the shelves back in place. The thing outside slammed into the barricade and knocked her back, where she landed hard on the floor. Darius fired through the shelf again, collapsing the upper part of it.

For an uncomfortable amount of time, they waited and listened. The sounds of summer slowly returned, but there was no sign of the beast. Darius looked outside and saw the thing was gone.

"Let's get these boards back up."

In only a few minutes, the barricade was back in place.

"You're bleeding. A lot."

Once mentioned, Darius became aware of the pain and warmth of blood on his upper arm and shoulder blade.

"Take your shirt off."

Darius did as instructed. Sarah gathered a first aid kit from one of the shelves and began to tend to Darius' wounds. She had to resort to digging in his many lacerations with tweezers to remove fragments of glass before cleaning with alcohol and bandaging the area as best she was able.

"You're probably going scar. You'll have a bruise on your shoulder too."

He sat down and leaned against the counter.

Sarah took her shoe off and wrapped a bandage around her ankle.

"Are you hurt?" he said.

"I just twisted my ankle. I'll be okay."

He reloaded the shotgun.

Sarah put her shoe back on and tested her weight on the injury. She nodded. "We're not going to get out of here alive, are we?"

Darius placed a final round in the chamber of the weapon and left the safety off. "We'll get out of here. I don't know when or how yet. But we will, even if it means waiting it out."

They ate a lunch of canned pasta and candy bars in silence. Through the afternoon, they saw no signs of life.

They were alone in a sea of lifeless summer. Their only companion was some unnamable creature. If they could keep the barricades intact and maintain a supply of food and ammunition, they just might survive this.

When the sun sank low, Darius returned to his perch on the counter. The sky behind the mountains turned purple and faded to darkness. The moon rose behind the store and changed the world once more to a land of silver and shadow.

He thought long and hard. How the hell were they going to get past that thing?

Sarah put a hand on his shoulder. He turned to face her. Her eyes were sunken and dark although she wore a hard expression of stubborn determination. Darius knew the look well.

"I'm not dying here," she said. "Don't give me those sad puppy dog eyes. This isn't some kind of 'oh I forgot your birthday' kind of times."

"Sarah ..."

"You shut it, mister, I'm serious. I'm not dying in some dusty, little shithole because you wanted to be *among the mountains*. Wedding stress or not, this was a terrible idea."

He nodded. "I don't disagree."

She stalked away and he returned to his vigil.

Everything was quiet.

*   *   *

Darius snapped awake, suddenly aware that he had fallen asleep on watch. Behind him, Sarah stirred and sat up. From the back of the store, there was a loud crash. Darius moved toward it, anxious about the coming conflict, the shotgun against his naked and sore shoulder.

The ancient, steel desk braced against the door jumped with another loud crash. Darius reached the doorway to the back and waited for an opening he could shoot through. Then the banging stopped.

In the room beside him, the stack of beer cases exploded in a shower of shredded cardboard, aluminum, and beer. The mass of shadow oozed through the small window, its almost canine-like head stretched forward. Darius spun and put a shotgun slug into the thing's flank. Black blood splattered across the wall and the mass of fur dropped back through the window. Darius' second shot missed entirely, destroying a case of beer.

He waited, his ears collecting nothing but a painful ringing. He glanced around. Across the building, the front window exploded inward. Glass and wood shrapnel tore through the air in a dangerous volley. Sarah dove for cover behind a shelf and pulled herself up tight.

The great, furry shadow landed on the counter where Darius had been sitting only a moment ago. He ran forward, firing at the beast twice, his second round tearing apart a rack of cigarettes above the register. The beast leapt to the floor and landed between two of the shelves. Its bulk slid into the space that was too narrow without the slightest disturbance to the goods stacked around it.

Darius ran forward and put himself in a straight line to the thing stalking toward him. With a clear line of sight and no longer running, he placed three well-aimed slugs into the bulk of shadow. A spear that he thought was a tongue lashed forward. He threw himself prone and fired again. Black blood sprayed across the shelves.

The thing spun in the too small space and leapt to the counter and out the window. Darius rose to one knee and fired again, but only took a big hole out of the top of one of the shelves as the thing made its escape. He ran forward to the window and brought his gun to bear on the fleeing beast, but the gun merely clicked on an empty chamber.

Suddenly the world spun, fuzzy around the edges, turning blacker with each second. Darius staggered and almost fell. He tried desperately to draw air into his lungs but he felt as if he had been dealt a massive body blow and the wind had been knocked from him. He staggered toward Sarah, who caught him as he fell. He gasped but the air wasn't there. She said something he couldn't hear.

She disappeared for a moment and returned with a small aerosol inhaler. She shook it and held it to his lips. He sucked in the medicine, and after a moment, felt the air begin to come more easily. He took a second puff, and after another excruciating moment, slowly could breathe again.

Sarah sat and held him until his breathing relaxed. His heart pounded. She was talking to him. The words were difficult to understand.

"Just breathe. You're going to be okay."

A moment later, consciousness left him.

* * *

When Darius woke up the sun had risen. Its light did not yet stream through the front window. It was still morning. The barricade over it had been repaired, and much of the glass and splinters had been swept into a far corner. Sarah was propped against the wall nearby, her nose in a book.

"What time is it?"

Sarah checked her watch. "Ten thirty. How are you feeling?"

"Like shit."

"I didn't know you had asthma."

"Neither did I."

Gingerly, he stood up. He hurt even more than the day before. His muscles were sore in ways he didn't know was possible outside the body aches of a bad stomach flu. His bare shoulder was a swollen mass of purple bruise. His back burned. His hands ached with cuts and abrasions, but Sarah had cleaned them while he slept. His lungs ached and his ears still rang distantly.

Sarah stood up and gently hugged him. "We can't keep this up."

He nodded. "I know."

"We're almost out of lamp oil and the ammo is running low."

Darius limped to the window and peered out. The town was clear.

"It stalked around for a while this morning but left again."

Darius sat down hard in one of the chairs. "We need to get out of here. We won't survive the next attack."

"That thing is still out there."

Darius rubbed his unshaven face. "Yeah. Ideas?"

"The keys are still in the truck. We can make a break for it."

He scoffed. "Because that worked so well last time. We'll get eaten before we get that far."

She sighed and rolled her eyes. "Not if we set a trap for it."

"What?"

She stood up. "If I run out first it should come after me, but then you come out and shoot the hell out of it."

"There's almost a hundred feet between the door and the truck."

"Well then I guess you better be a good shot. Now grab that hammer and help me."

Together, they dismantled the barricade, watching and listening carefully for any sign of the beast. Once the door was clear, Darius lifted the gun to his shoulder and scanned the area. That thing was out there somewhere, and they were going to die.

Sarah took a deep breath. "Now or never."

Darius' eyes remained fixed on the world beyond the door. Sarah slapped him hard across the arm.

"Focus!"

A stern finger pointed at his face. "Darius, be ready and pay attention. I know you're tired, we both are, but if you shoot me I swear to god I will murder you in your sleep."

He nodded. "You ready?"

"No," she said and darted into the sunlight.

She was in the open for several paces before the beast emerged at a run. As soon as it passed, Darius stepped out and put a slug into its side at close range. Black blood splattered and turned to dust in the air. The beast skidded as it spun around on the gravel.

Sarah leapt into the truck and started the engine. Darius rushed and fired at the beast again, hitting it low and staggering it. The truck started to move. Darius fired another round, missing wildly, and leapt into the bed of the truck.

The engine roared and the truck skidded around, throwing gravel and tearing grass, sending dust and sod in big arcs behind it. The beast recovered and darted toward them. Their tires smoked on the asphalt as they slid to the side, before catching and surging them forward. The beast was close behind.

Darius fired again but only grazed the thing and tore chunks from the asphalt. The truck raced away and the world rushed past. The beast moved impossibly fast, closing the gap between them. It leapt as if they were standing still. Its front legs reached forward with wicked claws. It landed hard on the tailgate of the truck and tore it from the bed. The discarded chunk of steel crashed and tumbled away behind them.

The thing was upon him. It was in uncomfortable definition. The creature was a mat of slimy, black fur. Wounds dripped viscous blood on the truck bed. The maw that opened beneath its blank, black eyes yawned larger than the snout seemed able to accommodate and glistening teeth unfolded from within.

The beast lurched forward and Darius brought the gun to bear. The shotgun roared. The unnatural head exploded in a shower of blood and flesh, scorching Darius' skin where it hit him. The headless beast snapped backward with a boneless flailing of appendages, fell from the truck, and slammed to the blacktop, an amorphous, tumbling blob of shadowy fur. It came to a rest as they sped away. As the distance grew greater, the thing seemed to crumble and blow away on the breeze. In only a few moments, the thing had vanished completely.

Darius collapsed in a heap in the back of the truck, grateful when they left the valley behind.

❋　❋　❋

The world that passed by was one of stark, unending green. No civilization to be seen. His body and soul ached. Nothing would ever be the same.

When they passed a handful of silent houses, Darius began to fear the worst. The next home however, had two men resting comfortably on their front porch, a cooler between them and cans of beer in their hands. One raised a hand and waved as they passed.

Darius was too tired to respond.

A LOVELY LITTLE NASH

Leon Roy

Four young women are driving through Augusta, Maine heading south towards the bright and lively coastline of Boothbay Harbor. Dorothy, sitting in the back-right passenger seat, is mourning the recent passing of her father. Her friends Jackie, Frances, and Ruby are taking her to the *Spruce Inn Resort and Spa* for a much-needed weekend getaway. Jackie, who is behind the wheel of her old Cadillac, rolls down her driver side window to smoke a cigarette.

"Do you guys really think so?" Dorothy says.

Ruby turns around in her front passenger seat to address Dorothy while blowing on her freshly painted fingernails.

"Of course, we do sweetie," Ruby says. "This will turn out to be exactly what you need right now, you'll see."

Frances finally stops scrolling through her news feed before tucking the phone into her bra.

"Yeah, absolutely," Frances says. "We can stay up late —"

Dorothy looks back and forth between Ruby and Frances.

"— sleep in —"

"Walk on the beach with the sand beneath our toes and dip our feet in the water." Dorothy twiddles her thumbs, waiting for a chance to speak.

"See the town too, right?" Dorothy says.

"Of course."

Jackie flicks her cigarette ash out the window, some of the ash cascading through to the back seat and onto Frances's dress. She quickly wipes it away.

"There must be a decent place for a beer too I hope," Jackie says.

Ruby sighs as she touches up her lipstick in the small mirror on the visor.

"That would be what you're most concerned with wouldn't it?"

Jackie obnoxiously sighs back at Ruby who is now applying more cover-up.

"Just keep powdering that face *Ronald McDonald*. All I'm saying is a little drink would be appreciated. I'm sure as hell not spending this entire weekend sober while you girly girls curl each other's hair."

Ruby closes the visor and turns to Jackie, putting her make-up back in her purse.

"You know what? You can drink all you like just as long as we can all agree that at the end of the day we're all here for Dorothy."

"Obviously," Jackie replies.

Frances lashes out towards Jackie while placing her hand firmly on Dorothy's inner thigh.

"Jackie!" she yells.

"No guys. It's okay she's right. Regardless of everything I see no reason why we can't have a little fun. Sound fair?" Dorothy says.

They all agree.

Ruby reaches her hand around back to Dorothy and locks her pinky with hers sharing a brief smile.

Frances removes her hand from Dorothy's thigh and waves away some of the cigarette smoke, lingering in the air.

"Besides Jackie, while we girly girls are busy with our slumber party ... you know, pillow fights, manicures, and curling our hair, there will be a very large jetted bath tub. You can dip your toes in that," Frances says.

Jackie rolls her eyes and flicks her cigarette butt out the window.

Gazing out the window, a car show in a local church parking lot catches Dorothy's eye. There is a sea of classic cars, one stands out though: a cherry red 1950's *Nash Rambler* with a white drop-top and whitewall tires.

"Stop the car!" she yells, causing Jackie to swerve.

"Why what's wrong!?" Jackie says. "Are you okay?"

"I'm fine, just pull over. At the car show ... there!"

Jackie turns around and pulls into the church parking lot. Before the car comes to a complete stop, Dorothy jumps out of the car and sprints to the far side of the parking lot, running straight for the *Nash Rambler*, a big smile stretching across her face.

Jackie catches up to Dorothy first. "What ... the ... hell?" she gasps, bent over with her hands resting on her knees.

Mesmerized, Dorothy lightly drags her fingers along the sparkling hood of the car.

"It's perfect," Dorothy says softly.

"Yeah ... they all are baby doll," Jackie says short of breath. "That's kinda the point."

The trunk of the *Nash Rambler,* which was open, abruptly shuts. Standing at the end of the car is a young man about the same age as the girls. His attire matches the car's era. He's dressed in black boots, black jeans, white t-shirt, black leather jacket, and even sporting a 1950's style rockabilly haircut. Dorothy winces at the unexpected loud bang of the trunk.

"Oh, I'm sorry. I didn't mean to —"

The young man takes out an extinct brand of cigarettes, *Lucky Strikes*, and interrupts Dorothy.

"— Mean to what?" he says.

Dorothy stares at the young man as he takes a drag.

"My father always wanted one of these," Dorothy timidly says.

"He teach you about cars, did he?"

"He tried to."

The young man extends his hand to shake. "Names John," he says. "But my friends call me Johnny."

Jackie, not impressed by his mystique, hisses his name under her breath.

"That's my name little momma, don't you go and wear it out now," Johnny says.

Johnny smirks at Dorothy, waiting for her to shake his hand and she finally does.

"It's nice to meet you Johnny. I'm Dorothy."

Shaking Johnny's hand, chills shoot down her spine, like some sort of sixth sense warning her off danger.

"Dorothy?" Johnny says. "Now there's a name not thrown around much anymore. Unless you're from *OZ* that is." He winks.

Jackie chuckles under her breath. Johnny glances over and notices the tattoos on her arms.

"Nice ink," he says. "Never could get any myself. Thought I'd always be scratching ... So, are you queen bee then? Where's your king?"

"No king, just loyal worker bees," Jackie says.

Frances laughs.

"Yeah. You're queen."

Jackie, still gasping a little, surveys the other cars and realizes Johnny has parked his *Rambler* in a secluded corner of the lot.

"Are you even a part of this thing?" she says. "Couldn't you have parked a little closer to the church?"

Johnny sighs, shrugging his shoulders. "Well I've always been a bit of an antichrist."

Dorothy steps in front of Jackie. "So, what's the secret to restoring a car into such fine condition?"

Johnny takes a long drag from his cigarette. As he blows out the smoke he whispers in Dorothy's ear. "I sold my soul sweetheart."

Frances grabs Dorothy by the shoulder and tries to pull her away. "Come on, let's go."

Just as the girls begin heading back to Jackie's Cadillac, Johnny says, "Say ... Could I interest you ladies in a car?"

Dorothy breaks free from Frances and runs back to Johnny. "This car!?"

"That's right."

"He's joking, sweetie!" Frances yells.

"Au contraire, doll face!" Johnny says.

Johnny reaches into the back seat of the *Nash Rambler* and removes a thick stack of paper. He drops it on the hood of the car with a loud thump.

Dorothy looks down at the stack of paper. "What's that?"

"A contract," Johnny replies.

He holds out a red pen in front of her face and clicks the top revealing the ballpoint tip.

"What kind of contract?"

The girls all peer down at the "contract."

"Today is your lucky day girls. If you would like to drive away in this pristine masterpiece here, all you have to do is sign right here on the dotted line. All of you. Then ... the car is yours to do with as you wish for twenty-four hours."

"What's the catch?" Ruby asks.

"No catch," Johnny says. "You all sign ... you take the car ... and in twenty-four hours I shall return to collect. I do it all the time."

"Excuse us," Dorothy says, pulling the girls off to the side.

"Certainly."

"I think we should do it," Dorothy whispers.

"What are you crazy?" Jackie says. "We can't trust this guy."

"I would normally disagree with her, but *James Dean* here has trouble written all over his face," Ruby says.

Dorothy looks back at the car then back at the girls. "Look guys, can you just do this for me? Please? My father always wanted to restore one of these and this may be my only chance to ever drive one ... Frances?"

"Alright." Frances nods. "For you and your father."

Jackie and Ruby sigh as Dorothy squeals in delight. She walks back over to Johnny, trying to remain calm.

"So, do we have a deal?" Johnny asks.

"Deal," Dorothy says.

Johnny's grin grows to a sinister smile.

"Well then," he says. "Let's get this show on the road."

Dorothy and Frances sign the contract first, followed by Jackie and Ruby. Satisfied, Johnny rolls up the contract and tucks it under his left arm.

Jackie returns to her Cadillac and drives it over to transfer their luggage into the trunk of the *Nash Rambler*. Ruby and Frances let the white drop-top of the car down. Once properly stowed, Jackie tries to read the license plate at the rear, which reads: "BLZBUB."

"What does that say?" Frances asks Ruby, tilting her head confused.

"I'm not sure," Ruby replies, also confused. "Must be some kind of car thing I guess. Come on, let's go."

Ruby and Frances hop in the back seat of the car.

Johnny jingles the keys in his hand. "Now then, who's driving?"

Dorothy is already in the driver's seat. "That'd be me," she says with a smile.

Johnny tosses the keys to Dorothy.

"Don't you need to know where we'll be staying?" Dorothy asks.

"Just meet me back here tomorrow," Johnny says. "Oh, say ... high noon. You just enjoy your one night. The sun sets fast."

"Thank you," Dorothy says.

Johnny's sinister smile re-emerges as he leans on the open driver side door. "Don't thank me yet."

Johnny slams her door shut, backing away from the car. When Dorothy starts the engine a cloud of yellow dust escapes from the exhaust pipe, smelling of brimstone.

"Ew, something smells like rotten eggs," Jackie says, plugging her nose in disgust.

"Okay, do you literally have to take the fun out of everything?" Ruby says with disapproval.

As Dorothy drives out of the parking lot she takes one last look at Johnny through the rear-view mirror, who is lighting up another cigarette, and is reminded of the sense of menace she felt when first shaking his hand.

❊　❊　❊

The girls cheer, waving their hands in the air while they speed down the road in their borrowed *Nash Rambler*. Once they near town though, Dorothy is forced to slow down due to high traffic.

As they drive up and over a hill they enter the Harbor and can smell the sea water. Dorothy can even hear the faint sound of boat horns coming from the lobsterman entering the Harbor after a long and hard day's work at sea.

While Dorothy drives, the girls take in the many beautiful sights of Boothbay Harbor. At the top of a hill is a large, old, but stunning chapel. Below that and closer to the docks, are multiple restaurants and a location where part of the musical *Carousel* was filmed. The *Novelty* is returning from a tour around Burnt Island where the oldest lighthouse in the state of Maine has firmly stood since 1821.

Eventually the girls pull into the parking area of the *Spruce Inn Resort and Spa*. Dorothy parks the car and after grabbing their luggage from the trunk, they all enter the lobby of the hotel. Jackie vigorously scratches at her right arm, at one of her tattoos.

"Man, am I glad you talked us into taking that car," Ruby says. "The risk was worth the ride."

"You're welcome. I'm glad you enjoyed it," Dorothy replies with a hint of sadness.

"Your father would have loved it," Frances says.

Dorothy notices Jackie scratching her arm raw. "Are you okay Jackie?" Dorothy asks.

"I think so," she says. "My arm is just really itching me."

At the front desk a young woman named Maggie obnoxiously chomps on a piece of gum, chatting with her girlfriend. Maggie frowns in disgust at the sight of Jackie scratching her beet-red arm.

Ruby begins to dig through her purse. "I have some lotion in my bag you can use."

"No, I think I'm just going to take a bath when we get to our room."

Jackie approaches the front desk first, but is ignored by Maggie. "Excuse me? Hello … I'm talking to you!"

With a smug look on her face, Maggie finally acknowledges Jackie. "Can I help you with something? Do you need some directions perhaps?"

Jackie shakes her head. "No. I don't need any directions. We're here for check-in."

"You're late," Maggie says. "Well?"

"Well what?"

"You gotta name?"

"Dorothy," Jackie says. "It's under Dorothy. Dorothy Paige."

Maggie glances at the rest of the girls and Dorothy raises her hand.

"Hi," Dorothy says.

Maggie finds their reservation. She takes out their room keys and when a scratching Jackie reaches for them, Maggie pulls away and hands them to Dorothy.

"Thanks," Dorothy says.

Maggie glares at Jackie. "You know; you should really get that looked at before it spreads." She grimaces. "We like … have guests here."

Before Jackie has a chance to react Frances steps in and pulls her away while Maggie resumes talking to her girlfriend.

At the door, Dorothy fumbles with the room key while Jackie's excessive scratching worsens.

"Stop it Jackie!" Ruby says. "You're going to scratch right through your arm."

They enter to a luxurious room equipped with two queen-sized beds, a fireplace, the large bathroom with a jetted tub that Frances had described earlier, and their very own private balcony. Ruby jumps onto one of the queen mattresses and rolls across. She suddenly feels pain in her fingers and stands up off the mattress. With her back turned to the rest of the girls, she sees that all her fingernails have begun to peel away from her skin. Her new nail polish is melting away and blood rises from the base of her nails.

Ruby's eyes begin to tear up, becoming hazy. She brings her hands to her mouth and starts to gently glide her bloody fingertips across her lips. Her mascara and bronzer melt from her face, which begins to bubble as more make-up runs off her cheeks.

One by one she removes her loose fingernails with her teeth, each dripping blood as she rips through the last flaps of cuticle connecting the nail. Ruby begins to suck on her fingertips even as they seem to ooze more and more yellow pus. Tiny individual holes begin to appear all over her hands giving her skin a webbed appearance. It spreads up her arms as if she were being burned alive.

Dorothy sets her bag by the bed and sees Ruby has moved into the corner of the room facing the wall.

"Ruby, what are you doing?" Dorothy asks.

Ruby turns to look at Dorothy and appears completely normal, except for her watery eyes. She looks back at her fingers and they also appear to be normal. Confused and slightly afraid of what has just happened, she says the first thing that comes to mind. "Sorry … I thought … I thought I broke a nail."

"Over react much?" Jackie says behind her breath. "I'm going to go take a bath and see if I can't get rid of this rash."

Dorothy heads towards the door, but Frances catches her.

"You're just going to leave without saying anything?" Frances asks. "Where are you going?"

"I'm just going to go for a quick walk in the Harbor. I won't be long."

Dorothy exits the room as Jackie is setting up her *iPod dock* in the bathroom. She leaves the bathroom door cracked open and begins blasting loud heavy metal music as she undresses. Ruby quickly becomes annoyed by the loud music, reaches over and closes the door.

Once Jackie is fully nude, it's clear that the rash is not isolated to just her arm. Unbeknownst to her, it has spread to the right side of her back and upper right shoulder. While Jackie steps into the bubbling warm tub she reaches around her shoulder and tries to scratch her back. She lets herself slowly sink into the tub, sprinkling around more bath salts while dipping her arm in and out of the water.

Jackie tries to resist scratching her arm any further, but can't control herself. She digs through her purse to look for anything that could help, but all she finds is her pocket knife. She opens the blade, spellbound by the shine of the stainless steel.

Jackie slowly begins to cut away the skin on her right arm, peeling it off into strips and dropping them into the bubbling water. When she feels she has removed enough skin, she begins to scratch at her bare flesh with her nails again turning the bath water into a bubbling bloody red cauldron. Eye watering, she remains relatively calm, seemingly in no pain just as Ruby short time before.

Just outside the bathroom door though, Ruby sits at the end of the bed complaining to Frances about Jackie's loud music. Frances ignores Ruby, flipping through the channels on the television, finally stopping on nothing but static.

"That's it, I've had it!" Ruby screams.

She jumps up from the bed. Frances seems to be in a trance, blankly staring into the static on the television screen. As Ruby nears the bathroom door, Frances's eyes begin to bleed. Ruby enters the bathroom, closing the door behind her, nothing amiss but the rash. Jackie sits in the tub with the pocket knife hovering over her right arm and tears streaming down her cheeks. Ruby turns the music down and frowns in disgust.

"What the fuck are you doing?!" Ruby screams. "Drop the knife! Right now! What's wrong with you?"

Jackie looks up slowly, her face filled with horror. "I don't know ... I ..."

Jackie rises up from the water and bright yellow pee runs down her legs. She steps out of the tub, dropping the knife, and barely makes it to the toilet in time to vomit. While Jackie wretches, Ruby picks up the knife, suddenly transfixed on the stainless steel blade.

Outside the room, Frances stands up and approaches the body length mirror by the entrance. She looks into the mirror, tears of blood streaming down her face. Her image reflected back at her slowly begins to resemble Dorothy.

Meanwhile, Dorothy is walking across a passenger bridge that stretches to both sides of the Harbor. The sun is setting and with the sea breeze she experiences a slight chill. She rubs her arms and turns back to the resort. Along the way, the rolling waves seem to whisper to her.

"Dorothy ..." the voice whispers.

Dorothy looks around and doesn't see a single soul. The voice whispers again, this time from a greater distance, almost as if it's traveling with the wind.

"Dorothy ..."

Frightened, she hurries back to the safety of her hotel room.

Back in the hotel room, Frances is coughing up blood, spitting it onto the mirror. She watches the blood and mucus slide down the mirror and drip to the floor. From bottom to top she licks the blood and mucus away from the mirror, while sensually swaying her hips. When she reaches the top, she kisses her reflection, smearing blood and gore across the surface, blood leaking out of her closed eyes. When she opens her eyes, the image of Dorothy has reappeared, staring back at her.

The room spins and the mirror disappears. Frances and Dorothy reach out to touch each other. As Frances leans in to kiss this mirror image of Dorothy, her eyes begin to glow of a deep neon red, even transforming the colors around the room.

Ruby emerges from the bathroom carrying the knife. Blood runs down her arm, dripping from the blade.

She sees Frances kissing a reflection of herself in the unblemished mirror. Frances opens her eyes and through the mirror sees Ruby approaching, her eyes also aglow. Frances and Ruby step toward each other and Frances grabs the bloody knife in Ruby's hand and proceeds to lick the blade.

"Do you think I'm pretty?" Ruby says softly.

Frances nods stiffly while Ruby exposes her neck. Frances gently slides the flat side of the knife against Ruby's neck, wiping the blood from it before leaning in open mouthed to kiss Ruby, leaving behind the bloody lip prints of some seductive vampire.

"Jackie didn't think so," Ruby says.

Frances gently places her hands on Ruby's cheeks. Staring into Ruby's neon red eyes, she passionately kisses her like a demon possessed.

By the time Dorothy makes her way back to the room, Ruby and

Frances are standing out on the balcony. A few blood droplets are sprinkled on the center of the floor. Dorothy squints her eyes as she looks down at the blood droplets, curious. With the room lit and the balcony dark, just the silhouettes of Ruby and Frances are visible to Dorothy.

"What are you guys doing in the dark?" Dorothy asks.

Ruby and Frances say nothing. Dorothy approaches them, but stops at the end of the bed when she notices their eyes glowing bright red in the darkness. She takes a step backward.

"Frances?" she says. "Ruby?"

"We were wondering when you'd come back to us," Ruby says, speaking softly in a drawn out relaxed tone.

"We were worried," Frances says.

"What's wrong with your eyes?" Dorothy asks, her voice cracking.

Ruby and Frances slowly step into the room and when they do Dorothy takes another step back. At that moment, Jackie's bloody arm pushes open the bathroom door and she drags herself out into the open, crying in pain.

"Oh my God ..." Dorothy whispers, shocked. "Oh my God!"

Dorothy rushes over to Jackie to help her up, but Jackie, who is still fully nude, falls to the ground. Jackie is missing her left leg and right arm from below the joints, which appear to have been more torn than cut. Pieces of her flesh dangle from where the limbs should be, dragging along the floor.

Waves of terror tremors shake Dorothy.

"Jesus ..." Dorothy says. "How could you do this!?"

Dorothy slides down to the floor, leans up against the wall and cradles the distraught Jackie in her arms. She pushes Jackie's hair out of her face to find that her face has been slashed deeply multiple times. Dorothy looks over the rest of Jackie's body to find she has deep cuts from head to toe.

Ruby and Frances stand a few feet away staring at Dorothy cradling Jackie, bemused. Dorothy glares at them.

"You're sick!" she screams. "Both of you!"

Jackie reaches up to touch Dorothy's face, just barely dragging her fingertips across her cheek.

"Do you hear it too?" Jackie whispers.

"What?" Dorothy says. "What did you say Jackie?"

Dorothy gently places her hand on Jackie's head.

"Do you hear it?" Jackie whispers even a little softer.

"Hear what Jackie?"

"The voices ..." She says. "Am I a ... bad person?"

Dorothy begins to rock Jackie back and forth like a small child.

"No," Dorothy replies. "Of course not. You're every bit of good —"
Dorothy whimpers trying to stay strong.

"— I'm so sorry. This is all my fault."

Dorothy begins to softly sing "*Somewhere over the Rainbow*" while
quietly whimpering. She leans her head back against the wall and closes
her eyes. Halfway through the song, blood suddenly splatters across her
face. Dorothy opens her eyes and is horrified to find that Ruby has
walked over and slit Jackie's throat, putting her out of her misery.
Dorothy screams while Frances giggles and playfully bites down on her
thumb.

Ruby grabs Dorothy by her hair and drags her across the floor over
to the beds while the dying sound of Jackie gargling on her own blood
haunts her. Dorothy breaks free of Ruby's grasp and scurries toward
the bathroom. Jumping to her feet, she shoves Ruby away and rushes
into the bathroom only to slip on Jackie's blood, which has pooled
around the door. Reaching back, she shuts and locks the door.

In shock, shaking, and full of fear, Dorothy tries to wash Jackie's
blood off her hands in the sink. As she thoroughly scrubs her hands,
the voice she heard earlier on her walk calls out to her once more.

"Dorothy ..." the voice whispers.

Dorothy looks over her shoulder and the breath of the voice is
gently blowing her hair near her left ear, as if a ghost is whispering to
her. Slowly, she calms down until she finally drops the soap onto the
floor, leaving her hands uncleansed.

Dorothy's reflection now reveals eyes that glow the same deep
neon red that she first saw on Ruby and Frances.

The door of the bathroom opens and Dorothy steps out. Ruby and
Frances are each sitting on separate ends of the queen-sized beds.

Everything around is some vibrant crimson hallucination. The contrast of the colors in the room change becoming darker in some areas
and brighter in others, like a rave. To the left of where Dorothy is
standing, the electric fireplace spontaneously sparks to life.

"Come sit with us," Frances says coaxingly.

The blood shines bright as Dorothy approaches them. Electricity
is in the air as the colors of the room grow richer in depth, more unreal

Dorothy sits next to Frances and Ruby moves over beside her.

Ruby begins to lightly drag her fingertips along Dorothy's arm, moving up to her chest.

"She wasn't like us Dorothy," Ruby says.

"She didn't belong," Frances adds while gently removing Dorothy's sweater. "But you ... you're special."

"Pure ... untouched," Ruby says.

"Innocent," Frances whispers, nibbling at her ear.

Frances tosses Dorothy's sweater to the ground and Ruby removes Dorothy's hair tie. Her luscious blonde locks cascade through the air.

Frances leans in close to Dorothy placing her hand on her inner thigh, pausing just before her lips touch Dorothy's. Dorothy kisses Frances and starts to remove her clothes. She turns to kiss Ruby removing her clothes as well. As Frances moves her hand up Dorothy's inner thigh she slides her hand under Dorothy's panties. Dorothy opens her mouth to moan and as she does Ruby sticks her tongue in her mouth and kisses her.

"It's okay Dorothy," Frances says. "Just let yourself go."

Heavy metal music suddenly erupts from the *iPod dock* in the bathroom. The three of them continue tear off their garments, in the throes of passion. They begin to chew on each other, tearing away bits of skin and flesh, moaning, finding pleasure in their pain. With each bite the blood spreads and they smear it all over their bodies, continuing to tear each other apart.

Ruby reaches for the knife on the bed side table.

"Be gentle with me," Dorothy moans.

"Don't worry," Ruby promises. "I won't cut too deep."

Dorothy, Frances, and Ruby take turns with the small pocket knife cutting off bigger and bigger pieces of flesh, dropping them to the floor. They drown in their lust until they finally collapse into pieces on the floor. Blood, flesh, and bone have been scattered around the room, gore and viscera covering the floor. When the nightmarish orgy ends, the music shuts off and the fireplace extinguishes.

* * *

The following morning Johnny cheerfully approaches the *Spruce Inn resort and Spa*. He walks down the busy streets of the Harbor waving and greeting people that walk by. He whistles an upbeat tune from the musical "*Grease*" while flipping an ancient looking coin in his hand, occasionally rolling it between his fingers.

Johnny reaches the *Spruce Inn* and just outside the door a dog aggressively barks at him.

"I'm sorry," the dog owner says. "He's never like this. He's actually quite friendly."

"It's quite alright," Johnny says. "I can sometimes have that effect."

Johnny winks at the dog owner and enters the *Spruce Inn's* lobby. He approaches the front desk where Maggie is once again chatting it up with her girlfriend. However, this time Maggie takes an immediate interest in her guest, flirting with him.

"Oh, hi."

"Hi, there," Johnny replies, flashing a smile of gleaming white teeth.

"Um, can I help you with something … anything?" Maggie giggles.

"Well aren't you just the cutest thing."

Maggie smiles and playfully twirls her hair around her finger.

"I'm actually looking for my friends," Johnny says.

"Oh, okay. I'm sure I can help you with that. Name?"

"Dorothy," Johnny replies. He flips his coin one last time before stowing it back in his pocket.

"She checked in last night with her friends," he says.

"I remember her," Maggie says. "Her friend had some kind of weird rash or something, it was pretty gross."

"Well that's a shame."

Maggie looks up Dorothy's name on the computer while occasionally looking back at Johnny and smiling.

Maggie's girlfriend notices a yellowish powder on Jonny's left shoulder. "You've got a little something," the young girl says. "On your shoulder."

Johnny glances down at his shoulder. "Huh," he says, wiping away the yellowish powder into the air.

"Your friends are in room 204," Maggie says. "Would you like me to walk you there?"

"Thanks, but no thanks," Johnny replies. "I should probably go up there alone, but I'll be back in just a minute … I promise."

"Okay," Maggie says, giggling again.

"You know; woman would kill for cheekbones like that." Johnny points to Maggie's cheeks.

"Thanks. You really think so?" Maggie says, still chomping on her gum.

"Definitely."

Johnny leaves the lobby and walks up to room 204. When he reaches the door, he pauses, taking out his pocket comb. He slicks his hair back and takes a deep breath before entering the room.

Johnny opens the door and steps inside, firmly closing the door behind him. He looks around the room seemingly amazed by the carnage spread across the floor and walls.

"My, my, my," he says. "What a mess."

Johnny takes a few steps further and nearly slips on a piece of skin that slides across the bloody floor. Johnny sighs while shaking his foot to remove the bits of flesh stuck to the bottom of his shoe.

"Hello again girls. Am I interrupting anything?" Johnny waits and looks around the room as if he were waiting for an answer.

"No?" he says. "Well then ..."

He takes the coin back out from his pocket and holds it up into the light. Johnny utters something in a strange language then flips the coin into the air. While the coin is in the air it seems to hover, pausing at the point where gravity is about to take hold. As the coin hovers in the air, suddenly a beam of flashing blue light shoots up from the floor and is sucked into the coin. Just as soon as the light is sucked into the flipping coin, the coin falls back down into Johnny's hand making that signature metallic sound.

"Jackie —" he says.

Johnny flips the coin into the air again and another beam of blue light rises from the floor before being sucked into the coin, landing back in his hand.

"— Ruby —"

He flips the coin a third time with the same result.

"— Frances —"

Johnny flips the coin into the air for the fourth and final time, once again sucking in a beam of blue light.

"— and Dorothy. My favorite."

He tosses the coin gently a few inches into the air, catching it back in his hand, feeling the now heavier weight of it before stuffing it back into his pocket, smirking.

Johnny looks to the other side of the room and sees the car keys to the *Nash Rambler* on a side table.

"Damn," he says.

Johnny tip-toes and hops to the other side being very careful not to step on anything. He treads lightly over to the blood-splattered keys. Johnny reaches into his inner jacket pocket and pulls out a red handkerchief with a black pentagram design printed on the front. He uses the handkerchief to pick up the keys and store them in his jacket before making his way back to the door. Before exiting the room, he checks his pockets like any normal person would do before leaving the house to make sure they didn't forget anything.

"Ahhh ..." he says.

Johnny enters the bathroom and sets the song "*Beep Beep*" by *The Playmates* to play on the *iPod dock*, a song about a *Nash Rambler*. He smiles, exiting the room.

On his way back down to the lobby he dances through the halls causing a few passing guests to look at him funny, but in his mind he can hear the song, "*Beep Beep*" playing loud and clear. Johnny stops dancing once he reaches the lobby and heads briskly for the door.

"You're just going to leave without saying goodbye!?" Maggie calls.

"No time to waste, darling."

Just as Johnny pushes the front door of the hotel open he stops, quietly chuckles to himself, then turns around to face Maggie and her girlfriend.

Johnny takes a deep breath. "Say ... could I interest you ladies in a car?" he says.

"How much?" Maggie replies.

"Not much at all. Just requires a little signature."

Johnny smiles.

LIARS AND LIES

Angi Shearstone

"He's a witch!"

Ethan called out the stranger and roused the entire village in their seats. Nobody much liked these roaming merchants, though none had taken up grievance as yet. This Sebastian constituted the worst of them, and he had come to sit alone among them.

Ethan redoubled his accusation, as all the town paid mind: "Did you see his eyes? He's cast a witchery upon good Sarah!"

Ethan's townsmen sprang up, ready for confrontation: A witch!

Just as Ethan had hoped.

The traveling fur trader had caught Sarah's eye when he first passed through with his rough companions. They were brutish and manner-less, but somehow Sarah grew entranced with their spectacle.

Bewitched.

Weeks ago, on his first visit, Sebastian had lured Sarah from the dining hall. None could account for where they went. The next morning, she had taken ill, while the trader had remained absent all day.

Again tonight, the strange, small man with the thick accent coaxed Sarah to him.

Again tonight, Ethan felt the hot coals of jealousy within him.

He'd seen something unnatural in the man's beckoning. The man had devilish eyes behind his tinted spectacles. They shone like molten silver, and had no separation of the pupil, the iris, or the whites. He directed those eyes at good Sarah and Ethan could not abide that.

The accused took flight, abandoning coat and belongings. The village gave chase. Ethan felt justified: No innocent man would flee justice.

Sebastian fled, heading for the woods faster than any man. They might have lost him in the mist, but the stranger fell in his attempt to clear the churchyard fence.

They surrounded him under the sudden light of the bright moon, and one man hit him on the head with a shovel. The blow left Sebastian unconscious and gashed.

They dragged him to the witch's cell beneath the church and secured him into the chains reserved for witches.

Waiting for the town leaders to arrive, two of Ethan's companions humiliated the accused for his poltroonery. They sheared the coward's hair from his head with their knives and would have gone further, if not reminded by the constable that guilt had not yet been proven.

They resigned themselves to wait for the Magistrate, and left the constable to guard the accused.

Ethan stepped into the moonlight. Did he truly believe his accusation? Jealousy or no, the stranger's presence made Sarah act strangely, and Ethan feared for the young woman's well-being. He could not fathom how Sarah was attracted to the stranger with his vulgar jests and habits.

Ethan's accusation may have come out of spite, but let the magistrate question the defendant and decide the truth of it. Ethan would make his peace with the Lord, regardless.

He wondered where Sarah was now.

"Dear Sarah fainted and her mother has taken her home to bed," the minister spoke, as if he knew Ethan's mind. "Tell us what led you to make this serious charge, young Ethan."

Before Ethan could begin, a call rang out from the underground hold.

They found the prisoner spread and chained between two posts.

He now stood fully conscious, and with his head wound fully healed.

"Don't look at his eyes!" The constable sprawled along the floor, frightened.

The accused directed his furious attention at Ethan.

"*You!* Wretched stripling! How dare you accuse me falsely! Filthiest of liars! I will thrust my most thorough vengeance upon you, you whoreson!"

The defendant spat terrifying threats and wicked obscenities upon all present. Ethan shuddered to imagine this coarse language striking dear Sarah's sweet ears.

But was indecency equal to witchery? Ethan's heart faltered as the man accused him of fouler feats than false witness.

The trader spewed black insults until the minister and three assistants fastened the branks on him. Ethan shuddered, chilled by the charge the prisoner had leveraged against him: *Liar.*

The iron gag did little to silence the accused. He screamed and worked his jaws like he meant to break the device by voice and tongue.

The rig held fast, but the small man kept at it. He strained until blood filled his mouth and dribbled down his chin in a most unholy way.

The blood came dark and slow, oozing, giving off a vile and festering odor. The gathered stared in horror.

The minister bid one man to strip the captive to the waist, and another to test a few lashes on the fiendish man's back.

Ethan could scarcely believe his eyes as the seeping wounds healed within minutes.

They *had* caught themselves a witch!

Ethan's heart leapt with relief, but not with joy. Malodorous blood? Wounds that vanished as they watched? He had never heard of witchcraft such as this.

The abomination now redoubled its efforts to break from bonds and branks. The devices held, but the grisly vocals disgusted all who heard them.

"We have seen this devil's craft for our own eyes, and the Magistrate will bear witness when he arrives." They left the fiend to suffer its strangled curses in solitude.

❋ ❋ ❋

At the first light of dawn, Ethan ran to the cells to await the Magistrate's arrival, fearful and flushed. The constable and deacon looked agitated when he arrived. Alarmed, Ethan rushed down the stairs.

To his relief, the accused still hung there. But to his dismay, the creature appeared lifeless and breathless.

"It went weak and silent just before dawn," the constable said. "Its skin proves cold and unresponsive to the touch. But better a dead witch than a live one."

Ethan did not believe that. The woods to their west — near the base of Bauneg Beg Mountain — had become haunted by way of a witch not properly executed.

To the consternation of the whole village, the magistrate's *apprentice* arrived midmorning, alone.

Magistrate's Apprentice Camilla Birdsley assured them of her qualifications. "I possess full knowledge and authority granted by the Magistrate to assess this case in a serious manner."

Birdsley did arrive by wagon, prepared to transport a prisoner as needed. An educated woman of the city, she shamelessly did not bother with further formalities.

"Who has brought these accusations to bear?"

Ethan's knees moved like jellied currants. "I did, ma'am. Ethan Tinsdale."

"Good. I will have questions for you, and you will bear witness to the exam. First, I must meet your suspected witch."

Ethan detected a tint of derision in the woman's pronunciation of *witch*.

In the witch cellar, the fiend's condition did not give the apprentice pause.

"Do not be fooled," Birdsley said. She appraised the security of the witchery chains.

She circled the inanimate witch without contact. She used gloved hands to lift its head and pull open its eyelids. Ethan shuddered as he now looked directly at those eyes.

They swirled in shades of gray like tarnished silver now, not sparkling like Ethan had seen directed at Sarah.

Next the apprentice tested the iron around the accused's jaws. Dried ichor caked the bridle near his mouth, but no blood remained on the skin; perhaps absorbed back into the man's unholy flesh.

Satisfied, the apprentice pushed the witch's lips back, and Ethan nearly loosed his bowels at the gruesome sight within.

Grotesque and malformed fangs lined the intruder's gums. Some stood straight like thin arrowheads, some curled back like talons for ripping and scraping.

How had he missed such a sight, as they had wrestled the apparatus into its maw? How had they not seen it, fighting to control those very jaws?

The apprentice let the head loll and stepped back.

"You have a powerful abomination among you. Count yourselves fortunate for young Ethan's watchful eye." She looked to all present. "I have tracked this villain for months, and many good folk have gone missing in his wake. His execution will serve a great justice."

"But the fiend is already perished," the minister declared.

"A powerful deception."

Birdsley circled to the suspect's back, and she struck several lashes. It woke to jerk with each blow and yelp with some, and fell deadly quiet when they ceased. As before, the gashes healed, even as the heinous thing seemed dead.

She seized a torch and held it to Sebastian's face, nearly setting alight what remained of his hair. The prisoner screeched and sprung to life. Birdsley waved the fire around its form, and it cowered from it to the limits of its bonds. All the while it shrieked, now fearful rather than furious.

Birdsley put the flame away and the prisoner's shaking halted. Ethan feared it might return to its fury, but it sunk back into its chains, limp and expired enough to bury.

"This creature will succumb to no death save by *fire*." Birdsley turned to leave. "I have seen enough."

The entire anxious village waited in the churchyard.

"I confirm: You have captured a witch. His execution will provide a most overdue justice." Birdsley approached her wagon. "I will make ready to transport the prisoner."

"We have the means here," the minister gave protest. "And we captured him, we should see this through to the end."

Birdsley made to argue, but the constable intervened. "He violated our trust and acted against us."

"The Magistrate would wish to certify the charges —"

"Then send for him," the minister said. "The monster will keep until he arrives."

"Gentlemen, you have a most dangerous evil in your custody. I am eager to rid the world of this stain."

"And soon we will. You brought confinement to convey a known witch?"

"That I did."

"Let us display him in cage and chains until the magistrate arrives, to deter all who would consort with the devil."

The apprentice reluctantly acquiesced.

"If you wish to delay justice, so be it. Send for the magistrate at once. Let us return to the cellar and secure the convict without further delay."

The gibbet cage was a monstrous thing, with devices to hold the condemned centered within the frame, legs spread, arms bent, and wrists secured at shoulder height.

Into this nightmare, they packed their corpse-like captive. Then the apprentice checked all the locks. To Ethan, such measures seemed wasted on the small fur trader. But Birdsley performed the tasks as if securing the devil himself. She turned to the town's leaders.

"I must question him before you take him to your gibbet. I will watch here until he wakes, and would question Ethan alone while I wait."

They left, and Ethan looked on while Birdsley checked the locks again.

"He doesn't seem to warrant all that."

"No. But he would break most any other prison. Remember, he did seem a witch to you, and that matters."

She turned to Ethan with torchlight glinting off her eyes. "Tell me how you came to your suspicions."

Ethan told the apprentice of Sebastian's eyes and Sarah's odd behavior.

"I will speak to this Sarah, too."

"Please be gentle, she's taken ill again."

"You like this girl."

Ethan nodded.

"Do not worry. This thing's influences will vanish with its destruction."

"I could not see its teeth last night."

"They can hide them, or cause people not to notice things."

"Like its eyes."

"Yes."

"He's not a witch, is he?"

"No."

"What is he, then?"

"We will get to that tomorrow."

Ethan asked no further questions.

＊　＊　＊

Birdsley showed no surprise when, upon sunset, the devil came to life again. It rattled and brayed against its enclosures, enraged at its impotence within them.

"Calm yourself!" The apprentice grabbed the branks and forced the witch to meet her eyes. "I would confirm your *true* identity, *witch*."

Again, she said *witch* in that tone.

The form's struggles stilled to a tremor. Ethan mistook the quivering as fear, but the creature's face banished the thought. The fiend's eyes were not frightful, but leveled in purest rage.

"You are no witch, and cannot speak your name."

She spoke as if the two of them, interrogator and prisoner, shared some secret knowledge.

"But I know who you are."

She paced a half circle around him.

"Your physical stature ... the reports of your accent and obscenity ..." She paused to flick at the branks. "... and the arrogance that presses you to *keep* your name, or similar, through the *ages*."

She locked eyes with the prisoner; his now *glowed* with fury.

"You can be none other than *Sevastianos*, first Turned outside Athens, nearly seven centuries ago."

The witch drove the branks against the bars, over and over. He meant to break his muzzle, one way or another. But the structures would never give way, not in a lifetime of clanging.

"Finally here, I end your bloodthirsty madness."

The thing shook, and *barked* through the gag, once.

"If I had found you first, you would already be ash under my feet. But these folk will shame you for your crimes first." She gestured at his butchered hair.

"They will hang you in cage and chains both forged by my father's hand. They will display you on the eastern edge of town, and pelt you with stones, rotten food, and feces. They intend to execute you for your *witchery* when the magistrate arrives, around noon I should expect.

"But we both know you will not live to see his arrival.

"You will withstand their humiliations and contemplate your atrocities in silence through the night.

"And then the sun itself will rise and claim you. Good riddance, Sevastianos."

* * *

The village of Hearthstowne had caught themselves a witch.

Magistrate's Apprentice Camilla Birdsley knew very well he was *not* a witch, but for her purposes, the designation would do. She climbed the stairs with young Ethan, ready to relinquish the prisoner to the people.

"He has revived," she told the leaders of Hearthstowne. "You may put him up as you wish, but I must insist: Do not loosen his bonds one inch."

"We would not dream of it." The minister sent several men down into the cellar. Birdsley watched, wishing this affair was done and over.

Terrible things existed in this world, and Birdsley recognized them when she saw them. She had debated the magistrate for an hour to gain approval for this investigation when this strange village had caught themselves a witch.

The rational magistrate did not believe in witchcraft, and halted many inquiries before they could start. But Birdsley's years of study, patience, and service came to bear, and the magistrate agreed she should look into the matter.

Birdsley confirmed the village had caught something far worse than a witch. Few had notion of this particular evil, let alone name for it. But due to a poorly contained incident in Serbia, a new word now trickled into the world from Slavic languages: *vampyr*.

Birdsley hated the term.

Hearthstowne's witch was one such creature, a thing that stalked only at night and drank from the veins of natural mankind.

Birdsley suspected another dwelled nearby, in the wood towards the mountain to the west. She would investigate that soon, but not by herself. Those who pursued blood-drinkers alone met their end swiftly.

Even now, her husband Thomas hid just outside town with several of their colleagues, ready to give aid should Hearthstowne's *witch* free itself. Once Sevastianos was dust, the group would hunt the other.

But here, Birdsley would not need their assistance.

Her clandestine efforts through the magistrate's office had worked, culminating in a victimless capture and restraint of Sevastianos. The successful containment pleased her but she did not gloat over the fiend's humiliation.

She and her colleagues had created and funded the plot. Under the seal of the magistrate, Birdsley sent sets of consecrated chains to towns throughout the region, with instruction on how to contain a witch. The contrivances did no worse to a human than regular restraints, but would hobble a vampyr for as long as necessary.

The ploy took advantage of the unwitting magistrate, as well as the credulous commonfolk. Popular superstitions sometimes led to the harm of innocents, but Birdsley and her colleagues could not change that, so they put such folklore to good use. The triumph over powerful Sevastianos proved well worth it.

Witchhunting provided an effective ruse to hunt these demons, and burning brought them to a sound end, whether through application of flame, or by virtue of the sun.

To be true, witchcraft did exist, just not in the way the unlearned suspected. Most practitioners used their talents not to the detriment of mankind, but against the blood-drinkers. Some of the bloodthirsty devils performed spells themselves, and those were the most dangerous of all.

Birsdley's husband Thomas had talent for the craft, while she herself did not. She had instead great aptitude with the legal complexities and subterfuge required for working the courts. It was uncommon for a woman to hold a public position such as this, even in the city, but she proved her worth greater than any others.

She stood next to Hearthstowne's councilmen as the cellar door opened again. The time had come for the end of the diabolical Sevastianos.

Five men dragged the heavy cage from the basement, and the minister addressed the condemned:

"Sebastian Stranthos, merchant and former guest of this village: We have witnessed your possession of abilities that could only be granted by the devil.

"You used some of these against our own, after we offered you hospitality. You are found guilty of witchcraft, and will hang for it on the morrow, when the magistrate arrives.

"In the face of justice, you have shown nothing but cowardice and vulgarity, and so, until your most deserved death, let your display send a message to all who would similarly transgress."

He stepped back and gestured for the village to do as they would.

A group of the town's unrulier young men set upon the condemned. They poured hot dark pine pitch through the cage and onto the immobilized felon. They covered his chest and back, head and face, arms and feet, anything exposed. The muted howls of outrage turned to cries of pain and protest, more pitiful than otherworldly now. The blood-drinkers possessed great powers and superior faculties, but had also a heightened sense of touch, and felt pain worse than any man.

It would take Birdsley days to clean the mess from the bars, but she would not mind. The pitch would shield the creature some, when the sun struck and ignited its skin. The protection would prolong the time between first sparks and critical ash, and Sevastianos would burn a slower death with it. Birdsley would not regret his suffering.

The boys floated feathers until Sevastianos was well covered, all the town laughing and jeering.

The most brutal Sevastianos, near seven hundred years old, now stood shorn, tarred and feathered, branked and gibbeted. Even worse, he'd been discovered by way of a boy's jealousy, captured by superstitious townsfolk, and convicted completely independent of his true crimes.

Ludicrous.

Birdsley could not join in the mockery.

She could not even smile, and would not relax until the monster had crumbled to dust. She learned young that one does not trifle with blood-drinkers. One catches them and kills them quickly, and then moves on to the next. There was no joy to be had, as there was always another, somewhere.

Her ancestors had tracked this one's atrocities across hundreds of years. They'd last sighted him in Lisbon in 1506. Not one report mentioned his very peculiar eyes, unique even to blood-drinkers. While Birdsley wondered what could have transformed them so strangely, she could not bring herself to release his tongue to answer. He would only plaster the village with more of his profanities.

The townspeople loaded their convict's coop onto a cart, and paraded him through the streets. The whole village followed, and dogs, goats, and chickens joined the line as it went. The procession ended at the gallows at the east edge of town, where they strung the cage high and took aim.

The cage shook against rotten vegetables, rancid meat, stones, rusted nails, and worse. The teenage boys used large sticks to beat upon it, spin it around, and rock it back and forth.

Slowly, with each indignity, Sevastianos' rage gave over to despair.

Soon the night grew cold, the villagers tired, and their putrid ammunition low. Intermittent groups made their way to their beds and left the beast to the exposure of the cold October night.

Before long, the apprentice stood alone with the young accuser, and the more distant watch of the night guard.

"You do not need to stay, Ethan. I will watch him until light."

"I do not want to leave until it can threaten Sarah no more."

The fiend still flailed against the inevitable. Ichor dribbled from where it bore the worst of its struggles. Its muted voice had gone hoarse behind its bridle, yet it would not cease hollering and writhing.

Birdsley gestured to the display.

"What do you think of him now, Ethan?"

"I think even an animal would have given up by now."

"He wants to live so badly he traded his very soul for it. Once, he was like you and I. Now possessed by pure evil, he murders to survive, and cannot bear the thought of perishing."

"You must rejoice in his torment."

"No. Were it not for your leaders' interference, I would have rid of him the moment we left the village. Only a fool takes chances with his kind."

Birdsley considered ending Sevastianos now, rather than wait until dawn. She could set an arrow alight, and shoot straight into the abomination's chest. An easy target.

But she could not allow the boy to bear witness, nor the watchman; she had an official position to maintain. Come morning, the folk would find only ash and think he had escaped. Better they see their witch catch fire in the light of the sun.

The two kept vigil to the futile exertions, until some hour after midnight the creature finally fell silent. It ceased struggling and surrendered into the unyielding structure of confinement.

This prompted no relief in Birdsley, but alarm. Sevastianos could rage for a week undiminished, if daytime could allow his tantrum to continue unabated.

"Something's wrong," she warned. She drew her hidden firearm, and hoped her team took notice.

A terrible stillness fell to the trees, Birdsley caught the flicker of glowing red eyes, but it was too late.

✱   ✱   ✱

Burned as a witch.

Sebastian would burn as a witch if he could not determine a way out of this ... *outrage*.

A rotten potato covered in horse manure cleared the bars to strike his shoulder. More rage burst across his body, and every muscle quivered against the devices that held him. He shouted the most foul curse he knew, but the metal spikes that pinned his tongue distorted it beyond recognition.

Burned as a gods-damned witch!

These simpletons would not burn him, they need not produce a single spark nor pyre. But he would burn nonetheless, come sunrise, to their benighted shock and satisfaction.

Sebastian was not a witch, and had no interest in the craft. He had no need, not with his *inherent* powers.

It was an insult how this jealous dunce and that mendacious wench caught him, by naught but a series of flukes.

If Sebastian had chosen any other direction to run; if he had not tripped into consecrated ground; if the accursed moon had not emerged and dazzled his vision, these mortal maggots would not have captured him.

If they had put him anywhere but that chamber, in any fetters but these or cage such as this; if anyone had questioned him but this hunter in disguise, this herd of peasants would be dead or dying by his hand.

One of the youths used a stick to spin the cage around, and another hurled a bucket of warm piss up as it spun.

He kicked and pushed and fought again with all his might, but not one single hinge did give in the slightest. The crafter of this thing knew what it had to contain.

Sebastian was no witch, but neither was he human. His strengths and powers came from his transformed blood. Centuries ago, he passed through death to the other side, to join they who thrive on the blood of inferior mankind.

That woman was no Magistrate's Apprentice under the surface. Her ruse put her in convenient position to hunt Sebastian's kind. She abused her title, sending out such devices and directives to these gullible half-wits.

If he could but accuse her of witchcraft, they would find enough oddities on her person to question her intentions. It would not free him from this, but her pretense would crumble.

But iron kept him from speaking, and reduced his roar to a trickle. Still he forced his voice around it, in summons for one who might give aid.

Another of his kind lurked in the woods to the west, he was sure of it. That curious detail drew him back here in the first place.

That and Sarah, the girl who looked like his absent Simone. Or Clarabelle, or Margueritte, whatever name the object of his desire now used. If Sebastian could only find her, he would remind her who she was — *his bride*.

He meant to have her again, and to destroy that louse she had Turned two hundred years ago. But first he must destroy this village, all who bore witness to his humiliation, save Simone's lookalike.

A rancid turkey leg struck his eye and scattered maggots across his face.

He would disembowel them all one by one, with his teeth. He would feed the entrails of each victim to the next, on and on until every last one was a smear upon the soil.

Every last one!

The night's chill set in, and the villagers left one by one, until only the hunter, the liar, and a blundering night watchman remained. Sebastian thrashed again; a madness now ate at him, and grew with each ineffective effort.

The gallows post would rot and fall before this infernal contraption would waver. The thought crazed him all the more. He let loose another roar, and again it stayed trapped behind the branks. His strength faltered.

That was when he felt it — her? — the other like him watching from the woods. She had heard him! He could not see, the cage faced the wrong direction. He caught sight of her when she moved for a better vantage point on the liars below.

Sebastian quieted upon viewing her monstrous beauty, a misshapen warrior demon who could never walk amidst humanity again.

His rage rested as his inner strength returned. He need not worry, he need not struggle. He would have his revenge upon each and every peasant. He simply had to wait for his warrior to set him free.

* * *

The dolts thought they'd caught themselves a witch.

Marionne almost snickered from the bushes that hid her.

They hadn't. They had caught themselves something much worse. Marionne knew, because she was *both*.

She worked the craft and drank mortal blood. She was both witch and what some called vampyr.

As for the villager's witch, he might be both, too, but Marionne could not recognize a practicer of the craft so easily. None could, regardless of the popular and widespread trials.

Those travesties tormented the guileless and mocked justice more than anything else, and Marionne watched with delight whenever she could — not as often as she preferred, as most took place during the day. She took pleasure in the howled pleadings pitted against the false truths. The interrogations stank of fear and desperation; scents that stirred Marionne's appetite.

She arrived too late to see what specific crime put this vampyr on display. But she heard the taunts of the villagers tossing filth and rot: Witch, demon, sorcerer.

Weeks ago, she felt this vampyr visit this town between the lake and the mountain. But he left before Marionne could lay eyes on him. He had returned, and now stewed in desperate fear. It didn't smell nearly as good as mortal terror.

They had overpowered him, stuffed him into a cage, and hung him up high. He swung like mad, an exposed and stinking criminal or blasphemer. Marionne tried not to giggle at their foolishness as their rotten supplies dwindled.

They intended to finish him tomorrow, by daylight. He would catch fire, though they would not take action to burn him. He would burn, and they would commend themselves for unearthing an abomination from their midst. They would thank their god for saving them the work of building a pyre.

But Marionne would not let him burn. She knew she could gain something if she gave him aid.

She also felt compelled, though, by strong curiosity: The world held very few of their kind, and he seemed much older than she. She could learn so much from him. And he would owe her for this rescue.

And, of course, Marionne rejoiced in toying with the commoners' fears.

Finally, the villagers grew bored, and left him there undefended to the chill of the night. Only three remained; the hunter, the accuser, and the night watchman who wandered the streets.

Marionne knew only a hunter would line a cage with gold, and etch the locks with symbols of power. Only a hunter would stand through the night, to keep eyes on a blood-drinker until he burned to dust.

Marionne moved closer, and the prisoner ended the beautiful dull and smothered howls that had attracted her. He must detect her here, just as she detected him from miles away.

In that quiet instant, the hunter knew something was wrong. She reached for a concealed firearm, and Marionne made her move.

She leapt upon the boy and the hunter, bashing their heads together. The two fell, knocked cold before they could react. The night guard walked the other side of town, and heard not a thing.

Marionne took the two unconscious mortals and fixed their heads and hands into the pillory, side by side. They would die tonight, but at the mercy of their accused; Marionne wanted very much to see his vengeance.

She looked up at the prisoner as he struggled to stare down at her. Even helpless and humiliated, he watched with proud, predatory eyes.

Marionne liked him very much. And soon he would owe her.

She pulled the keys from the hunter's pocket, dropping them when they burned to the touch: The damnable hunter even consecrated her keys! But Marionne knew how to fix that.

She dug a fingernail across the boy's cheek, smearing his blood across her fingers and palms. She recited a simple spell to bind the coating to her skin. The keys gave her no further trouble. Marionne would enjoy this hunter's death, and considered she might make a point of hunting these hunters.

Marionne lowered the cage to the ground, leaned it against the gallows post, and locked eyes with the prisoner.

He stared at her, eyes pools of molten silver, flickering and flowing in the light, his expression unreadable. She understood his plight: He could not beg, but he dared not offend her, his only chance to escape death.

She did not know why, but she afforded him his dignity. She averted her eyes and set about unlocking his hands.

Marionne only felt indifference and cruelty towards others. Were any other being in such a bind, she would laugh and mock at his plight.

But she dared not laugh at this one. Even through fetters and feathers, she knew she should honor him.

She unlocked one hand and he flexed the cramps from it while she worked on the other.

She considered which lock to try next, but he seized her hand and grasped it and the keys tight. Somehow, they did not burn him, but she still felt fear in his grip. Shaking, he took the keys from her and groped blindly at the branks, trying to locate its latches.

Marionne felt no affection or empathy for any other creature, but somehow this one reached into her, this bound and helpless god of darkness. Her kin. It would be a sin to let this powerful vampyr suffer these indignities another moment.

She held his hand in understanding. She then took the keys and set about removing his muzzle.

Presently he tested his voice and tongue with slow, exhausted groans. His wounds would heal, though he would need to feed soon.

"Before you know it," she whispered, "we will howl and feast upon their nightmares."

He reached for her shoulder and met her eyes again. "Thank ... you."

"Let me finish."

One by one, she opened every lock until the last fetter came undone. The prisoner fell from the enclosure, covered in filth, feathers, blood, and exhaustion.

When he looked up again, all trace of fear had vanished from his eyes. He got to his feet, and Marionne was overcome by his aura of might, though she stood much taller than he. She fell to her knees and reveled in his glory.

"Tell me your name."

"Marionne."

"You have my gratitude, Marionne. You may call me Sebastian, and I will reward you greatly for this service." He beckoned her to stand. "First, let us extract penance and contrition from these contemptible dogs."

Sebastian then examined the unconscious and pilloried liars.

He worked the branks onto the woman's insensible head, and shoved a rotting gourd into the boy's slack mouth. He drew a bucket of water from a nearby horse trough, and doused the pair until they woke. Sebastian set his eyes aglow; Marionne followed his lead.

The hunter neither flinched nor showed fear when she realized her overturned circumstance. She looked back at her enemies with defiance and guile.

The boy soiled himself.

Marionne snickered.

Sebastian stood before them, a hand under each jaw, forcing the two to look up at him.

"Lustful, jejune liar," he looked to the boy.

"Charlatan harlot," he cast his eyes on the woman.

"Know that I will not kill you quick, now that my rage is released." A terrible power collected around him as he spoke.

"My fury burns long and slow, and eternal, like *hell*." He squeezed their faces harder with each word.

"When you are finished, I will locate, torture, dismember, and behead your accursed kin — every last hunter until they are no more." His hands shook with rage as he gripped their faces.

He placed his hands on the top of each head, gentle now like a benediction.

"Tonight, I will save you for last. You will watch everything I do to these people. You cannot warn them, or stop us, or cry out as they die."

He gestured at the sleeping town.

"I will burn this village to the ground."

He returned to the pillory, and crouched in front of their faces.

"Then and only then will I deal with the two of you."

The night watchman rounded a corner and stopped in his tracks, petrified and unable to shout for help. Sebastian gestured to him.

"Exquisite Marionne, consider this my first gift to you."

"Gladly."

The guard stood transfixed as Marionne claimed each of his weapons and broke it before his eyes. She ran her nails down his cheeks until he almost found his voice again. Then she sank her fangs deep into his throat.

When she finished, she found Sebastian occupied with a teenage girl, one that had his scent on her already. Perhaps he had started to enthrall her, and perhaps that had got him caught. He bound her unharmed to the base of the pillory, with fine cloth tied across her eyes and mouth.

The rest was a wild haze of carnage and pleading. Sebastian and Marionne prowled from house to house, silencing each human swine before they could scream, then crippling them for a slow death piled upon the scaffold. Between the broken and dying, Marionne poured lamp oil and scattered gunpowder. Tonight, the superstitious would die upon the very pyre they reserved for those they condemned.

Sebastian took his time with a select few, forcing garbage down their throats before disemboweling them and adding them to the heap.

Many of these he maimed directly in front of the pilloried prisoners. The hunter and the liar watched powerless at the waking nightmare, with the one soul spared the sight of it at their feet.

The village was small, but it made an impressive mound.

Marionne had just wrung an old man's neck — the minister, perhaps — when she heard Sebastian shout.

She ran to him, and found him standing between the pillory and the pile of bodies. His wrath burned bright enough to light the pyre.

The pillory was empty. The liar, the hunter, and the innocent; they were gone.

Marionne sniffed the air, but the wind kept shifting. She could smell no trace of them through the scattered rot and incendiaries.

With fury and haste, Sebastian threw a torch upon the groaning heap of wounded and plunged into the woods.

Marionne tore after him, intent on killing at least one hunter this night.

The chaos started with a musket blast. Then a flaming arrow. Then two more shots and another arrow, all from different angles. Not a single one found a target, but now they knew: This hunter had not come alone.

In the distance, several horses broke into a gallop.

Sebastian started toward the sound, but another line of fire struck between him and the getaway. Marionne took to the trees.

The assault was not an offensive attack but rather a defensive deterrent to allow the escape.

Marionne felt the pang that announced dawn was not far off. Sebastian looked to her: He felt it, too.

They might engage with the rear guard, but they stood no chance at catching the fugitives. They would have to take shelter from the sun first.

Marionne traced an arrow's route back to its origin, sneaking among the branches tree to tree, more silent than death. She pounced from above, broke the bow, and garrotted the bowman with his own bowstring.

She stood behind a tree, listening for another target. This one found her first, but also found her laughing.

He pulled the trigger on his rifle, but Marionne moved too fast for the shot. With one leap, she was in a tree again, only to drop to the ground right behind him. She broke this one's neck.

She felt the pang again, and noted the faintest light in the east. They needed to leave, soon. She sniffed the air for the rot that covered Sebastian. The wind had died down, and she detected him easily.

She found him elbow deep in one of the hunters.

"We must go. We have just enough time to reach my shelter, before the sun shows."

Sebastian nodded in silence. He had fed from the villagers, but he required rest.

"How far?" He made to stand, but already the sun's approach affected him.

"Not far. We will make it." He passed out, and Marionne carried him the entire way.

* * *

Magistrate's Apprentice Camille Birdsley opened her eyes to sunlight on her face.

Her head felt like a gourd split wide open and hollowed out. A great stomach sickness set upon her when she tried to sit up. Her head was bandaged and bruised and she feared it quite damaged.

She tried to call out, but her throat and tongue burned with illness and infection. Fever likely worked against her faculties, hand in glove with her injuries.

She breathed slow and deliberate, until the swirls of the ceiling slowed and stopped. The room was silent — too silent. Should she not at least hear birds?

Two figures entered the room. For a moment, she could not make sense of the faces, even after she managed to focus her eyes.

Sound came, muffled and distant, as the voice of her husband, Thomas. His face came first into her knowledge, but she took several minutes to recognize the other as their doctor.

Memories of the village returned while the doctor spoke quietly to Thomas and left a tonic to drink.

With the doctor gone, she clutched at Thomas' shirt, drawing him close. She tried to speak again, but thought better of it. She gestured for a writing slate.

'What happened?' she wrote.

"Are you well enough to hear this?"

She glared hard and brought a new swell of pain to her head. She winced but bade him on.

"The entire village burned, none survived, with most charred beyond recognition. The magistrate believes you to be among the dead. Were you to visit his office, I fear all would speculate on the circumstance of your survival."

Birdsley's heart fell. She worked hard to secure that station for herself, and it had just started paying off. But Thomas had the right of it. Her reappearance would implicate her, as a witch or as otherwise.

"We need decide nothing until you are well and ready, but our talents would best prosper with a transfer and new personage."

She picked up the chalk again: 'The others?'

Thomas hesitated again, but moved on before she could blink.

"We lost three. Smitherns, Brimsley, and Drummone. What did you see of the second creature?"

Chalk: 'Tall, shadowy, hard to see'

"Well, that sets it apart from every other vampyr." He smiled but she was not amused.

Chalk: 'Don't call them that. Hate that word.'

"We cannot stop the tide. The name has spread, and more folk believe in the deathless fiends that drink blood."

The thought made her sick all over again. Sometimes their war felt completely unwinnable. She reached for chalk again. She could not recall names, but knew others were with her. She had to know:

'Boy & Girl?'

"The boy survived. His head's in better shape than yours, though neither as appealing, nor as cunning."

She ignored his levity. 'Has sharp eyes. Possible recruit.'

"I'm sure Arnos will bear that in mind." He paused. "The girl ... has not yet spoken, nor taken food, nor even slept."

'*Sevastianos.*' She underlined it and tossed the slate aside.

"We will get him. Perhaps not you and I, but our brethren, some-day." He pulled her close again.

"And then there is always another."

CONFESSION

James Graham

The distant patter of rain and the humming of Father William Primrose was all that could be heard within the chapel of St. Peter's Catholic Church, which was out on the edge of the quiet town of Oldmill, Maine. He was humming a half-forgotten song of his youth as he began the long process of extinguishing all of the many candles throughout the chapel. It was mid-week and he was tidying up a bit before he shut the doors for the night. It was a confessional night and a rather slow one at that, just a few of the older women of the parish who regularly attended mass and whose sins were hardly sins at all.

The priest was born and raised in Maine, originally from Portland. He had decided to move away from the bigger city and live in a more rural community. He was now past the prime of his life, and aside from his love of the church, he was also an avid outdoorsman, more specifically, he loved to fish. He would cast his rod into the water every single chance he had. There was something calming about it, some base instinct perhaps, or it may have been that it was, in his opinion, a noble and almost holy pastime. He never felt closer to God than when he was on the bank of a river or in small boat on a lake.

He had just finished snuffing the candles and was taking one last look around before he locking up, when suddenly one of the heavy double doors into the chapel slammed open from the outside. The Father looked up with bewilderment and was astonished to see that it was Freddy Wilks, the son of Betty and George Wilks. Betty Wilks came to church every Sunday faithfully, as did George when it wasn't football season, but it had been several years since Freddy had come with them. Freddy's own son's Baptism was the last time in fact, if Father Primrose remembered correctly.

"Hello my son, how may I help you?" Father Primrose asked, trying to sound jovial but also a bit worried. He hoped that the man's parents were okay and he said a silent prayer for them.

"I was hoping for a confession Father. But if it's too late ..." The man said hesitantly.

"Not at all my son, come in. Come in. Just follow me over."

Oh dear, He's cheated on his wife. Stop that, don't assume or judge. That is reserved for God only, not you Billy Primrose.

He led Freddy over to the confessional booth and stepped into his side. Through the dark screen, he could just make out movement on the other side.

"Forgive me Father, for I have sinned," Freddy began in an anxious voice. "It has been several years since my last confession."

"Tell me your sins my son, so I may absolve you of your burdens." He had always liked to step out of the traditional script of confession to make it seem more personal.

"I have sinned countless times since my last confession, and I do not wish to take too much of your time. But there is one sin I have committed, that was most egregious."

This confused the priest because he had never known Freddy Wilks to be a man of large words.

"Go on," he said encouragingly. "The seal of confession is absolute."

"I have broken one of the Ten Commandments, the highest of holy laws. I have killed someone Father," Freddy began, sobbing. "I killed Thomas Raker last week."

"My son," the priest replied hesitantly. "Thomas was found at the bottom of Stanly's Drop. You weren't ..."

"I killed him, I strangled him and then I pushed his car off the cliff. I wanted him to die, and he died. I choked the life from him and watched with a smile as the light left his eyes."

Thomas's death had been ruled a suicide, so he hadn't had a Catholic burial because of it. But if he had been murdered ...

"My son, I insist that you turn yourself in to the authorities."

"I can't do that Father, but if you could pardon me of my sins ..." He trailed off.

"I must insist ..."

"I can't!" the man shrieked, sounding agonized. "I can't, my family ... They can never know."

The faint shadow of the man bent over and the priest heard him sobbing in earnest.

"The Lord forgives you, your penance is set at one hundred Hail Mary's and one hundred Our Father's," Father Primrose said evenly. "I must also recommend that you spend an hour a day in prayer and silent reflection. But again, my son, for your sins to be fully absolved in the eyes of men as well as God, then you must turn yourself in to the proper legal authorities. I am certain that some amount of leniency ..."

"Thank you very much for your time Father, please pray for me ..." Freddy paused as if unsure if he should go on, then with a new-found conviction, he continued. "I think I may be the Devil."

Without another word, Freddy Wilks got up and walked out of the Confessional booth. The priest however, took a moment to clear his head.

By the laws of the church, Confession was a confidential place where men could be forgiven in a discrete manner. But it was also not illegal for him to come forward about it. The thought was a bitter one. He was torn between two choices that were morally ambiguous. Did he wish to turn from the edicts of the faith and trust the law to see this man safely behind bars or perhaps even better, in an insane asylum? The final words Freddy had uttered would certainly be taken as a sign of insanity by the authorities. Or did he wish to keep his vows to the confidentiality of the Confession and disregard what the law told him was right? Neither choice seemed right to him.

But he couldn't sit and do nothing, he knew that. Perhaps he would go and visit the man in a couple of days, see if he could get a better sense of him. Perhaps it was over a dispute and more of an accident than a murder. But he couldn't shake that final statement that the man had made.

I think I may be the Devil.

Father William Primrose rose from his seat and crossed the room. He went immediately to the large wooden doors and locked them. His shaking hands made the process difficult, but he made sure they were closed fast. He was terrified.

I think I may be the Devil.

* * *

Aside from his duties at the church the thing Father Primrose enjoyed most in life was fly-fishing. He went as often as possible, sometimes by himself, and other times he went with his friend Roland. Roland was an avid outdoorsman, hunting and fishing every-thing there was to hunt and fish. In years past he had even trapped in the winter, though now that he had grown old he had lost interest in trapping.

It was an odd friendship to be sure, mainly because Roland was one of the foulest tongued men the world had ever produced, and he was far from a religious man. But the two had hit it off fairly well when they had run into each other down at Cutters Stream several years previous.

Roland had been standing in the middle of the running water with his dark green hip waders when he had first met him, swearing about how his flies seemed to be ineffectual in luring in a fish. Father Primrose had called out and offered one of his own to the man, who had accepted graciously as possible when every other word was a curse. The two had spent the rest of the afternoon talking of fishing, the town, and how the hell the Father was so damned good at tying together a good fly. They had been the best of friends ever since.

The priest knew that Roland did his best to temper his tongue around him, and he was grateful for the older man's effort. It was certainly nobody's place to judge except God's, in Father Primrose's opinion.

Many people rediscovered the Lord in their advancing age, but repeated attempts to bring Roland back into the flock had thus far been unsuccessful. God was a forgiving lord to his people, and he would gladly take them back. But if old Roland only spat and said a brief blasphemous joke when asked about his faith, then it was a good day. Father Primrose couldn't help but smile at the thought of his old friend.

A couple of days had passed since Freddy's confession, and the priest had gone on a short fishing trip with his friend Roland. It was a much-needed break to clear his head.

He always found solace while he stood knee deep in the water as he was now, casting his rod over and over into the water. It was silent and relaxing, and helped him put things into perspective. He spent most of his time on the trip thinking about the events of the last couple of days.

Thomas Raker had only lived in Oldmill for a short time, less than a year anyway. It was unlikely that he could have had much time to get to know Freddy Wilks. What would the motive have been? It just didn't make sense. How could he grow to hate someone so quickly that he would want to kill them in less than a year?

Tom had of course attended church every Sunday since his family moved here, he had two daughters and a young son. His wife was pretty in a plain sort of way, and they even had a small yappy mutt. Father Primrose had blessed their house the first week that they had moved in. He had always seemed so devout that it had been a shock when he had found out that the man had committed suicide. His wife had never believed it. She even caused a large scene in front of the whole congregation the day her husband had been buried when she had overheard a muttering about how a suicide shouldn't receive a Catholic burial.

But the trip was not entirely silent. Roland had known something was wrong with his old friend but had kept his mouth shut about it for the most part. That was, until a few beers had brought out his courage.

Roland was a Coors man, in fact it was all William had ever seen him drink besides the occasional hard stuff. How long had it been since Roland had drank water?

William always drank O'Doul's, a non-alcoholic beer, when on these trips. He had been taking a swig off of one when a half-drunk Roland had finally sloshed through the water to him.

"Alright you damn whoreson," Roland had said. "What's got lodged in that arse of yours?"

He had spat out the beer and laughed for a second at the older man's language.

"What were you, raised in a barn full of sailors?" William had replied.

"Don't change the damn subject. We're friends ain't we? We're supposed to be able to talk to each other, right?"

"I can't really speak of it Roland. I am sworn to secrecy."

"Oh, I see," Roland had said in a thickly sarcastic voice. "Old Catholic secrets."

"I just don't know what to do about a situation I am in." He paused for a moment trying to think of a way to convey some of the tale without breaking custom. Roland could have some impressive wisdom about him when he was drunk enough.

But before he could come up with anything Roland had downed his beer.

"Alright then, keep your damned secrets. But don't say old Roland never tried helping you out." He finished speaking and turned immediately toward the shore. He slipped and almost fell, splashing water in every direction.

"Don't be an ass," Father Primrose had said. "You are scaring all the fish."

"Oh Jesus, did you steal one of my Coors? A priest that is blaspheming."

"Ass is in the bible," he had joked back.

"Well this old donkey is going to take a piss and then he is going to catch a salmon as big as his pecker."

He had laughed so hard at Roland's analogy about how large a salmon he was going to catch that it still made him smile a couple of days later.

It was now Saturday night and he was in his office, putting the finishing touches on his preparations for the next day's sermon.

The fishing trip had done little to alleviate his worries, although they had begun to feel a bit more distant. He still intended to visit Freddy in the next day or two to follow up with him, but it seemed somehow less urgent to him. Maybe the man had been overwhelmed with guilt, perhaps he had seen Thomas Raker's car go over the ledge and he had not reported it for some reason. He could have been driving drunk or something. And as for his haunting words before he left, perhaps the man's sanity was wavering under such stress and pressure.

A feint knocking in the distance brought him to the present.

His office was down the hallway from the chapel and there were two doors in between him and whoever was knocking. He hastily rose from his chair, went around his desk and opened the door. Peering out into the hallway and looking about, he saw nothing out of the ordinary and was about to step out when the knocking came once more, this time much louder.

He jumped again, his heart pounding. He hadn't been truly scared since before he had taken the vows of priesthood, and now twice in a week his heart was working double time. Though he couldn't think of any rational reason to be afraid, it didn't stop the hairs from raising on the back of his neck. He took a step out and walked slowly down the hallway to the chapel door.

He hesitated for a second to compose himself. There was almost never a visitor at this time of night.

Except for Freddy Wilks.

It's just one of the choir members, or someone who had left something here earlier. It's only eight o'clock. It could be anyone. It won't be Freddy Wilks.

He looked down and saw that he was now gripping his crucifix so tightly that his knuckles were white as a ghost.

"The lord is my shepherd ..." He whispered, beginning his favorite Psalm.

The knocking came once more, louder still.

He cringed for a moment and took another second to compose himself. Whatever was out there, he was going to face it like a man of God. He took a deep breath and found his courage as he finished the prayer. He opened the door and stepped out into the darkened chapel.

The lights were out and only a couple of candles still burned.

He walked over to his podium and switched on the lights of the altar. This filled the room with a faint light, though the corners were still shadowy.

He walked over to the large double doors with his shoulders held high, feeling as brave as he ever had. He wrapped his faith around him and felt its weight like armor.

He got to the doors and unlocked one before pulling it in strongly.

There was no one there.

Father Primrose took a step outside and looked around the deserted parking lot. He saw only the church-owned van over in the corner. His own car was in the back nearer to his office.

He looked all about and saw nothing.

Confused, he slowly closed the door and locked it. He took a deep breath and chuckled at himself as he began to turn.

A hand clapped down on his shoulder.

He screamed in terror, and whipped about in panic. Sure enough, the hand belonged to Freddy Wilks.

"I am sorry I frightened you Father," Freddy said. "But I need another confession if you have the time."

Freddy's manner was different now from the previous visit, when he had seemed calm as a cucumber. This man's visage was that of someone who had completely snapped.

Father Primrose swallowed hard before he responded.

"Of course, my son. The Lord forgives all who truly wish forgiveness."

"Of course," Freddy said with a disconcerting smile.

Father Primrose led the way to the confessional once more. Freddy sat in one booth and he sat in the other and once more he could see the faint outline of the other man.

"Forgive me father for I have sinned," he said.

"Confess your sins my son, and let them be washed from you."

"It has been three days since my last confession."

Father Primrose's heart dropped. Had the man done something else?

"I killed Doris Heywood."

A bit of anger coursed through the priest at that. Doris Heywood was a plump woman who moved to Oldmill six months ago, to care for her elderly mother.

"She was here just an hour ago, practicing with the choir," he retorted. "How is this possible?"

"She walks home you know. It was a shame really; she was in the wrong place at the wrong time. I smiled at her as she died. When I drove my car into her I only broke a leg, so she was fully aware as I snapped her neck."

Father Primrose erupted out of his seat and screamed through the mesh divider.

"You will not get away with this!"

"If you were going to inform the police then you would have already. I know that you can't tell anyone as long as I am in this box when I tell you. Now, how many Hail Mary's Father?"

"There can be no forgiveness without remorse. I must again advise you, more sternly than before, that if you are truly guilty of these crimes, then you must turn yourself in!"

"I am most remorseful, I assure you. These acts have not been easy for me. But they were necessary. Now, I am begging for forgiveness, please ..." Freddy's voice was filled with mock pleading.

"I will set your penance much sharper than before, though I doubt very much you will follow them. But I say that you must spend six hours contemplating these crimes daily. Another hour spent of Hail Mary's and Our Father's. *And you must turn yourself in*!"

Freddy seemed strangely relieved by the words.

"Thank you, Father, I appreciate the time as always."

He then rose from his seat and casually strode over to the large double doors and opened them before stepping out. But before he was fully gone he turned and said one last thing.

"I think I may be the Devil."

Then the door closed cutting off Freddy's laughter.

The man is insane, Primrose thought. What am I to do?

For the first time since his mother had died, Father William Primrose cried. He wept like a child and did not care.

He had to go to the authorities, he had to. God would surely forgive him for breaking the sacred vows if it meant that innocent lives were spared.

Once more the words ran through his head.

I think I may be the Devil.

❊   ❊   ❊

The next day, after a very restless night, Father Primrose was nearing the end of his sermon. It was time for communion, and everyone slowly rose from their pews and formed the lines to come and receive their bread and wine. Despite how hard he tried to look strong, he knew he must look exhausted because half of the people who came to him asked if he felt okay.

Perhaps they also thought that it was because of what had happened to poor Doris. He had called for a moment of silence, though it had been interrupted by several sobs from her friends. He too was nearly overwhelmed with emotion.

Late in the night when a police officer had taken his statement about the death of Doris Heywood they seemed to think that it was a hit and run, probably someone just passing through.

He had almost told them right then that he knew who had done it. But not only did he risk his livelihood by doing so, he realized that he had no real proof of any of it. For all he knew Freddy was just taking credit for the deaths for attention. Of course, he did not believe that for half a second. No, in his mind Freddy had snapped.

Maybe he was possessed.

That didn't make sense either, because from everything Father Primrose knew of possession, the possessed never willingly entered a church, nor even touch a holy artifact. Freddy had done all of that, so it had to be insanity. Of course, some evil could not be purified by exorcism. Sometimes it simply had to be stamped out like a spark landing in dry grass.

He was about halfway through the communion when Freddy Wilks emerged from the crowd, wearing a large smile and looking as though he knew a secret that nobody else did.

Father Primrose knew what that secret was.

"Hello, Father," he said in a near mocking tone. "Are you well? You look a bit under the weather."

Father Primrose could not help but spill a little of the communion wine when his hands began to shake, both out of fear and anger. He was absolutely terrified of this man, not because of what he would do to him, but because of what he was capable of doing to others. He was angry at the audacity of the man, flaunting his sins about like this. He was a lunatic.

Freddy reached out with his left hand and took the wine cup from Father Primrose and took a small sip from it, eyes on the priest the entire time.

When he handed the cup back his mouth looked to be dripping with blood. He leaned in close to whisper in the priest's ear.

"I think you ought to stop by my house tonight Father. There will be something fun happening around nine o'clock. My wife and kids would love some company."

The easy way that the man said the words was very disheartening. He was evil. He was insane. But he wouldn't hurt his family, would he? Who could tell what the mad were capable of until it was too late.

"By the way father, I think I may be the Devil."

With a light chuckle the man walked away. Father Primrose had all he could do to stand there and finish the service. He knew any words he had said from then on were hollow and weak, and he hoped that everyone passed it off as something poor that he had eaten.

When he finally retired to his office, he had brought a bottle of the communion wine with him. Once he was certain that nobody was left in the church, he poured himself a large glass. Tonight would likely break him, no matter what happened. What was he going to do?

He had no real evidence.

He had finally decided to go and seek the wisdom of an old wise man, one that had all of his confidence. One that he hoped had the answer which he so desperately searched himself for.

Roland.

He could go to his friend for anything. In fact, he should have confided to the man when he had asked in the first place. Doris might still be alive if he had not been so shy of seeking help.

* * *

Upon reaching Roland's house, William was greeted by the man's two German Short-haired Pointers, a pair of beautiful black and white dogs, whose stubby short tails wagged back and forth with fervor upon seeing an old friend. He even smiled a little as he patted their heads.

He walked up to the door of the small cabin and knocked.

"Hold your damn horses!" came the irritated yell of his old friend.

A moment later the door opened to reveal the older man.

"What the hell are you doing here on a Sunday afternoon?" he said with a confused smile upon his face.

"I need your help."

The older man nodded slowly then held the door open wider to allow his friend to enter.

Animal heads adorned the walls, as did several large fish and a few pelts. A large bear skin rug sprawled out near a now vacant fireplace. There was a bookshelf on the wall nearby with some dusty old leather-bound books. Across from the fireplace was his kitchen and the only door in the whole room led to the bedroom and bathroom which was only accessible through the bedroom. A large puffy chair sat near the fireplace, making up what living room the man had, next to the chair was a pair of puffy dog beds covered in fur.

His friend was a simple man, living a quiet existence. In fact, William had always admired the older man's reclusive ways, and if it wasn't for his love of the church he believed that he might lead such a life.

They walked over to the table in the kitchen which had only two wooden chairs. One chair was older than the other, the newer one not being built until William had begun coming over for dinner on occasion.

Many a night they had spent exchanging old fishing stories, many indeed.

William walked over to the old refrigerator before joining him.

"Want a beer?" he asked.

"Yes, please."

Roland seemed a little shocked.

"I don't have any O'Doul's ..."

"Coors will be fine."

"Well now, it must be serious indeed. Come on then and let's hear it."

They both cracked open their beers took a few long sips. Several minutes passed with Roland looking thoughtfully at his troubled friend, stroking his beard and drinking his beer.

Finally, William downed his beer and began.

"You know about Thomas Raker?" the priest began.

Roland nodded.

"And about how late last night Doris Heywood was killed?"

Once more Roland nodded.

"They weren't accidents. They weren't suicides. They were murders," William said in an uneven voice.

His friend stared at him for a couple of minutes before rising from his chair and walking across the kitchen. This time he opened his freezer and pulled out a bottle of liquor. He always kept a large bottle of Jägermeister in there to keep it ice cold. He had even gotten William, who typically abstained, to indulge from time to time. At first Father Primrose found it to be a foul, syrupy drink. But after toasting to their fishing adventures a few times he had grown to love the taste.

Roland poured some into a couple of shot glasses and grabbed a couple more beers before sitting back down.

"Alright Billy," said Roland, using the name that only he used. "Out with it. All of it mind. If I am to help you I'll need to know everything."

The priest picked up the shot glass and stared into it for a while. It was not so easy to set aside one's holy vows after all.

He knocked it back and slammed the shot glass down on the table upside down.

"The night before we last went to the river ..."

Nearly an hour had passed by the time his story was finished, and aside from the occasional break to grab another beer he had Roland's complete attention. The old man was completely absorbed by the story, and no matter how ridiculous it must have sounded he never doubted the priest for a second.

"… So, I have no idea what to do. He hasn't told me anything outside the confessional booth that's damning, so I can't go to the police, but I can't sit back and let more murders happen Roland, I can't."

The priest felt old as he looked down into the dark lip of the can of Coors. He felt tired and worn, and on the cusp of tears.

Roland stared at the table thoughtfully for a long while, not moving except to bring the can to his lips. Even the dogs seemed to sense the tension, because they lay quietly on the wooden floor beneath the table.

Finally, Roland broke the silence.

"It seems there is only one real choice then. I'll go there tonight around eight thirty and I'll make sure that nothing happens to his family, and if he insists on hurting them, then I'll do what needs doing."

"My friend," William began before choking up. "I cannot ask that of you."

"Nobody's asking me, but it needs doing and I am up for it. I know that your vows prevent you from … certain things. But I am unhindered by such. I'll go. You can come with me if you want, but I am going."

"I … I can't … Of course, I will come with you my friend, though it pains me to bring this evil upon you."

"I know, but you are my friend. Dress-wearing and sober though you are, or were I should say. And I'd help you with anything Billy."

The priest nodded. "Thank you."

Roland looked at his watch. It was nearly three in the afternoon.

"I'll tell you what, you go and get some rest or pray or whatever you need to do and I will pick you up at the church at eight o'clock."

"Okay, that sounds good."

"Make sure you rest in some fashion, alright? I will want you at your best. And no more drinking, for either of us. The old man finished his beer and walked over to his old coffee maker."

"A cup for the road?"

William nodded.

As he drove back to the church to pray and beg forgiveness he found that he couldn't get Freddy's words out of his head.

I think I may be the Devil.

* * *

Father William Primrose spent the next few hours on his knees before the large cross at the head of the chapel. It had been a long time since he had spent so much time upon his aging knees in prayer, and they ached something awful. But his prayers were calming.

He knew that he had broken his vows, and was going to break them further.

He went through several Psalms and several passages of Corinthians.

He prayed in silence, and he prayed aloud.

He called out as loud as he could at the son of God who stood nailed to the cross above him.

"Please, let everyone turn out fine in the end. Let Freddy see the light and above all, forgive him my lord!"

He begged and pleaded. He cried and wept.

But all the time he was haunted.

I think I may be the Devil.

"Why Freddy? Why are you doing this? You were such a good man; how could you have fallen so far. Please lord, let him see the light!"

I think I may be the Devil.

His knuckles were aching and he realized he had been pounding the carpeted floor with his fists. He had even drawn a bit of blood which he wiped on his clothes.

His watch beeped at him, reminding him of the time. It was seven thirty, and it was time for him to make himself ready.

I think I may be the Devil.

He stood up and made the cross over his chest. He then walked over to the pool of holy water and dipped his finger in before again making the cross over himself.

"In the name of the Father, the Son, and the Holy Spirit. Amen"

He walked around to the door and went into his office. He stripped himself out of his street clothes and put on his finest robes. He wore them only on the most special of occasions, but tonight seemed as good a night as any.

He also grabbed the old tattered copy of the bible that had been his from childhood. He decided that it would be his shield tonight, faith would be his armor, and duty his sword.

He glanced at his watch and saw it was time.

I think I may be the Devil.

He walked through the chapel on his way out, fearing it was for the last time. He looked about at the decorations, the art, the stained-glass windows and the hand-worked wooden pews.

He was quite proud of this place, and even more so of his small congregation. His flock had grown about fifteen percent in his years here. In a time where more and more people were walking away from the faith, that was an outstanding number. They loved him, and he loved them.

It was time for him to prove his love, and be the shepherd of his faithful flock.

Roland's truck was waiting for him as he stepped outside and said his farewells to the church.

I think I may be the Devil.

✳ ✳ ✳

Roland was mostly silent on the way to Freddy's house. It was a quiet part of town, just on the outskirts. His nearest neighbor was at least a half mile down the road.

The dogs had been left at home, though the old beat up truck always carried their hair and smell.

When they reached the house, they parked on the side of the road a hundred feet from the driveway. They went the rest of the way on foot, silently. Father Primrose held his bible in his hands, and Roland held an old revolver in his.

It was dark and there were a couple of lights on in the house, though not as many as he normally would have expected, just after eight o'clock.

Freddy had probably made sure that his family went to bed early.

They reached the front door and looked at one another.

"Last chance to turn back Billy," Roland said.

"Last chance to turn back Roland," he replied.

His friend chuckled a little under his breath.

"All right then, let's get to it."

The door was unlocked, as were most doors in this part of Maine. Roland's old hands were plenty nimble, and he opened the door without a sound.

William had been here on a couple of occasions, the last being when their little girl had been baptized. They had had a quiet little gathering afterwards and he felt that he remembered the general layout of the house.

It was a single-story ranch with a half-finished basement. Three bedrooms and one bathroom. The living room light was on, as was the muted television, but nobody was there.

They moved quietly across the room and into the kitchen, which was also empty.

Then they stalked down the long hallway, passed the bedrooms and bathroom. Roland suddenly held out his hand to keep the priest from moving.

Then the priest heard it too. It was a muffled sob coming from the end of the hallway. The priest's throat tightened at the sound. It was real, it was actually happening.

Roland took a few quick steps down the hall, abandoning caution. Just as he was passing the linen closet outside the bathroom, the closet door opened and Freddy slammed into Roland knocking him to the ground with a loud thud. Roland's pistol went sliding across the hard-wood floor as it was knocked from his hand.

Freddy climbed atop the old man and began raining blows down upon him with heavy fists.

William rushed forward and lunged into Freddy's side, sending them both sprawling.

"So, there is some life in you huh Father? But not enough for you to come alone. You really should have, now I'll make you watch him die."

As the priest tried to pick himself up, he felt a hard kick in his rib-cage and he spat out a cough as he dropped once more to the floor, groaning in pain.

Freddy had abandoned him for the moment and went back to Roland. He wrapped his hands around the old man's neck and began to laugh as he choked the life from him.

William tried to stand, but couldn't. He pulled himself along desperately, beginning to weep.

Suddenly his hands smacked down on something cold.

It was the old revolver.

He didn't have time to think, he lifted it up and put Freddy in his sights.

"God forgive me," he muttered as he squeezed the trigger.

The flash and report was over in an instant and Father Primrose was temporarily stunned.

Freddy fell off of the older man, who immediately gasped loudly and tried desperately to catch his breath.

The priest ran over to his friend and helped him up. "I am sorry Roland."

The old man shook his head.

"Don't be sorry, you saved my life."

They both looked down at Freddy who now lay in a growing crimson pool. His breath was shallow and he coughed and sputtered.

"Thank you, Father, I was afraid I was the Devil." He chuckled one last time and then coughed for a second before expiring on the floor.

Thank you, Father, I was afraid I was the Devil.

* * *

A week had passed since the night of Freddy Wilks death, and three days after the funeral of Doris Heywood. The town was in full mourning; it had been years since three people had been killed so close together. The violent manner in which they all died took a harder toll as well.

Father Primrose was tidying the chapel before he went home for the evening.

The police report read that he had been driving back to Roland's house from Bangor, about forty-five minutes away. Roland had wanted a companion for the journey and offered to buy dinner if his friend tagged along. It was well known that the pair traveled in each other's company so it did not seem suspicious. They had been driving down the road when they had heard a loud scream coming from Freddy's house, and instead of going into town and alerting the police they decided to check it out themselves. Roland had grabbed the old pistol out of his glove box and led the way.

They had knocked, but nobody answered so they decided to let themselves in. After checking a few things out they were set upon by the maddened Freddy Wilks whom, after a brief struggle, was shot and killed by Roland. A clear-cut case of self-defense.

They had then discovered Freddy's wife and children tied up in a walk-in closet in one of the bedrooms. They were terrified, but relieved to have been set free.

It was a hard thing, for Father Primrose to lie to the authorities. But he had done it, and he had repented for it every day since. It still did not sit right with him, but he had done it and could not take it back.

Roland maintained that Freddy was simply a madman, and not possessed, so he refused to come to church to pray with him over the matter.

He was about to call it an evening when there came a knock at the loud double doors. It jumped the priest for a second, but he walked briskly over to the door, no longer haunted by the fear of Freddy Wilks.

He opened them up and there stood one of the older women that came for confession quite often. She had a grave look on her face.

"What is it Mary? Is everything okay?" he asked genuinely concerned.

"Yes, I am fine. If it's not too much trouble though Father, I have come for a confession," she said with the faintest of smiles.

"Of course, of course. But then you must allow me walk you to your car. It's too late for you to be out and about alone."

She nodded and accepted his offer. Then they walked over to the booth together.

I wonder what sin she could have committed that she needed a confession so late. Her last confession included several thoughts of a sexual nature involving the host of a gameshow on television. Primrose thought.

"Forgive me Father, for I have sinned," the old lady croaked, seeming to be in a better mood now that her burdens would be lifted.

"Tell me your sins daughter, that I may help you reach forgiveness."

"I have this very night done something that is most terrible." The old lady said, almost giddy now.

Oh my. He thought. *She must have had a particularly bad thought toward the poor fellow on the gameshow.*

"I have this very night killed Gladys Brown."

The priest couldn't help but jump at the words.

"What? What do you mean? You two are friends."

"I know, best friends for over thirty years Father. But tonight, I killed her. We were watching old T.V. shows, and I poisoned her soup."

Father Primrose began to lean away from the dark mesh divider between the booths. But the shadow of the old woman grew darker, and he could make out some of her features as she leaned closer to him.

"You know something Father," she said, beginning to sob. "I think I may be the Devil."

THE PHIPPSBURG SCREECHER

Lynda Styles

Ezra knew it was the right place the moment he laid eyes on it. It had been nearly twenty years since he had last visited the camp at the Basin and almost nothing had changed. Huge pine trees left a covering of pale brown needles on every surface. The road going in wound right and then left, and he felt the familiar, warm tug in his belly coming around each bend as he had every single July when they came to ride the waves at Popham Beach, explore the stone fort at the end, and catch fireflies in mason jars. He came over the hill on the rust-gold, bumpy dirt road and swung left into the driveway. He opened the door to the car and breathed in the crisp, green air.

Uncle Joe had passed away in March of last year, and as far as Ezra knew, no one had been there in at least that long. He chose not to discuss his visit up to Maine with anyone. He knew where the key was and how to use the place without burning it down. He had as much a right as anyone to be there.

At a glance, it did not appear the place had been tampered with and Ezra felt tremendous relief at that. He kicked aside the pine needles, leaves, and sticks that littered the steps leading up to the deck, carrying a bag on his arm. He felt above the door frame and grew nervous when he didn't find the key. He put his bag down, feeling along the edge with both hands starting in the middle, until finally his index finger pressed against cold metal.

The door to the cabin opened with a creak and Ezra breathed in the stale but familiar air. The entrance led into a square main living area with light wood-paneled walls decorated with family photos, fishing magazine pictures, and the occasional kitschy sign offering wisdom like 'All fisherman are liars except you and I and I'm not so sure about you.'

A kitchenette stood at the back, with a small rectangular table and two wooden chairs. The dark wood plank floor was coursed with scratches and grooves from decades of life, dotted now and again with a braided rug.

Ezra stood in the kitchenette area with his bag swinging and bouncing gently off his knee, filled with peanut butter, Fluff, bread, chips, salsa, Clif bars, and some packets of iced tea mix. He had grabbed these from the cabinet and planned to stop for ice and other necessities, but he figured he could set up and then go back out for whatever else he needed. He felt with his left hand for the light and flipped it on. One old, incandescent lightbulb spurted to life overhead, and he lifted the bag — a Red Sox reusable tote — up onto the old tiled counter.

Ezra pulled open a drawer near the fridge and grabbed a flashlight, then went seeking the hot water heater and the water valve. He found it right away in the corner behind the bathroom and switched both on, wiping a cobweb from his face. He closed his eyes with relief for a moment, thankful that the system seemed to be working and there were no surprises thus far.

Heaving a sigh that no one would hear, he walked back to the kitchenette. He turned the water on at the sink and let it run before looking for a pitcher. The cabinets were mercifully, tightly closed and latched, so no animals had gotten at any of the well-stored dry ingredients. There were Tupperware containers with nuts and dried raisins and berries. There was instant coffee and even a bottle of Za-Rex leftover from who knew when.

He found an old pitcher in the cupboard that he didn't remember from childhood and filled it halfway with the water, hoping it was still clear and potable like it was decades before. He poured a scoop of the iced tea mix into the pitcher and stirred it with a wooden spoon from the drawer. He found a relic of a plastic glass with Fred Flintstone and Dino on it and filled it. When he opened the small refrigerator to put it away, it breathed out hot air at him.

"Ah crap," he said, and looked behind the fridge for a plug. He found it and plugged it in, and the refrigerator hummed to life. He exhaled and looked around, wondering what to do next. It felt strange being here without his mother knowing, but in time he would feel like talking again and give her a call. She had been paying the taxes and electric bill at the camp since Uncle Joe passed away, and she'd want to know how the place was.

Ezra stepped into the little bedroom that sat off of the living room and set down his bag of clothes. He unzipped the black duffel and pulled a clean tee shirt free. He changed his shirt and stretched his legs, then walked back out and slid into his sneakers again.

He could see through the back window into the stretch of forest behind the cabin. He watched the forest quietly, grateful that he wasn't standing in downtown Boston anymore, grateful that he had this place to recover and begin to sort out the mess that his life had become.

That familiar rip of pain tore through his gut as he pictured her face, held lovingly in the hands of Todd Stipple, leaning up to kiss him. He still couldn't accept that everything she had said was a lie. Lisa had cheated, after six happy years, and now it was over.

It was then that he saw a gray blur dash past the window and into the forest, gone and covered by leaves again before Ezra even realized he had seen anything at all. His brow furrowed and he leaned closer to the window while his brain worked to rectify what he had seen.

A deer? But this animal appeared to be on two legs. Maybe a bear? Not unheard of. But bears are pretty brown in this neck of the woods. Probably one of these neighboring camps or houses has kids and they think no one is here. Ezra walked to the window on the other end of the room and peered out. The leaves were still shaking where the animal had run through, but he couldn't see anything. Must have been a neighbor, Ezra told himself again.

Ezra ate a handful of peanuts from the container in the cabinet and checked his phone. He saw with annoyance that there was no signal out here to make a call, not even using data. He thought about going to the center store and using his phone just to check in on Facebook — to let anyone who cared know that he was still around — but he wasn't sure he wanted them to know where he was. She may come for him if she knew he was here, and the truth was, he had nothing to say to her. Not anymore. He decided to get the few supplies he needed, including ice, and get started on some time at the beach, where he would consider his next move.

When he pulled off Route 209 and into the little parking lot, Ezra felt grateful to see only a handful of cars parked at the General Store. He did not want to run into someone who may recognize him and mention his visit to Uncle Joe's camp. Ezra wanted peace, anonymity, and a short stretch of time to hide and lick his wounds. If Ezra understood anything about Maine, it was that people talked to one another a lot and it was a *very* small world.

* * *

The Phippsburg General Store was an oasis with only the most important things one might need tucked into every corner. The wooden steps leading inside were unpainted, like the shingles out front. Paper signs dotted the front wall and fluttered in the wind: offerings for cottage cleaning, firewood, tree removal, fresh eggs, animals, and all sorts of items for sale.

A wave of oregano, tomato, and cheese hit Ezra directly in the taste buds when he stepped inside. He felt his mouth water and his stomach rumble. Figuring he had plenty of time on his hands, he walked over to the pizza case for a quick slice. He paid the cashier for the pizza while making very little eye contact and stepped back into the darkened area of the store, staring intently at the local ads on the wall and a fishing license poster issued by the state of Maine. He devoured the slice efficiently and wiped his mouth, disposing of the napkin in a neat ball.

Stepping up into the main part of the store, Ezra eased around two women buying snacks, and gathered milk, beer, Spaghettios with meatballs, oatmeal, and a bag of pretzels. He found a basket of fresh fruit near the register and heard his mom in his head, asking him to eat more colors. He grabbed an apple and a banana and waited for his turn.

The cashier, whom Ezra noticed had rather kind blue eyes, said, "Well, hi there. You're cleaning us out tonight, huh? There's a Shaw's

Market in Bath, ya know. If you need much more, I mean." Ezra returned her smile as she started ringing up his items. Two younger guys appeared behind him, discussing their options at the beer cooler.

"You staying in town awhile?" the cashier asked.

"Ah, yeah, I'm visiting family for a bit," Ezra said, feeling absurdly like she knew that he was lying.

"Oh yeah, nice. Where are you staying at? Down the beach?" Man, this lady was not afraid to be nosy.

"Out in the Basin, a family camp," he said, and immediately regretted it when her eyebrows shot up. *Oh, so you're a tourist, but not really*, her eyes said.

One of the two guys at the cooler glanced his way from under a Carhartt baseball hat and after a moment he said, "If you're staying in the Basin, watch out the Screecher don't get ya."

His buddy laughed and punched him in the arm. Ezra looked at the guy and laughed, fingering the keys in his pocket, wishing for an escape.

"Oh yeah?" he asked.

"Yuh. There's something in them woods in the Basin. You ever stay out there before?"

"Yeah," Ezra nodded. "I grew up coming here every summer. I don't remember anything weird." This was so much more conversation than he was hoping for tonight.

The punchy sidekick friend said, "When you were a kid, didn't you ever hear sumpin' like an owl or a bat, but real big? HeeeeeeeeYAH HeeeeYAH!" The guy cawed madly throughout the place and the cashier made a face at him like he was drunk or stupid. Maybe both.

Ezra shook his head, feeling confused and embarrassed for the guy's friend, who stood staring at his buddy, a wide smirk spread across his face. "It ain't no owl or bat, nope. That noise is a pissed off ghost," he nodded and scratched at his hat.

"A ghost? Oh, now *that* I can believe. What's it pissed about?" Ezra couldn't resist.

The cashier spoke next and surprised them. "They say it's a girl who got attacked and killed out there, back in the forties, I think. Very sad. Nothing to joke about, right Cal?" She looked at the Carhartt kid with those kind eyes and the guy settled instantly.

"Well, if you haven't heard that sound, then you probably will soon. You ain't never heard a sound like that, I am telling you. Just about make you fill your drawers." He laughed, but his eyes were wide and dead serious.

The other one added, "Probably nothing at all but people's way a keepin' out the tourists. You ain't stayin' out there by yourself, right?"

"No, I'm not," Ezra lied.

"You should be okay then. The Screecher seems to like people best when they're all alone." The guy turned away from him and placed his six pack on the counter with a bag of chips.

Ezra shook his head and offered one more good-natured, skeptical smile before paying the cashier and picking up the large paper bag with one hand and the six pack of Sam Adams with the other. He nodded at the locals and pushed open the door.

The sun had fully set when he pulled back onto Basin Road. Rocks and dirt crunched beneath his tires. He yawned and glanced at the clock. Not even eight and it was black as pitch. It was early June, and the sun was starting to set later, but he had misjudged how long it would last. Ezra knew he would sleep well in the quiet, and he pushed away any thoughts of his former life. He was done torturing himself with that noise.

He turned off the engine and sat a moment, taking in the sounds around him. The night was dark and the forest felt attentive, watching, pushing inward against him, like it had to try very hard to be still. Ezra put the bag and beer down so he could unlock the door. The only sounds he could hear were the peepers, little frogs that sang after dark, and the diligent, constant high chirp of the crickets.

A while later, with his belly full of canned pasta rings and a cold beer in his hand, Ezra stepped out onto the screened porch and patted the chair to make sure no spiders waited there. He left the light off and settled into the chair, his weight stretching and expanding the white wicker.

He breathed in the quiet night and looked up at the stars above the trees. He did not invite any thoughts in, especially not the ones that tore his heart to shreds. But he felt it there, in the dark recesses. It was a raw, hot, nauseating pain that twisted him into knots, lurking like a monster behind a paper-thin door.

Ezra tried to focus on the times he'd spent at the camp as a kid, or swimming at the beach. His memories were a sun-bright myriad of family gatherings, birthday parties, weddings, funerals, and all of it a speeding freight train that he never felt truly present on. After a while, he succumbed to the grief and allowed himself to picture that moment once again when he had witnessed the love if his life in the arms of another man.

He took a long pull from his beer and swallowed hard, blinking away the tears and wondering where it had all gone wrong. He could still smell her, could feel the silky, familiar warmth of her skin. How could she throw everything away like that?

Then, Ezra heard a shrieking, piercing scream that filled every particle of the air around him. He felt every hair on his body stand on end. A fight or flight panic tore straight through him.

He was on his feet in an instant, brown eye sharply focused on the dark forest outside, suddenly painfully aware of the flimsy screen that separated him from it. Then, as fast as it had come on, the screaming stopped.

Ezra stood perfectly still, his heart galloping in his chest. He didn't know what to do — was someone hurt? The sound was inhuman and visceral, and so he just stood frozen, waiting, thinking of what weapons he had available. There was a rifle in the bedroom but he didn't know if it was loaded, and besides, was that a woman screaming? Or an animal?

Then, as human minds are wont to do, Ezra's brain began to make excuses. He was coping and rationalizing before his fear took over. He told himself it was just a bat — okay maybe a big bat — and when the noise didn't happen again, he reasoned that maybe he had nothing to act upon.

Moments passed and the night remained still, as though whatever had made that shriek had never been there at all. Ezra slowly felt his bearings returning and focused on his feet, standing firmly on the floor, as Bert, his bass-voiced therapist, had told him to do so many times when he was younger. *Your feet are here, right in this moment. You can get through this.*

Ezra moved slowly, backing into the house and closing, then locking, the door. He shook his head, knew he was being silly, and turned around to check the front door anyway. The ticking of the clock in the living room area was deafening.

You're going to have to get a hold of yourself if you intend to stay here, Ezra thought.

The night remained still and soon Ezra calmed down, laying on top of the quilt on the queen bed next to his bag, reading a *National Geo-*

graphic. He thought about leaving and getting a hotel room, about what the guys at the General Store had talked about, and reasoned with himself some more. *Haunted, wild animals, or whatever, where else are you going to go?* His wife had frozen the checking account right away, saying smartly that if he wasn't going to forgive her, that they would have to work "everything else" out. He was left with one credit card and very little cash. It was almost as though she had planned it.

Despite it all, Ezra slept well that night, in a deep, dry-mouthed slumber that went uninterrupted. In the morning, he lamented the lack of Wi-Fi while he made a small pot of coffee, wishing to see the Sox score at least.

⁂ ⁂ ⁂

The sun rose early and glowed golden yellow across the landscape. Ezra smiled when he looked out the bedroom window and saw that familiar sparkle in the huge granite stones all around the property. He began feeling more at home than he had all night.

The returning thought of that abysmal shriek he'd heard the night before startled him, and he prayed for a moment that he'd dreamt it. He recalled the two characters at the store and wondered if they'd followed him and crept up to the house to scare him, tourist as he was. But that didn't make sense. You could hear a mouse crap in these woods — chances were you'd hear a grown man approaching from a hundred yards away.

Ezra packed up some beach gear and spent the first half of the day at Popham beach, pondering life, breathing salt air, and sipping iced tea while people-watching. He had to stifle a yelp when he touched the water. It may have been June, but the water felt like ice.

Hiding his smile, he witnessed aggressive seagulls breaking into bags and stealing chips and sandwiches. The mothers would get angry and chase the birds in a comedic ballet of futile, maternal effort, and the kids would scream bloody murder the whole time. But the memory would stay with them, and those children would chase seagulls away from their families forever after, every time they visited the beach, in dramatic and furious anger.

Ezra took the afternoon to go into Bath and stock up on a few supplies and, with great dread, check his email and Facebook to see if anyone was looking for him. He didn't want to hear from anyone, but he didn't want them worrying too much or getting any crazy ideas, either.

Not for the first time, he considered that there was no landline at the cabin. No connection at all, unless he drove out of the basin. He considered what had happened the night before, how that sound had really shaken him.

Crossing over the tiny bridge back into Phippsburg, he eyed the tide in the Winnegance Creek and felt a calm come over him. His car hugged the turns, the air smelled delicious and clean, and there were very few people on the road. He pulled into the driveway a short while later with the sun dipping past the horizon of the trees and a pink-blue glow layered the sky. Ezra popped the trunk of his little silver car to retrieve his bags.

He heard a branch crack behind him and spun around, catching the sight of something taller than he was backing away into the woods. But then it was gone again, a charcoal-gray blur amongst the dancing green leaves.

Ezra swallowed hard and held his keys tight in his right hand. He took his bags and leapt up the front steps like a child jumping into a bed so nothing could grab his ankles from beneath. Fumbling with the bags, he listened for any sounds.

Feeling ridiculous, he stood in the doorway with the door locked behind him, just listening. He was freaking himself out again, he knew, and he had to pull it together, especially since daylight would end within a very short time.

Ezra began to tell himself a great deal of non-truths. So, he saw a shadow from the corner of his eye, and maybe it was a ghost. So what. He could live with that. He had been here for years and never had felt that panic before. But, did the ghost scream like that last night? If not, what was it? Most importantly, would it bother him again?

He shook the thought away and closed his eyes. He knew the answer, and that if he *saw* it, it *meant* for him to see it. It may even be taunting him. He didn't think of his wife or what she had done during this momentary terror, and there was something to be said for the respite from that ache in his chest. He walked to the table and placed the bags down next to his cell phone and keys.

He walked to the bathroom and stood there peacefully, digesting the eerie feeling that had overcome him. Then, his phone rang. It had not made a sound for days other than while on his trip into town, but there it was, laying there, vibrating and ringing on the blue gingham table cloth across the room.

He finished fast and walked across the room. His jaw locked when he saw incredulously that it said Lisa. He reached for the phone without a thought and swiped his finger across the green circle. Ezra put the phone to his ear and whispered, "Hello?"

No sound. Nothing. He could hear a connection, could feel the seconds ticking away in white on the screen.

"Lisa? Can you hear me?"

Nothing. Ezra sank into the chair with his phone and stared at the door. He could not relax just yet, but in time he sank into the blanket behind him and took several deep breaths.

Then, the front door of the cabin behind him shook and banged violently, and Ezra jumped to his feet. He dropped the phone and sent it clattering across the floor, the battery springing free and tumbling under the table.

Ezra moved toward the couch and crawled across the floor, staring back at the door handle, knowing (praying?) that he had switched the bolt into its home and that he should be safe. But then it jiggled, to his dread, and the blood pooled in his chest like pudding because he hadn't heard any cars or footsteps approaching, as he most assuredly should have.

He thought about calling out to the person, but something filled him with fear at the thought. He felt rather than heard the movement on the little porch outside as whatever it was pressed against the door. He heard a sound like a sharp inhale of breath, then the sound of a thousand banshees filled his ears again and sent involuntary tears to his eyes.

Ezra fell back onto the floor and covered his ears. He pushed his way back toward the bathroom on his elbows and feet and pulled the door closed behind him, hands quaking, legs weak. He switched the light on and pulled himself to his feet, leaning against the door with all his weight. He faced the small medicine cabinet and caught a glimpse of the sheer panic on his face.

The window of the bathroom was small, about two by three with a white curtain which had four panels, edged jauntily with tiny, round, white and fluffy pompoms along its border. He could feel the dark night on the other side, pressing in.

Ezra stood statue still and stared at it, unable to see the window itself. Was it open? Was it locked? Was there even a screen? Ezra bargained with himself, not daring to go near the window yet fearing the idea of his back staying too long against the door.

He felt like crying, absurdly wished for his mother, and then finally settled on the fury he felt toward Lisa. Wasn't this her fault? And who was this? Who was doing this? Maybe those weird guys from the store, planning to rob him, or maybe even just playing a prank. But Ezra knew better. People in the Burg do not skulk around and prank one another, because it was likely they'd wind up with an extra hole or two.

Ezra caught his face in the mirror again and felt his stomach turn. He pressed his lips together and muttered, "This is crazy," before setting fear aside and pulling open the bathroom door.

In that moment, Ezra had a bright, fleeting memory. His older sister sat in the little twin bed next to his at the camp, brushing her hair and smiling at him as though he were something she could play with ... like a mouse toying with a cat. The light from the lamp beside her had lit up her profile eerily, illuminating her eyelashes, soft cheeks, and rounded nose.

"Can you hear those noises out in the woods? Listen, Ezra. They said he was half-owl or something. They said he escaped from the circus sideshow when it came to Maine, a loooong time ago. Uncle Joe told me so. It lives in the wood and screams. It's mad at people because they took him from his family. It happened when Uncle Joe was little like us."

"You're a liar, Cora," he had said.

"No, it's true. He said you'll hear it at night sometimes if you lay awake, or if you are ever alone."

"Welp, I'm never being alone here!" he had shouted, his eyes aflame with fury aimed at his sister's mean attempt to frighten him.

Returning to himself and his current predicament, Ezra peered into the living room area and saw nothing moving. Nothing had changed at all. He leaned out of the bathroom doorway and listened, hand firm on the brass doorknob. He thought of his dad's hand on that same doorknob when he'd blown Ezra a kiss goodnight, standing there in the doorway in his pajama pants so long ago. His wistful heart wished they were all here with him now. But his father could not be here, he was six feet underground in a cemetery down in Salem, Massachusetts.

He reasoned for a moment with this newly found treasure, brought from the depths of his subconscious. His father had never talked about anything in the woods here, not that he could remember. He went into the bedroom and listened again, but nothing happened. There was no sound.

He smelled the air like a hunter, seeking evidence. Nothing stood out per se, but when he quieted his heart, he could hear, plain as day, a rhythmic rush of air. The sound of breathing somewhere in the house. Or had he become so paranoid that his mind was now playing tricks?

He backed into the bathroom again and felt his hands shaking as he closed the door, pushing the lock into place. If something *was* in the house, then maybe he could get to the car. Maybe he could make it out that small bathroom window and to the car before whatever it was figured it out. If he were to turn on the shower, whatever it was would think he was in there, vulnerable, unaware of its presence.

Ezra pulled back the shower curtain and reeled for a moment, unsure of what he was seeing. Before him, crouching in the tub, was a massive shape covered in brown hair or feathers or both. White puckered skin was visible in balding patches. Its two winged arms reached up toward the shower curtain rod, grasping with rock-taloned hands. Huge yellow eyes stared back at him from beneath a v-shaped brow, set into a very disturbing forehead. Ezra's jaw went slack as he took in the beast.

He felt his arm move before the thought ever crossed his mind. He pulled on the lock with great stealth and speed. The damned painted lock stuck firmly in place, and Ezra's heart sank into his bowels. He made eye contact again with it, and felt as though he were staring into the eyes of all the lost ages of the world. Finally, the lock slid, and Ezra pulled the door open. He sprinted down the hall and out the door, spotting the car maybe twenty feet away.

He was whimpering before he reached the car, blubbering in clips and phrases and then yelps of fear. He longed terribly for what had once made sense to him. Ezra's legs were filled with lead as he pulled himself inside the car and closed the door behind him, clicking the locks.

He reached into his pocket for his keys and felt nothing. He patted his pants, checked the back pockets, and bit his lip hard enough to taste blood before roaring a wild "NO!" into the blackening night.

He panted, staring at the house and wishing it would just go away. He couldn't stay here, not after this, but he wanted to get his keys and flee. He knew he dared not go into the house while it was still in there. How had it gotten in there? What the hell *was* it?

Ezra thought that he should run away now, before this thing made a move, and that he could make it down the road to another car before anything happened, but he had seen those wings. He knew that animal could fly. Owls were predators, and maybe running off was enough to evoke it into moving. For all he knew, it could be perched on the roof of the cabin, waiting for him.

He resolved to stay in the car until morning, then he would either sneak in and grab the keys or run for his life down the road. He put his face in his hands and pressed hard on his eyes, his heart hammering in his chest, feeling more tired than he had ever felt. Then, the blip-blip of the car's locks sounded and he jumped in the seat, watching in horror as the locks rose on every door. It was then that he remembered his keys and fob clicker, sitting inside the cabin on the table.

He opened his eyes and pressed the lock button down twice, his finger hovering and waiting for it to happen again. He tore into the glove box seeking an old phone he thought he had, or anything with flame that might scare the thing. Sitting on top of his registration was a tiny metal box, one that belonged on the back bumper, containing his spare key.

Ezra's cold fingers fumbled with the metal slide on top of the box. He pushed harder and slid the top off, tossing the key into his right hand. He shoved the key into the ignition, started the car, and had the gearshift in drive before looking back toward the cabin. He felt the car lurch forward and then kilter to one side, as though the tire were caught in a rut — or flat. Ezra tried to reason with himself — drive to town on a flat tire? Get out and look?

Ezra sat with his hands clutching the wheel, maddening frustration taking over. He put his fingers to his temples, opened his eyes, and watched the house again. Nothing. It must still be in the cabin, he thought. He tried pressing the gas again, not wanting to call attention to himself or the car by revving the engine too loudly. The car rolled forward slowly and Ezra exhaled as it bumped up and over the rut in the ground.

He stepped on the gas with ferocity once he left the driveway. He flipped on his high beams, panting with the sense of freedom, and near-crying in the knowledge that he was safe in his car.

Images of that thing floated through his mind while he drove down the Basin Road. He had *seen* it. He'd smelled it. He'd felt it in the same space as him and he knew now that monsters were real. Nothing would ever be the same for him now. He slowed near a bend in the road and it was then that a brown mass landed on the windshield, crunching the glass, sending spider web splinters and cracks outward from the point of impact. He thought for a moment that he'd hit a moose, but he knew he was wrong when the head of the huge animal spun around and placed two glaring yellow-round eyes against the mess of the windshield.

Ezra shrieked over and over and stepped on the gas, swerving left then right to make the thing fall off his hood, but it held on with human hand-sized talons, gripping the top of the hood with little trouble. It opened a horrible beak-mouth and exposed a thick dark throat before letting out, just two feet from Ezra's face, a horrifying screech. A moment later, it's beak poked through the broken windshield like an excavator drill and came within a foot of Ezra's chest. He screamed back at the beast — his own brown eyes locking with those awful yellow orbs.

Ezra pressed the pedal harder to the floor, aware but not aware of where his car was on the wide dirt road. He came around a bend almost on two wheels but the beast hung on, and finally, he hit a larger rock that was exposed in the road and the car lurched into the air before thunking down again. Ezra was sure that the tire would pop, but the car kept rolling. He came around another bend in the road, swerving to stay with the road but desperately trying to get the beast off.

Just after the rock painted with the American flag, Ezra heard a huge boom come from his left and he instinctively ducked low into the seat. There was a silent moment when everything seemed to slow down. The owl-beast went flying to the side, and a burst of huge feathers and blood covered the windshield. Ezra slammed on the brakes and looked left, incredulity and shock on his face, searching for where the boom had come from in the faint light from the headlights.

Carhartt Hat and his punchy friend from the General store stood in the woods there, the former still gripping a 12-gauge shotgun, his eyes narrowed in concentration. When he and Ezra locked eyes, he nodded and pursed his lips. Ezra couldn't see out the windshield anymore, but his heart pounded when the two guys walked in front of his car and toward the thing on the ground. Ezra yelled "Don't!" but this did not deter them.

He almost swerved around them and hightailed it out of there for good, but they had saved his life and he saw that he couldn't leave them there. He inhaled sharply, blew it out, and put a hesitant hand on the door. The two friends stood there over the shaking mountain of feathers and beast. Carhartt Hat nudged it with the toe of his work boot and turned to Ezra, saying slowly, "We gotta stop meeting like this, bro. I told you to watch out for that thing." He nodded at Ezra and turned right, walking away back toward his truck, parked off the road just ahead, his friend close in tow.

Ezra got into his own car, decided he simply could not go back to the cabin even to lock it up, and after running the windshield fluid and wipers until at last he could see through the dark red muck, he drove toward town, not looking back in the rearview, and not seeing when the bloody, injured beast stood up and staggered into the woods.

IN THE ROOT CELLAR

GD Dearborn

Part 1: The Last Pages of a Diary Found in the Woods Inside of a Paisley L.L. Bean Backpack

November 4

We wait, and wait, and wait. Mommy says we must. "No use fretting when there's chores to be done." So I found the chopper and diced the turnips, chop, chop, chop. But I'm afraid when the dark comes. I think it might come in.

November 5

We're luckier than most. Mom and Dad were ready. Daddy dug a "root cellar" a couple years ago. It's actually a *lot* bigger than an ordinary root cellar. It's a bunker, really, but he didn't want people to know that. We have lots of vegetables from the farm down here: taters, carrots, parsnips, onions, and turnips. I *hate* turnips!!!

We've got plenty to eat down here. Anyone left alive who didn't prep like us must be hungry and have to scavenge for food. I feel bad about that, but I'm glad my parents were ready.

November 6

Daddy spends most of his day on the radio. He broadcasts for ten minutes and then listens for ten. Back and forth, all day long, that's what he does.

Daddy says someone will come for us if they hear us call. That's what I'm afraid of! He says *Them* are very smart, smarter than most people. If Daddy can hear *Them*, can't they hear us too?

Mom and Daddy had an argument about that last night. Daddy told Mom that it's vital to link up with "The Resistance." Which would be great, but there is no Resistance yet, at least not so far as Daddy can tell.

He's surprised that none of the military and civilian security bands he monitors are transmitting anymore. When we first got here, things were normal for a little while. Then the airwaves exploded with activity, more than Daddy could monitor. Then a few hours later, silence.

Daddy listens to *everything* on the air — marine, aviation, business, even some frequencies he would get in trouble for, if the government was still operating — but he hasn't had much luck. Just snippets of conversations that fade in and out, static, sometimes a few seconds of Morse code. Sometimes he will hear someone talking clearly for up to a minute, but then they fade away. He tries to talk back, but no one seems to be able to hear him clearly either. He's so frustrated; I hope it doesn't make him start drinking again.

So Daddy now concentrates most of his time on monitoring local civilian radio: shortwave, CB, and the FRS/GMRS bands. He wants to know if there are any civilian survivors in the immediate area, and if there is a Resistance enclave we can link up with.

Them sometimes talk over the radio, and they drown out any humans on the band, their transmissions are so strong. Daddy says they don't need radio to send each other messages, but for some reason they're on the air anyway. It's not just to jam our transmissions, because they seem to be able to silence any human transmission they want.

Their voices are creepy! Sometimes they sound like a steel saw being played with a fiddle bow. Other times, they remind me of a badly out-of-tune woodwind ensemble, or a fight between hornets and scorpions. It usually makes my ears hurt.

But once, their voices were so beautiful that I zoned out while listening and saw the sounds as colors. My dad found me, staring off into space, singing along with the alien song. He shook me awake and told me not to listen to the radio anymore if he wasn't there.

November 9

I heard someone thumping on the root cellar door last night, a little after midnight. I used my Kindle like a flashlight and went to the ladder. I guess I should have woken Mom and Daddy up, but I didn't. I wanted to make sure that I wasn't just dreaming and that someone was really there.

I heard a voice. "Hello? Hello? Is anyone there? Please, if you are, open the door."

I started climbing up the ladder, but three rungs up, I froze. Who was out there? Maybe just one scared teen girl, like me, but it could just as well have been a gang of survivors who wanted to take our stuff. I hoped that maybe, if I was quiet, they'd go away. I didn't think it was the Army, or some rescue team. The voice sounded too desperate for that.

So, I just stood there, on the bottom rung of the ladder, as quiet as I could be. The voice said, "Please, I'm hungry, and the creatures could find me. Open the door!" They started banging louder. Then the banging stopped.

I went back to bed. I didn't sleep a wink.

Should I tell my parents? No, it would just freak them out.

November 11

I read a lot when I don't have chores. My Kindle is my world now. My parents got it for me for my birthday. We do a lot of stuff the old-timey way, but my parents aren't luddites. They like technology just fine, so long as it keeps working.

About fifteen years ago, my parents started learning how to do things like the pioneers did them, because we couldn't count on technology working after *Them* arrived. They taught us those ways as we were growing up.

Most of our tech is working fine so far, except that the solar cells aren't producing enough power, and the radio reception is poor. We don't know why; they were okay when we got here. The internet and cellphones stopped working right away, of course. If my Kindle stops working, I'll probably die.

I'm lucky that the Kindle doesn't use too much juice. Daddy says the wind turbine is still working okay, but he gets less and less power from the solar array every day. Unless he turns off all the radios, the reserve batteries never completely charge anymore. He never turns them off while he's awake.

He lets us play our DVDs for only an hour a day, and if he can't figure out the power problem, we'll only be allowed to watch TV once or twice a week. He says finding the Resistance is more important than movies. When we link up with them there will be plenty of power, and we can watch movies whenever it is R&R time.

After so many days without contact, I am wondering if the Resistance is only wishful thinking, just another story to tell in the dark. I told that to my parents and Daddy got upset. He insists there *will* be a resistance movement and that we will be rescued. We may have to bug out again at a minute's notice. Mom smiled with tight, thin lips and said, "That's right, Hope, don't give up. You will get to wear that dress someday." But I don't think she has much hope anyone will ever come, and that suits her fine. She *likes* living in this little hole, all by ourselves. Sometimes I hate her.

The Kindle has lots of books on it, which is good. If Mom's right, they're all the books I'll ever get to read. Well, unless I write one myself, I guess.

November 12

We lived in Portland, Maine, before *Them* came, but now we're at Grandpa's farm in Norway, about 50 miles north of Portland. My father was an astronomer at the University of Southern Maine, so that's how he knew *Them* were coming. He heard them talking to each other on the radio telescope years ago, just after Mommy got pregnant with me. I asked him, "Daddy, if you knew the aliens were coming, why did you and Mommy have more kids after me?" He said, "Because kids are hope." I guess that explains my name.

November 13

The twins are creeping me out again. They were in a dress rehearsal for the Halloween play on the day of the bug out. They were wearing their skeleton costumes — black leotards painted with glow-in-the-dark paint — when Mom ran into the theater and yanked them out. They have other clothes to wear, but they won't. They'd rather dress up in their skeleton costumes and sit in the dark. I wish they'd didn't wear their masks.

November 15

Mom and I were in Macy's at the Maine Mall when she got the call from Daddy. I was trying on evening gowns for the Autumn Dance. Jeff, a Junior boy on the soccer team, asked me out. We weren't even friends or anything. I think he saw me checking him out in the caf and that's why he asked. It was going to be my first real date.

I had found the perfect gown, for just $60. I was showing off to Mom, twirling and making pirouettes, when her cell rang. Mom turned white as a ghost. I stopped mid-twirl. She grabbed me by the wrist, and we ran from the store. The theft alarm went off, but Mom didn't even slow down.

She gunned the motor and burned rubber leaving the parking lot. I saw the store manager chasing after us on foot in the rear-view mirror. I left my best jeans and my purse in the dressing room. :-(

We raced to the theater. She double parked and left me in the SUV in my stolen dress. The twins said the director came over to talk to her and Mom shoved her out of the way, grabbed them, and bolted. We drove to the farm in Norway as fast as we could, stopping only for gas. The boys ran into the mini-mart and got junk food, which they know Mom doesn't allow them to eat. She didn't even care.

As soon as Mom pulled into the gravel driveway at the farm, we started getting things ready. It went quickly. Mom just had our bug-out bags and a couple of plastic containers of essentials in the SUV, but most everything we needed was already there at the farmhouse. My parents had planned ahead. For years, we'd go up to Grampa's almost every weekend, during the school year, and spend our summers there, growing food and prepping.

We were all worried about Daddy. He was at work when he got the call from his contact at the observatory. He said he needed to grab some things from the physics lab and from the townhouse in Portland, but he was overdue. He pulled up ten minutes after the cell phones stopped working. I cried when I saw him.

November 15, before midnight I think

I lay awake most nights, reading my Kindle, and nap in the day.

Down in this hole we never see the sun, so "night" and "day" seems kind of arbitrary to me. I can't sleep at night anyway, everyone snores. But I'm also worried that something from outside will find its way in. It's better if someone is awake when everyone else is asleep. So, I stay up and read, even though Mom tells me I shouldn't.

The boys are snoring in their bunks, in their damn costumes, glowing in the dark.

November 20

I thought I lost this stupid thing, but I think the boys stole it. I found it under their bunks. I asked them if they had taken it, but they lied and said that they hadn't. I bet they were hoping I was writing really personal stuff in it, about kissing or something. I haven't thought about anything like that for a while. I hate that stupid dress!

November 21

I hope Jeff is okay. I hope *all* my friends and their families are okay, but I was thinking a lot about Jeff yesterday. I imagined what the dance would have been like. Maybe he would have called me the next day and asked me to go to the movies or a party or something. He could have been my first real boyfriend. I'm not sure that I'll ever have a boyfriend, if we don't hear anything on the radio soon.

November 22

The twins are driving me nuts. I know before I used to say that to everyone, like all the time. But, back then, I just meant that they were wicked annoying. They used to tease me half the time, and then bug me to entertain them and make them food the other half. Really, how hard is it to make a PB&J? Or cook bacon? Plus, they used to tell really dumb jokes. I frickin' *HATE* shaggy dog jokes! But I'd gladly listen to one now, if they would just tell me one.

They don't talk to me anymore. They spend most of the day sitting on the bottom bunk of their bunk bed in the dark, crisscross-applesauce, staring at each other, making expressions like they are having a conversation. At least they don't wear their masks anymore.

The only light in the room is from the glow-in-the-dark paint on their H'ween costumes. It is the creepiest damn thing I've ever seen. If I turn on the light, they sit on the edge of the bunk and just stare at me, faces completely slack, until I turn the light off again. Then they go back to what they were doing. Weirdos!

I've tried telling Mother and Dad, but they don't believe me. The twins act perfectly normal around them. Actually, around the 'rents, they are a bit too polite, not like the turd bags they used to be. I pointed that out to Mother, but she said "I, for one, appreciate how polite and calm they've become. It's a sign they're growing up." Right. I think they're going crazy, or trying to drive me crazy, or both.

November 24

About half the day went by, business as usual, before I realized that today was Thanksgiving. I told Daddy and he stared at me with a stupid look on his face for a second, and then he laughed. "Go tell your Mother that we must celebrate the holiday properly." He pulled a bottle of bourbon from the desk drawer and poured some in his coffee.

I thought it would upset Mother when I told her what day it was, but instead it was like the best news she'd ever heard. I think she was glad to have an excuse to cook too much. She set me to peeling potatoes, chopping onions, and making biscuits. I couldn't think of anything to be thankful for, but then I realized that we were going to have a pretty good Thanksgiving dinner, and most everyone else was starving. I felt grateful to be alive, but a little ashamed too. Why did I get to live?

The boys, for once, were acting like their old selves and were making bad jokes about how *Them* were eating survivors for their Thanksgiving. I stuck my tongue out at them, but I thought it was sort of funny. Sick, but funny.

November 25

Oh my God! Jeff is alive! He's alive!

After the big feast, everyone was sleeping. I got up around 3am and went out to the common room to sit by myself and read. But I couldn't get into my book, so I went into the radio room. I put on the headphones (Daddy calls them "cans") and turned on the radio. I found a *Them* song on a police frequency. It gave me a headache, lots of buzzing and clacking and high-pitched squeals. I don't know how Daddy and his friends decoded any of it; it just sounds random and awful to me. But then it turned strangely beautiful, so I switched it off before I fell into another trance.

I turned on the plain old FM radio. Daddy told me never to listen to it, ever, but he was asleep, so I did anyway. I heard voices, speaking in English. I got really excited, but then I realized it was actually *Them* talking. I think there were two of them talking, like a pair of weird morning-drive shock jocks. One of their voices sounded *almost* human, but not quite right. The other one sounded like they were using some sort of device to talk with, like the gadgets used by people who lose their vocal cords from throat cancer. They wanted all of us "fine American citizens" to know that everything was all right, no cause for panic. They were our friends and they came to help us with global warming. The President of the United States was right now in a diplomatic meeting with their leader. We all needed to make our way to Bangor, Portland, Manchester, or Boston, where we would be given assistance.

Bullshit!

I turned it off, and switched on the FRS/GMRS. All the channels were static, but I said "Happy Thanksgiving!" on all of them, one by one. When I got to channel 20, someone said "Hello" back. It was Jeff! I couldn't believe it. He said that he couldn't talk right then, but he'd call again on that channel soon.

I ran to the bedroom and woke Daddy up. I thought he would be pleased, but he wasn't. He said, "Pumpkin, I am glad your friend is alive, but you can't talk to him, not now. We can't take anybody else in here, and we can't give away any of our supplies. I'm trying to find us a group that we can join to protect us, but we can't help refugees, except to tell them where to find the Resistance. I'll monitor that channel and learn what I can. You understand, don't you? Now please stay away from the radios, unless I tell you otherwise."

I said I understood and promised I wouldn't use the radios in the radio room anymore without permission. But when he went back to bed, I took one of the walkie talkies out of the cabinet. Technically, I'm not even breaking my promise.

December 1

I made contact with Jeff again. I've been trying to find him on the radio. I have to do it in the bathroom or in my bunk, with the curtain closed. I speak softly and wear my earbuds. I'd just about given up, but I finally got a response on Channel 20. He said that he was happy I'm alive and wanted to know where I was. I told him that I was happy he was alive too, but I lied and said I didn't know my location. "My parents kidnapped me and are holding me hostage!" is what I said. I thought it was going to get a laugh, but he just said, "Well, try to find out. I will rescue you." That made my heart skip a beat.

He said that he and a few soccer players and cheerleaders got in a bus crash on the way back from a game, the day *Them* came. They figured out what had happened and decided to hide in the woods, because it was safer than being in the cities. Sometimes they steal stuff from empty houses, which is how they got the radio. Daddy started banging on the bathroom door then, so I told Jeff I had to sign off, but we arranged that he would call every day at midnight. I am so, so happy now, I could die!

December 2

I told Jeff that I was glad he was safe and I was really sorry that we didn't get to go to the dance. He said "Me too," and that I was all that he could think about. I asked him why and he said it was because I was so beautiful, which made me blush. Good thing we weren't on Skype! He said he liked my hair and my face and my big brown eyes. I said "Derp!" and he said "What?" and I told him my eyes were blue. He laughed and said of course they were. I'm not mad because that's a pretty small thing, considering he's living out in the woods and being hunted by aliens.

I hope he finds a better radio. His voice sounds kind of messed up on it. I asked my dad some radio questions, nonchalantly, and he said sometimes radios with a faulty component can buzz a little. He offered to tell me more about radios. I batted my baby blues at him and said, "Sure. Later, Dad!" and blew him a kiss.

December 3

Jeff didn't call today. Why am I crying? He's safe. He has to be.

December 5

Jeff called again. Yay! He said that his group was on the move, which is why he couldn't call. Also, it isn't always easy getting batteries, so I shouldn't worry if he skips some days, just keep monitoring the radio at midnight. That made me sad, but it makes sense. I asked him if I could talk to some of the other kids, but he said they were all asleep. I wanted to know who else was there with him, but the radio cut out then. The battery probably died.

December 7

Daddy left the cellar today and went outside. Mom didn't want him to, because she didn't think it was safe, but he said he had to go to check the antenna and the solar cells. Even the little bit of reception we used to get on the radio was gone — nothing but static — and we weren't getting enough power.

Unexpectedly, the solar cells tested fine; connections tight and no breaks in the wires. Nothing was covering them up either. Daddy said that of course he didn't expect to get a lot of juice so close to solstice, but we are getting much less than we should. He doesn't know why that is, or at least he isn't saying so if he does.

We found the antenna lying on the ground, which explains the bad reception.

December 8

Daddy brought me and mom outside with him a little before noon, and we got the antenna strung back up. He got much better reception after that, and even heard some people broadcasting, but they're too far away. Too bad, I've heard Tampa's nice in the winter! :-)

We went out around noon because that's when the sun is highest. He says *Them* don't like the light. I don't know how he knows that, but he says he's been listening to *Them* for fifteen years, and he and his internet friends figured some stuff out.

He tried telling some important people about *Them* once, but it almost lost him his job. He's listened "on the down low" ever since. He shared what he learned in anonymous chatrooms for alien invasion preppers on the dark web. That's why he says he knows something about *Them*, and also why he thinks we aren't the only ones left. The government didn't want everyone to panic so they kept it a secret, but they were getting ready for the invasion too.

December 9

Daddy lets us out of the root cellar for an hour every day now, but only around noon. He doesn't think there are any people around anymore, so it is safe.

December 12

It's been a week since Jeff called. I listen for him every night. I only heard static for days, but last night I heard one of *Them*. It was singing one of their creepy-ass songs, so I was about to switch off, when I heard it say, "Hope. Nyar-nyah. Hope." I must have been hallucinating. I wish Tumblr was still working so I could make a meme: "That moment when you are getting razzed by an alien." I'd LOL now, but it actually isn't funny. :-(

December 13

Jeff called again, finally. He said he was very sorry for not calling sooner, but his radio wasn't working. He got a new one, but it's hardly better than the old one; it's just as buzzy.

We talked for a long time. Jeff said he loved me and that he was spending all of his time looking for me. He asked me again if I knew where I was. I really, really wanted to tell him and I almost did. I said "I'm in Nor ..." but a little shiver went up my spine and I stopped. I cleared my throat and said, "Excuse me, I had a tickle in my throat. I'm North of Portland, I think." Jeff pressed me for more information, but I just played dumb.

I like — love! — Jeff, but his taste in music is lame. He was obsessing about Rihanna, Beyoncé, and Brittany Spears and wouldn't shut up about them. Everyone I know was way over those singers by the sixth grade.

It doesn't really matter. Even if it is just a romance by radio, I have a *hawt* boyfriend!

December 14

Goddammit! My Kindle is broken. :-(This sucks. Fortunately, my dad is very techie and was able to download some of the books in my library to my cell phone. I hadn't used that thing since Bug-Out Day, because it isn't much fun if there is no cell service. There was an app on it for reading books, so that's what I'll use to read. The screen is tiny, but it's better than not being able to read at all.

December 17

I asked Jeff if we could switch times when we talk. Since I'm out of the cellar around noon, I could talk to him then. He said that wouldn't be possible. I asked him why not and he didn't say anything or reply to my hails for a couple of minutes. Then he came back on and said that radios work better in the dark and *Them* can't block transmissions at midnight. That only made half-sense to me, but I let it go.

December 21

The days are really short now. Actually, tonight is the winter's solstice, the longest night of the year. It's almost Christmas. I'll give Santa a pass if he doesn't find us. :-/

Now that I go outside at noon almost every day, I find myself missing the sun the rest of the time. I feel like the Dark is a real thing, like a person, and it wants to get in. Even the electric lights in the root cellar seem too dim. The Pilgrims brought their God with them to the New World. Did the aliens do that too?

Christmas Eve

Today Daddy allowed us to go out after dark. I thought it was earlier, but the sun had already set. We went in the farmhouse and the place had been ransacked. It looked like someone had been sleeping there for a while. We found a knapsack with some dirty clothes in it. There was a Casco Bay High hoodie in it and a pair of jeans that fit! Merry Christmas! I'm not keeping the underwear, LOL. :-)

We cut down a little tree and set it up in Grampa's living room, just like we always do on Christmas Eve. I built a fire in the fireplace. Daddy and Mom had some presents for us. I got an embroidered apron from my mom. Daddy gave me a gun belt and holster he made himself from the buck he shot in October. He'd hand tooled Celtic knot work on it and made it beautiful. I was kind of dumb and said "What's this for?" He smiled at me and said, "It's for when you go outside, to carry your Glock in." Then he handed me another present: a Glock 19! I have the best dad ever!

December 27

Mom is sick in bed. I was taking care of her, but Daddy said I should take the boys up top at noon instead. They wanted to shoot their air rifles, and I wanted to try out my Glock. Daddy taught me how to shoot last year. I didn't like it at first, but it's actually kind of fun. The twins wanted a try with it, of course, but Daddy told them they couldn't. Not like I would have let them anyway.

I thought they'd be less creepy in the daylight, but they aren't. When mother is feeling better, I'm going to insist that she make them bathe and wash their hair. Most of the time they don't seem to care about much besides staring at each other, but they did seem to enjoy Christmas. They were talking normally and blinking and everything. Did

I mention that already? Sometimes they don't blink.

I almost caught hell just before we went up. Dad made us each take a walkie talkie, and one was missing. I almost panicked, but I pulled the one I borrowed out of my bag and said, "No, Daddy, I got it right here. I already packed it, when you told me I was going to be in charge of the boys." He said that I was a good girl and liked how I think ahead.

I left the boys to visit the outhouse and turned on the radio to see if I could raise Jeff. I wasn't expecting to get him during the day because of what he had said before, but he answered right away. He had great news: he figured out where we were! He and his gang were in the woods, right on our property. In fact, he said he could see me as we spoke.

My heart started racing like crazy, like it was going to explode in my chest. I told him I was going to run into the woods to see him. He told me I couldn't, it would ruin his plan. He wants me to gather up all the stuff I'll need and then sneak out at midnight. I said that my mom was sick. I can't leave the family now, but I can go in a few days when she's better. His radio started squealing and I told him to adjust the squelch if he could. He got it under control, but the buzz was very bad. I thought he'd be upset, but he said he understood and that he'd talk to me every midnight until I could get away.

He begged me to hurry, though, because his group was anxious to move on. That worried me a little. I asked him if they were planning on looting our root cellar. I begged him not to and warned him that my dad had guns. Jeff started cracking up (it sounded like "zotz-zotz-zotz" because his radio's so bad) and said "of course not." In fact, his group had learned about a government shelter, and he said that when we got there, Army guys would come back and bring my family in to safety. I told Jeff I loved him. I am the happiest girl on the planet!

December 28

Everything is ruined. There is no hope. I just want to die.

My dad was tuned into Channel 20 and heard Jeff's plan. He took my walkie away and locked it the cabinet. He is going to also padlock the radio room when he's not using it. He forbade me to talk to Jeff anymore. If Jeff was on the level, *he* would contact him.

Then I got a twenty-minute special: I could have put the whole family in danger, how much do we really know about Jeff and his group, what was I thinking, blah, blah, blah. When dad starts lecturing, he just won't stop. He said that I was way too old to be this disobedient, especially now that we all had to pitch in and act like a team. If I was going to act like a little girl, he said, I ought to be punished like one. I was scared that he might actually hit me then, but he said that there were too many chores to do. Taking care of mother and the boys was the priority.

I started to cry. I told him I was sorry and didn't mean to do any harm. I hate lying, and it felt good that everything was out in the open. But that good feeling went away when I realized that I might never see Jeff, or even speak with him, ever again.

Dad took the Glock too. It's in the gun cabinet. He never locks that.

December 29

Mom's fever broke, she's going to be okay. But the twins have me frightened. They just sit on the couch with their eyes rolled up, so only the whites show.

They chant loudly now. Crazy stuff. "Ayuh! Ayuh! Hope, he has come! The Dark! The Dweller in Darkness! The Crawling Mist! Ayuh!"

I screamed at them, and shook them, then slapped them both, but they just kept chanting.

Dad's gone topside. He took his shotgun. I think he's looking for Jeff and his gang. He's probably just going to chase them away. But what if there's a scuffle? What if he shoots one of them, or if they attack him? Everything has gone to hell.

December 30

Daddy didn't come back last night. I was so scared. He came in early this morning.

I'd locked the twins in the bathroom. I couldn't get them to shut up and it seemed the best thing to do.

Mom is up and around, but she looks tired and feeble. She had terrible nightmares and fever dreams for three days. Now she seems like a shadow of herself. She's started to stare and mumble sometimes, just like the boys used to do.

Daddy is out cold now. He started drinking when he came back. He let the boys out of the bathroom. He said "Let'em chant. Keeps them off the streets," then laughed a great big horselaugh.

He hugged mom and me and told us that we should make the

best meal we could, considering Mom won't be able to help much. I asked him about Jeff and the kids and he said "Pumpkin, I looked and looked. There is no camp, there are no kids."

I did what Daddy told me to do — what else was there to do? — and cooked another big meal, just like Christmas and Thanksgiving. It took me all day. I had my earbuds in and blasted tunes from my cell phone so I wouldn't hear the boys being crazy.

We got the boys to sit at the table, but they wouldn't stop chanting, and they wouldn't eat. Mom ate a little and said it was wonderful that the whole family was together again. Daddy had a whole bottle of wine at dinner. He stumbled into bed and has been out like a light ever since.

I have to make a plan. I need to find help.

December 31

New Year's Eve. This may be my last entry for a while. I'm bugging out. Not the whole family, just me. I'll go and find the army and bring them back, to rescue my family. I'm their only hope.

I don't think I'd have the courage to do this by myself, but Jeff is going to help me. He saved me in my darkest hour. I was the only one left that wasn't insane or dead drunk, and I didn't feel safe. So, I took my Glock out of the gun cabinet, checked that it was fully loaded, and strapped it on my waist.

My mind then went into a very dark place. I didn't want to think about it — couldn't think about it — but I'd had enough. The gun would take care of things, one way or another. I pulled the gun out of the holster and stared down the barrel. My finger squeezed on the trigger, but not hard enough to shoot. I couldn't move a muscle. I shouted to my mommy and daddy and said "I love you guys!" and then the phone rang.

I just about jumped out of my skin.

Jeff was on the phone!

How was this possible? Because of the best possible thing: *Them* are gone now!!!

There will be a lot of hard work ahead rebuilding civilization, but it's all going to be okay. Jeff is waiting for me, just outside the door. We will get help for the twins, Mom, and Daddy. We'll have to get back to Portland, but that'll be no problem if we take the SUV.

We always have our go bags ready, in case we need to leave in a hurry. I'm just going to write a note, grab my bag and my dress, and I am gone. The nightmare is finally over!

Part 2: Hope Lost in Twilight

It was his boys' loud chanting at the foot of his bed that woke Dr. Winship from his alcoholic stupor.

"Darkness rises! *Iä! Iä!* The Whisperer has awakened!"

The acidic smell of his own vomit and his headache told him that he'd fallen off the wagon, hard. His head throbbed, yet it was clearer now than it had been for a week. The voices were silent.

His wife lay in the bed next to him, her body rigid. Her eyes were rolled up, showing only whites. He checked her pulse and breathing and heard a faint whisper. She was chanting, almost inaudibly, in unison with the boys. *Brain damage?* He left her there in bed. He needed to take care of the boys.

The boys offered no resistance as he led them out of the bedroom. He feared that there was nothing left of them in their heads, just the alien choir. Winship had tried to drown it out with drink, but his poor sons were defenseless. Vocalizing chants did nothing to relieve the psychic pressure.

Winship considered tying them up and gagging them, but then he saw his daughter's note. In the brief time it took him to read the note, the boys continued chanting, unmoving.

For expedience's sake, he locked the boys in the bathroom. They didn't seem to care, and he hoped that their mindlessness meant they'd not harm themselves or their mother. It'd have to do. He needed to find Hope before she got too far.

He grabbed his hunting jacket and his shotgun and raced up the ladder, two rungs at a time, praying he wasn't too late to rescue his daughter.

It was twilight when he got out of the hole. He read his watch: eight minutes until noon.

A shot rang out. He raced through the woods in the direction it came from. In the near darkness, it was hard to avoid the branches that tore at his clothes and whipped his face. He shouted her name and was heartened to hear her shout "Daddy!" back.

He emerged from the thicket into a clearing and saw his daughter. She was lying supine on a blanket of pine needles, holding her pistol up with both hands. She was bathed in violet light. Above her was a thing — not a machine, or a person, or even one of *Them*, but a synthesis of all three — and it had caught her in its spotlight.

The scientist instinctively tried to categorize what he saw, looking for any vulnerability. It walked on spindly mechanical metal legs, not unlike those prostheses worn by para-Olympic runners, but powered. The torso, made of some glassy substance, had several mechanical arms attached, also spindly. Some ended in pincers, and some were like spikes — some sort of probes, he guessed. A protrusion on its back — probably the power unit — was made of the same metal as the arms and legs, with a strange luster to it.

Inside the crystalline polyhedron of the torso was one of *Them*. To Winship, it looked like a rosy chanterelle mushroom crossed with lobster and a wasp. Hideous.

Hope fired her Glock at it again and again, but the bullets bounced off the torso without making any impression on the diamond-hard surface at all. The creature only wobbled a bit, slowing its advance, but quickly regained its balance.

At the top of the hybrid, above the torso was an ellipsoid head, made from the same crystalline substance as the torso, and attached to it by a flexible metal neck. Winship could hardly understand what he was looking at, it was so uncanny. Glowing gemlike objects, wires, machinery, piping, and a tubular capsule were visible inside. The violet light that trapped Hope suffused the interior of the head and emitted from a lens at the top of it.

A human brain floated weightlessly within the capsule, suspended in fluid. A mesh of bare wires poked out of it, like gossamer threads, woven into a cable that went into the neck. Winship tasted fresh vomit when he finally comprehended what he was seeing: *the human brain was cybernetically linked to the creature in the torso.*

But the atrocity didn't stop there. On the front of the head, framed by a metallic bezel, was a human face. It spoke to its beloved.

"Hope, we can still be together. It's just the beginning. We can live together forever."

Winship raised the Mossberg and shot at the face, destroying it on the first blast. The bezel now surrounded a hole in the head. The hybrid froze. The scientist pumped the shotgun and fired into the hole, over and over, until he was sure that the poor boy's brain was destroyed.

The violet light went dark. Hope scrambled to her feet and ran to Winship. "Daddy!"

Before she covered half the distance to her father, a metallic ten-tacle shot out of the thing's arm and wrapped around her waist. She screamed. The thing from beyond ran off into the woods with its prey, whistling and buzzing and crackling.

His baby was gone. Only her backpack remained.

Winship took no time to mourn, but only enough to chamber a shell into his shotgun and fully load the magazine. He turned on the flashlight mounted on the barrel and charged into the woods after the monstrosity that had snatched his daughter away. It was high noon and he had less than an hour of twilight left.

ABOUT THE AUTHORS

Martin Campbell is the author of *Maine After Dark: A Collection of Nightmares*. He has had a deep-rooted love for horror ever since seeing the 2001 cinematic classic Wendigo. Martin hopes to complete his next book while completing the Wade Boggs challenge.

Duane E. Coffill grew up in Freeport, Maine. He started writing when he was twelve. His favorite author is Stephen King. He has written many novels and short stories, including his soon to be released novel, *Nightbeast*. He founded Horror Writers of Maine in 2012. He has appeared on numerous podcasts and radio shows such as, "Positively Maine" at the Portland Radio Group. He currently resides in Windham, Maine with his beautiful family.

Peter N. Dudar is the Bram Stoker Award-nominated author of *A Requiem for Dead Flies* and the recipient of the Solstice Award for his 2015 novella *Where Spiders Fear to Spin*. A graduate of the University at Albany in New York State, Dudar now resides in Lisbon Falls, Maine, where he has been writing and publishing fiction for the past twenty years. When not writing fiction, Dudar also pens a film review column for Cinema Knife Fight, and keeps a blog on WordPress called "Dead By Friday". He is a proud member of both the New England Horror Writers and the Horror Writers of Maine.

GD Dearborn, for one, welcomes our new alien overlords. He lives and writes in Portland, Maine.

E.J. Fechenda is the Amazon bestselling author of *The New Mafia Trilogy* and she released the first book in the *Ghost Stories Trilogy* in May 2016. She's had short stories published in *Suspense Magazine* and several anthologies. E.J. is co-founder of the fiction reading series, "Lit: Readings & Libations," which is held semi-quarterly in Portland, ME.

Jeremy Flagg: Jeremy Flagg is the author of the *Children of Nostradamus* dystopian science fiction series and *Suburban Zombie High* young adult humor/horror series. To find out more, contact Jeremy Flagg at www.remyflagg.com. Be sure to vote for whatever award John M. McIlveen is up for or we'll never hear the end of it.

Joshua Goudreau emerged from the 1960s New York fashion scene where he worked as a runway model until a freak zipper accident brought his career to a grinding halt. He wandered for a number of years until one night encountering an ancient mystic who trained him in the shadow arts of Wu Fei. Today he stalks the north dealing justice to those who seek evil and where his boots touch the ground, the forces of darkness tremble.

James Graham is an author from Brewer, Maine where he lives with his wife and two young children. When he is not busy playing with the kids, bugging his wife, showing up at his mother's house in the middle of the night to scare the shit out of her, or walking his enormous dog, he can usually be found watching the Boston Red Sox or any football game that's on. Somehow though, in that chaotic schedule of his, he finds the time to take all the weird, frightening, or downright disturbing thoughts in his head, and turn them into tales to entertain both himself and others. Or at least he tries to.

April Hawks is a coffee addict, a minecraft enthusiast, and an avid reader. She has a zombie plan, but it is a preciously guarded secret. April's first publication was in *Bleed* from Perpetual Motion Machine Publishing and several more short stories in anthologies. April's big projects in the works are a fantasy novel and a mystery novel. She can be found on Amazon, Twitter, Facebook, Wordpress, Pinterest, and Instagram.

Harold Hull lives in Presque Isle, Maine, with his fiancée and son. He holds a bachelor's degree from the University of Maine and works for a local non-profit. He's hard at work on his first novel, a young adult retelling of Frankenstein. He can be found on Twitter at @harold_hull.

Leslie J. Linder, M.Div. lives and works in Downeast Maine. Her nonfiction work has appeared in Circle Sanctuary Magazine, Sage-Woman Magazine, and Witches & Pagans. Her poetry has appeared in publications like Wicked Banshee, Forage Poetry, and Rat's Ass Review. Her debut novel, *Revenant: Blood Justice,* will be out through Black Rose Writing in May, 2017. Leslie's writing updates and links can be found at www.lesliejlinder.com.

John McIlveen wrote a novel. It is called *Hannahwhere*. It won an award. It is called The Drunken Druid. It almost won another award. That one is called the Bram Stoker. John has a new novel coming out. It's called *Gone North*. Maybe it will win something.

Holly Newstein's short fiction has appeared in Cemetery Dance Magazine, Lamplight Magazine, and the anthologies *Borderlands 5*, *The New Dead*, *In Laymon's Terms*, *Epitaphs: The Journal of the New England Horror Writer's Association*, *Evil Jester Digest Vol. 2*, and *Haunted Maine*. Her collaboration with Rick Hautala, "Trapper Boy" appeared in *Dark Duets*, an anthology edited by Christopher Golden, published by Harper Voyager in January 2014. Her story "Eight Minutes" was part of *Anthology II*, published October 2013 from The Four Horsemen Press. "Mischief Night" will appear in *Halloween Carnival: Dark Tales of October*, publishing in 2017 from Random House/Cemetery Dance.

She is the coauthor of the novels *Ashes* and *The Epicure* with Ralph W. Bieber, published originally under the pen name H.R. Howland. She lives in Maine with her dog, Moxy.

Dale T. Phillips has published novels, story collections, non-fiction, and over 60 short stories. Stephen King was Dale's college writing teacher, and since that time, Dale has found time to appear on stage, television, in an independent feature film, compete on Jeopardy, and lose in a spectacular fashion.

David Price tried to become a Doomsday prepper, but it was too much of a commitment. Rather than interact with the real world, he spoons with the monster under his bed. He is a proud member of the New England Horror Writers, the Science Fiction and Fantasy Writers of America, the Horror Writers Association, and the Horror Writers of Maine. David's debut fantasy novel, *Lightbringers* is available now, the sequels soon to follow. @_David_Price_, www.davidpriceauthor. Com.

Glenn Rolfe is an author from the haunted woods of New England. He has studied Creative Writing at Southern New Hampshire University, and continues his education in the world of horror by devouring the novels of Stephen King, Jack Ketchum, Hunter Shea, Brian Moreland, and many others. He and his wife, Meghan, have three children, Ruby, Ramona, and Axl. He is grateful to be loved despite his weirdness.

He is the author of *Becoming*, *Blood and Rain*, *The Haunted Halls*, *Chasing Ghosts*, *Boom Town*, *Abram's Bridge*, *Things We Fear*, and the collections, *Out of Range* and *Slush*.

He is hard at work on many more. Stay tuned!

Visit him at https://www.glennrolfe.com

Leon Roy is a writer of short fiction, screenplays, and some poetry. Following a two year absence from his home state of Maine in Okinawa, Japan, Leon joined the creative writing community alongside groups like Horror Writers of Maine, and Portland Screenwriting Meetup. Leon dedicates time between two night jobs to display an artistic view on varying genres, *A Lovely Little Nash*, set in Boothbay Harbor where he spent many summers. Leon can be found playing piano during his downtime and contacted via private email at tquirion1992@gmail.com.

Angi Shearstone is an award-winning professional artist with an MFA in comics, a small herd of cats, undeniable geek tendencies and a great love for ska-core and punk rock. In addition to writing horror, Angi blogs about creativity at Amazing Stories Magazine and creates and sells fine art. Learn more about her writing at www.blooddreams.com

Katherine Silva is the Midcoast Maine author of the *Monstrum Chronicles* series, is a connoisseur of coffee, and victim of crazy cat shenanigans. Her second book in the series, *AEQUITAS*, was nominated for a 2013 Maine Literary award. She is a member of the Maine Writers and Publishers Alliance, New England Horror Writers Association, Horror Writers of Maine, and founder of the Midcoast Maine Halloween Readings series. Find out more at www.monstrumchronicles.com.

Juss Stinson is 25 years old, a mother, an oddity enthusiast, a life consultant, and an author! She has always taken great pleasure in being quirky and loves the creativity that blossoms from it into her world of writing. Juss has proudly self-published five books including two paranormal romances, a horror poetry/short story anthology, a children's book, and a free verse horror story. There will certainly also be much more to come! You can find Juss Stinson on AuthorJuss.com and on most social media.

Wicker Stone has had two short stories published in a magazine called, "Fang." He covered Stephen King's movie, *Thinner*, for the magazine, "Cinefantastique," and had his own column in the central Maine newspaper, *The Morning Sentinel*, for six years.

Lynda Styles is an author living in Bath, Maine with her husband and family. Styles is a graduate of the University of Maine and the author of *On Gallows Hill* and several short stories. She enjoys exploring, swimming, and hiking the forests and beaches of Midcoast, Maine, especially Phippsburg and Popham Beach.

Morgan Sylvia is a writer, a metalhead, a coffee addict, a beer snob, an Aquarius, and a work in progress. A former obituarist, she lives in Maine and is now working as a full-time freelance writer. Her work has appeared in several anthologies, most recently in *Wicked Witches*. In 2014, she released her first book, *Whispers from the Apocalypse*, an apocalyptic horror poetry collection. Her debut horror novel, *Abode*, will be released from Bloodshot Books in late spring 2017.

Jeremy Simons lives with his wife and daughter in Grayson, Louisiana. He writes constantly in his spare time and aspires to one day become a full time novelist. His works have appeared with *Carnage Conservatory*, *Aphelion-webzine*, *The Horror Zine*, *Voices from a Coma*, *Hellfire Crossroads Volume 4*, *Short-Story.Me*, and *October's End* and the *X3* Anthology (both anthologies from Horrified Press). His debut novella *Buried Alive* is now available for purchase via Amazon and Smashwords in both paperback and eBook format. You can find Jeremy Facebook at Facebook.com/jeremysimonsauthor or follow him on Twitter, twitter.com/@jeremi1986. His website is jsimonsauthor.webnode.com.

Born and raised in the small town of Milo, Maine, **Thomas Washburn, Jr.** discovered a passion for writing, art and storytelling at a young age. Fueled by an over active imagination he spent countless hours working on his creations, getting lost in the worlds of the stories he created.

As Thomas grew older his passions changed from writing, literature and art to music. He spent several years from 1995 to 2012 playing in various bands, playing hundreds of shows around Maine, New England & Canada. Writing lyrics for the bands he played in gave him a chance to tell stories through a different medium. During that time period he also wrote several unpublished screenplays. After semi-retiring from music in 2012 Thomas rediscovered his passion for writing and in 2013 released his first novel *The Returners*. Thomas is the author of over a dozen independently published works.

www.ingramcontent.com/pod-product-compliance
Lightning Source LLC
Chambersburg PA
CBHW070845260626
47170CB00007B/2510